Justice

Tomorrow

JACKIE ROSS FLAUM

This book is a work of fiction, and does not represent real events. Characters, names, places, and incidents are works of the authors imagination and do not depict any real event, or person living or dead. All rights reserved. No part of this book may be used or reproduced in any manner whatsoever without written permission by the publisher, except in the case of brief quotations in a critical article or review.

Copyright © 2020 Jackie Ross Flaum

Published by Jackie Ross Flaum
ISBN 979-867-5497-9-04
Printed in the United States of America

All rights reserved.

ACKNOWLEDGMENTS

Thanks to Cheryl Nelson Deariso in Georgia for her editing and suggestions, and retired Sheriff Deputy Jay S. Hinton Jr. in Florida for his advice on firearms, police procedures— and his lifelong friendship.

No writer makes it alone. Malice in Memphis A Killer Writing Group, helped me learn and grow. Its members pushed me, corrected me, and cheered me along these last few years. I cross the finished line with their help.

Big thanks to the gentlemen in my original Malice in Memphis critique group: Larry Hoy for teaching me to write fight scenes, Richard Powell for his editing and production help, and Lynn Maples, who not only straightened out my writing but designed the cover, my website, my ads, marketing, and my business cards. Writers all and very talented ones. They were hard on me and I appreciate it.

The photos in the book were taken by Sandy Johnson Vandenberg of Maryville, Tennessee, high school friend and Smoky Mountain amateur photographer.

Finally, and without doubt, the biggest thanks, goes to my editor Ann E. Hall of Andover, Mass. We began as reporters for *The Hartford Courant* in Connecticut. If you like this book, send her flowers.

DEDICATION

To David, Stephanie, and Becky
always and forever.

CHAPTER ONE

Barking hounds and sporadic gunfire spurred Madeline Sterling through the Alabama woods. With each step, her wound throbbed and her sides ached. Low branches of pine needles slapped her. How far had she and her partner run? She fell against an oak, grabbed a few gulps of air, then pushed deeper into the forest. Finally, she tripped on a tree root and couldn't rise.

Barely missing a step, six-foot, two-inch Socrates Gray wrapped her good left arm around his neck and hauled her up a rise. He was so much taller than Sterling her feet skimmed the forest floor.

A boom behind them quieted crickets, angry squirrel chatter, and bird songs. Even the mob and their dogs fell silent. Then came the sound of whoops, gunfire, and yelping dogs set off on a hunt for the couple. Thick black smoke swelled over treetops behind them.

"Burned our car," Gray panted. "Come on, Sterling."

No one had called her Madeline since she entered training to become a civil rights investigator for the top-secret organization Justice Tomorrow. Odd thing to remember as she and Gray ran for their lives.

They scrambled down the rise, along a ridge, and up to a clearing at the top of the hill where they could see a lake in the distance. Surrounded by an ocean of green leaves, the blue water promised relief from the hellish heat and humidity. Sterling licked her dry lips, mesmerized by the patterns of light across the water. Ducking between the trees below them, a shallow rocky creek thirty to forty feet wide wound around the base of the hill and headed to the lake. Gray adjusted his grip on her hand and her waist.

"Pickup . . . there?" She wheezed. "Lake in Little River . . .?"

No answer. Broad-shouldered and stronger than anyone she knew, Gray's labored breathing huffed in her ear. Rivulets of sweat stained his blue shirt as he half-carried her down the hill. The muscles in his brown arm strained with the effort of helping her along.

"Leave me," Sterling panted. "Th-hey won't shoot a white woman. They'll kill you — or worse."

Gray rested her against a maple overlooking the creek they'd seen from the hilltop. Strands of her red hair snagged on its bark and tugged on her scalp. But blessed relief. The wound throbbed less when she lay still.

"Go . . . please."

"I'll get water." In two or three steps Gray jumped into the creek bank. She inhaled fresh pine then choked on a God-awful stench.

"Phew-w." With some effort, she turned from the sickening odor of something dead or dying. Suddenly a wet strip torn from Gray's shirt whipped across her face.

"Your shoes." Gray yanked them off her feet without waiting for her and ran back the way he came.

Sterling let water drip into her mouth then sucked it from every fiber. Enough moisture remained to wipe off a little. Better. What could she remember from all those weeks of Justice Tomorrow self-defense, survival, and interrogation training that would help? She reached in her jeans hip pocket for a red bandana she'd worn around her neck when this day began.

Wincing, she peeled away a bloody wad which used to be a white handkerchief. Gray had stuffed it against the wound in the moments after a bullet blew through the upper part of her shoulder. Pretty disgusting, but she might use it later somehow. She tucked it in her shirt pocket. Next, she dabbed the edges of the bullet hole with the damp cloth. Finally, she tied the bandana around her arm, trembling from the effort.

Light-headed and nauseated, she leaned her head back against the tree and admitted she'd never make it to the lake. She would die here like whatever rotted close by. She would die a year from becoming twenty-one, a legal adult. Without graduating from college, being an FBI agent, or taking a lover. She'd never go to Paris, vote Lyndon Johnson out of the White House, or taste *crème brûlée*.

The barking and howling sounded clearer. Closer. She closed her eyes and willed herself to die before they tore her apart.

Another death in the fight for desegregation in America. No doubt Justice Tomorrow would investigate her murder. Which of her teammates would uncover her killers and preserve the evidence that would lead to a conviction someday? How long would her family wait until the day these white murderers could be convicted in an Alabama courtroom?

Her poor mother. Sterling had resented her father's forbidding her to join

Justice Tomorrow—a man who marched for civil rights and pounded protest signs in his yard to the horror of their Boston neighbors. But her mother's words had seared her heart: "Danny's in the Marines. I already have one child in harm's way. Please. Don't do this. For God's sake, you're only eighteen!"

Odd how easily she accepted death. She never thought of it back then. Sterling imagined herself stronger. Her shame kicked at her exhaustion in hopes of jump-starting the will to live. She'd given no thought to death when she signed with Justice Tomorrow. Instead, she celebrated the righteousness of the cause, the excitement of learning investigative skills, the joy of having someone value her talents.

Sterling dragged in a breath. Where were the angels of God the priests talked about? All she heard were dogs. Where were the angels?

"Hey, open your eyes." Gray thrust her shoes at her and hauled her into his arms. "Got an idea."

The forest spun in crazy colors. Of course, Gray had an idea. Next to her father, Gray was the smartest person she'd ever known — even though he went to Yale.

He carried her down the steep creek embankment until they reached a hole gouged into the side of the bank. Covered by broken branches, piles of leaves, and rocks left by the last spring storm, the hole in the creek bend was deeper than it seemed at first glance. And God, the awful smell.

"You okay?" His mouth twisted with concern.

"Hunky-dory."

The half-eaten deer hung over the hole surrounded by dozens of scattered paw prints left by predators who'd feasted on the body. Besides the bugs and worms, the gnats swarmed around it.

Her nose wrinkled. "Gross."

"Complain to the management." Gray laid her in the hollow with the top of her head nestled under a small overhang, dropped dry branches across her, curled around her then sat up enough to throw leaves and rocks about. Some leaves and twigs he tossed in the air fluttered down on them. Then he peeled himself away with care. Puzzled, she sat up to slip on her shoes. The world spun like a Tilt-A-Whirl.

"Don't move!" Gray tried to obliterate his footprints with a pine branch and handfuls of forest debris. "I'll be back quick as I can. I gotta gather branches and stuff from the other side of the creek. Then I'll walk backwards in my footprints. I already made your prints."

"Tear this . . . nasty thing in pieces." She handed him the handkerchief in her pocket with shaky hands. "Tie on a rock. Might confuse dogs."

"'Gross,' 'hunky-dory,' 'nasty'—does Justice Tomorrow know you talk like that? Lay down."

3

She stuck her tongue out at him and eased into the hole again. Tired. Her eyelids fell. The noise of splashing water, the faint crash of stones or wood thrown into bushes, more splashing, then a strained grunt as though Gray struggled against a herculean force. Suddenly a suffocating weight fell across her. Her head swiveled to find a deer eye staring at her. With a shriek, she clawed against the weight, her mind a terrified blank.

The deer's body lifted enough to let Gray scrape his way underneath it. He slapped a hand over her mouth as he grabbed her in a sideways embrace. She twisted and heaved and screamed. When she sagged against him at last, he leaned forward and threw handfuls of rocks and leaves where the deer's body had been. Satisfied, he rearranged the hiding place to cover him and snuggled around her again.

"Be still." Gray's lips moved against her ear they lay in the hot putrid hole. "No matter how close they come, how the dogs bark, how the men talk, don't stir or make a sound."

Every time Gray moved or dug, the darkness in their small pit grew until she saw only specks of light, felt the wetness of perspiration or blood, the smell of dirt and decay. Her hearing became acute.

The men drew closer. Drunken voices hollered, "string 'em up," "nigger," "nigger-lovin' whore." Why did all these voices sound familiar, all the words the same? Had she said 'hey' to them on the street? Gone to church with them? Shared a joke with their wives?

A green leaf slid down next to her lips, then another. She let them stay. The men and dogs crashed through the underbrush and down the embankment.

Gray gripped her tight and sent a "sh-h" of air in her ear. Adrenaline lanced through her and created a fiery resolve. The seconds ticked in her head: "*one one-thousand, two one-thousands, three one-thousands. . ..*"

A dog's sniffing nose burrowed so close the hairs on her head moved. Another dog dug near her throat. With the racket the dogs sent up, she heard only fragments of the men's words.

"God . . . John," hollered one man. "Thought ya had a tracking dog. He treed a dead deer." Laughter.

"Come on, boy," another man grunted. "She-et. Git! What's . . . with you, dogs?" A dog yelped. And another. Men stomped around the deer. Swoosh, crack, whoomph noises sounded like men beating the hounds away.

"Stinks. Phew-hee. Poke it, Charlie. See something move beside them maggots."

More raucous laughter.

"Give me another swig, John."

Sterling clenched her teeth, waiting for gunfire. Instead, a whack—the blow vibrated down the deer carcass and through Sterling's injured shoulder. A vast blackness punctuated by pulsing stars and burning pinwheels burst in her brain. Only Gray's soft breath against her earlobe kept her grounded.

A crunch-thud-thud outside sounded like running. "Hey, y'all! Got footprints cross the crick. Bring 'em damn dogs yonder."

"I'm tired traipsin' all over hell and half of Alabama," whined a deep voice.

"We must a kilt the girl, let the nigger starve in these woods." The second man's complaint trailed away.

Sterling craved light, to see what happened outside this hell. It became urgent, powerful. She closed her eyes to control the darkness, to make it her decision when there was light. The seconds ticked by. She counted them, "*One one-thousand, two one-thousands, three one-thousands, four one-thousands . . ..*"

CHAPTER TWO

Mrs. Woolworth, the same middle-aged woman who recruited Sterling for Justice Tomorrow, approached the hospital bed as though expecting the patient to drop her magazine, rise, and throttle her. "How are we feeling, dear?"

"Get me out. I'm not kidding. My parents think I was only 'slightly' injured in Alabama." Sterling tossed aside *Time* magazine with her free arm. "A week! I'm going crazy in this hospital."

"I spoke to your mother and reassured her," Mrs. Woolworth said. She still wore the haughty cloak of old money, breeding, and privilege.

The first time Sterling met her handler she had slogged home from Radcliffe College in a snowstorm with a bruise on her chin from a segregation protest march. Her visitor was sitting in a place of honor in her parents' living room drinking tea from her mother's best china. Wary at first, the passion in the woman's green eyes drew Sterling in.

For more than an hour Mrs. Woolworth, who never gave her first name, spoke about a secret organization formed by wealthy donors horrified by the unpunished murders of people in the civil rights movement. They created Justice Tomorrow with networks in southern towns—men and women afraid or unable to act on their own but willing to help in secret.

"The youth of our investigators is both a blessing and a curse," she had remarked to Sterling's parents. "We decided on young investigators because, well, who would suspect kids of collecting evidence in a murder? On the other hand, young people want their cases to come to trial immediately. We sometimes have trouble persuading them to wait until there is hope for conviction from a white Southern jury. After all, there is no statute of limitations on murder."

Her parents had been fascinated but not enough to bless their daughter's involvement. Sterling, however, threw her studies out the window and signed on the moment Mrs. Woolworth promised, "You'll be a fully qualified investigator when your service is over."

That day seemed so long ago. Longer than two years. Sterling rearranged the sling on her right arm with an exaggerated sigh.

"I can bring more magazines," suggested her handler. "Or hand you another case."

Sterling's cheeks flushed so red her freckles vanished. "Home."

"We'll arrange a short visit."

"A month." Sterling snuggled under the white blanket, feeling a twinge in her wound and a powerful wave of homesickness. She pictured her brother Danny off in Vietnam as a Marine advisor and imagined how lost and alone he must feel.

Mrs. Woolworth paused for a deep breath. "Sterling, we need—."

"I screwed up." It was a whisper.

The handler tsk-tsked. "Why are we women ever ready to accept blame, but never credit? You took one risk too many, as we covered in debriefing. You're inexperienced. That's why we retrain our team after every mission. A talent like yours—well, you have a future in law enforcement. Perhaps the Federal Bureau of Investigation. J. Edgar Hoover can't run it forever."

Sterling refused to be handled and pouted. The harsh light from the goose-necked lamp on the metal bedside table cast surreal shadows around the sterile hospital room in Philadelphia.

"Gray is hoping to work with you again." Her handler added softly, "You didn't break, Sterling."

"You sent Gray out already?" Her mouth flew open. "He looked awful when he came to say goodbye." She never mentioned what he'd done to save her.

"He's on R&R. I believe he's with his brother Aristotle, Silver as you call him."

Good. Gray deserved it after the escape from the woods. When she came to under a tree, he had redressed her wound. A day of torturous hiking to the rendezvous lay ahead with her feverish and babbling about hearing maggots. A Justice Tomorrow operative drove near at the appointed time in his green Dodge— why were their rescue vehicles always green? She and Gray slipped in the back, scooted in the seat below the windows, and they drove Route 21 to a clinic. There a doctor stabilized her, and another volunteer took them north to the hospital used by Justice Tomorrow.

How far did the organization's influence stretch? The question occupied hours of her convalescence. The network of training, research, and resources she had already seen made her think it was vaster and better funded than the FBI. Every time she asked, however, Mrs. Woolworth referred her to the pledge of secrecy she signed.

"Retraining's in a few weeks. You, Gray, Silver, and the others. We've a new man to work into the team," Mrs. Woolworth said.

"New?"

"Roots in Georgia. Ah-em, Silver found him."

Sterling frowned. "Silver recruited him?"

"He's quite a good catch."

Too late. Sterling heard the woman's hesitation.

Justice Tomorrow selected its members with care. No agent recruited another.

"Sterling? Listen, I'll give you two weeks off, possibly more after retraining," her handler said. "We have a—."

"Time for me to be back in school." Sterling kept her voice level.

"Do you want to be?"

Sterling held the older woman's gaze.

After an aggrieved sigh, Mrs. Woolworth rose. "Get rid of the sling, I know you don't need it anymore. I'll drive you home."

To her embarrassment, Sterling burst into tears.

CHAPTER THREE

Sixteen-year-old Henry Johnson dreamed of young love.
Humming to himself he pressed the gas pedal of his father's 1958 sedan, then cranked down the driver's side window to let the Georgia breeze blow in. Couldn't let his starched white shirt wrinkle or worse, get sweat stains. He wanted to drive up to the Mt. Moriah AME Church in Crossville looking cool. A certain girl was sure to be there.

Henry squared his shoulders wishing he had the body girls fell for: light brown skin instead of blue-black, muscular and broad in the chest instead of lean with a short torso and long legs. Thankfully, for today anyway, Henry had the Chevy and an important errand to catch her eye.

Polished until it shone, nobody but the pastor of Mt. Moriah ever drove it. This once Reverend Johnson made an exception for his son. Folks being evicted from their farm needed his help. Since his congregation planned a canvas to encourage Black voters, he told Henry to take the car. The church folks needed the flyers on the new 1965 Voting Rights Act, which made it difficult for states to keep Negroes from the ballot box.

As he approached a section of the two-lane darkened by arching pines, Henry popped on the car's headlights. County deputies laid in wait for motorists along Callie's Cutoff. His uncle got beaten for not paying a 'ticket' one deputy issued him. Today, however, Henry's thoughts weren't on the man, but a girl. He rehearsed how he'd drop into the conversation real casual-like how his father talked on the phone with the Reverend Doctor Martin Luther King Jr. himself. Elections rolled around soon, and Reverend King wanted Pastor Johnson to rally everyone around Crossville to register and vote.

Henry figured he'd carry the box of flyers in as easy as you please, set it on a table with a satisfying thud to show it was heavy, and then invite everyone to take one. He'd nod serious-like as folks took a flyer or two until it came to her turn. Her love light shining on him made Henry squirm in the car seat.

A red light filled in his rearview mirror.

Henry's stomach dropped. His dreams of impressing a girl vanished. By the time the Bell County sheriff's cruiser pulled behind him Henry had sweated through his shirt.

A siren wailed.

Panicked, Henry stomped on the Chevy's accelerator and shifted into high gear. The old car didn't have much to give, but if he reached Parson's General Store, he might be safe.

He never made it.

A Ford pickup carrying a bed full of armed white men pulled out of nowhere as he approached the curve and cut him off. He had to stand on the brake to keep from ramming them. He whipped the car around, sending voting rights pamphlets and the box of flyers sailing off the bench seat into the floor. Blocked by the cruiser across the road on one side and the truck on the other, Henry flung open the car door. He leapt out and headed for the trees, praying his long legs would save him.

A bullet took him down inside the tree line. He skidded along the forest floor shrieking in agony. Fire sizzled up his right calf, but Henry kept his hands and one foot moving. He had to find a way through the pine needles, dried leaves, and dirt.

He heard brakes squeal behind him, then a car or truck backfired.

"What's goin'—." White man's voice, one Henry didn't recognize.

Henry hollered a strangled cry for help.

"Git out! Go on!" another man shouted.

Car tires spun on the gravel. Henry heard the car speed up and knew no one was coming to help. The sound of footsteps breaking twigs and banging something hard against tree trunks spurred him into crawling faster through the woods.

Too slow.

A lanky sheriff's deputy and two or three men hemmed him in a semi-circle then watched him struggle a few more feet before they kicked him. Henry doubled up and covered his head with his arms the way he learned in Southern Christian Leadership Conference classes.

The blows stopped. Henry peeked between his arms to see Sheriff Martin Boyd had made his way into the pines. He was a well filled-out man, and right then loomed gigantic to Henry. For a moment, silence except for a tiny voice in his head whispering over and over, "MamaMamaMama."

10

JUSTICE TOMORROW

Boyd slapped a bunch of the voting rights flyers against his palm, huffed, and kicked Henry in the ribs so hard the wind whooshed from his lungs.

"Goddamn it, Alvin! This nigger's the son." Leaning down close enough for Henry to smell sen-sen covering the whiskey on his breath, Boyd grabbed the boy up by his shirt collar. "This look like a full-grown man to you?"

With a gasp, Henry torqued his body, swiped blood against the sheriff's shirt, and clawed for support. Boyd knocked him off like swatting a fly on a horse, but Henry had a grip so tight Boyd's uniform epaulette tore off. The boy hit the ground and doubled up in pain, jamming the ripped cloth under the dirt and leaves beneath his side. His digging in the ground ripped off most of a fingernail, but the pain of it didn't register. Every inch of him hurt worse.

"This ain't my fault," Alvin whined. "You said the pastor's sedan, and that's what I pulled over."

The sheriff poked his finger in his deputy's chest. "But it isn't the right boy in it, now is it?" Boyd shook his head in disgust and pointed further in the woods. "Stuff every one of them votin' papers down his throat and string him up."

Terrified, Henry struggled to get up, run. Boyd smacked him on the head and Henry hit the ground. He felt nothing after Boyd hauled off and kicked his skull in, not the rest of the beating or the rope around his neck.

CHAPTER FOUR

A strong scent of pine filled the blue Impala as the driver slowed the car to a crawl. Sterling rolled down her passenger side window and stuck her head out far enough to catch a breeze. She hated the smell. Still, she drew the cool air deep into her lungs to push down the bitter taste of dread. Feeling this way was natural at the start of an investigation, but the close call on her last assignment made it worse.

So did this month-old crime scene.

Tall forests of pine on either side of the two-lane whistled an ancient tune conducted by Georgia breezes. The loblolly and slash arched to form a tunnel that made the last stretch of road into Crossville dim on the sunniest day. After driving miles and miles of woods where trees stood tall and straight as soldiers in a green army, Callie's Cutoff jarred the senses.

The woods cut into Sterling a little deeper than most travelers, awakening her alarm to dark and fearful dangers, conjuring images of the dead and dying. After so many hours reviewing files of what happened, she sensed Henry Johnson's last desperate moments, saw where his father's car was pounded into scrap, felt the hate swirling among the brown pine needles. She shuddered, knowing what it was like to fight for your life in the woods. Henry was only two years younger than her.

Tom Foster, her driver and new partner, inspected the area and hissed against his front teeth. "Even if I didn't know somebody died here, this place is creepy."

"Two somebodies. Henry is the second unsolved murder in Callie's Cutoff." Sterling fingered the bleached blond teased hairdo which recently replaced her

JUSTICE TOMORROW

red hair.

"Great."

"Back in 1865 somebody murdered Callie Epson, daughter of a big Crossville landowner, and her lover," Sterling said. "Legend says the killer scalped her lover to throw the blame on Indians, but everybody knows the son of another landowner did it."

"Everybody knows who killed Henry Johnson too." Tom's upper lip curled. "The county sheriff and his Ku Klux Klan buddies."

"We don't know for sure it was the sheriff. Justice Tomorrow sent us here to find out." Although three years younger than Tom, she felt older from the moment he came into training camp. Gray once quipped that time in the field aged people fast.

Tom steered off the pavement onto the dirt shoulder of the road and threw the car into park. Dust swirled ahead of the tires along the roadside, adding another dirty coat for dying wildflowers to wear.

"Even if we get proof the sheriff did it, nobody will care."

"Someday," she said. "Someday, it'll be possible. We'll testify, have our evidence ready."

"Sterling, I don't want to be a vigilante." Tom picked at threads on his blue suit jacket. "But when I hear the news it makes me crazy. I mean, the police arrested nobody for bombing those poor little colored girls at the church in Alabama."

"But you see what happens when a case goes to trial these days. Not a week after Henry died in September, a jury let the white killers of a Negro Army Reserve officer go scot-free. And the FBI had all the evidence in the world for conviction." The injustice rankled even more since the trial of Lt. Col. Lemuel Penn's killers happened a few hundred miles from where she and Tom sat.

"Proves what I've been saying." Tom pointed his finger at her. "White prosecutors and jurors gonna let their friends and neighbors go."

"It-it won't always be like this."

"How does Gray stand it? Or Silver? Or any of the other colored men in training camp?" Tom cried. "I want to drive into town and shoot the sheriff myself. Why don't they?"

She once asked her old partner the same thing. She gave Tom the answer she got from Gray. "Ever hear of Nate Turner, Red Summer, or-r the Houston riot of the Black Third Battalion, Army Infantry? Check it out. Every time Negroes take up arms there's more of them murdered, hung, and laws passed against them."

"Damn." Tom smacked the roof liner of the car with the flat of his hand.

13

"If you don't believe in Justice Tomorrow, why finagle your way in?" Sterling snapped.

Tom appeared unfazed by her temper. He leaned atop the elbow resting on the driver's window a moment then blurted out, "My father's a sonvabitch, thinks he can run everything. Treats everyone like property he owns, especially coloreds."

"Oh-h-h." Sterling's breath eased out.

Personal experience cradled everyone's idealism. When she was nine a southern university fired her father from the history faculty for his anti-segregation views. His own students chased him from campus. Fearing more violence, the family fled town in the pre-dawn hours. The sting of the night lingered, in part because she loved the little college town. She had friends, and for once life mirrored the wonderful stories her mother told of growing up Southern.

After she partnered with Gray, she discovered there were worse stories than hers. She chewed on her index fingernail.

"Wait, now. I believe in equal rights and nonviolence. 'Course I do," Tom added.

She gave him a reassuring smile she didn't feel. All this talk was filling space, taking time before they hit Crossville and the mission started. His nerves were as raw as hers. It was his first mission. "It's okay to be a little scared. I'd think you were touched if you weren't."

"Oh, I'm sane." He cleared his throat.

"Me too. Sane as can be."

Tom scoffed. "You're not afraid. You're the toughest woman in the world."

Nice. Not only the compliment, but he and the others in camp treated her as a full member of the team, not a wounded, delicate flower they must protect. Tom was okay, but no Gray. She trusted her old partner. After a half dozen investigations together, why separate them?

It was the first of many questions she had about this mission. Justice Tomorrow sent her with a white partner, not a Black. Someone from her team must be in the Black community gathering information. Who? Bookman? Leggett? Ashford? The names of her Black teammates rolled through her mind. It was unusual to have everything so compartmentalized. And why the added secrecy? The afternoon breeze picked up, tossed a candy wrapper to the sky.

Tom took her hand. His blue eyes, a match to hers, studied her. "We'll do great. Hey, we're Sterling and the brothers."

Sterling was the only woman in this particular training session, so someone—probably Gray's brother Silver—gave the team that nickname. Back in camp learning self-defense, marksmanship, survival skills, and interrogation techniques they seemed invincible. They planned to start their own detective agency together: Sterling Brothers Limited—limited to those who served in Justice Tomorrow.

Today she wanted—needed—to believe in Sterling and the brothers. Outside her passenger window the bold red, yellow, and green leaves shook on their tree limbs as though warning her away.

"Let's check out our crime scene." She had already pinpointed the likely location of Henry's murder, the path he and his tormentors took to the tree, spots for the ambushers to hide.

"It's getting dark." Tom craned his neck to see around her. A whiff of Old English after shave drifted in the air. "You wanna check it out?"

"Don't you, Foster?"

"A new bride should call her husband Tom. Or Honey. I like Honey," quipped Tom as he got out of the car.

Sterling guffawed, reached under the seat, and brought two folders into her lap. She opened the one marked Home Recipes to check a location marker in the Johnson dossier. In another folder labeled "Places to See," she wrote a note about the cutoff. Busywork to give her jumpy stomach time to settle.

Outside the windshield, the man playing her husband for this assignment stretched his six-foot body. He had cut his brown shoulder-length hair short yesterday, and a shapeless blue business suit hid firmly toned muscles. She remembered him bare-chested, hair tied in a ponytail with a strip of leather, body straining to break holds in self-defense class.

"I'll walk along the side of the road, see what I can see." He slid a pack of cigarettes from his pants pocket, jiggled it until one fell out. Jamming it between his lips he fished for and found a silver lighter from his other pocket. With a flick the flame lit the tobacco, he inhaled and exhaled smoke. A nearby black cloud of gnats dissolved, reforming further into the woods. Why did there have to be gnats?

"I'll try to see where the body was found." She climbed out, slammed the car door.

Tom reached across the passenger side fender to hand her a small paper bag to store evidence. "In case you find something."

Their fingertips touched and they exchanged a grin. Sterling took a deep breath and forced herself into the woods, to concentrate on the crime scene. She picked her way up an incline to avoid dirt or briars, always scanning for broken twigs, cigarette butts, scraps of cloth or thread, holes in the ground, any and every piece of evidence that might have miraculously survived a month in open air.

The shade of the trees cooled the afternoon warmth. Why hadn't she taken her jean jacket? Her heart beat quickened. Her steps slowed. Feeling the sweat on her back she chided herself for being so nervous. Within moments, she became so attuned to the scene she saw Henry's struggle here, his clawing the ground under her feet, his terror.

With every step into the scene she sank deeper into each leaf, rock, and pine needle. Scary, though no longer a shock to her. It happened during re-training. Gray quipped she'd gained supernatural powers. She laughed, knowing what Gray called her "voodoo-feeling" was insight wedded to research.

Tom's cigarette smoke wafted to her. Blended with the pine it smelled clean and masculine. She squatted behind a clump of bushes where a pattern of dry leaves and needles drew her attention. Her heart raced. Nothing extraordinary, yet hard to ignore.

What was so familiar about these trees near the rise? Her body felt almost weightless. She relaxed and allowed her mind to project the crime from photos, reports, and sparse interviews onto the woods until she knew how it happened, almost as though she'd been a witness. She crouched over the spot where Henry Johnson died.

The notion so startled her she fought for air. She wanted to let it be. Still, her hand reached out one last time. She lifted the edge of a green leaf and check what lay beneath. She swatted the bugs with a free hand, noted indentations in the dirt. The disturbed earth might be the work of an animal digging or if Henry's body was hanged on the oak tree to her right the broken soil . . ..

Tom laughed too loudly. An alert, not humor.

Tires crunching road gravel and dirt, squeaking brakes. A car door slammed. She froze.

Then, she smelled more cigarette smoke, heard muttered voices down on the road.

Peeking between the underbrush she glimpsed a black and white police cruiser parked behind their car. The officer approaching Tom was older by two decades, a little taller, and outweighed her partner by least fifty pounds. Tom blew cigarette smoke toward the woods as the two men talked.

The new arrival matched photos of Sheriff Martin Boyd. Age flecked his dark brown hair with white. Still, his thick, wavy hair was bound to impress female voters in Bell County. He replaced his uniform cap, and his best feature disappeared.

Sterling smacked the heel of her right hand against her head. What could possibly be her excuse for tramping around in these woods? To mark the spot, she found two rocks, piled them up under the bush with the green leaf between them.

Thinking fast she tugged a piece of her pleated blue skirt into the leg of her underwear, rustled the bush, kicked a few noisy dry leaves to the side, then stood and walked into the open.

She picked her way down the incline, adjusting her white blouse into her waistband and yanking down the skirt she just tucked up. Then she glanced at the car and skidded to a halt. Her mouth formed an "O," and her hands flew up, hitting her cheeks a little hard to be sure they showed a shameful red.

Tom gawked. The sheriff focused on his cigarette as though smoking required intense concentration.

After stomping his cigarette butt into the road gravel Tom walked far enough toward her to take her elbow and draw her close. His hand was cold. "Sterling, honey, this is Sheriff Boyd. He saw our car and wondered could he help."

Sterling fluttered her lashes and gave the officer a shy giggle. "Pleased to make your acquaintance."

Boyd tipped the black bill of his cap with a grin. "Mrs. Foster. Your husband was telling me y'all just got married and are moving to Crossville. He's gonna sell real estate with George Thompson."

"Do you live in Crossville?" She wondered what else her partner said.

The sheriff nodded toward town. "My wife and I go to First Baptist up the road."

"We're Baptists too. Small world. Well not small, really, in the South most folks are Baptist." Tom rocked back and forth on his feet. "I've been to small towns where they had two or three Baptist churches."

Sterling beamed at her husband hoping an adoring glance shut his mouth. "Is your wife in the Women's Missionary Union, sheriff?"

"Yes, ma'am."

"I expect we'll be seeing you at church then. Not this Sunday since we're just moving in. I hope y'all have a dandy preacher. Sterling and I are used to a good sermon." Tom extended his hand. "Well, nice to meet you."

Tom put his arm around her waist, and they watched the sheriff drive away. When the cruiser's taillights receded, he exhaled a big breath and gave her a squeeze. "Now what? I'm Catholic. I've never been in a Baptist Church. I thought it was a mortal sin. Do they handle snakes?"

"No idea. I'm Catholic too. I just know about the Missionary Union from typing letters at the Boston YWCA. I worked there part-time to earn extra school money." She scooted back to the car. "Why do Southerners always want to know about your church?"

"It's a way of tellin' how much money you have," Tom said. "We should have told him we were rich Episcopalians. He'd have been more respectful."

Her heartbeat way too fast, and she wiped wet palms across her skirt to dry them. Still, Sterling felt a little better. Her first encounter and she didn't freeze, curl up in a ball—or give in to her new "voodoo" feeling. She survived. So did Tom. She gave him a nod as he climbed behind the wheel. He wore a satisfied grin, his biceps flexed, and his square, dimpled chin lifted.

She ought to explain why an investigator shouldn't prattle on with a potential suspect. Who knows what small thing he might give away? He shouldn't have volunteered they were newlyweds, and he should have been combing the roadside for anything to help their case. Instead, she clammed up. Tom didn't need a lecture and he sure didn't need to know she doubted him. She wasn't alone in her doubts, either. Justice Tomorrow had sent her at the last minute to watch him.

She wondered aloud, "We have to come back here. What excuse can we use?"

****

Sheriff Boyd chuckled as his patrol car drove from Callie's Cutoff. Been a long time since he'd seen a woman as embarrassed as the one he glimpsed in his rearview mirror.

He recalled his momentary alarm when he saw the Impala on the road's shoulder. Foolish really. He and his officers combed these woods for anything left behind after the Johnson boy got disciplined.

Nobody ever found the epaulette from his uniform. He discovered it was missing when he got home—shows how pumped he was. Hell, his uniform may have ripped earlier in the morning. Boyd pretty much knew where he and the boy tussled, but damned if he found anything there.

Boyd wiped his sweaty palm on his pants, gave the couple in his mirror a final gander. Handsome pair.

The man, Tom Foster, impressed him as the kinda fast-talking salesman type who'd do well at Thompson's Homestead real estate office. The wife acted cute, innocent, and eager to please. While not beautiful, she appealed to him. Welcome additions to the town. And he'd enjoy admiring Mrs. Foster's legs. He got to see more of them than she intended.

Lust. The devil's tool. He accepted he was a sinner, but his wife Peg—and Jesus—kept him on the path to heaven.

"Through the blood of Jesus, I'm saved," he confessed to the empty cruiser.

CHAPTER FIVE

The facade of Parson's General Store on the outskirts of Crossville needed repair, but it boasted a shiny metallic Coca-Cola sign and new gas pumps. A patchwork of poverty and prosperity. The houses sitting back from the road on either side were like the store, half fading in and half faded out.

Tom pulled to the side of the road to let an army convoy pass. The trucks full of men and munitions rumbled by homes with rusted metal roofs and sagging front porches where half a dozen children played in the yard. Crossville lay between military installations that were too far away to help the local economy.

Sterling leaned her chin on an elbow jutting from the open car window. What was life like for those kids, for people who never left Crossville? What must it be like to live in one place all the time, raise children there, die there? She lived in five college towns before her father settled at Harvard.

When the last military vehicle passed, Tom followed it on the road to Crossville. Three old white men fingering their suspenders sat on the porch out front watching with undisguised interest as Tom and Sterling's car drove by Parson's. A lanky Black man in overalls and a holey blue shirt lounged against a fence post on the right. A Black woman shooing a toddler came out the side of the store and made her way through tall weeds toward him. The door swinging shut behind her said in crooked letters: "Colored Women."

Sterling lifted her head. "You see the bathroom door?"

Tom glanced in the rearview mirror, puzzled. "Ah, what was wrong with it?"

She hoped segregated bathrooms and water fountains were norms she never got used to. To be fair, such things might not be so startling had she spent her whole life in the South like Tom. The sensation of traveling back in time left her weary. Isolated. Captured.

"Almost there," he said.

Houses with weathered frames and crumbling porches hinted of hard times in Bell County. Weeds and mailboxes askew dotted the side of the road. Plowed fields carved out of pine forests dotted the acres between houses and looked as tired as the farmers she noticed. Even bigger homes with siding and mowed front yards carried telltale signs of stress: gates off a hinge, screen doors sprung open, flowers drooping in cracked planters.

Until they drove past acres of pasture and woods on the opposite side of Main Street.

"Gateway to Crossville business district. Nice, huh?" Tom said.

A restored plantation home with white columns sprawled back from the road on their left as they passed the city limits. Sterling wondered who on earth lived in such a mansion amid the pine trees until she noticed the cross on the door and read the sign out front inviting her to services at First Methodist Church.

"Huh. The Methodists have muscle," Tom mused. "Interestin'."

Further down the street business fronts sported bright white paint, washed red brick, or some combination. Green shutters shining tacky with fresh paint accented the hardware store, a Black man painted red trim to brighten the department store windows. Down the road on the right, the white columns of the courthouse and smaller public library next door sparkled in the sun.

Since it was Monday the A&P grocery store near the Methodist church bustled with shoppers who needed to restock after Sunday closings. People carried loaded brown paper bags into cars parked facing meters. New streetlamps stood along clean sidewalks. The town square looked like it was expecting company.

"There's my office." Tom pointed to a rectangular building next to the bank. "Homestead Realty."

"Can you sell real estate?"

His eyebrows arched. "Honey, I can sell anything. Wait here. I have to pick up the keys to our furnished rental here."

He parked the car out front, neglecting to feed a nickel into the meter, and left her to examine her new hometown. A Black mother in a maid's uniform and her sullen son walked by, each carrying a brown paper sack of groceries.

Nice. Homey. Evergreens and grass in a park-like strip between the two main business streets, flowers in white wooden boxes flanking the bookstore, the A&P, and a dress shop.

JUSTICE TOMORROW

How long would she be in such a lovely spot caretaking Tom and investigating Henry's murder? A month, two months, four?

Catty-corner to her sat a narrow wooden building with a brown roof. "Emporium," the sign read. She squinted and read in smaller letters: "Crossville Historical Society." A punch of interest tingled along her spine into her fingertips.

An American flag waved in front of the Emporium, and over its roof, she glimpsed part of the flying red horse sign of the Mobil gas station building behind it. A closer inspection showed the flag marked the entrance to the U.S. Post Office next door, a building much like the physique of her Aunt Bridget, narrow in the front and wide in the back. Like most buildings she could see in Crossville's business area, the Emporium and Post Office were separated by a small alley barely wide enough for a car. Quaint wooden rain barrels sat off to one side of each alley.

Two wiry Black men talked outside the Post Office, one in overalls and the other in a tan uniform. They took a half-step to the side to allow a white man in a suit to stride down the middle of the sidewalk. They never stopped their conversation.

Sterling got out of the car and let a milk delivery truck pass. Jaywalking towards the Emporium, she crossed over the grassy, parklike strip separating one side of the business district from the other. Two Black women paused for her to go in front of them, then picked up their animated conversation further down the sidewalk.

Someone had taped a homemade sign advertising the Crossville Methodist Church Carnival on December fourth to an inside window of the Emporium. Next to it hung a more professional-looking sign that reminded folks only they could prevent forest fires. A soft bell jingled as she entered.

"Be with you in a minute," a woman's muffled voice came from the other side of a curtain stretching behind the front counter.

"Take your time," Sterling called and strolled around, inhaling deeply. The place smelled like home.

Her first impression was lemon. Not a scent she associated with cooking or baking, but with a furniture oil her mother used. She also recognized the musty odor of old books and antique cabinetry so typical of her father's study.

Shelves and display cases of ladies' scarves, earrings, necklaces, lace or cotton detachable collars, shawls, and sweaters jammed one corner. Vases, tablecloths, glasses, and silverware for setting a proper dining table crammed into another. Neither had seen a dust rag in months.

The entire back half the store, the part clearly lavished with love, reminded her of her father's office. She didn't have to be a detective to figure which where

21

the owner of the Emporium spent the most time.

Except for the heavy blue curtain hanging on an archway behind the counter, the rear half of the Emporium sported little color. Books, bound in black or the occasional red or blue, and framed historical newspapers lined the walls and shelves. Pale wooden tables trimmed sat around the room in no clear pattern. She ran her hands along the spines of handmade family genealogies, printed local history, and crumbling census books as she walked the creaky wooden floor.

In the far corner, a lamp illuminated a small but properly set dinner table. A delicate bud vase in the center held a single rose. She grinned.

"Do you like it?" a woman's voice asked. "The flatware's on sale."

A rotund woman old enough to be her grandmother approached. She wore an easy sweet smile, a pink sweater with a matching cardigan and a brown skirt. Just seeing her warmed Sterling. The woman fingered one pink-flowered earring and pointed to the table.

"Some of these items have an important story to tell about Crossville history."

"It's nice." Heart in her throat Sterling added softly, "I-I love sterling. If flatware's on sale, a salad fork might interest me."

The woman's hazel eyes widened.

"Really? I'm Harriet Cook, owner of the Emporium and historian here. Volunteer historian." She licked her lips as though they'd suddenly gone dry.

"Sterling Foster. My husband and I just arrived in town. While he was getting the key to our house, I popped over."

The woman stole a glance at the front door. "How lovely. You know, sterling silver fell out of favor after the 1940s."

"I like to set a table with sterling," Sterling answered dutifully.

"Many young women do." Harriet said.

How wonderful to discover her local contact with so little effort. Relieved, Sterling picked up a fork and waited for Harriet to acknowledge her code.

"I-I see you like the feel of sterling silver," Harriet choked.

Sterling's breathing eased. Harriet must be the person who called Justice Tomorrow to Crossville.

"Glad to meet you, to have you here at last," Harriet whispered. "We get a lot of company in here, so we need to be careful."

An odd relief replaced the tension Sterling carried in her neck.

"If you like this piece," Harriet pointed to the fork in Sterling's hand, "I have lovely silver in the back from my great-grandmother's collection. A tea service. Care to see?"

"Sure." This wasn't part of the sign and countersign. Puzzled, Sterling followed Harriet through the heavy curtains behind the front counter.

Boxes, wooden chests, an old dressmaker dummy, a rusted-handle sink, and a few scattered chairs filled the large storeroom beyond the curtains. A rustic key rested in the backdoor lock as though someone had forgotten to remove it decades ago. Harriet snapped on a light, which did little to illuminate the room, then craned her neck. "Hello?"

A Black man eased out of the shadows from behind piles of cardboard boxes and Sterling flushed. Armed with a flashlight, Gray looked like he'd been hunting for something. Since she last saw him, he'd cut his Afro to nothing. A dingy white shirt hung off his wide shoulders as though he'd thrown it on without time to button it right.

His eyes widened and his mouth dropped when he recognized her.

"Gray, when you finish with those boxes wash the outside windows." Harriet massaged her hands as though they ached.

"Yes ma'am. Soon's I finish up here." He did a poor job of sounding subservient.

"All right. Ah, Gray does odd jobs once in a while." Harriet wiped her hand on her skirt. "The sterling tea set is in the top box. Get it for Mrs. Foster."

As soon as Harriet parted the curtain and ducked out Sterling grinned. "They told me I'd have no trouble finding my contact. How are things?"

"Whoever thought jeans were comfortable?" He grimaced.

"The sacrifices we make." She almost laughed out loud when he growled at her. Gray did like to dress well. "Anyone here besides you, me, and Foster?"

"Silver. We've been here almost month and have more questions than when I arrived."

"Swell."

"Ajamu Watts got here five days ago."

Sterling stiffened. "He-who-fights-for-what-he-wants?"

"Appropriate African name he assumed, don't you agree? Nigerian. I also took the trouble to look up the meaning of his name after I made his acquaintance." Gray rubbed his jaw like it hurt.

"Sucker punch?" It wasn't hard to imagine Gray in a fight—an aura of violence hovered around him. Hard to imagine him losing even to a Black militant famous for his quick temper and quicker fists.

"He's got kin around, but he's not acting like he's here for a family reunion. His being here complicates matters. He attracts violence—or he creates it." Gray took down a cardboard box, opened it to reveal a sterling silver tea set, and pointed.

Sterling exclaimed loud enough for anyone beyond the curtain to hear. "What lovely sterling pieces, Mrs. Cook."

"Thank you," she called back.

"Harriet's dedicated. She insists we stay in character even when alone," Gray half-whispered. "Not a bad practice. I do odd jobs for Harriet, but not often. I work next door at the Post Office. Again. When Justice Tomorrow assignments are all over, I might qualify for a Post Office pension."

"Are you the college boy around here?" No matter where their assignment was, Gray picked up the title.

Gray's nose wrinkled in a sour look. "I'm getting good at acting dumb. Reminds me, what are you doing —."

The front bell jingled. Harriet greeted someone.

"I'll see how Harriet feels about my coming by more often. For research." Sterling straightened her belt. "I have to meet Tom. We're moving into our new house."

"Tom?" Gray scowled. "Look, there's more going on here than anything we've seen. Black folks evicted, threatened."

"How many?"

Gray counted on his fingers. "Four, no, five Black farms gone so far."

"What does this have to do with Henry Johnson?"

"No idea." He shook his head. "I'm thinking the situation here goes far beyond what we've ever seen. Sterling, you have a problem."

"Mrs. Foster? Your husband is here." Harriet called.

Quick as a thought, Gray slipped out of the back door.

Sterling frowned at his abrupt departure, then parted the curtain to find Tom glowering in front of the counter.

She heard a faint toe-tapping on the floor as though he were impatient. He played the part of an irate husband well.

"I told you to wait in the car. When you were gone, I went ape. Where did you go, and it getting dark? Then I saw the sign." Tom turned to Harriet. "She loves jewelry, history, and old things."

"Then she will love me," Harriet cocked her head toward Sterling.

Tom pointed out the left front window. "I didn't think to ask George Thompson, but is the Methodist Church over there at plantation mansion?"

"Yes indeedy. Our resident contrarian built it almost a hundred years ago and left enough money to the church for years of upkeep," said Harriet.

"'Resident contrarian'," said Sterling. "Sounds like a good story."

Harriet chuckled. "Oh, yes. John Cross was a wealthy man. He had a son, but none of his descendants live around here anymore. He got mad at the Baptists and left the house and a nice sum to the little band of Methodists. I

JUSTICE TOMORROW

researched it once."

"Mrs. Cook, may I do research with you? Tom's right. I love history."

Harriet put an arm around her waist and drew Sterling close. "You must call me Harriet. Come anytime."

The doorbell tinkled again. A woman in a black shirtwaist dress accented by red heels and a red scarf swooped in. Judging by the brown age spots underneath the powder and rouge on her cheeks, she and Harriet were close to the same age. She examined jewelry displays in passing and sniffed as though something unpleasant reached her nostrils. The tilt of her chin, the slight arch of one brow, and her thin lips made her appear like a queen inspecting her troops. She sauntered to the counter, removed her black leather gloves, and tapped them against her palm.

Amused, Harriet said, "Alice Peterson. You are just in time to meet two of our newest citizens." She made the introductions, nodding to Tom and Sterling, "Alice is the wife of the bank president."

"What are you doing in Harriet's lair?" Alice's height made Sterling feel small. She imagined Alice knew what affect her height had on people and used it.

"I came to volunteer, Mrs. Peterson. I have an interest—."

"In what," Alice put her leather handbag on the counter. "The origins of Indian tribes around town? The decline of timber industry?"

"I'm interested in a local legend. The one about Callie Epson and Callie's Cutoff."

Both women stared as though she'd grown two heads.

Alice collected her purse. Through tight lips she said, "I'm an Epson on my mother's side."

Sterling's hands flew together in a prayer pose. "Can you help me?"

"Family history's a personal thing, young lady," snapped Alice. "But I won't forbid you."

"I imagine she's relieved to hear it," said Harriet.

Alice ignored the sarcasm. "Harriet, the bake sale is Saturday and I have no idea what you're bringing. This is getting to be a habit with you."

"I always bring sugar cookies. You're here because you miss seeing me."

Alice huffed. "Are we still on for bridge tomorrow?"

"Noon at my house. See you then."

Alice examined Sterling from hairstyle to shoes. "Do you play? Few young girls do."

"I'm actually pretty good."

A wisp of Alice's brown hair, badly dyed to mask the grey, dared to fall out of place and cross her forehead. She disciplined it with a swat of her hand.

"My daughter has a group of younger women who play. Perhaps she will call you to substitute in their group."

"Perhaps," said Sterling.

"And you sell real estate." Another of Alice's blunt remarks, this one aimed at Tom.

"I also play bridge."

Alice put the strap of her purse on her arm. "I am impressed. You both may stay. Good afternoon, Harriet."

"Good afternoon, Alice. You always leave me warm and fuzzy."

Alice waved her off as she opened the front door.

Harriet laughed. "Alice's family has lots of money, one of the founding families in town. We've been the closest of friends since forever. I love her beyond reason, but she can be off-putting."

"Left me all warm and fuzzy," Sterling murmured.

"You'll do fine in Crossville. Alice likes you." A shadow crossed Harriet's face and she frowned. "See you later?"

"Yes, tomorrow."

"Come in the morning. I have bridge later."

CHAPTER SIX

Gray's heart pounded so fast once outside the Emporium he had to stop, suck in some air, slow things down. What the hell was Sterling doing here?

The sight of her in the Emporium storeroom gut-punched him. He expected Foster, so why had Justice Tomorrow included her? She'd earned a longer rest after being shot. Besides, she might be in danger.

Justice Tomorrow had sent word that the state police had issued a multi-state alert for a young, educated, light-skinned Black man and a petite, red-haired woman with freckles known to be traveling around the South stirring up Civil Rights agitators and stealing. Somehow their other work in South Carolina, Mississippi, and Tennessee got linked to what happened in Alabama. Though small and dying, the Klan commanded members or sympathizers among police officers throughout the South. Word of civil rights agitators spread rapidly through law enforcement.

Did Sterling know about the alert? He started to ask, then Foster showed. Just thinking of her made him grin like a fool. He had missed her. Quick-witted, sarcastic, smart, and so pretty. No. Nope—life was dangerous enough, painful enough without thoughts like those. He booted them to the depths of his soul, kicked a rock, and followed its bounce down the alley. Staying in the shadows of the store, he crossed the alley behind the buildings, where cars were parked. He leaned against the Post Office on the corner to check and see who was out and about on Main. Threads of his shirt caught on the brick building as though tying him to a place he hated.

The Crossville postmaster made Gray's life so miserable that his cover grew more demeaning and tedious every day. But he had to stay with it. He spit on the brick, taking out his disgust on the building.

The local Post Office served as the investigation's communication lifeline. Information flowed to the Justice Tomorrow team in ordinary envelopes watched over by one of the two senior investigators assigned to the case. For this assignment, Gray swept floors, stacked sacks of letters and circulars near the mail slots for the postmaster and read as many of the addresses and return addresses as possible. Gray watched for the envelopes addressed to Harriet Cook from Cousin Mabel Justice in Virginia. Cousin Mabel's letters contained Justice Tomorrow information meant for him. Sometimes they got delivered to Harriet and she sent for him to do an odd job. Most often he slipped the letter inside his shirt with little fear of discovery.

But he wasn't just looking for Justice Tomorrow messages. He also scanned the mail for any odd letters or packages or return addresses from known segregationist groups. Sometimes an investigator got lucky—working as a postal clerk Silver once spotted a letter which suggested an unlikely killer.

As important as the Post Office was, investigators had other ways of communicating. White primary investigators had a handler who pretended to be a family member calling weekly to chat. Sometimes the weekly talk carried coded instructions that no one overhearing on a party line would understand. Since Black investigators often stayed with people who had no phone, their handlers, posing as family, called the local church to ask about them. Silver worked for Reverend Johnson for that reason.

Failure to report or acknowledge communications brought the Justice Tomorrow cavalry. Or, as Sterling noted, the green escape cars.

Burying his hands in his pockets, Gray left the Post Office corner and walked across to Reverend Johnson's Mt. Moriah Church. Maybe Crossville would be his last assignment. It sure as hell should be Sterling's.

A car slowed, and somebody shouted a cheerful, "Hey, man." Gray waved and trotted across to the shadow of the church steeple. On the other side, he settled on an old tree stump to gather his thoughts. The stump had a clear view of the Emporium's back door where Harriet left signals for a meet. He could not go to the Emporium often to avoid being linked to Harriet, so he fell into the habit of sitting by the church. People got used to his loitering there.

Gray put both hands on his knees and swiveled his head toward white Crossville. Clean, neat, prosperous. Next, he turned to the aging wood buildings of the South End, the potholes in the street, the run-down school two blocks away under the cover of trees, the neglected shotgun houses and farms sitting off the gravel roads intersecting with Main. A throbbing pain began in his sinuses. His landlady's two-story house across from the barbershop was one of only three two-story buildings in his part of town. The houses at the far end of Main still had outhouses. Why didn't white people see the injustice?

Change was coming. Someday. For his children—or their children. But weren't those words the same as his mother and father spoke when they left teaching jobs in Connecticut for the rural South? And what did it get them besides pain and death? Gray stayed on the stump longer than he planned, unable to resist peeking at the Emporium door. Hoping to see Sterling again.

She had looked good. Relieved. Even happy to see him. They worked well together, sensing each other's moods and plays. Although she took so many risks, she alarmed a cautious man like him. One of his recurring nightmares was the time she crawled behind bushes to overhear a conversation between two suspects. Or the time she challenged a white man's treatment of a Black woman–he broke into a sweat remembering it. And Alabama. Always the Alabama woods.

The smell of onions cooking drifted from a house Southenders patronized for special occasions like anniversaries—when they had the extra money. His stomach rumbled. He rose, headed for the barbershop, but only took one step. Down the street in front of the barber pole Ajamu Watts was talking with— no, recruiting—three young Black men. As usual, Gray's younger brother Silver hung on the militant's every word. Silver would be glad to know Foster had arrived. Gray had doubts about the guy.

Foster had no idea how to pull Sterling back from the edge when she inevitably threw herself into a dangerous situation. He would be too busy flirting or saving his own ass to care about anyone else. Gray ground his teeth. Where others saw inexperience in Foster, Gray found selfishness and cunning.

The increased size of the investigation in Crossville gave Gray pause too. His report on the evictions of Black farmers, Ajamu, and the suggestion the land grab held the key to Henry Johnson's murder must have triggered an alarm. Or maybe his bleak assessment of the morale in the Black community caused Justice Tomorrow to figure new brains might jump-start the case.

He glanced once more toward Carl Poke's barbershop, then jogged across Main toward the room he rented from the widow Carson, his Justice Tomorrow contact. Dust flew over his jean cuffs from passing cars.

"Gray!" The change in Silver's pocket jingled as he crossed the street. "Church's having a supper. Wanna swing over?"

"Oh, you got time to talk to me? We're supposed to be friends now?" Gray kept walking. "Ajamu must have left town."

His brother ignored the jab and whispered, "Hey, Yale beat Harvard. Us Yalies gotta love it."

"Don't give a damn."

"What's eatin' you?" Silver scooted in front of his older brother. A good three inches shorter and fifteen pounds lighter, he stopped Gray in his tracks. Gray hadn't noticed, but his little brother was developing muscles and letting his Afro grow back.

"Sterling came with Foster."

"Cool."

"Now there're four of us here for one murder, counting Foster as a real investigator."

"Uh, huh. You still don't like him." Silver gave his brother a crooked smile.

"I don't trust him."

Silver snorted. "Remember, when I recruited him he was in the hospital 'cause he got hurt in Freedom Summer."

"You didn't recruit him," Gray scoffed. "He horned in on Justice Tomorrow."

"He's here now laying it on the line," Silver bristled.

"He's preppy, cocky, self-absorbed, and oh, so very white."

"Except for the white part, he could be you." Silver chuckled.

Gray swore. "He's . . . a con artist."

"A good thing in our present line of work."

"Well, he played you."

Silver's grin vanished. "I'm glad Sterling came. Now you have somebody you trust to talk to." He whirled and jogged into the street.

"Sorry. Hey, Silver . . ." But his brother dodged a car and kept going as though he hadn't heard.

Gray trudged up the outside wooden stairs to his room feeling lower than snake spit. Much as it pained him to admit, Silver got a few things right. Foster may have tricked Silver to learn about Justice Tomorrow, but no denying he had a way of winning people over—even people he was using to get his way.

And Gray did have Sterling to talk to. Senior investigators did have a way of communicating with each other. Part of his job meant meeting with his white counterpart for sporadic updates. They would rendezvous at a designated safe house, saving the Emporium for an emergency. Until today he figured his contact was Foster. Contentment spread over him.

Gray decided to wash, head over to the church supper, and patch it up with Silver. He worried about his little brother. Now he had Sterling to worry about too.

30

CHAPTER SEVEN

In the gathering dark, Tom and Sterling faced a dingy clapboard house enclosed by what might be loosely called a white picket fence.

"Every woman's dream," she muttered. "I bet it has rats."

"You'd think we'd get better from a rich organization like Justice Tomorrow," Tom groused.

Sterling's lips vibrated in derision. He had the decency to hang his head.

"'Course as the new man, I don't know how rich it is or who all's involved in Justice Tomorrow. I bet you do," he said.

"No idea."

As they stood in silence, Sterling drifted to her college days working part-time at the Boston YWCA, learning about the civil rights struggle, and meeting at night with Black students in a small group affiliated with the Southern Christian Leadership Conference.

"You okay?" Tom asked. "You look whipped."

Sterling dropped her head to hide tears. Discouraged, afraid, homesick, and, yes, whipped. She should have listened to her mother and turned down this assignment. Her brother should never have joined the Army. They both ought to be home.

Tom nudged her. "Well, let's go." He walked to the rear of the car and opened the trunk to pull out their suitcases. Sterling took hers, noting how Tom's arms and hands jerked anxiously. He acted like someone having second thoughts about the job too.

She glanced around the neighborhood. It wasn't much. "A bit deserted out here."

Their house and two other buildings intruded on a paved street where weeds, briars, and trees grew wild. On one side of their rental sat a well-maintained home built like theirs and to the left, sat an abandoned store. She blinked in surprise.

"My boss told me a girl came over today to clean it and make beds after the movers put our things inside." Tom leaned over to whisper, "The biggest bedroom has a double bed."

She grabbed her throat and pretended to choke.

"Hm-m. Not thrilled. Okay," he said. "Well, we live next door to a building which might collapse any minute and our house backs up to a creek that floods."

"If you're trying to sell me, your pitch needs work."

The dilapidated general store next door was her safe house, somewhere to hide in case of trouble and meet Gray when needed. Awfully close to home. Bushes hid the lower half of the safe house from the street. The ramshackle wood frame probably rested on brick pilings, but it slanted. Or maybe her weariness put her off-center. She tilted her head until the building straightened.

"What are you doing?" Tom frowned. "Oh, the abandoned grocery store. Eyesore. Well, see how the windows in our rental are near to the ground and almost hidden by weeds and bushes? Those side windows are a good way to slip out of our house."

"Why do we care?" She wisecracked to cover the panic of thinking Tom knew the location of her safe house.

He threw her a puzzled glance.

Sterling's spine prickled with the voodoo feeling. Sometimes these spells heightened her senses until she saw sounds and heard colors.

Nobody but the other primary investigator should know about her safe house. She didn't know Tom's or Silver's. All their lives might depend on it. Did Tom know about the old store? She couldn't tell.

What had been an earlier suspicion for Sterling crystallized into fact. As usual, Gray got it right. Something about this assignment was different. What was Tom doing on an assignment so soon? Why hadn't she and Tom gotten the same information? Why was a known militant like Ajamu in Crossville of all places? Until she got a better handle on things, she'd best be careful what she said. Especially to Tom.

Her fake husband, who had been all optimistic chatter on the way to the house, started telling her about real estate. He prattled on about how few people lived in the town, how people could build anywhere since zoning laws were lax, the recent county commissioner election, and similar topics until her eyes glazed over. She perked up to hear how much he liked George Thompson, owner of the real estate office. George apparently accepted Tom's story about being the newlywed friend of his college roommate's son's cousin. Sterling

32

always marveled how the most tenuous connections were embraced by Southerners—and it helped Tom's case that George was desperate for real estate help

But Tom's happy chatter had vanished. He stared crestfallen at the furnished rental.

Sterling picked up her small suitcase, noticing the smell of freshly cut grass. "Be it ever so humble, there's no place like . . ."

Tom grabbed her arm. "Can rats turn on lights?"

CHAPTER EIGHT

Fear incinerated Sterling's fatigue. She set her suitcase down and followed him into the yard far enough to let them peer through one of the two front windows.

"It might be . . . candles flickering," he hissed. "Someone carrying candles?"

People were after her, people inside the house waiting to grab her. She gulped away waves of sweat and nausea.

Tom grabbed a rake leaning against the front steps' handrail, stepped up carefully, and motioned her onto the porch next to him. Hands shaking, Sterling followed. She tip-toed across the wooden porch and slowly twisted the knob. The door opened without a squeak as though it had just been oiled.

She forced herself to slip inside behind Tom. Side by side they crept by the staircase in the entryway, past a small room on the left, and toward the living room on the right piled with cardboard boxes, then the dining room and kitchen.

As they got closer, a whiff of baked apples and something else delicious reached her nose. Her stomach growled in answer. Whispers came from the back.

"Honey, we gotta go. They'll be here any minute," a man's voice said.

Sterling and Tom crept closer to the kitchen.

"I don't know about leaving these candles burnin'. What if they're late and the whole place burns? What a great surprise!" a young woman said.

Sterling sensed Tom relax, and she peeked into the kitchen. At the same time, her relieved exhale startled the couple standing around a table set for dinner. An arrangement of wildflowers flanked by two Chianti wine bottles holding lighted candles decorated the table.

Tom fumbled for a wall switch and turned on the kitchen light.

At the far end of the room by a window stood a shocked couple: a rail-thin blonde in tan slacks, brown paisley blouse, and white apron leaned against a man who towered over her by at least a foot. Despite his pink colored shirt and blue jeans, Sterling took in the buzz cut of the man's brown hair and figured he was military. Both their mouths formed 'Os.' The woman recovered first.

"Surprise! Welcome home! We're your next-door neighbors, Nancy and J.T. Dawson. We wanted to make you feel at home with a home-cooked dinner for two." She chuckled. "Didn't mean to get caught."

"Hope we didn't scare you." J.T. stared at the rake in Tom's hand. Tom glanced at it, grinned, then leaned it against a kitchen wall covered in orange and yellow floral wallpaper.

"Tom and Sterling." He walked across the kitchen and extended his hand to J.T.

"The girl cleaning up today let us in. I use her sometimes on Fridays. J.T. cut the grass in the front, so it wasn't such a wilderness, and I unpacked some of your kitchen things, washed them up to use. I hope you don't mind us being forward, but we want Crossville to feel like your home." The bright red of embarrassment faded from Nancy's cheeks and the remaining pink softened her narrow features.

She squeezed her husband's hand. "Come on, J.T. We best leave you two to eat. Dinner's in the oven to keep warm. There's a Jell-O mold in the refrigerator for salad. Apple pie for dessert."

Sterling never liked a woman so much at first meeting. It was as though Nancy had opened a memory sweet as the apple pie on the kitchen counter.

She came over to take Nancy's free hand. "I never heard of anybody doing something so nice in my whole life. Stay and eat with us?"

Nancy shook her head. "No siree. Y'all are worn out from the trip and the move. I hope there'll be plenty more times to have dinner together."

"You can count on it," Tom said.

As he stiff-armed the backdoor to go, J.T. called. "You need anything let me know. I like to do carpentry when I'm not being a yard boy or deputy sheriff."

When the door shut, Tom rubbed his hands together. "Let's eat."

"Deputy sheriff?" She enunciated each syllable.

"Yum-m. Yes, Sterling, our neighbor is a deputy sheriff. Our back door and part of the side of our rental home is visible from his house. See why the side window escape is so cool? We can get out without a chance of his seeing us."

"Hm-mm." They did get different briefings from Justice Tomorrow. But Tom didn't seem to know that her safe house was next door: one example of standard procedure in an assignment sorely lacking them so far.

35

Sterling opened the oven door and pulled out dinner as her stomach and taste buds leapt to attention. After piling her plate with pieces of fried chicken, mashed potatoes swimming in butter, and green beans, she sat down and ate as if she had never seen food before.

Tom watched in wonder. "I like a woman with a good appetite."

She gave him the bird but didn't let the use of her middle finger interfere with lifting a drumstick to her mouth.

Tom chuckled. "You know, George and I talked a little about the market for land in Crossville. He's the only county commissioner. They needed to hire another person in the real estate office. Me. Apparently, there's a lot more action here than you'd think. Lots of folks from as far away as Atlanta are interested in farming here."

Sterling tried imagining an Atlanta banker plowing Crossville fields. Silly. She told Tom about seeing Gray, the troublesome appearance of a radical like Ajamu, and Blacks being tossed off their land.

"Do you think Gray's right about the land?" She pointed with a chicken thigh in her hand. "Don't you find it weird?"

Tom gazed with undisguised interest as she patted her mouth with her napkin.

"I said, isn't it weird?"

He jerked back from wherever he'd been. "For such a nothing town? I'm not into what's happening," his drawl became exaggerated "but I gotta think a sudden interest in farming shore ain't it."

She tried to sound casual. "Did you, ah, ask anything about Henry's murder?"

"Nope." Tom lay his fork down and leaned back in his chair. "I told George we stopped at Callie's Cutoff and met the sheriff there. George's big fat grin disappeared right away. When I asked if something was wrong, he said the place was snake bit."

Since Tom stopped staring at her, Sterling relaxed. He stretched out in the chair like he wanted to create more room for chicken. She didn't know him as well as she did the other members of her team. During the interminable drive to Crossville, he'd tried to make conversation. But instead of paying attention to her new partner she alternated between re-reading the files, studying the map of the town, and battling the fear of going back into the field. Dumb. To guide a new investigator, she had to know him. "Tom, why did you leave Georgia Tech?"

"I dropped out of Vanderbilt too." One eyebrow arched. "Does it matter?"

"Just wondered. I never asked where you went to school, where you were when you joined. You know, stuff a fake bride oughta know."

He fidgeted. "Originally from Atlanta. I had my whole life laid out for me from cradle to grave, life to death, single to marriage, and beyond. I woke up one day and didn't like the plan. You?"

"I actually went to the University of Georgia in Athens for one quarter."

"Aren't you from Radcliffe College?" Both his eyebrows shot up.

"I transferred. But I love the South. I felt a real sense of belonging when I lived there briefly as a girl."

"What made you leave Athens?"

"I was homesick. I was the youngest girl in my dorm. Only seventeen," she said.

He rolled his eyes. "You weren't homesick. Come on now. Why'd you leave?"

She took a long time to answer. "I liked it too much."

Tom laughed. "What kind of answer is that?"

"Maybe I got out of Georgia because, well, I had to be true to myself." She also knew the minute she felt comfortable and content, something uprooted her. Better to leave on her own terms. Control the darkness.

"And is that what Justice Tomorrow is for you? Being true to who you are?" Tom's voice dropped low and husky.

"Okay, I admit it. I get a rush out of investigations. I love finding out what nobody wants you to know then using it to turn people's lives upside down. People who deserve it." Saying it aloud warmed her. She'd forgotten amid the agony of her last assignment.

"For real?" Tom wiped his mouth and threw down his napkin.

"What about you? What do you want?"

"Nobody ever asked me. I never figured it out. I just eliminate stuff I don't want. I'll get at those boxes in the living room, so we can get settled." He pushed back his chair and patted her shoulder as he walked by. He didn't bother to take his plate to the sink.

She twisted around to watch him leave. Handsome and sexy, no doubt. Got some problems with his father too. Didn't he ever finish anything? She stood to clear the table.

By the time she'd washed and put up the last glass, blessing Nancy Dawson for organizing most of the dishes in the walnut cabinets, Sterling felt wrung out. More tired than normal. Grateful as she was for dinner, she questioned her new neighbors' motives. Why were a deputy sheriff and his wife being overly nice to newcomers?

From time to time over the clatter of dishes and splash of dishwater, she paused in her musings about the neighbors to catch the sounds of boxes being crunched, the front door opening and closing, and a grunt or two as Tom lifted something. When she heard his footsteps going upstairs, she decided she'd better go claim a bed.

At the foot of the stairs, she glanced into the study at the left of the staircase then turned right to look over the sparsely furnished living room. She reached for the light switch. The sudden flash of light reflected in the one large front window. Tom had made progress unpacking and setting up things. The small television set sat unplugged in a corner on a rickety table. Flattened cardboard boxes of all sizes lay stacked in a corner. She recognized none of the furniture or wall-hangings. But the framed photographs Tom set up on an oak end table next to a worn club chair and on the bookcase on the opposite wall rang true.

For one photo, she wore a long white peasant dress with a garland of wildflowers in her hair. Tom had on a blue suit and white shirt but no tie. They were standing outside a church door as though they had just gotten married. In the other picture, she and Tom posed in jeans sitting in front of tombstones in the Athens cemetery where University of Georgia students studied for fall and spring quarter finals.

She stared for a second at the long straw-colored wig she'd worn for the staged photographs and decided blond was more Nancy's color than hers. She'd worn the wig because she hadn't bleached her red hair yet and remembered how it itched.

The smiling faces in the fake wedding photos made her wonder. Could a wedding picture be real for her someday? She never dated much. Marriage and family lurked in the back of her head, but never reached the front. Happily-ever-after made her shiver in fear—or anticipation. Or exhaustion. Yes, she was "flat wore out," as her Mississippi grandmother used to say. Sterling snapped off the light, checked the front door lock, and climbed the stairs. Each step felt higher than the last.

The one bathroom in the house was on the second floor. As she climbed the last step, she heard Tom gargling inside the bathroom. A narrow hall the width of the house linked two bedrooms and the bath. To the right was a lighted bedroom furnished with a floral-covered chaise and double bed. Tom's bag rested on a chair inside the door.

She turned left, flipped on the light, and discovered a four-poster bed with matching cherry nightstand and dresser. The massive furniture swallowed any free space in the room. But the bed was made, covered with a colorfully stitched quilt, and she saw a clear path to it from the door. Good enough.

Even better, she found her suitcase atop the dresser. Thoughtful of Tom to bring it up. She snapped open the metal fasteners and opened it to drag out her pajamas, robe, and bag of toiletries. The new lace chemise she'd bought to wear under a short dress had caught in her pajamas. She untangled it, held it up to admire. Behind her, Tom caught his breath. Balling up the chemise, she thrust it into the suitcase and turned to him.

"We've gotta come up with another way to do things, Tom. People can't be seeing lights in two different bedrooms every night. Not in the home of newlyweds."

"No kidding." His voice from her doorway sounded thick and hoarse. His hungry look held no mystery. A funny ripple coursed through her.

"I mean, you're right." Tom turned off her light and waited in the hall.

The heat from his body created flutters in her stomach as she brushed by on her way into the bathroom. Once inside, she leaned against the sink and chewed a fingernail. Playing at marriage to Tom might prove harder than solving Henry Johnson's murder.

CHAPTER NINE

Gray burnt his tongue on hot coffee in his rush to finish lunch and get to his job at the Post Office. The burn put a Jim dandy exclamation point on a day he already dreaded.

The old cracker who ran the place had to be the whitest white man he ever saw. Albino. And he never showed himself outside in daylight, according to the men who gossiped at Poke's barbershop. They claimed the Postmaster squinted at his hired men and fired them almost as soon as they started working.

Justice Tomorrow considered Post Offices vital, so Gray struggled to stay employed. In Crossville, he not only learned what white folks were reading—business envelopes from a Congressional committee in Washington, banks in Atlanta, lawyers in Macon, and official packets from the military—but he saved the folks in the South End some trouble. The Postmaster didn't always put Black people's mail in their boxes. Gray sometimes rescued letters from the trash and delivered them later. One of several federal postal crimes which gave him not a minute's bother.

The key to keeping the old albino happy became obvious on the first day. Gray had to act dumber than his boss. The sixty-two-year-old Postmaster wore thick glasses that sat on the end of his broad nose and hooked around the back of his elf-like ears. Despite the glasses, he held letters and official flyers at arm's length, moved his lips as if sounding out the words, then crammed letters in mailboxes so slowly people who showed up in the morning never got their letters until the next day.

The Postmaster sure wanted nobody to know he read so poorly, especially a Black hired man. Gray pretended to be light in the head, something which took more effort than he imagined. Logic said a high school history teacher had to be smart, but such a notion didn't occur to the Postmaster.

JUSTICE TOMORROW

Not a lot bothered the old man. He rarely changed shirts or bathed. Maybe frequent soap and water chapped his skin, but there was no excuse for wearing shirts with grease stains or pants with mud on the cuffs. Gray could smell the Postmaster coming when he was halfway down the street.

The Post Office itself reflected its master. Even with Gray's daily dusting and sweeping—what he considered the equivalent of changing shirts—the old place stood disheveled and worn, unloved and untouched by paint, grace, or class. Yet despite, or perhaps because of it, the federal building drew older white men who picked up their mail from boxes or the Postmaster's own hand, then stuck around to lean against the counter or come around the counter to chew the fat in the side room amid unclaimed magazines and newspapers. Women didn't linger but received their mail or bought their stamps from a Postmaster who asked after their health and complimented their children.

The Postmaster never paid Gray any mind when he knocked on the back door, slipped in, then called, "Good day to you, sur." Instead, the old man grunted and persisted at the laborious task of sorting mail. Occasionally he'd drop a letter or catalog, and if Gray were anywhere close, he expected Gray to pick it up and hand it over.

In the beginning, Gray figured the Postmaster couldn't bend his enormous bulk enough to reach the floor. Didn't take long until he understood it was the albino's way of keeping the hired help in his place. Inside a week all the whites who visited the Post Office considered Gray part of the furniture, though the Postmaster always seemed to know where his hired man was.

This morning the Postmaster waved an overstuffed envelope at him first thing. "Git yourself to George Thompson's. The real estate office. This letter's Special D."

The Postmaster had three white delivery postmen, but when they were out and a special delivery letter arrived, Gray had to take it.

Gray reached out to catch the letter as it fluttered back and forth in the air. "Yassur."

"First, grab the broom and clean the sidewalk 'fore more folks come."

"Yassur."

"Then clear out them bags of mail so's folks can walk back here without trippin' on nothing," the man wheezed.

"Yassur." The postmaster must expect friends. Most of the boys who loitered in the side room were regulars. He knew one or two—they sneaked into the South End to sell their homemade brew.

"I brought ya a slice of pie from supper. You like pecan?"

"I shore do, sur." Gray grinned. "Thankee."

"Stop starin' like a goddam ape. Git the broom."

41

CHAPTER TEN

Sterling whimpered in her sleep. The stench of rotting deer meat, the feel of a heavy weight across her made her retch. Dogs barking. She wanted to run, but Gray told her not to flinch. Footsteps came closer, closer.

"Sterling. Sterling, time to get up." Tom shook her. "I have to go to work."

She flung the bedcovers off and sat up, gasping for air, rivulets of sweat running between her shoulder blades. She flung her arms out, trying to get oriented. Four-poster bed. Crossville. Tom. Gray. She visualized each person and thing to rid her mind of Alabama.

"You okay?"

"Yeah, bad dream." She crawled into a robe and padded to the bathroom. After a minute she heard Tom banging around in the kitchen. She hoped he was making coffee. She wanted some after a quick shower. Dreaming about her narrow escape made her feel dirty.

Sterling spent most of her first morning in Crossville at the Emporium trying to find out enough about the Epsons to justify her search of Callie's Cutoff. Since Gray thought it might be important, she also took notes on anything she found about local land ownership.

Harriet made her wear white gloves like the ones she wore to church when she handled old documents. Sterling hadn't seen anyone so thrilled by books and ancient papers since the last time she stepped into her father's study. She no longer thought of Harriet's domain as an emporium. It was really a historical society.

To Sterling's surprise, Harriet left her in charge when she headed to her bridge party at noon.

JUSTICE TOMORROW

"There's nothing worth stealing but lock up when you leave. You might drop off this letter next door at the Post Office. You can meet the Postmaster—the man never leaves the building in daylight." Harriet patted her pockets. "Where did I lay my car keys?"

A few barking dogs and the pleasant murmurs or shouts of passers-by disturbed the quiet of the Emporium throughout the afternoon. Twice Sterling did greet women shopping for jewelry or asking about Harriet. With the customer's help, she even sold a pair of earrings.

Mostly she spread relevant books and papers across a study table for easy reference. Always she kept an ear out for Gray's knock on the storeroom door. By late afternoon she buried her head atop her folded arms on the table. No blinding revelation in the paltry material she found, and no Gray showed up with news of land or voting rights.

She learned the town of Crossville was under one thousand citizens, almost a hundred years old, and named for the largest landowner in the county at the time it formed, John Cross. Surely there was more about the Epsons than she'd found. A published civic brochure had more. She took in all the boxes on the floor, books on tables, and papers dripping off shelves in despair. The historical society needed reorganizing.

Harriet acted surprised and delighted when she returned in the afternoon to find Sterling hard at work. She allowed as how nothing pleased her more than having help sorting through all the historical material.

She pulled up a chair next to Sterling. "Alice Peterson is amused by your interest in her Epson family. She's suggesting her daughter Jennifer invite you to lunch. By all accounts, you and Tom made a good impression around town."

"Any mention of Negroes being forced off their land?"

Harriet shrugged. "Most of the chatter was about a dinner party Alice is planning, and how many salt cellars she needed for the table. She and the mayor's wife are hosting Col. Reginald Taylor from the Marine Corps base in Albany. White tablecloth."

"Nice." Sterling wrote a few names such as Cross, Anderson, Epson and their addresses from the local census of 1860.

"'Course every time we play cards, we talk about LBJ and how he betrayed his raising with this vote bill for Negroes. There was talk of an outside agitator with the foreign name. Ajamu." Harriet went on. "I admit, Sterling, he scares me. They say he ambushed a state policeman in Mississippi."

Sterling scoffed. "I doubt he'd hurt a policeman, or they'd been hunting him down like a dog. I do think he's dangerous. I heard him on the TV news once. He preaches violence for violence, and he's gaining followers among young Negroes."

"Well, violence makes me sick. Crossville's a lovely town. Mostly we get

along, and when we don't, we make up quick. I like that about Crossville."
Harriet said. "I don't like how people treat our colored folk."

"I like Crossville too," Sterling confessed. "Still, there's bound to be
growing pains with any change."

"You aren't the only strangers in town. Maid says there are new folks
among the coloreds." Harriet peeked at the papers. "Any luck, dear?"

"Not much about the legend around here. I learned a lot about family trees
and who used to run sawmills back when timber was king. Not much about
Epsons."

Harriet frowned. "Something's outta whack. You know, my grandmother
used to tell stories her mother told about how the biggest land and slave owners
in early Crossville didn't get along. They liked to snipe and pick at each other.
Different philosophies of running farms and slaves. Cross was a bit more
moderate than his peers though he supported the Confederacy. I know there's
something about the families around here. Ah . . . Here's a little paper on the
Epsons that Alice wrote in high school English class."

With a flourish, Harriet presented her with typewritten pages drawn out of
a big book of maps on a top shelf. "And somewhere in this mess, I will find
the family history Margaret Anderson wrote about her family. Every year the
senior English teacher used to make the students write papers on their families.
I've got quite a few."

"I'm too hungry to read anymore." Sterling took the pages and checked the
clock over the front door. Good Lord, it was almost dinnertime.

Harriet walked up and down rows of books, her index finger touched every
spine. "Hm-m. I think I remember a local man who wrote about Callie Epson
and her lover. John Cross the third, great-grandson of the original Cross.
Published it himself and moved back to town twenty-five or thirty years ago.
Some scandal about it, I think. Didn't stay long. He came into some money—
rumor says they bribed him to leave town. Whoever 'they' are. I'm sure he gave
the society a copy. We were a new group then. I haven't read it, and I haven't
seen it in forever."

Sterling began replacing materials.

"Found it! Right behind a volume on Crossville business and agriculture.
Take this with you too. See what John Cross had to say about things." Harriet
handed her a thin book showing little use or wear. "Now what did I do with
those senior high genealogies?"

"Thanks. Harriet, why are you doing this?"

"Oh, I love history—."

"No, I mean helping me. Why are you helping Justice Tomorrow?"

44

Harriet licked her lips. "It scares me. A lot. But how folks treat Negroes never set well. Made my late husband mad too. A colored man saved his life in the war. Me, I opened my big mouth about desegregation enough to get crossways with folks. Doesn't matter much after my Leon passed away. He was all I had so . . . if not now, when?"

"How did you find us?"

"Hm-m, not supposed to say," Harriet pursed her lips. "And you're not supposed to ask."

Sterling chuckled.

Stroking her chin, Harriet returned to the wall of books. She and Sterling's dad would get along well, as historical scholars with the same love of books and justice.

"I've got to run. See you tomorrow."

Busy reading a book she pulled off the shelf, Harriet didn't act like heard. Sterling smiled. Just like her father.

Sterling flopped behind the driver's seat of her car and pulled away from the store. At the intersection, she waited for a convoy of Army trucks. Her head hurt from all the reading. Her stomach rumbled as loud as the armored vehicles on the road, turning her attention to mundane things like eating the rest of Nancy's fried chicken.

After a dinner of leftovers, Tom put on some LP records and Sterling washed dishes. Soul music drifted through the house and out the open windows. Cool October air blew in to relieve the stuffiness of the rooms. Sterling set the last clean glass into the cabinet, folded her kitchen towel over the oven handle, and searched for Tom. With a gulp of dread, she found him smoking in the front yard with J.T.

Tom leaned comfortably against the bottom newel post of the steps holding a can of beer. J.T. shifted his weight from one foot to the next often and alternated between chugging beer and shooting cigarette smoke from his nose.

"I wondered why I didn't hear boxes being emptied or bookcases being put together." She put her hands on her hips. "Evenin' J.T."

"The wife is a slave driver." Tom blew smoke rings.

"Evenin' Sterling." J.T. drew in a deep drag of the cigarette then expelled the smoke as though ridding himself of evil. His foot kept at impatient tap-tap-tap.

Tom reached, took her hand, and drew her down the steps into his arms. She waved a bug away from her nose with the other hand and turned to J.T.

"Nancy is a great cook. I can't wait to get to know her better."

"She's wonderful," J. D. stopped moving for a second. "I'm a lucky man."

Whatever was bothering him had nothing to do with his wife. "Soon as I get this house in shape Tom and I want you to come over for supper. Just expect nothing as good as you get at home. Tom married me for my money."

Tom guffawed a hair too loud.

J.T. lifted a Milwaukee Braves baseball cap to scratch his head. "I'm sure it'll be fine."

"J.T.'s a baseball fan," Tom said. "We've been talking about Milwaukee's move to Atlanta next season."

Little danger in Tom talking about baseball so she retreated into the house to read the book Harriet gave her. "I'll leave you to it."

CHAPTER ELEVEN

Right after she drove Tom to work in the morning, Sterling gathered Nancy's serving dishes and knocked on her neighbor's door. She opened it so fast she must have been standing close when Sterling knocked.

"It was all delicious." Sterling held out the Corning Ware. "And you were so right about how tired and hungry we were. We didn't even know it ourselves until we started eating."

Nancy waved her inside. "Have you plugged in your TV yet? You might be the lucky house in Crossville to get three channels without snow across the screen."

"Tom set it up, but we haven't really checked. Too busy."

"I noticed last night your place has a washer and dryer! I am so jealous. Going to the laundromat once a week is a hassle."

Sterling chuckled. "I haven't had time to notice. You're welcome to use my machines anytime."

"Bless your heart," Nancy cried. "I heard you were both working hard to get unpacked."

"I can't find anything," Sterling complained.

"Took me a month to empty all the boxes when we moved."

Sterling gulped.

"Never did find J.T.'s favorite shirt." The two women chuckled.

"Maybe he misses it. I don't know him well, but he acted on edge last night."

"Something's been eating him," said Nancy.

"You think he's sick?"

Nancy snorted.

"His job?" Sterling grimaced.

Nancy winced.

"Every man's job has bumps," Sterling hurried to add.

"He loves the work, Crossville, the people we know at the Methodist church. It's a nice place to live." Nancy folded her arms.

Sterling gazed around the place to give her time to change the subject. The Dawsons' home followed the same pattern as hers except the layout was reversed.

"I swear, your home makes me green with envy. Tom and I don't have much furniture and what we do have looks like Early American College Student."

Nancy motioned her to a chair. "Bought on the installment plan. About the time we get it paid off, it'll be broken. What do you have left to unpack?"

"I found my toothbrush last night. That's about all. I was stupid and told Harriet Cook I'd meet her at the Historical Society this morning." Sterling found the overstuffed chair so comfortable she never wanted to get up.

"Darn. I was hoping to meet some girls at the Tea Shop for lunch. I wanted to introduce you." Nancy pouted. "Why'd you get tackled up with Harriet?"

"Well, history was my major at Georgia—."

"Did you have Dr. Oliver?"

A stroke of luck. Her roommate had taken his class and fussed all the time. "Skinniest man I ever saw. Good wind should have blown him away."

"And the meanest. I like history too. But I flunked his class first time. I didn't know you had to memorize every piece of dirt and date he mentioned." They both laughed.

Suddenly Sterling knew how to use the deputy sheriff's wife to get to the site of Henry Johnson's murder right away.

"Miss Harriet's already got me interested in local history. I'm gonna research the Epson family then do a kinda archeological dig at Callie's Cutoff. I want to see if there is something out there to tell us who killed Callie Epson and her lover."

"Why on earth?"

"It's good to work outside, dig around, and get some exercise. Maybe lose some weight. Second thing, it's more interesting than gardening. What if I really found something!" Sterling's cheeks hurt from grinning.

"It might be good for your figure, but the other . . .?" Nancy's tone dripped suspicion. "The Epsons and Petersons might have something to say about it too."

"I met Mrs. Peterson. She didn't object." Sterling threw up her arms and rose. "Can't say how long I'll last at it, but I thought I'd study some and go out there. Want to come?"

"Today?"

"No. Maybe the next day or two." Sterling shoved aside her impatience to visit the crime scene. "I have to pick up stuff at the grocery first. You and J.T. can't be expected to feed us every night."

Nancy's chin dropped in disappointment. "No lunch then."

"I can scoot over after I go to the historical society. Is the Tea Shop far?"

"Right across the street. I-I'm so glad you moved in. It's been kinda . . . .. Well, J.T. and I were raised in Kentucky. Most folks around here grew up in Crossville." Nancy exhaled as though glad to get it off her chest.

Puzzle pieces slid together. People like Nancy who were overly friendly made Sterling wary. Now the dinner last night and the lunch invitation today made sense. Nancy was smart, lonely, and vulnerable. No wonder she and Sterling clicked.

"You just tell me where the Tea Shop is. Is what I'm wearing okay?" She twirled around in her blue shirtwaist dress and fingered her pearl necklace.

"It's fine." Nancy waved her off. "I will see you at noon. It's just across from the Post Office. A small place. Green door. You can't miss it."

"I've gotta go home and grab a sweater. If I can find one."

"From now on use the back door," Nancy grinned. "The front's for strangers and company."

Sterling bounded down the back step warning herself to respect Nancy's intelligence as she played her. Guilt washed over her. This part of being an investigator made her feel sleazy.

CHAPTER TWELVE

To Sterling's surprise, Harriet threw herself into the study of Callie's Cutoff. She confessed she'd always wanted to know more about the Epson women, but never asked what it had to do with Sterling's purpose in Crossville. She dragged out old census tracts, cemetery records, and books from places Sterling would not have checked.

At first, Harriet chatted about the history of the town as recounted by old people on front porches telling fascinated children about the good old days. Then she mentioned her love for her husband Leon. His long illness and death. Whose farm grew the best tomatoes. How nobody ever saw the Postmaster in daylight, his tortured childhood as an albino. Peterson's stranglehold on the social life in Crossville. The new Methodist preacher who was captivating young people, including daughter Jennifer.

As time went on, Harriet grew more on edge. They discussed people in town who might be sympathetic to civil rights for Blacks – like Jennifer – and which people to avoid, which was most everyone else. Harriet paced to the front door, adjusting things in their cases, fussing with scarves, peeking out the window.

At noon Harriet called, "I'm closing."
"What? Why?"
"Sterling, you notice nobody's come in today, nobody's on the street?"
"I-I thought it was a slow day. What's happening?"
"Some kinda trouble. Come see."

Sterling glanced outside at two sheriff cars parked in the middle of Main Street. County officers spread out along a block of the street, two abreast, all the way to the red and white brick county building.

"What in the world . . ..?"

"You don't want to get mixed up in it," Harriet warned. "I'm getting in my car out back and skedaddling. Need a ride?"

"I'm supposed to meet my neighbor Nancy Dawson and some others for lunch."

"Deputy J.T. Dawson is your neighbor?" Harriet shook her head. "He's the newest member of the county department. Be careful. I bet my Aunt Tillie's last tooth he's as crooked as Sheriff Boyd."

Sterling gathered two books she wanted to review and trotted outside. The front door banged behind her, and the "Closed" sign tapped against the door's windowpane.

From the sidewalk, she noticed the green door with the Tea Shop's name printed across a wooden sign. A deputy nodded at her, another touched his cap bill. Neither spoke. Both wore grim expressions. Several officers lined the sidewalk on the grass strip which separated businesses near the Emporium from the local five and dime store, the bookstore, and several others. Sterling started walking.

In the distance came the faint, familiar singing of "We Shall Overcome" lifted by dozens of voices. The officers stiffened, fidgeted with their nightsticks. Sterling stopped and stood on tiptoes to see, anticipating what came next. Lines of men, women, and children left the shadow of the trees and marched into sight. The whole South End must be singing, carrying posters, or holding hands on their way to the county seat.

The closer they came to Main the more white people scurried onto the street. Two soldiers, however, left the drugstore and ducked back inside. A Marine in dress blues opened the Bell County courthouse door, then executed an about-face. Sterling gripped the straps of her handbag to her chest.

At the Post Office, she saw Gray screech to a halt at the mouth of the alley as though he'd been running. He sagged against the brick and mortar without glancing her way. The next minute he eased into the shadows.

She suddenly realized she was standing in the open with no time to find cover.

The protest march came closer. In the lead, Ajamu helped hold up a handmade sign: "Justice for Henry Johnson." There was no mistaking the radical civil rights leader from newscasts or newspaper pictures. He was one of the tallest men she'd ever seen, easily head and shoulders above anyone else in the march. His orange and black dashiki set off his dark black skin and strong jaw. Long dreadlocks fell past his ears.

On one end of a long banner reading "Stop Stealing Our Land," she recognized the solid frame, gray fringed hair, and clerical collar of Reverend Johnson. He seemed older than the pictures she'd seen of him. The elegant, dark-skinned woman with tight, thin lips marching next to him must be his wife. She wore a two-piece suit and pillbox hat with a large picture of her son held high overhead. Her thin, angular features seemed flat, almost painted on. But her lips quivered. Sterling had to look away. How awful to lose a child.

Sheriff Boyd stepped into the street with a bullhorn. "Y'all are creating a disturbance. Go home or I'll arrest you." Around the edges of the crowd a man with a camera, a news photographer, snapped pictures of marchers and police alike.

Heat flew into Sterling's cheeks. Hidden in the folds of her skirt, her fist clenched. She pictured swinging an elbow into Boyd's fat puss, knowing it was wrong to even think of violence.

The march of a hundred or more people halted in front of the sheriff. Home-scrawled signs of "Vote," "Our Land, Hands Off" and "I Won't Be Moved" waved in the air. Silver held a "Peace" sign. He looked irate, and impossibly young, standing behind Ajamu.

"Who loves Jesus?" Silver hollered.

"Show us!" the crowd chanted.

"Who killed Henry Johnson?" Ajamu pumped his fist high into the bright blue sky.

"Show us!" the crowd responded.

The deputies patted their nightsticks against their palms.

"Who's stealing our land?" another Black man screamed.

"Show us!" the marchers echoed and flung their fists up.

Ajamu raised both arms and the marchers fell silent. "Who killed Henry Johnson? Show us, Sheriff Boyd."

The policemen and the whites in the street muttered. Someone shouted, "Kill the niggers!"

"Boy, you better watch your damn mouth," Boyd stuck his finger in Ajamu's face. He had to raise his chin to do it.

A glass bottle flew into the crowd of marchers from the sidewalk near the courthouse. Then another. A couple of rocks followed. One marcher's nose bled, another grabbed his chest in pain. Still, the marchers stood firm, silent.

Ajamu called, "Find Henry Johnson's killer. Stop stealing our land."

With that, he lifted his hand, twirled it in the air like a drum major. The marchers turned around and sang back the way they'd come.

None of the whites on the street moved, but rocks and bottles kept flying until the last marcher walked out of range.

Sterling shook off the trembling in her knees.

"They coulda been shot." The officer next to her muttered.

To her shock, it was J.T. Dawson. Pale. Shuddering. Like he'd seen something he'd just as soon forget.

"And have the national press come here? Then ole Martin Luther King?" She shook her head.

"Sterling, darling, what're you doing here? Thank you for taking care of her, J.T." Tom pushed his way through the crowd.

The young officer acted like a man awakened from a troubled sleep. "No sweat. She got scared and froze. Seen grown men in 'Nam do it." J.T. tipped his cap and left.

Tom put his arm around her. Behind him came a bald man as big around as he was tall. Tom introduced George Thompson, his boss at the real estate agency and the sole county commissioner.

"I was on my way to lunch with Nancy Dawson. W-what were they talking about, murder and stealing land?" Sterling asked George.

George took a handkerchief out of the hip pocket of his misshapen tan suit and mopped his brow. "Silly talk. Lot of these people been sharecropping for generations on the same patch of dirt and they think they own land. They don't."

Sterling crossed her arms and deepened her voice. "So ungrateful."

"We always treated our nigras good around here. Why, I've known most of those people since I was a kid. Couple of them worked in my house." George pointed down the road. Several sheriff cars crept down the street after the marchers. "It's outside agitators."

She wanted to ask how well Crossville treated Henry Johnson.

"Oh, Sterling, are you okay?" Nancy, breathless and wide-eyed, ran up and threw her arms around her new friend. "I saw you from the Tea Shop window."

"Nothing wrong with me money wouldn't cure." She gave a nervous laugh.

"My daddy used to say that." Nancy giggled, then turned to George and Tom. "Rose and Jennifer are already at the restaurant. If you gentlemen will excuse us, we're hungry."

Tom gave her a kiss on the cheek. "If you're sure you're okay."

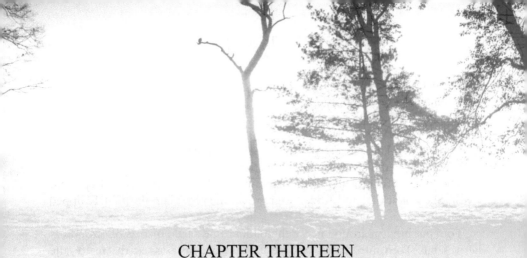

CHAPTER THIRTEEN

Nancy propelled Sterling toward the restaurant.

"Who was Henry Johnson?" Sterling asked.

"The Negro pastor's son from Mt. Moriah Church. He did some work for me in the yard once. Said he wanted to make money for college. Imagine a Negro boy from this lonely place wanting to go to college."

Now that Nancy mentioned it, Crossville felt more isolated than other small towns Sterling knew. "Who killed him?"

Nancy shuffled her toward the cafe. "They say the sheriff and some of his men—Klan still has a few members here. Doesn't matter who did or didn't. Nobody's ever gonna answer for it." She sounded a little bitter.

"Don't you care?"

Nancy sighed and opened the Tea Shop door. "I'm a little tired of it, yeah. Do you care?"

"Just curious."

"There're the girls," Nancy waved to two young women sitting at a round table covered with a white cloth and decorated with a vase of roses.

The aroma of freshly baked rolls teased her nose. Sterling took her seat and concentrated on the introductions, the recitations of husband and children's names, and where they all lived in Crossville. Her stomach begged for the yeast bread tickling her nose.

"I understand you're from Mississippi, Sterling. Do you know any of the Martins in Biloxi? We're third cousins." Rose Anderson Collins, like her first name, possessed red cheeks, petal-soft skin, a floral smell, and, as Sterling soon learned, a thorny disposition.

"All my mother's people are from Tupelo." Several times Sterling and her family visited her mother's family there. She found a cover story worked best when it lay close to the truth. "Granddaddy owned a furniture factory."

"Did you meet Elvis Presley?" Jennifer Lynn Mullins bore herself like the former beauty queen she was. Taller than any of the women, she had the thickest, blackest hair Sterling had ever seen. Her dark brown eyes and high cheekbones hinted at Indian ancestry and lent her an air of authority not unlike the one her mother Alice possessed.

"I hear they were white trash in Tupelo," Jennifer concluded with a sniff which assumed everyone agreed with her.

"Granddaddy knew the Presleys slightly." At seven Sterling wandered out the rear of Granddaddy's factory to pick flowers just in time to see a white supervisor slap a Black woman, then fall on top of her. Sterling choked, cleared her throat.

"You okay?" Rose's brow knitted.

"Something caught." She drank some water, rubbed her throat.

Rose leaned forward on her elbows. "Is Sterling a family name?"

"Great-great-grandmother was English. My father used to tease he named me after fine dinner utensils." Everyone chuckled. "Where are your people, Nancy?"

"Kentucky. My daddy reported for *The Courier-Journal*, but they moved to Ashland a few years ago. He's the editor of *The Independent* there."

Rose sneered. "Nancy wants to be a reporter like her father."

Nancy pushed her salad around with a fork.

"Well, there are lots of women reporters these days," Sterling said. "Pass me some peach jam for my roll, please."

"Lots of things aren't right these days." Rose passed the crystal jar. "Like women reporters—those nigras marching through the middle of town."

Jennifer's head shook side to side just enough to make her hair sway. She sighed as though the ways of mere mortals befuddled her.

For the next half hour, the women at the table chewed and stewed over the march. A common discussion topic of luncheon conversations all over town today, Sterling imagined.

"Do you think those people have any claim to the land?" she asked.

"Maybe a moral claim," Nancy blurted out, then added, "but not legal. I mean, they worked the same farm for almost a hundred years."

"They were paid," Rose sniffed.

"Not enough to feed their families, I'll bet," Nancy murmured.

"Are you on their side?" Rose's green eyes skewered her.

The rebuke hung over the table. The women turned to Nancy as one.

"I swear, you and Jennifer can't be going to the Methodist church! The new

55

minister's filling everybody's head with strange notions," Rose said.

One of Jennifer's eyebrows shot up, then she dismissed Rose with a glance and turned to Sterling. "Nancy's got an interestin' question. What about a legal claim? Some slave owners around here didn't just free their half-breed sons and daughters, they gave those chillun land to eke out a living. Back then men got real attached to those nigra women they slept with."

Rose gave her a playful tap. "You talk foolish."

"Maybe, maybe not. My grandmother always said there used to be deeds and records of it all before the county house burned twenty years ago." Jennifer worried a piece of roll between her fingers. "Might still be things tucked in family Bibles, who knows."

"Did y'all hear Shirley Wilson is gonna have a baby?" Rose put her elbows on the table.

Hisses of disapproval and tsk-tsking.

"How do you know?" Jennifer reached in her purse and took out her cigarettes.

Rose rested her chin on folded hands. "I know. Just like I know the father's not interested in marrying her."

Murmurs of disgust. Jennifer exhaled cigarette smoke.

"You wait. Shirley Wilson'll be feeling sick and heading to Kansas to visit her aunt for a few months recuperation." Rose confided to Sterling.

"What a shame. Her mother must feel terrible," Jennifer mumbled.

Rose adjusted the napkin on her lap. "Shirley needn't come back here and expect decent people to welcome her."

Her lunch companions finished condemning Shirley Wilson to the pit of social hell. Meanwhile, Sterling's head spun with the thought of hidden records in family Bibles. Her family moved so often her mother and father hardly kept Sterling and her brother Danny's school pictures, to say nothing of grandmother's letters or documents from her grandfather's business.

Throughout the lunch, the women annotated every local reference for the newcomer in such a gracious manner Sterling not only felt included but welcomed. Between the sweet tea, gossip, and pimento cheese sandwiches, more than two hours flew by.

"As soon as I fix up the house, y'all must come over," Sterling offered as they all made their way out of the Tea Shop.

"Rose has been living in their house for two years, and she still doesn't have it fixed up." Jennifer winked at Sterling. "She's aiming to get her house in 'Better Homes and Gardens'."

"I'd be okay with 'Southern Living'," Rose declared.

"Mother said you were interested in doing research on our family," Jennifer said to Sterling.

"I do not want an outsider poking around in my family history," sniffed Rose.

"For good reason," Jennifer drawled.

Rose harrumphed.

"Are you serious about studying the legend of Callie's Cutoff?" Jennifer went on.

"And I hope Nancy will be my assistant when I dig out there. Good exercise – and we might have a picnic."

"I can't help, I hate dirt." Jennifer waved to a lady across the café.

"At least the kind in a garden." Rose awarded Jennifer a smile.

"I always thought the story about Callie Epson's murder was really interesting," Nancy said.

"You know, everybody around here is related to the Epsons or us Andersons or the Cross family in some way," Rose said.

"Aren't any Crosses still in town?" Sterling said.

"No, because they were all terrible businessmen and lost what they had." Rose opened the front door of the café.

Once outside, Jennifer said, "Growing up I always thought some rich man who was married killed Callie Epson to keep her from talking about him. But my grandmother used to talk about the Callie's murder differently. When she was a child, she lived next door to the Winchester family—they were cousins to the Epsons, and all those kids used to play together. Word is Callie Epson's real suitor was a colored boy."

A collective intake of breath.

"No!" Rose clutched her heart. "Why would you say such a terrible thing? About your own kin!"

"It's just a mean rumor. I thought y'all knew it anyway." Jennifer consulted her watch. "Good gracious. I have to book it to the grocery, or I can't fix supper."

"I need to go too." Sterling seized the chance. Any Southern woman who didn't mind airing nasty rumors about her family history might also talk about who owned what land around town.

"Tag along then. I'll take you home. Nancy?"

Nancy waved good-bye. "I'd rather play in the middle of the road than grocery shop. You two have fun."

Sterling snickered. She and Nancy even shared a common dislike.

"Lunch was a great idea." Jennifer waved goodbye and took Sterling's arm. "Rose, try not to stomp on any more puppies."

"Hardy-har-har," Rose called as they walked away.

CHAPTER FOURTEEN

After the marchers retreated, Sheriff Boyd focused on dispatching his officers to various parts of the county with calm and strength. Kept his voice level. Never even pounded his desk. No one was gonna start anything on his watch. Nothing to bring attention to the town.

Still, it was clear his men felt the same as him — rage, fury, impotence. What busted Boyd's chops was the way coloreds turned on them.

There'd never been any kinda trouble until just lately. Reverend Johnson started it all with his voting drive. Then the nigger with the African name. Nobody hardly ever said a harsh word to the coloreds around here. Sent them food when they were hungry. And their own clothes when they out-grew them. Hell, he knew families who gave their maids or yard boys their old cars every time they bought new ones.

He wanted to kill them all right there. But he understood the importance of keeping the lid on everything. His money wouldn't come through until this project came to town.

He and his Peggy needed to get gone from here. Live in one of those adobe houses with a red tile roof somewhere out West. She loved the desert when they visited on vacation. And he loved seeing her happy instead of pinch-faced and hurting with arthritis. Crossville and her beauty shop wore her down.

Boyd signed a paper his dispatcher handed him, drank from a cup of cold coffee, and surveyed the officers milling around the station. Anger hung over the place like a stink.

Two of his officers and other Klan members had already asked what they were going to do. It was pretty damn clear they intended on taking action with or without him. Boyd ran his hand through his hair. He might as well be one of those tightrope walkers he and Peg saw at the circus in Savannah.

On one hand, his job was to keep everything under control until the land business was settled in Crossville—his dream of the desert for Peg depended on it. Couldn't move to Arizona on speeding ticket kickbacks. He needed the money he was expecting when this new development came through. Land was almost in the right hands. He was going to be rich soon. Maybe things were at a place where he could let the boys hit back at those sign-toting, marching niggers.

Besides, he couldn't let those nappy-heads run over him.

CHAPTER FIFTEEN

"I have only a few items to pick up. I'll just use your basket." Jennifer shoved a shopping cart at Sterling. "Nancy's got a head full of brains. Not much call for a woman with brains in Crossville, but she's nice too. You lucked out having her for a neighbor."

"Don't I know it."

"She's got a lot of different ideas about things."

Sterling put a bag of flour in the cart. "Like what?"

"Oh, like the sharecroppers." Jennifer concentrated on a baking soda box. What had Nancy said about the subject?

"She's probably right about them not making enough to feed their families," Jennifer continued.

Sterling reached for a bag of sugar. "Well, it's not very Christian."

"Hardly the point. Not the way things are done."

"Seems exactly the point. Do you think I need another bag of flour?"

Jennifer eyed her for a second. "No. You sound like the Methodist preacher."

"Is that good?"

All at once Jennifer waved over their basket. "Norma Jean! Hey, let me introduce you to the newest citizen of Crossville, Sterling Foster. Norma Jean Muller here's got two adorable little boys and her husband works at the bank with my husband John."

The shopping trip lasted longer than Sterling imagined what with all the introductions Jennifer made along the way. She learned Jennifer's mother Alice funded the historical society, mostly out of love for Harriet and a desire for space in her own house.

Sterling filled her cart with staples she and Tom needed while they lived in the Crossville house — eggs, bread, ham, salt, and cans of soup. Jennifer dropped in packages of bacon and two bags of cornmeal with a sad expression meant as a comment on Sterling's forgetfulness or culinary skills.

On the drive home, Jennifer didn't want to talk cooking or gossip.

"You always been interested in history?" she asked.

"One of my teachers said history predicted the future—I think he was right," Sterling said.

Jennifer's lips pursed in a thoughtful expression. "Crossville's history has lots of dark corners."

"Most every town does, I expect."

"You think people, or towns, can fix who they are?"

Puzzled, Sterling said, "If they want to badly enough."

"I dunno. Crossville's always been off the main highways and far from a city. We get only two TV stations—only one clear enough to see much—a radio station, and one weekly newspaper unless you order The Journal or Constitution from Atlanta. You, Pastor Allen at the Methodist Church, and Nancy are the first new folks we've had move here in, oh, ages." Jennifer's words trailed off.

"I haven't lived in many places small as Crossville. My family moved a lot. But everything here seems brand, spankin' new, so something's changed."

Jennifer perked up. "It's a great place to raise a family. Everybody knows the rules and plays by them."

"Gee, sounds like no fun at all." Sterling laughed, and Jennifer joined her.

"We might use our past to bring us into the modern times where everybody can do what they like. History doesn't have to be an anchor holding us down. I read a book in the Emporium that showed me a different way to look at, well, life in town. Crossville needs to change and open up a little."

Sterling arched an eyebrow. "Are you talking about Negro people too?"

Jennifer leaned out the driver's side window. "Hey, Marcy!" She fluttered her hand out the window while explaining to Sterling. "It's Marcy Perkins, the sheriff's niece. She babysits for me." A teenage girl in a plaid skirt and saddle oxfords waved back from the corner.

After Sterling thanked Jennifer for the ride and got out at home, she bounced into the house with her arms loaded. A productive day. Once she learned Alice Peterson was Jennifer's mother, she understood her better. Although, now that she had time to think about it, she didn't understand what

Jennifer was trying to say about Crossville's history and a book in the Emporium showing her something new. But Sterling shelved the conversation for a while and thought back to her lunch. All the women had been friendly. Thanks to Nancy's introduction and Jennifer's acceptance of her she had entrée into Crossville society. A break.

So why did she feel a little sad? Nothing lost. She never really belonged in a place like Crossville with girlfriends and a house she called home.

Once Sterling put away most of her purchases, she figured she'd better cook supper. Not a task she relished. Where to start? Cornbread. Bake cornbread. A recipe on the back of the cornbread bag suggested using a skillet.

Sterling hefted a crusted old black iron skillet from the stovetop. It would be a good weapon, she decided, but how was it used in cooking cornbread? Between canisters of flour and sugar, she found a red and white checkered cookbook. Betty Crocker. She'd heard of it.

She wiped sweat from her forehead and consulted Betty Crocker. Why cook cornbread in a skillet in the oven? Wasn't a skillet for frying?

She peered into a Crisco can full of bacon grease that Nancy had provided. Apparently, a can of grease was a prize all over the South. Sterling threw up her hands.

The thud-thunk of falling boxes, followed by a muffled howl had her grabbing the skillet for what she considered its best purpose. Heart pounding in her ears she crept down the hallway with her weapon, squatted down with the skillet ready overhead, and peeked around the stairs into the study.

CHAPTER SIXTEEN

Flopped across the pile of boxes lay Gray. "Don't wave that at me," he snapped. "I know you don't know how to use it properly."

"What's wrong?" She hissed, hurriedly closing the front door and drawing down the living room blind. She motioned him out into the hallway.

"Didn't you see the signal for a meet? I hid in the safe house waiting for a long while. It needs a good cleaning."

"I'll get on it right away." She dropped the skillet by her side. "I didn't get a signal."

"Pay attention to Harriet's back door next time. Did you know the store next door to your house used to be headquarters for the local KKK? Hope the cracker ghosts don't mind freedom-fighters taking it over." Gray moved down the hall away from the front windows.

Sterling heaved the skillet and pointed him back to the kitchen. "I'm starving, and Tom's coming home soon. What happened this afternoon?"

"The rally at Pastor Johnson's church got out of hand. Two of Ajamu's people came into town with guns, ready to arm everyone. They're all disciplined, tough, and plan to bring more in. He's got a hardcore following right here. I didn't realize . . . .." Gray plopped on a kitchen chair. "I don't like this."

"Holy Mother of God. And what's Silver doing?"

"He's supposed to be a friend of Pastor Johnson's working at the church as a handyman. In the two weeks Ajamu has been in town Silver has attached himself to the man. Spends most of his time at the barbershop with Ajamu. I can't tell anymore what's real and what's part of his undercover role. I warned him again about getting involved. We aren't here to protest – we're here to investigate."

"Silver is a good actor." Still, her own brother Danny claimed to be a pacifist like the rest of the family, yet he joined an elite Marine fighting unit now in Vietnam.

She scooped bacon grease from the can by the kitchen sink into the skillet, and Gray winced. She must be doing it wrong. How do you scoop out grease wrong?

Gray scrunched his mouth like he wanted to talk about something he knew she didn't want to hear. Sterling drew up, stuck out her chin, pressed her lips together. She refused to fight over bacon grease.

"How is it the march —?"

"What are you doing here, Sterling? When I last saw you, you were hurt, out of your head, and talking crazier than usual," Gray demanded.

"Can we focus on the case, please? I'm fine. Thanks to you." He opened his mouth to argue, so she hurried. "How did this march catch you off guard?"

"I never got word about it until the last minute." He scratched his beard stubble with both hands, a clear sign of weariness. "Call went out, sprang up, spread like the plague. People are angrier than I've ever seen on any assignment. Henry Johnson was the spark, but another farmer just got notice to vacate his home. Oh, give me the spatula. I can't stand it anymore."

Sterling handed it over gratefully and shoved the skillet towards him for good measure. "Cook and tell me what else you know. Tom will be here soon, and we can hear what he's learned. What's bacon grease for?"

"Cures burns. Fixes squeaky hinges. Cooks beans – and cornbread." Gray took the black cast iron pan and drained some grease back into the can. "Watch. I learned and you can too. It's a matter of survival in the South. Hand me the green beans over there. Ham too. And two of those eggs go in the cornmeal. You can fry up a couple of them to go with supper if you like. Get out some tea bags, you might as well learn to make tea before you blow your cover."

As he cooked, he described the thunderous mood of the Black community, their hopeless despair, Ajamu's blistering rhetoric, his own efforts to keep things calm. Finally, the conversation turned to the murder.

"I'm sure Henry's being in the pastor's car was bad luck, but the trap was well-planned. Doubtless, they expected Pastor Johnson. Later, no one was allowed around the crime scene except deputies and state police–big help they were. Get this ridiculous cookbook out of my way," he shoved at it with his elbow. "Set the oven to 400 degrees so I can put the skillet in."

"With only grease in it?"

"Two or three minutes . . .. This case is such a-a shame. All of them are," Gray shook his head. "But Henry–and his parents–are well-liked. I hear Dr. King is planning to come any time they want."

JUSTICE TOMORROW

"Ajamu and Martin Luther King? Two more different people talking on violence you will never want to see." Sterling watched him beat the cornbread batter and slice up the ham she'd bought.

Gray took two eggs from her. "A few farmers said they had papers their daddies and granddaddies handed down to them proving they're working land they own. I saw what a man named Morris Anders had. It was a hand-written note signed by Cross, the slaveholder who freed his mother. Looked genuine, but I'm no judge. He's reluctant to hand it over to anyone for authentication. Besides, he'd need collaboration of his claim from a court record or witness— and where's he going to come by that in Bell County?"

"This farmer, Morris Anders, what do you know about him and his folks? Who is he related to?" she asked. "Maybe I can come across his name or his father's name while I research the white families of Crossville."

When Sterling told him about Jennifer's remark on the family Bibles and records, Gray was cautious.

"Perhaps there are papers in enough families to prove their claims," he said.

"Wills. Letters to relatives. Odd keepsakes with land mentioned. Papers like Anders has," she said.

"Nobody lets those things outta their sight," he said.

After a minute she said, "Why don't you get a camera and take close-up pictures of the papers then?"

"Where would a poor Negro such as myself get a camera?"

She smirked. "Our employer gave me a fancy Brownie Hawkeye. I'll leave it at the historical society tomorrow. Bring the exposed film back to the society office and I'll send it to our employer."

"I'm not much of a photographer." Gray slipped the skillet into the oven.

"And here I thought you were good at everything." She snapped her fingers. "Tax records. Did the Black farmers pay taxes?"

"Yep. Got a few receipts. The Crosses, Epsons, and Andersons also paid them. Guess who has the prior claim?" he said.

"Nobody noticed the county double-dipping like this?"

Gray awarded her a sideways sneer.

"Why isn't this conversation about voting rights?" she asked.

"I believe the evictions, the land grab, started with voting rights. Once you take people's homes and land, they move. Fewer voters in the Black community."

"A pretty troublesome way to keep Black people from voting."

He frowned. "Yeah. There's more there. I know it."

"Why are the farmers being evicted? Why is their land so important to somebody?" she asked.

"When we get the answer, we might know why Henry died."

65

JACKIE ROSS FLAUM

"His death stalled the voting rights drive–reason enough."

"And speeded up the land grabbing."

"Well then?" She glanced at the clock. "I better fry the eggs."

"Do you want to eat them cold? He caught her eye. "Sterling, why don't you take a cooking class?"

"I have you." The truth of it swept over her. "I'm happy to see you."

"Hm-m . . . Tom will be too." He gave her a sour grin.

"Gray, everybody has a first mission. I can handle him."

"I know. You planted his white ass on the ground in self-defense class."

Sterling shook her head. "I can help him become a good investigator. You taught me."

"Truth?" Gray held up the spatula.

"Do you ever lie to me?"

"Okay. I don't like the way he found out about Justice Tomorrow. I don't trust him."

Sterling wanted to tell him Tom was searching for a purpose, something worth sticking with. Gray wouldn't care. He had a rigid view of right and wrong. "Don't you think Justice Tomorrow checked him out?"

"Eventually they did, sure." He used an orange potholder to pull the skillet out of the oven. "Shit!" Hot grease popped on his wrist.

A car pulled up outside. They both froze.

"Maybe it's Tom," she said.

The front door of the house opened and slammed. "Sterling? Sterling, how was your lunch with Rose Collins and Jennifer Mullins?" Tom called. He threw something on the floor in the living room with a thud then ambled toward the kitchen. At the sight of Gray, he pulled up short. "What the hell?"

"Hello to you, too, Tom."

"Have you lost your mind? You can't be alone in a white man's house with his wife." Tom quickly surveyed the house.

"Sterling and I are catching up. You know Black farmers are losing their land. Evicted. So, having you in the real estate office . . ." Gray began.

"Not their land. There is nothing to back their claim," Tom snapped. "George Thompson told me."

"Oh, George told you there was no truth in their claims. Guess that settles it then." Gray pantomimed washing his hands.

Tom started to say something but pressed his lips into a tight line instead.

"Tom may be half right." The notion surprised her.

"About what?" Gray scraped batter into the hot skillet with a great deal of force.

"I don't see how the sharecropper's land grab plays into Henry's death

66

unless the killers wanted to get rid of a troublemaker like Reverend Johnson," she drawled.

"They weren't sharecroppers. They were working their own goddamn land," Gray said.

Tom thrust a hand on his hip. "How do we know that, Gray?"

"Find out." Gray's grin showed all his teeth. "It seems to me somebody wants to own a big chunk of Crossville."

Tom reached over to a basket on the counter, picked up an apple, and bit into it so hard Sterling winced.

"Probably not for soybeans, pine, or peaches. Tom, is there a pattern to where land is being bought up?" she asked.

He thought a moment. "I've got a map in my briefcase."

Gray sneered. "You've got a briefcase?"

A police siren wailed out of the driveway next door. Startled, the three young people stared at each other. Finally, Tom rushed to the door and onto the front porch with Sterling right behind him.

"A fire! South of town." He pointed out the front door toward a billowing column of black smoke rising against the evening sky.

Despite the warm weather, she shivered. She backed into the house and collided with Gray.

"You know what's on fire, don't you?" He ran for the study window.

Suddenly, she did. In open-mouth horror, she wheeled and sprinted for the front porch and into their car.

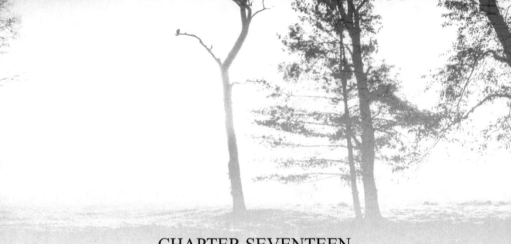

CHAPTER SEVENTEEN

Black billows of smoke brightened by sparks rose over the southern horizon and blended into the dying daylight.

Nancy Dawson shouted and rapped on the back door of Tom and Sterling's car. "J.T. took off like he was shot from a cannon. What's going on?"

Tom stuck his head out the driver's side window. "A bad fire."

"Are you going?"

Sterling hesitated a second. "You wanna go too?"

Nancy shrugged. "Small town life." She climbed in the back. "I did always want to be a newspaper reporter."

"More likely you're worried about J.T.," Tom smirked as he gunned the car into the street. "I hate this car. Has no pickup."

Tom raced down narrow town streets. The trees, white fences, and well-kept two-story houses passed in a blur. Ahead of them, giant flames shots into the night in the Black section of town. Smoke filled the air. The skyline, always dominated by the spire of Mt. Moriah A.M.E. Church, brightened. Tom dodged several people running to the South End.

By the time they arrived flames had engulfed the front section of the two-story church. The blaze crept toward the rear, which was partially hidden by smoke. Sparks popped onto the parsonage next door.

Sterling's vision narrowed and voices faded. She wanted to resist, lacked the strength. Instead, her senses sharpened. She saw dust rise from the ground in angry puffs as people ran toward the flames, smelled the aroma of charred wood and the sweat rippling down the men who ran past them. Rage smoldering in Blacks and fear lurking in whites rose higher than smoke or flame.

Suddenly a tidal wave of noise and heat built in her until Sterling thought she might come apart. She cried out and shook her head to make it go away.

Nancy leaned out her car window. "J-Jesus."

A dozen or more cars, plus the fire and police vehicles, were parked erratically along the street. When Tom pulled over to the curb across from the church, Sterling got half-way out. She clung to the car roof with one arm and leaned on the passenger door with the other as she strained to see.

"Stay there. Don't get too close!" Tom warned.

Fire trucks and an ambulance sat at an angle to the church. Firemen and frantic parishioners raced around the front and sides of the burning building. Across Main, lines of white men and a few women gawked as the undermanned volunteer fire department attached thick hoses to a hydrant almost a block away. On walls of the building not yet ablaze, firefighters leaned ladders to help them direct water onto the upper floor. Underneath the ladders and out the rear door, a line of Black men and women passed out books, vestments, furniture.

A small explosion blew from the church's midsection. Firemen, spectators, and people trying to save books or religious items ducked. Little pops followed the first explosion. And when everyone thought it had ended, another pop sent them ducking for cover again.

"Ammunition or-r dynamite." A short white man said it loud enough for his neighbors to hear. Judging from several stunned or angry voices around Sterling, he wasn't alone in thinking so.

"No, no, no," Nancy murmured.

Ajamu. He must have hidden weapons. Did Reverend Johnson know? Did Gray or Silver? Sterling, Nancy, and Tom elbowed through the crowd.

Sterling found herself stuck behind a tall man in overalls who hummed to himself while rocking back and forth, so she moved away. A moment later she realized she'd lost Tom and Nancy. She stood on tiptoes to search for them.

To her surprise, Jennifer Mullins stood in the street between the lines of whites and Negroes with her arm around an elderly Black woman. Their heads were leaning against each other's until the black of their hair blended. Puzzled, Sterling made her way over. The heat and smoke became more intense, the crackle and sizzle louder.

"Jennifer?"

"My mammy." The younger woman roused slightly. "My mammy's church. She used to bring me here Sundays when I was little."

The woman in Jennifer's arms shuddered.

"I am so sorry, ma'am." Sterling bent to whisper.

"I don't understand." Jennifer swiped at tears. The effort left streaks in the soot along her cheeks as she muttered, "We have more volunteer firemen. Where are they?"

Shouts of warning snapped Sterling's attention back to the church. A fire ladder in the back fell, nearly clipping a willowy white man in a clerical collar who carried out a lectern draped in purple vestments. She stepped back to get a better view of the men and women trying to salvage things from the church.

The smoking roof of parsonage suddenly sprouted flames. The line of people trying to save things inside the church fell apart as some folks turned to rescue things from the home and garage. They carried out everything from a silver chest, piles of books, and a toolbox, to armloads of clothes and piled it all in the street. A child's rubber bathtub toy, a tugboat, sailed into the gutter downstream of a leaky fire hydrant.

"Let's get out of the way," Sterling suggested.

"Baby, come on. Cain't do nothing but pray." Jennifer's mammy took her arm and pulled her away.

Sterling scanned the crowd. Why were members of the volunteer fire brigade and a man with a clerical collar the only whites who were helping? Were all the others afraid of the fire? Or didn't they care? The few remaining white women stared and gaped, fascinated or unsettled by the spectacle. Others flinched each time a spark popped. The men shuffled their feet, some searching the ground like they'd lost something. Some men stared at the spectacle with folded arms and raised voices. One or two grinned and nudged their companions. Sterling tried to memorize the most hostile faces.

Jennifer called to her to get back. She hesitated a second longer to turn, crane her neck, and search the whole church. The fire spread. Suddenly a second explosion belched from the belly of the church. Glass from a second-floor window of the building blew out onto the grass below. Smoke poured out. In the back nearest the parsonage, another window blew, and this time a wooden chair hit the ground along with glass.

Women screamed as a little head popped out amid the smoke, and then two more frightened girls appeared. Smoke swirled around them. Both sides of the street echoed with the gasps and screams of those who spotted the children screaming out the church windows.

CHAPTER EIGHTEEN

A few volunteer firemen hurried to disentangle and move fire ladders or direct sprays of water from the hose around the window where the children screamed. Tears blurred Sterling's vision of the tragedy unfolding in the church.

Her heart jerked as a familiar figure led other Blacks in grabbing up a wooden ladder pulled from the garage. They leaned it against the side of the building and Gray rushed up the ladder to the children.

Flames snaked out the first-floor window near his feet, but an alert man with a bucket scooped up mud and water from the ground and tried to beat them back. Others tried to toss mud and water on the flames with their hands or whatever they found.

A fire hose sprayed water on the downstairs windows. The force of the water split the flames sideways, away from the bottom of the ladder.

Gray grabbed one little girl around the waist and handed her to the next person on the ladder who gave her over to someone on the ground. He lifted the next girl down and was reaching for the third when Sterling realized the flames had shifted.

Did no one else see the danger?

Flames whooshed between to the middle rungs of the ladder like someone opened a window and fed the flames new life. Smoke wafted between cracks in the church's sliding as the fire weakened outer walls. Debris and sparks fell into the crowd at the foot of the ladder.

"Get back! It's gonna fall!" Someone's hoarse shout sent the crowd rushing from the church and leaving Gray on the ladder with a child in his arms.

"It's falling!" A chorus of voices yelled.

"Run!" A fireman waved folks back.

The fire suddenly shot higher up the ladder between the rungs. Gray tried to descend then retreated upward. More screams. Gray didn't see the danger he was in.

Sterling ran.

Along the way to the fire, she scooped a sweater someone had dropped, dragged it in water dripped by fire hoses as she ran. Again and again, she flung the sweater up the wooden ladder to beat down fire. A Black man joined her with a blanket. It was useless.

"Jump!" she screamed.

"Gray! Jump!" The man beside her yelled.

She back-pedaled for a better look, barely feeling the heat. She grabbed the Black man's arm and they linked arms to create a crisscross seat.

Gray tossed the child into their waiting arms. A sudden jerk wrenched her back and she yelped but held on. The fire roared.

"Help him down!" Sterling pressed the girl to her chest and ran. The child weighed more with each step and Sterling fought for enough air to keep going.

"It's fallin'!" Behind her came a chorus of alarm. Another holler and a small crash. It sounded like Gray had jumped, or the ladder fell with him clinging to it. She ran without looking.

When she thought she was safe, Sterling collapsed on the pavement wheezing, coughing. The child clung to her neck, hacking and hiccupping at the same time.

"It's okay," Sterling rasped, trying to free herself from the girl's arms and find out what happened to Gray.

With a tremor and deep-throated humph, the church collapsed. Flames, burning timber, and sparks flew in all directions. Sterling covered her head and leaned over the sobbing child in the wet street.

Five or six Black women swarmed Sterling. "Git cold water – clean water," a woman with a bandana around her head shouted. "Eunice! Your baby over here!"

"Praise to God, they safe!"

"Thank you, Jesus."

"Thank you, ma'am," one said to Sterling.

Sterling leapt to her feet. Scanning the inferno in front of her she searched. Safe. Two men had looped Gray's arms around their shoulders and were carrying him behind the burning parsonage.

Sterling hung her head to hide the relief. By the time she glanced up the whole church, parsonage, and garage glowed with flames the volunteer firemen tried to douse. People scurried in all directions.

Tom swooped her into an embrace. "Mother of God, what were you thinking?"

72

JUSTICE TOMORROW

Energy drained out of her as though someone pulled a plug. She stumbled, slumped against him. She turned her head away from Tom's chest and saw Nancy's astonishment. "They're little. Just little girls."

"Are you hurt?" Tom looped his arm around her waist as they walked to their car.

"I-I don't think so." She wasn't sure. Hidden by her powerful adrenaline rush, the aches and pains would come later. The after-action high was always like this, and in a flash of clarity, she recognized the feeling as a big reason she loved Justice Tomorrow. She wanted to be an investigator forever.

"You smell like a chimney and there's dirt – your sleeve is scorched! Is your arm burned?"

"Tom, don't freak," Nancy hissed. "Not here."

A dozen whites who had remained at the church parted slowly to let them by. When they reached the car, Tom opened the passenger door to help her in, and Nancy said, "I see you with a rock in your hand, Angus Murphy."

"I know where all y'all live," shouted a man's voice from the back of the crowd.

Sterling bunched her fists and might have turned to challenge the crowd. But Tom held her arm, thrust her toward the open door.

For what seemed like a long time the only noise in the car came from the pop, crackle, roar, and hiss of the dying church. If she closed her eyes, she heard Gray's footsteps crackling through the Alabama woods as he made his way back to her hiding spot.

The rear passenger door opened, the smoke grew stronger, Nancy got in, and the door slammed. Tom hustled to the driver's side. With a final glance at her, he backed the car away from the church.

"Shit!" He said. "Got a burn hole in my shirt."

Sterling coughed a half-dozen times, feeling the pain in her lungs plant her back in the present. But she wanted one more minute to revel in what had happened. She pushed her head and back against the car seat. She had saved Gray's life, fought a fire, dragged a little girl to safety – most people in the world lived and died having done less.

"Good Lord, Sterling. What did you do?" There was awe in Nancy's voice.

To her chagrin, Sterling cried.

CHAPTER NINETEEN

Gray was a hero. Gray and the crazy white woman. Everyone said so at the Missionary Baptist Church fellowship hall where members of the Black community gathered after the fire. Someone had opened all the windows to get rid of the smoke smell and cool the place off.

The pastor and his flock at Missionary threw together food and drink for the fire victims. Nobody had an appetite, but nobody wanted to go home. The incessant cough of those who fought the fire made the loudest noise.

Gray and a few other men sat on the cracked linoleum floor of the church fellowship hall and let the women have the chairs. His back rested against the wall and he wished he had chosen another, more secluded spot where folks didn't all stop to thank him. Acrid smoke and bitter defeat coated his tongue. Several women had brought him food, batting their lashes and swinging their hips. He had a plate of food he couldn't eat, and invitations he hadn't the energy to accept.

How would he eat anyway? He burned his hands. Although they hurt enough to make using a fork problematic, the wounds weren't bad. They rested on top of his bent knees slathered with pig grease and wrapped in gauze. To his surprise, the burns on his shins and feet were not as serious, though arguably more troublesome. It'd be hell to walk for a few days, and he'd need new boots. He also made a mental note to get an antibiotic and find sterile cream for his burns. To get it he'd have to visit a doctor in the next town who treated Blacks. He had to be more careful.

A deep breath seeped out. Sterling was neither careful nor cautious. He recognized a recklessness in her like his own. Gray, however, tempered the beast to serve the people and things he cared about. He wasn't sure about

Sterling. With the innocence of a child, she behaved as though right protected her. No arguing that she had saved his life and a little girl's too. He tried to relax his muscles, enjoy Sterling's gift to him.

"Coffee?" Silver rubbed his thick lips, once a source of embarrassment to him, and slid down the wall to sit on the floor beside Gray. He offered his brother a chipped mug, recognized Gray's predicament, and lifted it to his brother's mouth instead. Silver's large brown eyes, so like his own, flashed with humor.

"You give up that low-profile notion?"

Gray chuckled. "What happened to the church? Anything left?"

"Gone. And Reverend Johnson's house. Guess they'll live in what's left of his fancy ga-r-rage," Silver drew out the last word. "Sheriff Boyd stood on courthouse steps and told everybody it was an electrical fire in an old building. But it was Mollies, Molotov cocktails. Two, maybe three."

Anger gathered inside Gray again.

"Place reeked of gasoline." Silver said. "Children were gathering in the sanctuary for choir practice. The deacons had a meeting, and one of them was running late. He saw a dark blue sedan with three or four white men in it drive by and pause long enough to throw bottles through the front and far side windows. Then they high-tailed it."

"Anybody hurt?"

"You." Silver said. "All three babies. Painful, not permanent. Nobody else got more than cuts, bruises, and a punch in the gut."

"Reverend Johnson?" Gray asked.

"Lower than a snake's gut. He may be beat down once too often."

"Hmmm-m."

Silver poked a forkful of mashed potatoes at him. Gray hesitated then opened his mouth, only to discover the taste of salt, cream, and butter instead of soot.

"Sheriff took the deacon into his office for a talk," the young man went on. "I don't figure the deacon will recall who was in the car or even what kind it was."

"Until we talk to him."

"Hell yes. I know him well."

Gray hid his amusement. His brother was cocky, so sure of himself. Gray tried to remember whether he had ever been eighteen and oh, so confident. Not since he joined Justice Tomorrow. Not since their father got lynched, his mother died from grief, and Silver taught him how ignorant he really was.

"Are you writing all this down and putting it in the Justice Tomorrow box?"

Silver guffawed. He took a drink from Gray's mug and whispered. "Sterling's bad. Real bad. Folks talking 'bout her for sure. Arty over there? He

75

helped her catch Eunice's baby girl. He said he never touched a white woman until she grabbed his arm. The girl scares me sometimes. She's so far out, brother."

Gray wondered how bad Sterling's reputation would be if everyone knew how she cried once danger passed. She was probably crying right now. On their first mission he'd heard her sniveling in the back of the car on their way out of town. She'd done something similar the second time they worked together, and he'd put his arm around her for support. She'd gone limp as tissue paper, and her sobs rattled in his chest. Still did if he was honest. He tried to rub his mouth with a gauze-encased finger.

Gray rested against the wall again and let his eyelids drop. He practiced shutting the fire out of his head. He fixed his mind on concrete things – the wall, his ruined boots, a table leg — when his concentration slipped and he once again saw flames, smelled smoke, or heard little Black girls screaming for help. If he started now, maybe he'd be able to get some sleep in the next day or two.

"Brother Gray." Ajamu loomed over him. "You're a warrior."

Gray coughed. His head swiveled to Silver and he sensed a flash of jealousy in his brother. Silver's adoration used to be reserved for his brother.

Ajamu slapped hands with Silver and squatted in front of Gray. "We need you, especially an educated man like yourself."

Gray's muscles tensed.

"We have to strike back." Ajamu urged. "You've been silent. You gotta be the first to stand up after tonight."

Gray held up his bandaged hands then surveyed the big room. Everyone tried to be busy. Several of the younger men moved together, forming a hard knot in the room's center. Even Silver held his breath.

Gray wanted to say yes. He wanted to wrap his blistered hands around a gun butt and shoot up the bookstore or the A&P shouting, "How do you like it? How does it feel?"

Instead, he lifted his burned hands to the ceiling to testify to the truth. "Hate and violence never won a lasting victory." He struggled to his feet.

Ajamu, his face pinched in anger, rose too. "Eye for an eye."

"An' all you git is blind men! Ain't none of y'all gonna stop it." An elderly man spat and grasped the straps of his bib overalls.

Later, in the safety of his boarding house room, Gray replayed the evening and did not recognize himself.

He'd never been an orator, never cared to be a leader, and he never intended to violate Justice Tomorrow's orders to stay in the background. So, what in hell had he been thinking? He only knew both pastors remained silent when Ajamu and one of his gun-waving followers called for violence, revenge.

JUSTICE TOMORROW

Someone had to step into the vacuum. It shouldn't have been him—something else his landlady Mrs. Carson said while skinning him alive after the meeting.

"Ain't nobody called ya here to go scarin' folks and get them doin' things make they lives harder." Her foot tapped an angry beat to accompany her finger-wagging. "Y'all talked crazy tonight and, hear me— folks gonna git hurt!"

As he lay on his bed, Gray covered his eyes to erase the picture of him telling how violence against whites got his father lynched right outside the school where his mother taught. In daylight. In front of his mother, her students, and her two sons

What possessed him to demand a boycott of Crossville, to revel in the cheers he stole from Ajamu? He rolled over on his bed in a sweat, recalling how the idea took hold of the crowded church. Only a few, like his landlady, fought the idea as too much too fast.

Good luck he avoided serving on the boycott's steering committee and all the letter writing they wanted to do to other churches asking for support. Bad luck they wanted him to stay at the Post Office, to make sure any mailed contributions to the boycott found their way to Reverend Johnson. They all knew the Postmaster stole from folks in the South End and helped the Klan.

Smoke inhalation surely cooked his brain to have him talking farmers into bringing pages and papers from family Bibles and boxes from under their floorboards. Leave it to Silver to jump in and volunteer to record contents of the pages after the joint church service of praise the next night.

The pain in his scorched hands, feet, and heart forced him to admit the truth: he was sick of waiting. Tonight fired him up. Literally.

CHAPTER TWENTY

"What have I done?" Sterling mimicked Nancy's question as she limped down the stairs in her terrycloth robe. Her back muscles ached from catching the little girl and her old shoulder injury throbbed. Still damp from a shower, she wandered into the living room worried she'd be an outcast in Crossville. Worse, she wondered whether Justice Tomorrow would learn what she and Gray had done and consider them too visible in the community.

Her main job was to watch over Tom. Now it seemed she's the one who needed a keeper.

"Nothing like a nice, quiet evening," Tom said.

She tightened the robe around her and plopped down on the couch next to him. A towel turban kept her wet hair off her neck, but she removed it. The shower had washed away the soot and smoke, and eased some muscle soreness, but not her despair. Her hands reached for the black book on Crossville history that Harriet had given her earlier.

"I suppose I should finish this by John Cross's descendant. He has a whole new theory about Callie Epson's murder." Sterling opened the book with a sigh.

Tom leaned over to the side table, selected one of two glasses there, and handed it to her. "I added something to the Coke."

She smelled bourbon. "Tonight was a bummer." She drank two big gulps, enjoying the warmth spreading through her. She took another drink. "Hmmm." Her head dropped back on the couch, closed the book, and she swiveled to peer up at Tom.

No denying he radiated sex and sin.

"You are a crazy fool. I don't know what got you started across the street, but you saved Gray and the little girl. And I don't give a good goddamn what anyone else thinks or what else happens. You are —." He took her chin in his hand. As his mouth met hers, she plunged into his kiss. He also tasted of bourbon and took her in his arms to deepen the kiss. The heat from another kind of fire made her jerk away.

"What?" He said with a sly grin. "A man can't kiss his wife?"

"Foster, I'm not your wife." She put the drink down. She felt tingly and flushed.

Tom sighed. "Real life can be a drag."

She had to agree.

They both put their feet up on what served as their living room coffee table, a wooden board supported by two thick cork blocks. Lesson learned. Tom was not Gray. She could not play with them the same. Gray felt like coming home. Tom's arms sent her quivering between sex and caution.

"Hey. Don't sweat this thing tonight," Tom paused. "Act like nothing special happened. Call Jennifer Mullins and volunteer for the church carnival. Ask Nancy to go shopping."

"Your mother teach you all these social skills?" Her lips pursed in appreciation.

"She house-broke me too."

"We owe her a lot."

"She was a saint." He raised his glass in salute. "Too bad she died of neglect or I might have learned to give a damn about something."

For a moment neither of them spoke. He rubbed the birthmark on his right arm. Through an open window, a fresh October breeze ruffled the curtains.

"Was Gray right? Is this case about land grabbing and not murder or voting rights?" Sterling slid a finger along the side of her glass, following water droplets as they fell on her robe.

"We've seen church bombings and fires over civil rights—Birmingham, Alabama. Roscoe, Georgia. Meridian, Mississippi. None over land sales."

Her doubts lingered. The violence in this town escalated faster than usual. And the legal steps taken to evict Blacks from their land, which removed them from voting, had happened equally fast.

For once she almost wished for her annoying, scary spells to guide her.

"You think the Klan set the fire?"

"Who knows," Tom snorted. "After the march today, a big ole red flag in front of a bull's nose? Should have expected something."

She was about to agree when the telephone rang. They stared at each other in surprise. Tom rose and went into the kitchen to answer.

"Yes, she's fine. Few little burns. She's asleep." Sterling heard Tom pause for a long time. Who was calling so late? "I'll tell her and have her call you back first thing. Let me take your number. Okay . . . thanks."

He strolled back into the living room with a grin and lingered in the archway to rock back and forth on the balls of his feet. "Guess who it was?"

"Spill it."

"Jennifer Mullins. Her mother is —"

"Peterson. I know."

"She called to thank you for being so kind tonight. And she invited you to her house for lunch. She said you were interested in her family history, so she'd show you an attic full of papers." Tom slapped his hands together in triumph.

"Whew."

He sat and clasped one of her hands in his. "Yeah. I will go through the deeds of recent sales, plot them on my trusty maps, and see if some kinda pattern shows up."

Sterling took a sip of her drink. It was cold, sugary, and hit the spot.

"I'll go to lunch tomorrow and drop by the historical society again." She had a purse big enough to hide the camera she wanted to leave for Gray. "But the next day for sure I'm headed out to Callie's Cutoff. Maybe Nancy will come with me. I want to do a grid search of the Johnson crime scene."

"What possible reason can you have for being out there?"

"Oh, didn't I tell you? I'm doing an archeological dig for relics from the time of Miss Callie Epson's murder." She clasped her hands together under her chin, batted her eyelashes, and feigned innocence.

He snickered. "You think Sheriff Boyd is gonna let you dig around the scene of his murder?"

"I'm not asking. I've already established my interest in the Epson family history. I have John Cross's descendant's book to guide me. And my lunch date with Jennifer will give me more cover." Sterling patted herself on the back for her spur-of-the-moment interest in the local genealogy.

"Do you know anything about an archeological dig?" Tom asked.

"Not a thing. I'm pretty sure I need string and some sticks to mark off my search grids like we do for a crime scene search. And a shovel, rake, and garden trowel."

Those amazing lips twitched like he was trying not to laugh. She stared without blinking—and gave herself a mental slap.

"Take seeds and plant a garden while you're at it," Tom tried to cover his snicker with a cough. "Be honest. You don't hope to find physical evidence to help solve the Johnson boy's murder, do you?"

Sterling sipped the bourbon and Coke. "Doubtful. Still, that's what investigators do. They go over crime scenes, even old ones. I am really into solving crimes. Especially the digging up dirt part."

"No kidding? You don't want to marry a rich man and have his babies?"

Her head buzzed from the liquor. "I can't be an investigator, then come home to my houseful of kids, fancy mansion, and handsome husband?"

"What kind of husband would let the mother of his children have such a dangerous job? Who'd go to PTA meetings?" He put his arm around her.

"Hire someone to go."

"Good idea. I can't imagine anything more boring than a PTA meeting, except a board meeting at a bank."

"Or a group of lawyers writing contracts," Sterling muttered.

"Or accountants dividing up their bar tab. . . or anyone plannin' a wedding." They both laughed. Sterling thanked the bourbon. And Tom.

"Where did Justice Tomorrow find you?" It was a question normally discussed at training camp and she knew part of the answer. She'd never gotten close enough to ask Tom the rest of the story. "Silver, right? He found you."

"I got active in the Freedom Summer." He rubbed his birthmark again. "Got my clock cleaned, woke up in a hospital bed with the world's biggest headache. Someone in the curtained-off space next to my bed was whispering about a group they called JT. It was Silver and Jordan from camp posing as janitors and wishing there were someone in their group who understood a company's books. I peeled back the curtain and said, "Hey, I'm an accounting major."

"I was working at the YWCA, typing and filing. An older woman – she wore way too much rouge— came in my office, sat down next to my desk. Said she'd heard good things about me, and after a while she offered me a chance to join." Sterling said. "The woman became my handler at Justice Tomorrow."

"Huh! The one who calls every Sunday, pretending she's your mother?"

"And nobody listening on our party line telephone knows any different."

Tom touched his finger along her arm. "That's all you know about J.T.? I gotta say, I'm itching to know who pays my salary. A bunch of New York Jews? Some rich Yankee do-gooder? I'm surprised you aren't more curious."

"Does it matter?"

"You're the nosiest woman I know. And you never wondered who was behind all this?"

"Nope." A nibble of alarm poked her fuzzy head.

He arched his back and stretched. She remembered how good it felt when he pulled her next to him out on the street.

Sterling gave his knee a friendly tap. "You know those angry men at our car? I read this FBI memo about criminals coming back to the scene of the crime to see how the investigation was going."

"I think I know . . . yeah, I've seen one before tonight."

"Where?" She slid to the edge of the couch.

"Saw him walking by the real estate office two or three times today. George called him, ah, Jim. Jim Penix. Shit! I have to see George in just four hours."

81

He pointed upstairs.

"Dibs on the bathroom." She drained her glass and forgot about Cross' book for tonight.

CHAPTER TWENTY-ONE

A massive steamer trunk secured by cracked leather straps squatted in the middle of the walk-in attic like a sullen dowager. Jennifer Mullins cleared her throat and moved toward it as though afraid to disturb it.

"Do those creaks mean the floorboard is going to give way?" Sterling flicked away a cobweb.

"Can't rule it out," Jennifer said.

"Then I'm glad my last meal was so outta sight."

They halted inside the threshold, scanning the dusty attic in the light from the hallway. Jennifer moved sideways to grasp the light chain dangling from the rafter. The splash of light did little to dispel the ominous air.

Sterling scanned a room crammed with old lamps, boxes, stacks of books, a lopsided sewing machine, and broken suitcases. The unfinished space was stuffy, dirty, and she felt sure mice scurried in every corner. She grimaced.

"I thought you were kidding when you said there might be dead things up here."

Jennifer knelt in front of the trunk. "Nobody comes here unless it's to drop off more junk. My mother's attic is full, which explains why half this stuff is here. She knows I wouldn't come here on a bet."

"I'm honored."

"I can't be sure, but there might be something up here to help with your research on Callie Epson. This trunk is the oldest thing, so it's a good place to start. A-h-h!" Jennifer grunted from her effort to open the trunk. "Is the stupid thing locked?"

"Let me see. I had a locker in high school I had to open with a bobby pin."

Sterling got down on the floor, removed a pin from the back of her hair, scraped off one tiny padded end, and inserted it in the big brass lock.

The mechanism sprang open. Sterling sat back on her heels and grinned.

Jennifer shook her head. "You've got funny talents."

She had no idea. Strange talents defined Justice Tomorrow agents. Most, anyway, Sterling amended. At the real estate office yesterday, Tom mentioned training camp to George, and it took all her charm to cover his gaffe.

"Phew." Jennifer nudged her aside to peek in the trunk. She fanned away the odor of mildew with one hand while exploring the contents with the other.

Stacks of letters tied with pink or blue ribbon, a neatly folded christening gown wrapped in tissue paper, two tintype photos, a cracked white washbowl, yellowing white linen hand towels, and several leather-bound diaries secured by small gold locks filled the trunk. She tried to guess which item might give her clues about who gave what land to whom in long-ago Crossville.

Jennifer picked up a silver hand mirror to admire herself and then replaced it next to a matching brush. "You can start through this, while I take my life in my hands and explore. I hope you find something. It might be fun to find out the Epsons came from Yankees or Indians. Mother would come unglued."

Sterling selected the first diary she saw. "I don't want to know about any critters you find." Then she read the boldly written script inside the book aloud, "Alice Epson December 1925."

"Mother's. She devotes her life to preserving and polishing the family name."

Time had been unkind to the next book Sterling found. The leather binding was cracked, the writing faded, and the pages delicate. "Whose is this? The first page says, 'Amelia Jane 1865.'"

Jennifer straightened up from a pile she was sorting. "Amelia Jane? My great-grandfather's maiden sister, Aunt Amelia. She had to be fifteen or sixteen when she wrote it. Huh, I thought mother gave all her letters and diaries to the historical society."

"Harriet treats those things like valuable treasures," Sterling recalled the white gloves she'd worn to handle the old papers.

"Aunt Amelia wrote a lot about the Civil War time – what it was like at home, the battles her father was in, who married who, which Crossville men fought in what regiments."

"She was Callie Epson's sister, right?" Sterling's heartbeat picked up, and she carefully opened the diary pages.

"Technically Callie's my great aunt. But you know how we Southerners call every adult woman who is family—or close enough to be family—Aunt So-and-So. Heck, I called Harriet Cook "Aunt" Harriet until after I was married," Jennifer said. "Then she told me I was old enough to call her by her first name."

JUSTICE TOMORROW

It was too much to hope Aunt Amelia Jane would flat out say who owned what land, but she might have dropped one or two hints.

"Callie was the oldest, and then my great-grandfather John, then Aunt Amelia Jane. John served as county ordinary – what we call the county commissioner today." Jennifer's voice came from inside the large box she'd been leaning into. After a lot of banging and scraping, she drew out something heavy.

"What've you found?"

"An ugly picture in a pretty gold frame. Wonder why it's up here? I have a lovely watercolor – I'm gonna clean this up and use it." Jennifer held it up to show Sterling.

Hideous. No other word for it. "Doesn't strike me as your style," Sterling ventured.

"The box's full of dad's things. This picture's got to be his -- although this frame is all Mother."

"Hey, listen to what your Aunt Amelia wrote, 'Aug. 25: Word arrived Tennessee has been readmitted to the Union. Dear Papa worries the crops will be not be harvested since most of our slaves fled. Only Mr. Cross appears to have workers, owing to his giving them land.'" Sterling thought about the book by Cross' descendant that lay on a table in her living room. She read enough to know Jennifer's mother would hate the theory it suggested about Callie's murder. No wonder Harriet stored the book where no one was likely to find it.

"Hmm-m. You think this frame is too much for a delicate watercolor?" Jennifer asked.

"Ah, yes." But Sterling wasn't paying attention. The last sentence of Aunt Amelia's diary entry kept flashing in Sterling's mind as bright as a movie marquee.

Jennifer glanced at her watch. "My goodness. I told Mother I'd get my daughter at three. I have to go. Sorry to push you out."

"No sweat. I should go too. May I take this diary with me? I can drop it off at the historical society for you."

"Save me a trip." Jennifer held the grimy picture by the wire hanger at arm's length. "You're welcome to come back any time to go through this junk. Mother is agreeable to letting you poke around her attic too, though I'd wait until this church fire thing blows over."

"I guess she didn't approve of what I did." Throughout lunch, they'd danced around what happened last night. Their conversation touched on it, then jumped away to children, church, and husbands.

Jennifer's laugh sounded dry and harsh. "Do you care?"

"I enjoy looking into the past. But I don't think I'd like living there." She

85

hoped Jennifer wasn't offended.

"You try to blend in, but you're a rebel. Wish I was as brave as you . . . as you were at the church."

Sterling brushed the dust off her skirt nonchalantly, but the compliment warmed her. "Nobody else saw what the fire was doing, I guess. I like children. Want children of my own someday. I just—. Something came over me. Tell the truth, I didn't think about the danger."

"Hm-m. You've got good maternal instincts. What happens to me–the future I have, my happiness, the man I love–nothing matters but my little girl." Jennifer's mouth twisted, her chin lifted, and her cheeks flushed red as the words hung in the air. "That's what a mother's supposed to feel . . ."

How sad. Sterling and her mother disagreed — God knows, Sterling had tested every rule her parents laid down. Through it all there had always been love. Jennifer radiated resentment toward her mother.

The black and white drawing in its ornate frame twisted in Jennifer's hand. A glare off the glass bounced in Sterling's eyes until the frame twirled to the back. Brown paper sealed the art in the frame, and it bulged in the middle.

"What's in the back of your picture?" she asked. "Want to see?"

Jennifer ran a finger over the lump, gave a harsh chuckle and drew it from Sterling's reach. "Probably a note or letter telling where the picture came from. Mother saves every scrap. She refuses to throw anything away." She thrust the picture aside.

"That explains why she and Harriet Cook at the historical society get along so well."

"You're like a breath of fresh air in this stale town." Jennifer took one step at a time down to the second floor.

"Listen, ah, can I tell you a secret?" Sterling stammered. "I've got a-a problem . . . I'm embarrassed, and I don't know what to do or who else to ask for help."

Jennifer executed a pirouette. "What?"

"I-I can't cook. Tom and I are gonna starve to death. Can you teach me? Or know someone?"

"Oh, honey, I sure can solve your problem." Jennifer slipped her arm through Sterling's. "You know, it feels like I've always known you."

"Does feel like we've been friends forever." To her chagrin Sterling meant it.

As she drove away Sterling gave herself a good shake. She spent time lots of time in towns throughout South Carolina, Mississippi, Tennessee, and

Alabama. Those places had grocery stores, post offices, churches, and segregated water fountains like Crossville. They had grand dames and aspiring young grand dames, big movers and shakers, bigots and holy people too. Yet they faded into pale characters playing next to Alice Peterson, Rose Collins, Nancy Dawson, Sheriff Boyd, and Jennifer Mullins. She never wondered why this was so; she only knew everything in Crossville loomed larger than anything she'd known.

Sterling had hardly unpacked and felt at home already. The thought made her anxious. She wasn't here to settle down. Besides, whenever she felt like she belonged, things fell apart.

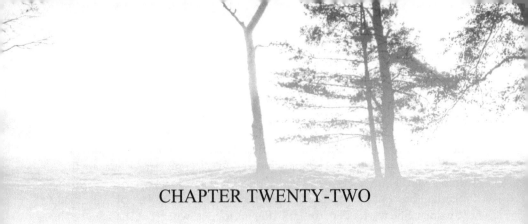

CHAPTER TWENTY-TWO

All Sterling's nerves bloomed at the hardware store, where she and Nancy shopped for string and a new shovel. She smiled too much and started to chew her fingernails but stopped herself in time. She had no idea what, if anything, she would find, but her fear of the woods had slammed into her before she even got there.

Once she decided to go, however, Nancy threw herself into it. Sterling giggled at her friend's running commentary as they walked aisles of nails, screws, wire, and hammers. No reason for dread. Her cover story for going out there was solid. Still, something made her stomach burn when she parked across the road from the area where she knew Henry had died.

Callie's Cutoff oozed evil.

"Did you know a boy from my church found a real arrowhead on Callie's Cutoff two years ago? I really don't expect to find anything. And I sure don't put stock in an old book claiming a rich man in town stabbed Callie Epson." Nancy unfolded the grid search map she'd drawn.

The sun brightened large patches of woods along Callie's Cutoff. The oaks and maples had already shed their shriveled leaves, but the faithful evergreens hung on. Wilted, dying plants littered the forest floor. Sterling clasped her denim jacket close and walked to the edge of the woods.

Following protocol and securing whatever her gut told her was there must be her priorities. Like Nancy, she never expected to find anything. Whatever evidence had been there surely must have been whisked away by weather or the police.

Beneath the sagging pine arch, Nancy hummed while she used string and stakes to plot a search grid. She wore her hair pulled back, an oversized blue shirt, and bellbottom jeans like Sterling's.

Where the grid began wasn't as important to Sterling as how far up it went and how it matched the probable site of Henry's death, but she consulted the book Harriet gave her written by John Cross's descendent as a guide. Nancy pounded in grid stakes, more interested in the site possibly being an Indian ceremonial location.

"I feel like I'm in your way." Sterling scanned the area.

"You know somebody died out here," Nancy remarked as they took a break.

"Callie Epson."

Nancy pursed her lips. "Henry Johnson."

"Henry Johnson? From the march?" Sterling displayed her best shocked expression. "On this spot?"

Nancy's free hand waved around the woods. "Someplace around here. I don't know where exactly, but J.T. said the Georgia state patrol and Sheriff Boyd's top deputies climbed all over Callie's Cutoff."

"Maybe it was across the road. Or back over there." Sterling hesitated, lowered her voice. "You think we oughta go?"

"Let's hang loose." Nancy surveyed her handiwork. "Why should they care? It was over a month ago."

"Did J.T. say the police found anything in these woods?"

"Like what?" Nancy's left eyebrow shot up.

"L-like an arrowhead . . . or any kind of relic."

"No-o."

Sterling sought inspiration from the sky. "I brought some peanut butter and jelly sandwiches and Cokes for lunch."

"I haven't had peanut butter in a long time," said Nancy.

"What do you and J.T. eat for lunch?" Sterling braced for a recitation of Southern foods she'd never be able to master.

"J.T. packs his own lunch." A few blond hairs fell on Nancy's forehead. "He might drive by today. This is his patrol sector."

"Let's dig. First, we skim the top of a grid square to see what's there. Then we dig down about five or six inches, I guess. Turn over each shovelful and pick the dirt apart to see what's in it." Sterling hoped she didn't sound as ignorant as she felt. "You can't tell when an arrowhead might have been pushed to the surface by frost."

"Doesn't sound like a scientific dig. I thought real archeologists used brushes and small trowels."

"We're doing the best we can with what we have to work with. Remember, exercise? A good excuse for the picnic too."

Nancy's steely look matched her tone. "Indians were removed from this area in the 1800s and marched west in the Trail of Tears."

"Many Creeks stuck around," Sterling dug in her heels. "Renegades, mostly, but they were loyal to the Confederacy. Are you suggesting the legend isn't real?"

"What do you really want here, Sterling?"

"Well, I don't want to make a fuss."

Nancy's laughter seemed to bounce around the woods and echo back. Sterling flinched at the sound that turned colors in the sun and radiated back in her eyes. Nancy didn't notice. "What a hoot. Who was beatin' out flames with an old sweater – and linking arms with a colored man to catch a girl jumping from a ladder?"

"It's a long-shot, I'll be honest," Sterling said.

"Can't you trust me?" Nancy touched Sterling's sleeve. "What do you expect to find here after a hundred years?"

"An old engraved cavalry sword . . ." Sterling lifted her chin and raised her eyebrows in triumph ". . . maybe still buried in a skeleton's chest."

"Downright disgusting."

"There's more." A mini tornado of pine needles swirled at Sterling's feet.

"I hope so after all this work."

"I didn't drag you here, Nancy Dawson. You volunteered."

Nancy folded her arms and cocked her hip.

"I heard about two star-crossed lovers murdered by Indians and how their souls haunt this land. Legend says Confederate Lieutenant Colonel Epson discovered the tutor he'd hired for his daughters, ah, courting Callie and threw him out," Sterling said. "The lovers eloped. Callie's old boyfriend, the youngest Cross brother Stephen, murdered them and made it appear Indians did it."

"Everybody knows the story," Nancy wiped the dirt off her jeans.

"Not the story this book tells." Sterling waved the thin volume in her hand. "It was written by a descendant of John Cross and claims the tutor, named Arnett, was nearly lynched when Callie's father learned he taught a young slave named Lucius Epson to read. Lucius's mother was Callie's mammy — she raised the two together."

Nancy's head snapped up.

Sterling opened the book, flipped for a page, and shoved it at Nancy. "See, it says Lucius became a freeman, and he took off the day Callie and Arnett died, Jan. 3, 1865. Here it is in the book, a copy of the public notice of a runaway Negro thief named Lucius published in mid-January. The Cross book says Epson discovered both his daughter and his newly freed slave missing when he sent for Lucius's mother."

"What about the Cross boy? I thought he killed Arnett and Callie?" Nancy read the part Sterling pointed out.

"The author claims his great-great-uncle Stephen was innocent, but no saint. He was supposed to be in Mississippi. But when he came back to Crossville, he

90

never put up much defense because he was busy dallying with another woman at the time of the murder."

"Then what was Arnett doing out here? Wait! No! Are you suggesting Arnett was helping Callie and Lucius get away?" Nancy's voice dropped low as though the conversation would shock the pines. "You're talking about Jennifer Mullins's family."

"That's why I'm sticking with the Indian arrowhead story. Nobody ever saw Lucius again. Cross, uh, the author of this book claims Lucius didn't run away. Somebody stabbed him to death." Sterling took out the book and opened it. "Listen to what the book says: 'Lucius died at the hands of a powerful man who stabbed him with a sabre. Nobody ever saw the prized sabre after Miss Callie Epson's death.'"

"Sounds like someone stole the sword. What a batch of baloney," Nancy smirked.

"Right here in this grid is where the book says it all happened, on the spot where Indians once held their sacred ceremonies."

"Suppose by some miracle we find something. What then?" Nancy said. "Tell Jennifer we found the family sword? Good God."

"I-I guess I hadn't thought about it. Tell Jennifer and let her decide what to do, I guess. It's history – her history first."

The zing of impending discovery, rocks singing for the dead, and pines mourning murder overtook Sterling. She tried to shake off the tunnel vision sensation and her enhanced senses. Still, she already felt the pull of the spot which drew her the day she and Tom drove into town.

"Hello. Are you hearing me? Jennifer might act like she doesn't care about family connections and pooh-pooh her mother's being in society around town, but tell her a close female relative loved a Negro boy?" Nancy whistled.

"Jennifer brought it up after lunch."

Groaning, Nancy tilted her head all the way back. She murmured so softly Sterling barely heard. "I don't want to do this again."

"What?"

Nancy eyeballed her grid handiwork. "I-I didn't really think you were serious. Oh, it was fun figuring how to do it, planning, talking about buying twine or string at the hardware store . . . Doing something with my brain for a change."

"Go to the *Crossville Caller*. Be a reporter." Sterling blurted.

Nancy drew a sharp breath.

"Sorry. Maybe you aren't serious about being a reporter."

Nancy flexed her fist around a shovel handle. "Serious? I left J. D. in

Kentucky and went all the way to Georgia for journalism school. Dean John Drury himself said I had talent."

Sterling's hands flew back in surrender. Nancy's yearning for excitement and adventure resonated. Shying away from it didn't.

"For the record, we are looking for arrowheads." Nancy thrust her shovel deep into one grid square. "I cannot believe I'm out here digging for colored bones."

"Pretty sure they're white like ours," grinned Sterling.

Nancy snorted.

"Besides, we probably won't find anything. I'm gonna start at the top." She left before her anxiety got the better of her.

From the rise, she called down to Nancy, who was visible from time to time through the bare trees and dying bushes. "Follow along the strings and study each square in the grid until we meet in the middle. We'll be here for hours."

"Oh, goodie." Nancy's sarcasm carried.

Sterling searched for the marker she left on the first day in town. Birds called overhead and a squirrel fussed at her. Until Alabama, she had loved the woods, found peace among the trees. Now the flashbacks—feeling the weight of the rotting deer over her, listening for footsteps, one step ahead of men with guns. It would end someday. Just not today.

Her breath quickened. Carefully she stepped into a grid box containing two bushes. A dried brown leaf lay between two rocks piled on top of each other.

The shovel in her hand dropped to the ground. She knelt to brush aside leaves, pine needles, and pebbles with the side of her hand. By the time she knew she'd found something, dizziness threatened to swamp her, and she'd skinned her knuckles. Panting and nauseated by the smell of overturned earth, she tugged at something half-buried. A scrap of brown cloth with an ensign or monogram. She held it up to the light. An epaulette from a military or police uniform?

She stuffed her prize in a small paper bag she'd tucked in her right pants pocket. Plenty of time later to examine it, mark the bag with the date and time of discovery, her name, and how she found it. Evidence secured, she sat back on her haunches, wiped sweat off her forehead, and tried to focus on white clouds drifting between tree branches until she felt better.

The queasiness passed. She bent to examine where she'd found the ripped cloth. The shallow hole she'd carved out held fine soil, small rocks, a torn maple or oak twig, and another crescent sliver so hard it resembled a rock. She took another bag and scraped it all inside. Better take everything and anything so she never had to come back. She hid the second paper bag under her shirt in the small of her back.

She found something important. Maybe two somethings if the rock-like crescent turned out to be part of the struggle Henry Johnson had with his killers. Amazing after all this time. Gray wouldn't believe it. Hell, she didn't believe it.

For the sake of her cover story, she jabbed her shovel into one of the grid squares and used one foot to press it down, overturning the earth to make it seem she'd been digging in the established grid. She dug until her arms ached. To catch her breath, she stopped for a minute, twisted left to survey her progress, and caught her toe on a rock. Off-balance, she fell sideways, and half her face plowed through the fresh dirt.

The earthy scent reached into her throat to smother her. Panicked, she pushed herself upright, ripped off her jacket to rid herself of its weight. She wanted to yell for Nancy, but she had to be quiet, keep the fear inside. She covered her mouth with one hand and concentrated on shallow breathing.

A blood-chilling scream ripped through the woods from the road below. It yanked her from her own terror into someone else's.

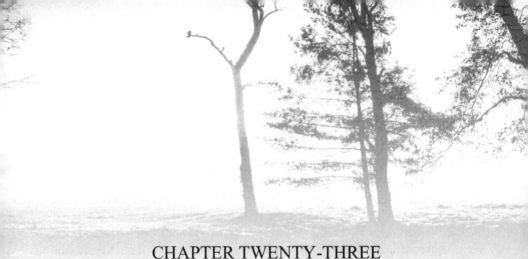

CHAPTER TWENTY-THREE

Sterling's hands lashed wildly as she ran, stumbling over strings, knocking over stakes, bouncing off tree trunks. The screams went on and on, whipping her into mindless flight.

Near the bottom of the slope, Sterling grabbed a tree trunk and slid the rest of the way down. Nancy shrieked and danced on tiptoes around a tiny circle of overturned dirt several feet from the road's edge. Stakes ripped out of the ground and carefully placed twine flew, some winding around her feet.

"Sterling! Good God!"

A dark reddish-black human finger bone pointed from the earth to blue sky.

Sterling plowed through the last string and grabbed Nancy in a bear hug. They both trembled.

"Wha—Is that a real finger?" Nancy's teeth chattered.

"I-I don't know. I think . . . .." She released her hold on Nancy and approached the find sideways. "It looks . . . old."

"I don't feel better." Nancy wailed.

The last vestiges of her episode in the woods evaporated. Sterling tip-toed closer to the bone and squinted to assess it as Justice Tomorrow taught her. Stripped of skin, the finger bone appeared flakey and brittle. A dirty gray fragment lay in front of it. A metal sleeve? Maybe it was a decayed hand or more bone?

No visible animal gnaw marks. So, the bone had been underground too deep for predators. She screwed her mouth in disgust for Nancy's benefit and used the heel of her hand to remove more dirt. The fragment near the bone was seven or eight inches long, flat and metal, wide at the top and narrow at the bottom. Sterling eyeballed the weird thing and came up with nothing.

Nancy sidled over to view her discovery. "I dug a few inches in this grid and when I turned the dirt over, there it was. Giving me the finger."

Sterling clapped a hand over her mouth to stifle the laughter, but it was too late.

Nancy snickered. "Oh, look, it's giving J.T. the finger too."

J.T. Dawson parked his cruiser by the side of Callie's Cutoff to find his wife and his neighbor supporting each other as they shrieked and hooted in laughter. He got out, slammed the door, put his hands on his hips to survey the grid for a minute while he shifted from one foot to the other.

"What in the name of all that's holy are y'all doing here?" He flushed, and his arms stretched to encompass the whole scene as he approached.

Both women howled, wiped tears, and waved their hands toward the bone.

He bent to see where they were pointing, then jerked upright. "What the hell!"

"It's a finger. Did it wave?" Sterling chortled, sending Nancy into peals of laughter again.

"Stop. My sides hurt," she pleaded.

"You're my wife, for God's sake, Nancy," J.T. shouted.

Nancy sobered in a hurry. "W-what? What are you talking about, honey?"

J.T. swore and slapped his uniform hat against his thigh.

"I-I don't get it." Sterling untucked her oversized work shirt to cover the paper bags hidden in her side pocket and small of her back.

Muttering to himself J.T. strode to his patrol car in three big steps and reached inside to unhook the mic on the patrol car radio. He spent several minutes relaying what he'd seen and returned to the women a little calmer.

"Don't suppose it crossed your minds you were trespassing. Now can one of you tell me what's going on?" He waved his hand across the grid, which was rapidly losing its shape thanks to Sterling's flight and the flimsiness of the twine. "What is all this?"

"I told you Sterling and I were planning a grid search for arrowheads."

J. T.'s nose scrunched up. "Here? Honey, you never said where."

"Did we do something wrong? Does this have anything to do with Henry Johnson's murder?" Sterling shifted her weight to another hip. "Oh no! This isn't HIS finger, is it?"

Nancy's hands slapped across her mouth. Her husband put his arms around her and pulled her close.

"No, no, it isn't Henry Johnson's . . . IF it is human at all." J.T.'s voice was a little too loud.

"Somebody cut off Henry Johnson's fingers?"

"God, no! Who—?"

"Did you see it?" Sterling grimaced.

"I didn't see a single knife on anyone that day —." J.T. stopped. "Hey, you there!"

A skinny Black boy gaped at them from across the road. He started at J.T.'s voice, eyes wide and feet poised for flight.

"Git out now. Nothing to see here," J.T. waved the boy away.

The teenager bolted into the woods.

"This-this is awful. I-I need to sit," Sterling wheezed. "And get a-a Coke. Nancy, want one?"

Without waiting for an answer, she lurched to her car, slid in the backseat where she'd put a red metal cooler and a wicker picnic basket. She leaned over the seat, flipped the cooler lid open to hide her movements.

By the time Nancy and J.T. reached the car, she had removed the paper bags, hid them under her front seat. They found her fumbling in the icy water of the cooler for a bottle.

Sterling felt ten feet tall.

CHAPTER TWENTY-FOUR

Nearly every day Gray opened the screen door of Carl Poke's barbershop next to the general store, jiggled the cranky knob on the outer door, and stuck his head to say 'hey.' The amount of cigarette smoke warring with sweet talcum powder smell told him whether there was news. What Gray learned at the barbershop had nothing to do with waxy pomade or lye-based relaxers.

Ajamu's young men often loitered at the shop in ones and twos. The rest were older men in overalls or worn plaid pants who sat in folding chairs or leaned against a side wall lined with hair care posters. They gossiped and pretended to look out the filthy front windows while they waited for Carl to finish with whoever sat in the single barber's chair. Gray loved hearing the stories of sharecropper days and tales their grandparents told about slavery on the Georgia land. But those stories came only after they'd decided to accept him.

The owner of the shop, Carl Poke, claimed he was old as Moses, and the cascading wrinkles on his face, arms, and hands offered proof of it. He not only cut hair but combed for nuggets of truth. The barbershop served as the communications hub for Crossville's Black men, a shrine with the red and blue pole as its talisman.

Gray's fondness for the widowed barber stemmed from how the old man helped Gray plug into the local community. Lots of strangers wandered through Crossville. Not all stayed or found a welcome. Ajamu did. He had a national reputation, and his cousin owned a piddly-ass farm a mile from Callie's Cutoff that got taken. Everybody figured his cousin called Ajamu about it. Reverend Johnson had welcomed Silver after a call from a friend of a friend. Gray wandered into town with nobody to vouch for him but the elderly Mrs. Carson. As his contact, she had to stay in the background.

On Gray's first visit Carl, who had to pump the barber chair as high as possible to work without stooping, observed him for the better part of an hour. Gray attempted small talk. When it was his turn in the barber's chair, the regulars picked their teeth and spat tobacco, while Carl cut his hair and peppered him with questions. Afterward, folks on the street spoke to him. Reverend Johnson invited him to supper. He got credit at Ferry's Grocery.

The barbershop grew to be home. The gossip made him laugh, and there was always a good-natured ribbing. On the other hand, their worries angered him, because he had heard the same gripes all over the South in one form or another. The springs poking up through worn seats of the colored section of the movie theater while the white seats were brand new. Food served buffet-style in the back room of The Tea Shop came out cold. Sisters, wives, and mothers gazed in the window of the new A&P with envy since they only shopped there in their maid's uniforms. Too many Black folks got arrested and too few went free. It was always the same outside the town limits, where Blacks built their churches, stores, homes, and garages in the South End. The town got money to build sewers, water lines, schools, and such. But when it came to getting county water, sewer, police help, school money, and jobs, South Enders sucked the hind tit. Nothing ever happened for them.

The first time Gray came into the shop conversation died. Today the folks lit up with welcome and laughter. Carl's scissors paused in mid-air in salute.

"You gentleman enjoyin' yourselves?" Gray said.

"Yassir," chuckled one elderly man. "Shore is."

"Ain't seen nuthin' like it since Bill Winchester paid off his sharecropping bill. That were fifty year ago," chortled another. "Story go ole man Cross—the last one—shore was surprised. Ain't no other sharecropper 'round here ever paid his seed and grocery bills and got himself free."

"What happened today?" Gray asked.

"Well, two white ladies dug up some kindly bone on state road," Carl guffawed. "Sheriff gets 'em and takes 'em to jail."

"Say what?" Gray's mouth dropped.

"Whose bone they find, Carl?" asked a middle-aged man straddling a beat-up folding chair.

Carl pretended to think for a minute. "Bone was black, or I heard, so-o lemme see those fingers. Hold 'em up."

His audience hollered and hooted.

"Where'd they find it?" Gray asked.

"My oldest grandbaby seen it from the woods." The elderly man in overalls said.

"Where?" asked Gray.

Carl snipped a stray hair around his customer's ear. "Where Johnson boy got kilt." For a minute, the only noises in the shop were shoe soles scuffling the floor and the buzz of Carl's clippers.

In the silence ran a familiar undercurrent—the one where Gray was the outsider with little understanding of local history. In previous assignments, he drew a straight line from slavery to the trials of whatever community he visited. It occurred to him Crossville might be a little different.

"Hey! Git da man a seat," Carl said. "How's your burn?"

Gray raised his bandaged hands. "I ain't gonna die."

"He afeared no more women cum tend them burns." A middle-aged man with a dozen dark freckles on his cheeks made his voice high and feminine to get a laugh.

"I heard he got no worries," snickered another. "Women likes them a big black he-ero!" Everybody laughed.

"I heard the gals ain't got no time for they boyfriends no mo'. They all got a thing for Brother Gray." The men in the shop hooted.

Gray chuckled. "Least they're paying attention when I'm teachin'."

The gangly man scooted off the folding chair and stretched. "When I was a young'un, I heard them was Indian graves in Callie's Cutoff."

Carl scoffed. "Mor' like slave bones—ones old Cross killed."

"John Cross? Thought he was . . . He gave land to former slaves." The news startled Gray.

Carl's left hand bent his customer's head to shave the nape of his neck. "Oh, did that too. But all them Crosses bad in the head. Fly off an'"—he snapped his finger— "somebody die. Give land same way. He weren't right." He tapped his head with the end of the comb.

"Hmm-m." The old man with freckles hummed. "Ole Cross kilt off more'n his share Black folks. Buried where nobody can't never find 'em."

"My granny say Lucas Epson in Callie's Cutoff." Carl pumped the chair up a notch with one foot.

"Who?" Gray asked.

The men shuffled their feet again. After a while, Carl's customer said, "Lucas an' his mama free, but they lives near Epson place after the war. One day he gone."

"Day Miss Callie kilt by Indians," Carl finished. "That ver-ry day."

A heavy silence reigned. Puzzled, Gray studied the men in the shop. Disapproval and disgust lay on every face.

The freckled·man rubbed his chin. "Lucas' mama was Miss Callie's mammy. Lucas and Miss Callie chilun together. My granny say he and Miss Callie —."

"Done it to hisself!" The lanky customer jabbed at the air.

"Stick to his own kind," said another.

All the men hummed and said, "That's right."

"Ain't right to go with no white woman." The man in bib overalls spat into an empty coffee can.

"Ain't no way to say. All y'all knows Indians mighta got Lucas too like they got Miss Callie." Several customers snickered and guffawed as Carl took the cape off his customer and flapped it in the air. "He weren't never seen no more. Buried Miss Callie an' the teacher in Epson cemetery. Lucas' mama never work no more for Epsons. She go on out to the cutoff ever' day and cry, my granny say."

"Lotta bones," the oldest customer muttered.

"Nobody want them bones dug up. That's why them white ladies gets drugged to jail. One was the white lady at the fire," the freckled-faced man said to a chorus of "noes."

Sweat ran down Gray's back.

CHAPTER TWENTY-FIVE

The pine bench outside Sheriff Martin Boyd's office hurt Sterling's butt. Hungry, tired, and, after being in the fresh air, nearly sick from the police station aroma of body odor and puke. Beside her, Nancy shifted and sighed as though she felt the same.

The sheriff brought J.T. into his office "to go over a few things." They summoned Tom to take charge of his wife. Just what she needed: cover from a bumbling, green agent. Unlike George Thompson, Boyd was no fool.

Except to point out she and Nancy were trespassing, no one explained why their little dig upset so many lawmen. Why, they even discovered something–Sterling would never get over her surprise at finding a finger bone.

The sheriff's office door had a wood bottom and a glass top with his name written on it in black letters. Even though it was cool outside, the sheriff's rotary fan atop a pile of books stirred papers on a metal file cabinet and ruffled the map of Bell County pinned to the wall.

Sheriff Boyd sat behind a massive desk with J.T. in front of him. J.T.'s body shielded the sheriff from outsiders, but the tenor of the conversation in the small office was easy to figure.

J.T. nodded so much Sterling worried his head might snap at the neck. Boyd picked up the phone and, while waiting to be connected, he glowered at the women.

As the sheriff talked on the phone J.T. shifted to the right slightly. Sterling glimpsed a brown paper bag holding the finger bone and a few pieces of rusted metal spread out on a white paper in front of him like Boyd was fixing to have them for lunch. There wasn't a rush to dig the land around the grisly find since everyone could see the bones were not from someone who died in the last twenty or thirty years. She nudged Nancy, winked at their bone, and grinned.

Nancy gazed at the ceiling, sighed, and clasped her hands on her lap.

The surrounding walls carried Wanted Posters, FBI announcements, State Police directives, a warning about venereal disease, and procedures to follow in case of a fire. Most of the paper curled yellow with age. Three or four desks for detectives and patrolmen who needed to write reports on black manual typewriters sat along an open hallway to the left.

The only busy person Sterling saw in the building was a dispatcher with a massive bun of brown hair, who wore her headset over one ear and commanded a wall of communication devices ranging from a telephone switchboard to the police radio system. Down the green linoleum hallway, Sterling spotted a refrigerator and couch through an open door. She punched Nancy with an elbow, inclined her head, and they rose as one to head there.

"Coke?" Sterling opened the refrigerator. Two lone peaches sat on the first shelf. From the noise coming from underneath it, cooling the fruit hit the limit of the refrigerator's abilities.

"I need a little water anyway," Nancy collapsed onto the soft but stained couch. She clutched her hands together in a tight ball. "What do you suppose the sheriff is jawing at J.T. about? They act like trespassing is a big deal. We uncovered something, maybe something important."

"The sheriff talks like it's a horrible crime for a deputy's wife to be trespassing." Sterling helped herself to two glasses of dubious cleanliness from the dish rack by the sink and filled them with cold water.

"Scoot over." She handed Nancy the water and plopped beside her. "I have no idea why the sheriff is so bent out of shape."

Nancy's forearms rested on her knees and the water in her glass rocked back and forth. Finally, she whispered, "I don't want to move again."

Sterling's head whipped around. "What?"

"Move. We had to move a lot since we married. J.T. likes police work, he's good at it." Nancy worried her bottom lip. "And he's been on edge for two months or so."

"What's going on?"

"J.T. was a new police officer while he was finishing at the University of

Kentucky. One night he drove up an alley and found a fellow officer beating a colored suspect half to death with his nightstick. Everybody knew this officer had a bad temper. When J.T. got out of his patrol car he saw that the colored man on the ground had no weapon, but the officer drew his service revolver fixing to shoot. J.T. pulled his own gun, hollered at him to drop it. J.T. was young and foolish and thought he could save the world."

"He turned the policeman in."

Nancy gave a sour chuckle. "The patrolman reported J.T. for not backing him up, interfering with an arrest, holding him at gunpoint. There was a hearing, but nobody even asked the colored victim what happened. It was in the Lexington papers, we had death threats. J.T. was 'allowed' to resign. The only job offered was in a little town near the Tennessee border. Policemen got a big network. They all know each other."

"So, what happened?"

"We moved to Tennessee. We were there almost two years. We decided to try further from home. I liked Georgia, so we moved here. It was hard at first. People aren't open to new folks in town. Now Jennifer, Rose, and some others are starting to accept . . .."

"You don't want to start over," Sterling finished.

Nancy shook her head, lifted her chin. "Every time J.T. gets moody, I wonder, 'Is he getting fired again? Should I pack?' I'm real tired of it. Can I trust you not to say a word?"

Sterling crossed her heart and hoped to die.

Nancy suddenly exhaled. "I'm going down to the *Crossville Caller* in the morning. Get a job."

Tom strode to the head of the hallway in a light blue seersucker suit looking both dashing and confused. His gaze flew over desks and down the hallway until he saw her. The two women went to meet him.

"What's going on, honey?" He examined her for wounds then kissed her cheek. "Are you okay?"

His concern touched her. Whatever his skill as an investigator, he had a good heart. When she told him about their day at Callie's Cutoff, Tom acted as buffaloed as anyone.

"I'll go speak to the sheriff," he said.

No need. Sheriff Boyd opened his door and strode down the narrow hallway toward the woman manning the switchboard. He gave them a curt nod before calling, "Delores, you see 'bout the missing persons files?"

Without a word the switchboard operator handed over two manila folders. Boyd scowled as he thumbed through the pages. "Hell, these the only cases we got open in twenty years?"

"Some cleared already, sheriff," Delores muttered.

103

Boyd slapped the files against his thigh and whirled around to his office. With a jerk, Tom followed. Sterling grabbed his arm, Nancy followed.

"Sheriff Boyd, what's going on?" Tom demanded.

"Nothing now. I called the property owner all the way up in Washington, D.C. on a Saturday to let him know what happened. You'll be happy to know he has no interest in pressing charges for trespassing."

"John Cross the fourth?" Tom asked.

The sheriff made a tent of his fingers and peered at Tom. "So happens."

Tom shuffled his feet, his brow getting damp. "I work with George Thompson at the real estate office up the street. He's teaching me a lot. Families are important in Crossville."

Boyd smiled. "Well, I thought your wife might be so upset she'd appreciate her husband."

"Mighty thoughty," Sterling had a bad taste in her mouth. "What's all the fuss?

"Trespassing is illegal. You don't know what kinda trouble you might cause the owner – damage and such issues." The sheriff reached down on the floor to retrieve Sterling's jean jacket and handed it to her by one finger. "We found this in the woods, Mrs. Foster."

"Why, th-thank you. I-I thought I left it in the car." Sterling stammered.

Boyd grumbled almost to himself. "Never mind outside agitators stirring up the nigras, I gotta chase silly women." He halted and jabbed a finger at Nancy. "Did you know you were digging up an old crime scene?"

She paled.

"Kinda the point, Sheriff Boyd. Callie Epson died there." Sterling jumped in.

Boyd leaned toward Nancy. "A recent murder."

Sterling touched Nancy's arm to grab her attention. "Did you see any crime scene sign? Anything to tell people to stay away?"

"I did not." Nancy squared her shoulders.

Boyd spoke a little slower. "Common sense should tell a deputy's wife not to go digging around in Callie's Cutoff after Henry Johnson's murder."

"Why?" Sterling's lips dripped ridicule. "Are you saying nobody can ever go around Callie's Cutoff again?"

Boyd's hands slapped against his thighs. "Mrs. Foster, I hear you were out there because you are interested in the legend of Callie's Cutoff." From his desktop he reached then held up Sterling's book by John Cross the third.

"Y-yes."

"And you were following this book by Cross, conducting some kind of dig to find a sword or arrowheads and such."

104

Sterling nodded.

"Do you know anything about archeology or the families of folks around Crossville?" The sheriff dropped the book and came around to the front of his desk He sat on the edge and clasped his hands together until the knuckles lost color.

"No, but I'm learning fast. It's so interesting."

"Sheriff, out of curiosity, whose bone did my wife find?" Tom folded his arms over his chest almost like he was hugging himself.

"Mr. Foster, Mrs. Foster," the sheriff began patiently. "You're new. John Cross and his family haven't lived here in years. There was bad feeling between him, his family, and several other families who still live in town. Let me give you some advice: folks don't like having old family stories dug up. Especially Alice Epson Peterson,"

Sterling's eyes bulged. "The finger belongs to Callie Epson?"

"No, no." The sheriff jumped to his feet.

"Henry Johnson?" Sterling hated to put her neighbor in a tight spot, but she needed to know if he was at the murder scene as he'd hinted. "But J.T. said he saw nobody use a knife on the colored boy before he was hung."

The sheriff's face flashed from red to almost purple. "Officer Dawson was nowhere near the murder scene the night the poor colored boy died, so he would have no idee about knives or missing fingers."

J.T. stiffened. "Sterling's misunderstood a fact I mentioned earlier. I said I never saw a single knife wound on the deceased. Wound. Fact is, sheriff, I saw the, ah, unfortunate boy when his father and mother came for his, ah, remains. Add to the fact this bone here is really old, I can say for a fact it is not his."

How many 'facts' could J.T. jam in one mouthful? But Sterling learned what she wanted to know. J.T. was on the scene when Henry was killed for at least part of the time.

"J.T., I guess I thought you were there like everybody else in the county," Sterling said. "Especially since it's your patrol area."

Sheriff Boyd chuckled. "Every police officer does not come running to every crime scene, Mrs. Foster."

The sheriff made it sound like J.T. wasn't around there at all. Stands to reason the deputy would have been there – unless it was his day off or he was lying. And why would he lie about being where he should have been? Unless he shouldn't have been there. She noticed Nancy stared at J.T. in disbelief.

Sterling concentrated, shut out the lights and noises of the station, to replay what J.T. had said this afternoon, his exact words.

"Mrs. Foster? Are you paying attention here?" The sheriff's sharp tone startled her. He leaned toward her, his gaze so penetrating it was as though he hunted for a flaw in her skin.

A familiar warning tingled in her toes and crawled into her belly. She winced, swayed.

Tom took her arm. "There is no call to be rude to my wife."

"Now we gotta seal off the area where you found this and send this bone off to Atlanta until we can find out what the hell it is. I mean, it ain't recent." Sheriff Boyd folded his arms and rolled his neck side to side. "Be our luck to wind up with a bunch of college professors down here blocking traffic, holding up development to dig all over the place."

Sterling swallowed a knot of fear.

"Some Harvard egghead dug up a pile of round Indian rocks in the woods northeast of here," Boyd went on, "and they had all this excitement about tourists, building a state park there, and such. Goddamn circus for nothing."

"We found Indian bones?"

Tom put a hand on her shoulders. "Honey, he doesn't know. Look, I get it. You and Nancy were having fun today playing scientists. But you were on someone's property."

"I thought it was county land."

"Well, the county doesn't give a hang what you do on your own property. But you have to get the owner's permission to lay a grid and dig a bunch of holes on somebody else's land." Tom put his arm around her and gave her an indulgent hug. "Since you found something, it's best left to the professionals like Sheriff Boyd and J.T."

Boyd beamed at Tom. "Leave it to the professionals."

Sterling's mind reviewed a few nonviolent solutions, yet all she wanted to do was maim the next person who opened their condescending mouths. She had to give Tom credit for his performance so far, but she'd endured enough.

"J.T., Nancy and I trust what you say. I-I'm sorry we didn't tell you what we were doing. It-it just didn't seem important enough to mention."

His uniform hat twirled in his hand. "It's fine."

She slipped her arm in Tom's. "Ready to get some supper, honey?"

"Past ready."

"Y'all need a ride to your car?" Boyd offered.

"After you called to say Sterling was here, George Thompson took me to Callie's Cutoff." Tom grimaced. "Kinda embarrassing to explain to my new boss."

"I'm so sorry," Sterling mumbled.

Tom huffed, "You've nothing to be sorry about. This has been a lot of fuss over a whole lot of nothing."

Boyd's chin snapped up. A satisfying warmth spread over Sterling.

"J.T., you want us to carry Nancy home with us?" Tom asked.

"Would you mind?"

Sheriff Boyd clapped J.T. on the back. "Na, deputy, go on home. I think we're clear on everything, and your wife has had enough hooray for one day."

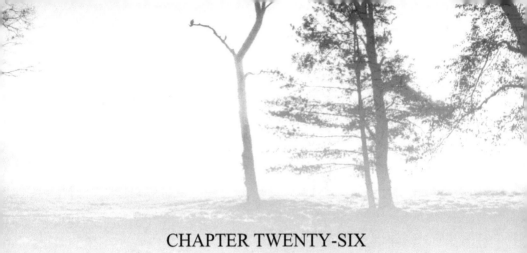

CHAPTER TWENTY-SIX

For a long time after everyone left his office, Boyd sat behind his desk. He unwrapped the bone and glared at it as though it were a living malignancy. He had to send the damn thing to Atlanta. Too many people knew about it to trash it.

He had no idea who belonged to the bone. Since it might be human somebody had to check it out. He might be unable to control the investigation once it got to Atlanta, or how quickly they did it. His friends in the state police had gotten mighty quiet lately.

The damn truth was an ancient Indian bone might really cause a delay in the Crossville development. He thought–no, hoped–it was too far along. All this on top of the boycott where no niggers at all showed up to work or shop. He'd already gotten a dozen calls asking what was going on and how he planned to end it.

Easy enough to find out what caused it. Anybody on the street in the South End acted real glad to say they weren't working in Crossville until the farmers got their land back and Henry Johnson's killers were found. Boyd shook his head, rubbed the back of his neck, and saw the bone again.

One thing. He didn't have to send the bone to Atlanta right away. Maybe in a day or two. Or next week. Hell, after what he'd already done to keep this project on track, holding onto an old bone was nothing.

From a small gold frame on his desk, Peg beckoned with a coy expression. He picked up the picture. Taken the day they met at a Sunday School picnic. Boy, he fell hard.

He wrapped the bone and rusted metal fragment in the evidence bag again and stuffed it in his middle desk drawer. A crumpled paper prevented his pushing it too far. With a frown, he clawed the paper out.

The written alert from Alabama authorities about the Black boy and white girl, grifters and thieves. Boyd chewed his bottom lip. He'd shared it with his department and even Penix, Murphy, and other boys, but he ought to mention it again. An image of Sterling Foster coming down the hill with her skirt tucked in her panties flashed through his mind. But she didn't have red hair, and he couldn't tell much about freckles what with all the make-up women wore.

Sterling Foster made him uneasy. She was digging right around the spot where Henry Johnson died. Found her jacket and a bunch of half-dug holes under the tree where they hung the boy. Something not right about the archeology story. Stupid enough for young women with no children to do. Then again, Boyd had been a lawman too long not take notice when his gut twitched.

At least Deputy Dawson stood strong. He'd had doubts about the man. But Boyd was proud to see Dawson had been quiet about anything he saw or heard in Callie's Cutoff while the Johnson boy was disciplined.

He tapped his finger on the desk near Peg's picture. And he chuckled. A crazy idea sent him bolt upright, his chair squeaking in protest. Peg was an expert on beauty, shit like hair, make-up, and nails. He'd sic her on Mrs. Foster. Should his instinct prove wrong about the Foster woman, at least she'd have a friend in Peg.

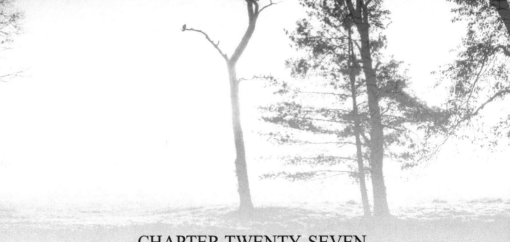

CHAPTER TWENTY-SEVEN

As soon as politely possible, Gray high-tailed it out of the barbershop and popped into Ferry's General Store next door. If Carl collected gossip from the men in the community, Langston Ferry and his pudgy wife had the inside track on what the women knew. Gray skirted three blue-flowered sacks of horse and mule feed leaning against the front of the store. He opened the door and stepped aside for a heavy-set woman with a baby on her hip and another with a toddler under her feet.

The little store bulged with women pretending to shop while they exchanged news of the boycott and compared recipes. Gray wandered around the store, fingering cans and hoping the crowd would thin. He wanted to talk with the owner, Langston Ferry.

Like most folks in the South End, Gray saw Ferry or his wife nearly every day. Their store served as the jump-off point for workers sharing rides to jobs in other towns —or, more truthfully, to search for other jobs. Langston acted as unofficial banker for the boycott since most folks spent whatever money they had on food.

The South End took pride in the store. It was once owned by John Cross and served Black sharecroppers. Like most landowners, Cross inflated prices and kept a ledger of what his sharecroppers bought. What they made when they received their share of the crop—or what they received from their share of cutting timber— never covered what they owed for food, clothes, and seed.

JUSTICE TOMORROW

When the last Cross heir left, he sold the store to Langston Ferry's father. Gray didn't know for sure, but he bet Langston was still paying on it.

"How's everybody feeling about the boycott?" He didn't want Ferry to know how interested he was in the white woman held by the sheriff by mentioning it first. "Many folks got jobs yet?"

Ferry grunted. A dark-skinned, fourth-generation Crossville native, his stinginess with words narrowly exceeded his tight-fisted business practices.

"Mr. Ferry, I gots to go," said a woman who pointed to a dill pickle in a jar and laid some coins on the counter. Outside a car horn honked. Ferry scooped out the pickle, wrapped it in paper, and handed it over in one practiced motion.

After the front screen door slammed behind the woman Ferry gave Gray the once over. "Not long 'fore whitey don't wanna clean they own mess. Boycott may be hard, but we ain't slaves."

Gray's head bobbed to acknowledge the truth.

"Whites ain't seeing the good in knowing what's going on. Never did." Ferry pressed his hands flat against the counter and leaned in.

Gray reached in his pocket, peeled off five dollars from his roll of bills, and handed over the rest of his $20 pay to Ferry. "For the boycott."

"Mighty nice, brother Gray." Mrs. Ferry murmured on her way by him. "Few families havin' hard time."

Ferry watched his wife sashay into the back. "George Thompson's maid say he fixin' to move. She working in Piperton now. Live-in."

"Thompson? The new county commissioner?" Gray fingered items on the wood countertop.

"He git lots a calls. Places like Atlanta and Washington," Ferry offered. "Buying that Moon Pie or jest petting it?"

Gray dug in his pocket and tossed a coin on the counter. He'd already noticed official mail to Thompson from Washington and business letters from Atlanta and said so. "I heard 'bout the sheriff holding two white women."

"Do say! I betcha sheriff's waiting orders."

Sometimes Gray could hardly keep from reaching over the wooden counter and choking Ferry by his apron strings until he squeaked out what Gray wanted to know.

"Orders?"

Ferry sold a sack of flour, a jar of molasses, and a peppermint stick. The store did good business though it was on the cuff until folks got money. No other way to sell things in the South End, and his wife saw to it he was more generous than his nature inclined.

"Sheriff don't shit without callin' somebody." Ferry drummed all but one of his fingers on the counter, the one with a purplish-black nail.

Gray checked out the jar of molasses candy waiting for his churning

111

stomach to settle. What in God's name had Sterling done to land in the sheriff's hands? Ferry didn't know or even he would have said by now. "You see my man Silver today?"

Ferry wagged his head to the right. Gray strode across the store and in his hurry to leave he hit the front door so hard it banged against the outer wall.

CHAPTER TWENTY-EIGHT

"Holy Jesus." Tom slid into the driver's seat of his car, exhaled, and grasped the steering wheel in both hands at arm's length. "I need a drink. Anything in the cooler behind me?"

"Coke's all, sorry to say." What a screw-up. The phone might ring any minute with the news her grandmother had died — Justice Tomorrow's way of ordering her out right away.

Tom shook his head and guffawed.

"You're enjoying this too much."

"Oh yeah. Having a ball." Tom's arms relaxed, but he stared up at the sheriff's office on the second floor of the county courthouse.

"No, I mean talking to me like a brainless housewife."

"Hey! I stuck up for you in there. Keep it up, Sterling! You're gonna get us killed." He chuckled once then muttered, "Here I thought I would be the big news today."

Sterling blinked. She had paid little attention to him, but she did now.

"Tom, did you put on a suit just to get me out of jail? I'm touched."

His downcast look reminded Sterling of a little boy suffering an unjust wrong.

"Boyd acts so worried about professors and Indian fingers." Tom put his hand on the back of the car seat and backed out of the parking place. He braked for a woman in a print dress who crossed the street behind him. "I bet I know what he's really thinking."

"Really?" She hesitated a fraction of a second and scooted next to him on the bench seat. Wives and girlfriends did sit next to their men. Truth is, she welcomed the warmth of her partner's body after the episode with the sheriff. "What is Boyd thinking about?"

JACKIE ROSS FLAUM

"Land. I bet he's thinking how to develop it." Tom grinned. "After you left, I shaved, went into the office — on a weekend, in a cheap suit."

"Oh, horrors."

"Turns out a real estate office is busy on Saturday. People shop for homes and land on a weekend. Anyway, I had Saturday off because we are supposed to be getting settled. I show, and right off George says I'm a real go-getter. No one ever called me that—I had to check to make sure I wasn't being insulted."

Sterling chortled.

"Anyway, we already know Black farmers are being evicted from their land by the original owners. I'm talking, original owners like the descendants of the Crossville founding fathers."

"Anderson, Cross, Epson." She ticked them off on her fingers.

"I still can't see how it plays into Henry's murder."

The connection still struck Sterling as far-fetched.

"Don't forget," Tom continued, "we have smaller original landowners who willed their land to their heirs. That's how Penix, Murphy, and so on came to be involved in the land sales. These small landowners have anywhere from a hundred to hundred and fifty acres each — and get this. Their land was given to their ancestors by Epson. Somebody wants the land of these small landowners and Penix, Murphy and the rest are selling it off at bargain basement prices. See, land hasn't been selling in Crossville for ages. No industry, no farming. Stagnant business. Nobody moving in or moving out."

She opened her mouth to ask something.

"No, I have no idea who is buying land from these owners. The real purchaser uses straw buyers."

"Straw what?"

"You know, people who buy the land with money from the person who really wants it. Later the straw buyer deeds over the property. It hides the real buyer's name. People buying large pieces of land for a housing subdivision do it to keep down the price of land they want. If you know a single developer is buying land around you, you can refuse to sell until you get a great deal."

"I get it. But don't folks know land is being bought up?" Sterling asked.

Tom shrugged. "Sure. By different people. And if somebody checked the dates, I bet this land buy has been going on for a while. I'd say Penix first. Black farmer gets evicted. Murphy bought out. Nobody noticed until a whole bunch of farmers got screwed."

"And did nothing about it." She made a mental note for "somebody" to sashay over to the County Clerk and check the dates of land sales over the last year, since it would not occur to Tom.

"If you do it right, I bet the transfer of the land title from the straw buyer to real owner would carry no extra taxes."

114

JUSTICE TOMORROW

"No kidding. How'd you learn all this in such a short time?" Sterling nudged him playfully.

"I asked George all about straw buyers and why an honest person would need one for the Cross land."

She inhaled sharply.

"Now what's the matter?"

"I hope you put it a little differently." Hadn't he researched the role he'd play in Crossville? He had no talent for undercover work.

"Listen, I knew something before I met you. Just not real estate." He gave her a playful nudge in the ribs.

What would that be, she wondered. Aloud she said, "You'd think the mayor or town council would be curious about all this land accumulation."

"Huh? Don't you know anything about Georgia? This town runs a few things like zoning in the city limits, the library, town schools, but most local government is county-based. Why do you think there's a county sheriff back there?"

"To aggravate me?"

Tom snorted, jerked his thumb in the direction they'd come. "Crossville is the county seat, and the sole elected county commissioner – used to call him the ordinary — is George Thompson. He makes sure the county collects taxes, oversees zoning, holds criminal court, and such stuff. Oh, there's talk in places about merging city and county government, but not around here."

Point for Tom. She did not understand the county government structure, though she remembered Tom saying George's election created the need for an extra hand in the real estate office.

"So, the county runs most things even in town?"

"Yep."

"Can you tell me why, after a million years, do the heirs of the original owners want their land back? They've gone to a load of trouble to do it." Except she already guessed the answer or part of it.

"Somebody needs it for, maybe, a development?" His eyebrows arched over iridescent eyes as they went by the Crossville Public Library. "I may not know much about investigating murder, but I do know legal action to take land or houses or cars or anything from colored people ain't a shit-load of trouble, especially for a county or a bank."

She chewed on that thought minute.

"I really need to show you on a map. Come into the office and have lunch with me Monday. Picture Crossville laid out wide at the north and narrow at the south." Tom tried to demonstrate with his hands while steering the wheel with his forearms. "We drove in via Callie's Cutoff from the north."

She imitated his movement.

115

"Remember how it's mostly empty wooded land, scattered fields, farms?" Tom said. "Even though it's all in the county, the land is the gateway to the town since it's on the main road. The real estate office, the new A&P, the Methodist Church, stores, and historical society lie on the end of the northeast side of the parcel. On the east, are streets with nicer homes behind shops and stores. And on the west, we have the bookstore, barbershop, more stores, and streets of houses – all of them nicer than our home."

"House. Not our home, Tom."

"The Negro section of town is to the south and some on the west. Coloreds who aren't farmers or sharecroppers or timber men live there, worship there, play over there. I think there may be a barbershop, small store or two."

"Okay." Geography never interested Sterling.

"Six or seven parcels of vacant land bought from whites or claimed from Blacks are grouped together in two spots in town. No pattern to who bought which acres when."

A bell jangled in the back of her mind. Something from the sheriff's office.

"I bet the sheriff knows." Tom pointed at her. "Remember he mentioned 'development'? Not a word that pops into your head when you're dealing with trespassers or finding a human bone."

It was her cue to cheer, and Tom deserved one. But she had more questions. "Right now, seven or eight buyers control one-fourth of Crossville —."

"—all taken from Black farmers or bought from white heirs who own small parcels of land. Bought at cheap prices, though. Those small landowners aren't smart." Tom jumped in.

"Who owns the big parcels, Tom?"

"I only know names on the deed. A variety of people. I can't tell whether the purchases are related or single buys. Should I find out?"

"That would be lovely."

He missed the sarcasm. "I know one buyer. A fellow in my office told me."

"A straw buyer?" Sterling guessed.

"Nope." Tom went on, "The largest acreage of land, which is in the center of the north side of town, belongs to John Cross the fourth. Handed down from the original John Cross. Who names their kid the fourth? Even my father wasn't so arrogant."

"The man who owns Callie's Cutoff? What does Cross do in Washington, D.C.?"

"No idea."

Sterling would find out.

"Should he and the neighboring owners on the north get together they would own land stretching from Callie's Cutoff to the historical society." Tom pointed his finger out the window to show her the property as they drove by.

"Six hundred, seven hundred acres of farm and timberland at Crossville's front door. Enough land to build damn near anything you wanted."

"Hm-m. Who—?"

Tom brightened. "George comes in couple of days a week. Almost every time he's here, he talks on the phone with this person he doesn't want all of us to know about. At least I'm pretty sure it's the same person every time. George says things like 'all quiet,' 'things are on track.'"

"Wow." Tom just thought to mention this to her?

"I never really thought about it, but they must be planning something big. I'll bet other people in town know about it. I mean, it's a small place, but folks are spending a lot to spruce it up and build new businesses."

She pursed her lips. What he said made sense.

Tom halted at a corner for a convoy of military vehicles to pass on the Main Road. "Anyway, there's more. Cross has a legal address in Atlanta, but it's a bank, not somebody's house."

"How do you know Cross gave a bank address?"

"I know Atlanta."

She grinned and patted his knee. "Way to go."

"That's the first time you've looked at me the same way you do Gray," Tom beamed.

"You care?"

"Yeah. I guess I do."

A tingle of heat rattled her. "Okay, who are these people buying land and moving to Crossville?"

"I feel like we're chasing our tails." He shrugged. "Don't know who's moving and who is holding land for someone else. I did find out that one or two of the names on deeds live in Virginia near Washington, D.C."

"Virginia?" Tom doled out clues like raffle prizes. Sterling wondered what else he knew. "We probably need to get those names to Justice Tomorrow to find out who they are."

"Another name is a bank lawyer in Atlanta. From what I know of him he ain't planning to raise peaches."

"How do you know him?"

Tom squirmed. "I'm from Atlanta."

"Turns out you know a lot. This land business is all Greek to me."

Maybe Justice Tomorrow knew what they were doing sending Tom to Crossville. She wanted him to work out, to be an asset for everyone. Handsome, sexy, plus clever would make him irresistible to a lot of women.

With a satisfied grin, he put his arm around her and drove with his left hand.

She inspected his hand sliding from her shoulder toward her breast. "Is this part of the doting husband act?"

JACKIE ROSS FLAUM

"Nope. I'm copping a feel."

****

Silver opened the door of his brother's upstairs bedroom at Mrs. Parson's house and fairly danced inside. "It's all copasetic, Gray. Sheriff let Sterling go."

"Copasetic?" Gray said, relieved beyond measure.

"She and Foster are driving around town casual-like. I saw them go by."

Gray perched on the edge of his bed, bowed his head and rubbed the top with both hands. "It's more than today. There's a police alert across the South on a short, young red-haired woman working with a tall Black man."

Silver stiffened. "For what crimes?"

"Grifting, stealing—anything imaginable. Point is —."

"She's got blond hair now, man. Trust the woman. She's good. Even Ajamu's heard about a white woman and a brother slipping around the south asking questions. He just came from Alabama someplace. They're calling you Ghost."

"Shit. Why the hell is she here?" Gray said.

Silver sat, clasped his hands into a fist. Somewhere in the pit of his stomach Gray already knew.

"They needed a white man at the real estate office —."

"And they assigned Sterling to watch him." Gray finished.

Silver thumped his chest. "I screwed up. Okay? Foster overheard me talking about Justice Tomorrow, and he got invited in. I ain't carrying that cross anymore. Tom Foster's as good as a white man gets."

"I screwed up too." Gray dropped his chin to his chest.

Silver clutched at his heart with both hands. "Not you! Not the invincible Gray?"

"I've got to meet with Sterling today. Now. I never told her about the police alert."

"Damn—better be the first thing you say."

"And she doesn't know about the boycott," Gray finished.

Silver pursed his lips and drawled, "Missrus Sterlin' gwanna kick yur Black ass fur shore."

****

Sterling and Tom drove slowly through town with cool wind blowing through the open windows. Sterling's mind whirled, while Tom hummed.

She said, "Do we know how many Blacks have moved out of town since the evictions started? Maybe Henry Johnson was killed because the killers wanted his father out of the way of the land grab."

"Gray said some people moved out of the county, but a few moved in with relatives. I don't think we're talking about huge numbers." Tom drummed a finger on the steering wheel. "I'm thinking all this is not about voting rights.

118

I'm with Gray. The murder's tied to the mystery development–the land, the sheriff, the hidden buyers."

Sterling had to agree. Tom—and Gray—made sense.

Why else would Boyd get in a lather over the far-out chance the bone was ancient Indian, which would attract the interest of university professors and bring tourists to Crossville? She would have thought the idea of attracting tourists was a good thing for this town of less than a thousand souls.

Crossville bustled on this fall Saturday. Sterling drew in a deep breath and surveyed the mothers with their children crossing Main, men going into the hardware store, a teenager with her ponytail secured with a yellow scarf. A soldier strolled with a young woman on his arm toward the cafe. American flags waved in front of the Post Office and City Hall. She frowned.

Something was out of place.

"You know of any development or rumors of development in Crossville right now?"

"I don't hear rumors. I'm the low man on the totem pole in the office," said Tom.

"What developments have started then?"

"Only one unless you count Paul Epson – Alice Peterson's brother." Tom had to take his arm away from Sterling to wave two overweight teenage boys across the street in front.

Sterling seized the chance to ease to the passenger side of the car in hopes of thinking clearer.

"As for developments, Epson's building a fancy new hardware store on the East Side, the grocery was renovated and turned into an A&P. One of the Andersons sank a big pot of money into a housing development in south of town. Your friend Jennifer's family is part of it." Tom went on.

"Jennifer mentioned Cotton Estates. What is it?"

"Much excitement in the local home sales world." Tom gave her a sideways grin. "The Andersons and Epsons are fixing to sink more money into Crossville. They're breaking ground on a sub-division on acres they own."

Sterling's hands played airplane with the air outside her window. "Can you slow?"

"Talking or driving?" Tom laughed.

"Both."

Tom obeyed and studied the scene outside the front window. "I like Crossville. It's a nice, prosperous town. Feels good here. Homey."

She agreed, sensing contentment maneuver for space inside her. "Someday I'll settle in a place like this. Grow roots. Join a-a book club. Have a handsome husband."

"I'm handsome," he quipped.

"You're a real snoop too. Wonderful quality in an undercover husband."

"You love being a detective, don't you? You ever wanna give up the life?"

"Someday. When I can have the top floor office in my own building of international investigators," she teased.

"Of course." He waved out the window at someone on the sidewalk.

She leaned back. Her town for a while, she could allow it. The bookstore boasted a good selection. A small but well-stocked record store sat next to it. A five and dime store opened a month ago but didn't have many customers today. Green grass. Clipped bushes. People smiling and going about their business.

"White! Everyone in town is white."

"What?" Tom made a right turn.

Rose Collins and an exasperated woman with a baby in her arms stood outside the public library in animated discussion but waved as they drove by. Outside the drug store, a man in a white coat searched the street, scratched his head then reached for a broom just inside his door.

"What the hell?" Tom turned down their street and passed the empty lots, the old store. "What's going on?"

"What does it have to do with voting rights . . . or murder?"

Tom parked in front of their house and killed the engine. For a moment they sat close, staring out the front window. What was going on in Crossville? Her mind wandered off in self-defense.

The poor run-down general store. Once parts of it must have been painted white. Today it was graying, splitting boards on a teetering foundation. The chimney had dumped a few bricks on the shingled roof. A storm might blow the rest of the chimney bricks through their roof or windows.

"I gotta talk to Gray."

Tom flung open his door and got out without a word. He stomped around the car, and in the rearview mirror, she saw him rap the trunk once with a fist. He opened her car door and offered his hand. "Let's have a drink. It must be five o'clock somewhere."

"Good idea," she said. "First let me call Harriet and tell her about my fun day." And arrange a meeting with Gray.

CHAPTER TWENTY-NINE

By now Sterling, like all of Crossville, must know about the boycott. Gray lounged on the stump in front of the blackened remains of Mt. Moriah Church so he could watch the Emporium across the invisible line marking white Crossville and his section of town. Not a single Black person crossed into white Crossville. This first day proved successful beyond Gray's wildest imaginings. Montgomery had ninety percent of its Black citizens stay off buses on the first day of its boycott, and Crossville surely beat them. Not one Black soul. On a Saturday shopping day.

Since he'd been sitting on this stump pretending to fix a brown leather mule bridle, he had seen a few cars and trucks driven by whites go into the South End and return with no passengers. Maids and yard boys weren't working today. Nobody was working except feeble-minded Silas Ramsey and two women who said it wasn't right to abandon the dying old man they tended.

Two fat white men in overalls took turns keeping an eye on him. He got an inordinate amount of their attention during the last two hours. One kept a newspaper in front of him, but the other had tiny eyes set way back under thin eyebrows and a nose like a hog snout.

Whites would try to hire help outside Crossville, but Gray doubted they'd find many takers. Word from neighboring Black pastors was nobody would work until the boycott ended.

He checked his clumsy bandaged hands and wondered how clever his ruse was. He lifted the bridle and it jingled. Any fool could tell it was hard for him to manipulate the leather.

The sun drifted lower in a cloudless blue sky and most folks started fixing supper. He figured he still had time to meet Sterling before his own dinner. He had accepted an invitation from a woman with eyes that beckoned and a butt that made promises. Gray licked his lips.

Like the barbershop crowd knew, his heroics at the fire earned him the attention of quite a few women, something he found amusing. And fattening. He had a cake and a pie sitting on a table in his room in the boarding house.

He had almost given up on Sterling when he saw Harriet Cook drive around to the back of the Emporium, park, and glance about. With an almost imperceptible nod to him, she opened the door and went in.

Presently, she came back out trailing a white strip of cloth. She slammed and locked the place, but the cloth hung like she'd caught it in the closing door. Then she hurried to her car and drove off.

In one hour, he would meet Sterling in the safe house. Had Harriet left behind two strips it would be two hours.

Gray scouted the sky to judge the time. It would be close. He would wash for his dinner and cut through the woods to the meeting. There was a trap door under the store's floor, made invisible by overgrown weeds. Thank goodness the floor was high enough off the ground, so he didn't need to crawl to use the hidden door.

He liked it better when their cover included his working for Sterling as a yard boy. Easy access, constant contact. The boycott made this difficult situation in Crossville worse. It cut him off from the historical society. The safe house would be the sole meeting place.

Pacifist or not, Sterling would kill him when she found out what he started. He vowed not to tell her about the boycott until he was ready to leave.

For the benefit of the pig-faced man across the street he hopped off the barrel, winced, and hobbled on the outer edges of his feet toward his boarding house. As he limped along, Gray ticked off the list of things he had to tell or bring Sterling. The boycott, a roll of film tucked in the ticking of his pillow, two more witness statements.

First, however, he had to warn her what Justice Tomorrow had told him earlier about the Alabama multi-state alert and their descriptions being sent throughout the South. His neglect was inexcusable. The mule's worn bridle jangled. He'd fixed the broken chin strap.

Sterling would be excited to hear what he found out about the timeline for Henry Johnson's murder. He'd mention what Ferry said about George Thompson's packing to move. He smothered a grin with his hand to think what she'd do when he told her. Her mouth in a tight O, skin pink with delight. She might get so excited she'd hug him.

Folks who lived along the road to Callie's Cutoff and others living on the far end of the cutoff from Parson's, gave him a pretty good idea about the timeline when Henry Johnson died. In his initial briefing from Justice Tomorrow, he'd learned what time Henry left home and when the body was found. He was also sure Reverend Johnson was the real target, not Henry. In three weeks of asking questions, he'd learned precious little else.

Since his heroics at the church fire, however, Gray found a woman who saw Henry drive into Callie's Cutoff. Or rather, she found him last night at the joint worship service where he and Silver read and photographed anything farmers brought in to show they owned the land they plowed. Silver did the camera work while Gray talked to the people about what their papers said. A few helpful passages leapt out, though it wasn't much.

For Gray, the best piece of news came from a woman whose farm wasn't far from Callie's Cutoff, only a minute or two from the murder scene. She saw bright taillights and the red light on top of the sheriff's vehicle as it pulled out of a road to follow the pastor's car. She knew deputies hid in their cars in the woods to take naps and catch speeders, so she thought nothing of it. She didn't get a good look at the deputy in the car except to say he was tall, fat, and white. Not much to go on. Later, she said nothing to keep from getting killed.

He wrote out her information, she'd signed it as true with her X. He didn't want to spook her, so he and Silver signed the statement as witnesses after she left.

Gray climbed the back steps of the house where he boarded, thinking about Callie's Cutoff. One end of the heavily wooded stretch of road where Johnson was killed lay close to Parson's store and lead to Crossville's front door. The other, the opposite end of the cutoff where the new witness lived, was in the middle of woods and farms and lead, eventually, to Batesville. Parson's teemed with Blacks and poor whites every minute it was open, so Gray thought it was logical that someone was around to see who came out of the cutoff around the time of Henry's murder.

So far nobody said anything.

Gray washed, applied new ointment to his feet and hands, and dressed quickly. Slow as he moved, he had to start early to be on time.

CHAPTER THIRTY

Sterling flung open the kitchen window facing the old store to allow a cooling breeze into the room. Ground beef smashed into odd-shaped patties sizzled in her trusty iron skillet. Water simmered in a copper-bottomed pot on the stove. When it boiled, she would drop a frozen block of peas in it. Chunks of peeled potatoes bubbled in another pot of water on the next burner.

"I've never felt better. Every day I wake up and can't wait to see what happens next." Tom leaned against the opposite kitchen counter. He saluted her with a bourbon and Coke, then drank.

Domestic bliss, Sterling thought with a touch of resentment. Even reading the torturous handwriting in Aunt Amelia Epson's diary was more fun than this. She hated cooking, yet here she was with a yellow apron around her waist and a spatula in her hand. Tom held the glass to her lips as she went by, and she took a big gulp.

Tom took the spatula to keep her from flipping the misshapen burgers again and gave her a sip his drink. "I feel like I can do anything with you and get by with it. Is that the way you felt working with Gray? Invincible?"

She cocked her head. "We're a team. We believe in each other, and we each know what the other can do."

Tom thought about it a minute and slipped his arms around her while she opened a package of frozen peas on the counter. "Like a married couple?"

"Not hardly." Sterling shook his arm off her waist.

Tom fed her another drink of his cocktail. "Would you date a colored man?"

Sterling's snort of surprise made Coke fly up her nose, and she coughed. "I usually hear that from a Black man."

"When I was growing up my family was strict about who I dated. They discriminated by religion because nobody, nobody, would dream of my dating a colored woman. My father ordered me not to marry anyone who wasn't Catholic." Tom pondered the melting ice cubes in his glass and went to the refrigerator freezer to get out an ice tray. "I didn't know I had to pick a rich Catholic girl."

Thanks to the clatter and crackle of emptying ice cubes from the metal tray, Sterling missed most of what Tom said. She understood discriminating by faith, though.

"I got the same from my father's family. Irish Catholics every single one." The water for the peas broke into a boil. She tore into the waxed box and a few loose peas scattered on the counter. "Our priest used to deliver sermons about divorce and faithfulness and the dangers of marrying outside the faith all the time. My friends and I joked his father must have been a Protestant who ran off and divorced his mother."

Tom offered his glass while she attempted to flip the burgers, but she shook her head. Grease splattered on the stove. "Are you a strict Catholic?"

"Fish on Friday, marriage, holy days of obligation, confession." Sterling wondered how long the potatoes had cooked.

"Now I know why you took the pepperoni off your pizza last night."

"I confess."

Tom pulled out a chair by the kitchen table. He sat down, let his arms fall between his knees, and leaned over to study his clasped hands. "I'm pretty strict too. I'm even feeling bad about going to the Baptist Church tomorrow."

"Gotta love Catholic guilt." Sterling poked at the hamburgers with a spatula. They felt firm.

"Did you date Gray?" He made it sound like an accusation, and it flew all over her.

"Are these questions about Black men generally or Gray specifically? Are you worried I'll marry outside the faith or my race?" She whirled on him, twirling the greasy spatula.

"Don't get so mad. Curious, is all." Tom downed his drink.

For several minutes she worried the hamburgers, then stabbed the potatoes with a fork and watched them disintegrate. As she poured the hot water off the potatoes, Tom rubbed the birthmark on his arm, casting about for something to say.

Every time Tom felt guilty about something, he rubbed his birth mark. Good to see him doing it now. The jerk.

She yanked open a drawer and clawed around for the wooden-handled masher. Standing on tiptoes, she drew the pot close and used the masher to take out her frustration on the helpless vegetables. In no time, the potatoes were white mush she scrapped into a bowl. All the water had boiled off the frozen peas, so they must be ready to eat.

"Set the table," she snapped.

Tom came up close behind her, leaned down to whisper in her ear. "Sorry, Sterling. I have no right."

Hands on hips she spat, "No, you don't."

His hands inched up her arms. "You're the most incredible woman I've ever seen, much less been around. Beautiful. Smart. Catholic. I would be a fool not to want the right . . ."

He kissed her. She closed her eyes anticipating the heat and grasped his waist. His lips nibbled on hers at first, then pressed firmer, more urgent.

The kitchen timer buzzed. They drifted apart.

"Timer. It's time . . . I-I have to meet Gray." Sterling stammered, suddenly anxious to get away, to find solid ground again.

"I'll go too."

"Your contract is Silver. I'm going out the back and through the woods to our meet, and I gotta hurry. Let's stick with protocol." She busied herself untying her apron.

Tom walked to the far counter, poured another bourbon and Coke. "I'll keep everything warm for you."

CHAPTER THIRTY-ONE

Gray's mouth dried up, his heart pounded so hard the pitted wooden countertop he leaned against should have echoed the beat through the store.

He stole another peek through the broken windowpanes toward Sterling's house in time to see her leave Foster's arms. Amid the play-acting every assignment called on them to do, he always recognized what was real. Sterling was real. That kiss was real.

Gray dreamed of kissing her so often the heat of it lay on his lips in the cool dark store. He wanted to reach for her hand, to feel her skin glide against his. His feet, wiser than the rest of him, pointed toward escape out the trap door.

Why did he want to run?

It would take more than one kiss to steal Sterling. They had work to do. He pulled up a filthy wooden chair and rolled a flour barrel that was missing a stave into the shadows away from any line of sight from windows. As an afterthought, he used his handkerchief to dust off both seats, then sat on the barrel to wait.

Her gardenia-scented perfume floated to him over the must in the store.

"Gray." She ventured further inside, closed the door, called to him again. "Gray?"

He didn't blame her. She was young, beautiful. Did he expect her to be celibate forever?

"Sterling," he whispered, gentle as a lover. "Sterling, over here."

An aura of sex, love, and lust filled the ramshackle store as surely as dust and spider webs. He'd never felt it so powerfully with Sterling. She felt it too, though neither of them said a word. Never acted like it existed. He wondered why, knowing the answer before the question fully formed.

She picked her way over broken boards and a fallen roof beam then gave him a little smile. "How are you ——-? Oh no! Were you burned badly?"

Singed by an unnamed pain, he'd forgotten his burnt hands and feet. "Ah, no, fine. Healing rapidly. Been worse if you hadn't stepped in."

"Let me see your hands. Did you put anything on them besides pork grease?" She started to grasp his wrists, and he jerked away.

"I applied burn ointment on them. Went one town over to the Black doctor and got tetanus and antibiotic shots. Stop fussing." He snapped, instantly regretting it.

She shrugged it off and sat on the edge of the chair beside him. "Nice shirt." She rubbed the material between her fingers.

"Comfortable. I take it your cover is still secure after the other night?" Gray shifted on the barrel lid.

Nodding, she said, "You were amazing. You inspired me."

"You jeopardized the mission." It came out harsher than he intended.

"You're welcome."

He grunted. "People are talking about the crazy white woman."

She rubbed her upper arm where the bullet scarred her; reminding her of when he had saved her. She glared at him, pinned him in the dim light. "What's going on, Gray?"

"The cops know about us, you and me. They have a vague description of a young Black male and a red-haired woman with freckles, a short white woman, maybe a college student." He heard her gasp. "I should have told you right off. You've got to watch out. They're not playing."

"We have to finish," Her voice trembled a little. Her hand played with an empty glass bottle lying on the counter.

"I'm surprised they sent you at all." To his relief, the frenzied static of desire softened.

"Who else do they have to send?"

"This might be your last mission in the South, Sterling."

"What about you?"

"You got any idea how many young black males are traveling around Georgia, Mississippi, Alabama? Hard to pick me out of a crowd."

"I can't—"

"We don't have all day. Take this film." He fumbled with his shirt to extract the roll of film there. He had forgotten how long he took to button his shirt.

"Oh, for heaven's sake. Let me." She got in front of him and grasped the middle button. Once it popped free, she reached inside his shirt, grabbed the roll wrapped in gauze with two fingers, resting the heel of her hand on his chest. Her fingers, her palm left a fiery imprint.

Longest five seconds of his life. Gray cleared his throat twice. How in God's name could she be so oblivious?

He slid off the barrel. "I've got witness statements in my back pocket. No! I'll get them out."

She harrumphed.

Thank God for tight jeans and dark rooms. Finally, he extracted the folded white pages. He lost sight of most of her expression when she sat with half her back shutting out the light from the broken window. What he saw hurt.

"Y-you smell nice. Aftershave?"

Was there a wounded tone in her question?

"Old Spice.," he said. "I've had it since Christmas."

"Hmm-m. You hardly ever wear it."

Gray gathered from the tilt of her head his answer was unsatisfactory.

"So, what is this?" She unfurled the gauze and held the black and orange roll between her thumb and finger.

"Two of the sharecroppers brought me old written letters from John Cross, man who owned their grandmothers. These men are descendants of Cross and two slave women. Cross freed the male descendants and gave them each acres of land right next to one another and bordering on land he claims he gave to the sons of two other slave women. Mr. Cross apparently spent the lonely winter nights siring children on his slaves. Silver took pictures of the documents, as the owners refused to give them up."

"I don't blame them. Well, I'll add all this to our evidence box. I had a great day. Got hauled into the sheriff's office." Sterling wrapped the film in a tissue and carefully lodging it between her bra cups with the same fingers she'd run over his chest.

Did he moan aloud? No. Gray dragged his mind back to the business at hand with difficulty.

"Since you're not wearing prison stripes, I assume all ended well." Grateful for a distraction he mounted his barrel seat again.

"I managed to bag a scrap of torn cloth near the base of the tree where Henry hung. A sheriff's epaulette or-r the rank patch from a uniform? The rest of the material I'm sending to Justice Tomorrow is twigs and such. Let them sort it out."

Sterling related her adventures with Nancy, concluding with her suspicion J.T. Dawson had seen some or all of Henry Johnson's murder.

Since it dovetailed into the story of the woman who saw a deputy sheriff's car the day of Henry's murder, Gray told her about it.

"Do you think J.T. was in the car the farmer's wife saw?" Sterling didn't sound convinced.

"I don't know. She didn't have a good description of who drove the patrol car. It would be helpful to know where J.T. was since he was not on his regular patrol." Gray said.

"I'm already on it."

"'Course." Gray snorted. "Silver and I are running down the folks who frequent Parson's to find out what they saw the night of the murder. Can you check on the whites?"

"Yep. Tom has done a good job pulling together maps, deeds, and getting us a clue about why sharecropper land is in such demand." Sterling inclined her head toward her house, then told him what Tom discovered.

Gray grunted. "Not much. He needs to keep digging."

"How is it straw buyers and a big unknown development on John Cross's land don't interest you?" No mistaking her irritation.

"I meant no disrespect of the enormous work that your partner" — he leaned a little heavy on the last word — "has done thus far."

Sterling jumped to her feet. "What are you so pissed off about?"

He slid off the barrel careful to land on the edge of his feet. "Why are you so touchy?"

"I'm hungry." She huffed. "We shouldn't stay here long. But I need to know: what's up in town? No black people anywhere."

"I convinced everyone to start a boycott. Until the land grab ends. Until they hand over Henry's killers. I didn't mean to do it, rather surprised myself. I acted like you for once, rushing into something without thinking."

"Damn, Gray!"

"I know. I know." He had already kicked himself a dozen times for getting caught up in the moment. "I . . . Reverend Johnson folded, gave up, surrendered. Can't blame him, really. No one but Ajamu was talking."

"I'll stand by you when Justice Tomorrow goes ape."

To his shock, she threw herself against his chest and hugged him as though she'd never see him again. She'd done it dozens of times: good-byes, escapes, the discovery of crucial evidence in a case.

But now? His cheek rested on her head and both arms wrapped around her. He heard her breathe and started to tell her how good it felt to hold her. As a man holds the woman he adores.

Instead, he squeezed a painful wheeze from his chest. "I don't think Justice Tomorrow should have risked sending you, even to babysit Tom. Get out of Crossville sooner rather than later."

She drew back, puzzled, hurt.

"Sterling, you and I act on facts, not what we want."

"I am a good investigator."

"Silver and Tom count on us to be realists." Gray tried to draw her close one more time.

"Old Spice, my ass." She shoved him. "You've got British Sterling on your 'comfortable' shirt — and I gave it to you for your birthday."

Sterling threw a small, slender, stiff shadow as she tromped around the fallen beam and out the back door. The oh-so-briefly opened door allowed in a red sliver of sun. Her slam rocked the rotten frame.

Gray gaped after her, wondering what just happened. He was the one wounded, so what was she so mad about? What he needed right then was to taste a double-serving of his dinner hostess's ass through both bandaged hands.

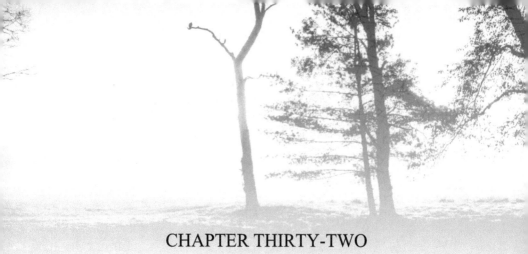

CHAPTER THIRTY-TWO

Gray's shutting her out sounded as real as the door she'd slammed. Sterling still heard it in her ears, felt it bam against her chest. Outside the store, she plunged through the fading light, through the weeds. Each stride fueled an anger and hurt she refused to acknowledge.

At her call, Tom trotted down the front hallway of their house from the kitchen and peeked into the room off the staircase. She lay half in-half out of the open window, kicking her feet in the air, pushing cardboard boxes aside, and clawing for a grip on the inside sill.

"What the —? Why didn't you come in the back door?" He raced over to grab under her arms and haul her into the study.

She huffed, brushed the dirt off her paisley shirt and blue jeans. "I wanted to know how hard it was to jump, grab the window, and climb in."

What was Gray thinking? Rescuing children was one thing. But Justice Tomorrow would pull him from the assignment for starting a boycott. And he didn't remember what she gave him for his birthday. It stabbed to the quick. Dumb. Gotta be the blues before her period. No, she calculated she had a week or so to go.

"Sterling? Are you okay? Sterling!"

She jerked her head up, still thinking of Gray. Instead, it was Tom eyeing her with more concern than Gray had.

"He convinced the black community to start a boycott of Crossville," she sighed.

Tom recoiled. "Justice Tomorrow will go ape."

"My very words."

"Maybe they won't find out."

"What a mess."

"Yes, you are." Tom leaned down to kiss her cheek and stepped back with a handful of cobwebs from her hair, which he dangled in front of her.

"Yuk! I need a shower." She jumped away. "Fix me a drink, would you? I'll tell you more when I finish."

Without waiting for an answer, she brushed by him, sickened by the swirling odor of aftershave, mildew, and sweat around her.

"Don't you want dinner?" Tom followed her to the foot of the stairs, and she knew he watched her hips as she climbed. "I left it in the oven. I even cleaned the kitchen. A once-in-a-lifetime thing."

"I'll applaud later." She started to swipe his kiss off her cheek. Unprofessional to kiss her. Yet sweet. And, okay, welcome. Was it so terrible to want a little human affection?

She banged the bathroom door at the top of the staircase behind her. For a moment, she gritted her teeth and leaned on her hands and arms, staring at her reflection in the wide mirror over the bathroom sink.

What was the matter with her? She snapped at Tom, who only meant to be playful and charming. And why was Gray upset from the moment she came in? Surely his wounds weren't so terrible. He was walking, using his fingers. Was he lying to her about his pain? Or something else? He never lied to her. Never tried to send her away.

Tears puddled. A hiccup and wheeze of loneliness. The quivering lip of an abandoned child. Finally, a tsunami of homesickness nearly felled her.

She missed her mother's hug, her father's outrageous laugh, her brother Danny's teasing, the free-wheeling love they showed each other. She missed feeling protected, meeting nervous young Harvard boys, being confident of who and whose she was. Right now, she craved the sight of someone who cared about her.

She yanked her clothes off, piled them in a corner, turned on the shower, and sat naked on the edge of the tub. Slowly she peeled back a corner of her mind to peek at her memories of Gray. Their adventures. The inside jokes. The all-night talks. The comfort his hugs brought.

More than anyone else Gray taught her to be a good investigator. She traced the puckered bullet scar. Gray nursed her through it.

Hot water never lasted long. She poured a handful of shampoo and scrubbed her hair harder than necessary. Scalp tingling and eyes closed to keep out the soap, Gray's face teased her. Water sloshed down her body, warm at first then tepid. She shut it off and fumbled for her towel.

She and Gray got too close. She wasn't naive enough to miss the attraction they shared. He never let on he saw it. And he never asked, yet she freely gave him too much of who she was. Foolish. Pointless. Reckless. Just like her.

The world wasn't changing fast enough for her — or Gray.

The powerful, wealthy organizers of Justice Tomorrow created clear rules for agent conduct. Seal and sign every bag of evidence. Do not murder or steal to further an assignment. Investigate without drawing attention. Agents will not be involved with each other.

None of those rules mattered now. A compromised agent was as good as gone. Maybe forever. Henry's death deserved all her time and energy. Whatever time was left for her in Crossville.

From downstairs, the music of Smoky Robinson and the Miracles bounded upstairs and lifted her. She wiped the steam off the bathroom mirror and examined her bleached hair for reddish roots, her cheeks for freckles, her eyes for signs of willful blindness.

Time to admit it. No matter how much people wanted to change the world, beliefs and prejudices they grew up with remained burrowed inside. Even inside those who sought change the most. She never ate meat on Fridays, regardless of how much she craved it.

Gray was right about something else: she was a realist.

The sound of Wilson Pickett dropped on the hi-fi turntable downstairs. She hummed along. The shower dripped in rhythm.

She tightened the towel around her and opened the door to tiptoe into her bedroom for clean clothes.

Tom stood in the middle of the staircase with a glass in his hand. "Thought I'd leave this on your dresser. You looked like you needed it. Was the rest of Gray's report bad?"

"Ah-h. The boycott is bad enough."

He nodded. "Their answer to the church burning."

"And Henry's murder. And the land grab."

He climbed to the top of the stairs until he was close enough to hand her the drink.

"Thanks, Tom." She reached for the glass and their fingers brushed.

"That's my real name, you know. Tom." He put one hand over one of the big yellow daisies splashed on the floral hall wallpaper and rested against it. "Is Sterling your real name?"

She stammered, "I-it's a family name."

"Any brothers or sisters? Been vaccinated for measles? Do you have a dog?"

Her heart sped up. "A brother Danny. He's my hero. All my shots. And no, we never lived in any town long enough to have a dog. Did you enjoy Georgia Tech? Do you have brothers and sisters?"

She babbled, hoping he'd step back. Hoping he wouldn't.

"I'm an only child. A prince. My father the king is desperate for an heir." His free hand gently traced her jawline, the side of her neck. Her breath caught. "His quest for a rich, fertile Catholic maiden to secure the kingdom for the royal line failed. While he railed and ranted, I ran away to fight dragons with the smartest, sexiest woman I've ever known. A woman who makes me earn the right to feel like royalty."

His kiss tasted of whiskey and promises, full of yearning and insistence.

Her knees weakened, the towel slipped. She grasped it, whispering something silly to lighten the mood, "Sir Knight, no trifling."

"I'm a prince, goddamn it." He unbuttoned his shirt and tossed it on the floor. "Princes do not trifle." He inserted three fingers under the top of her towel. She quivered. He tossed it aside, drew her against his bare chest. In his embrace, she felt wanted and deliciously in danger.

CHAPTER THIRTY-THREE

First Baptist Church took up a big slice of the street running parallel to Main and behind the real estate office. The white wood and red brick building occupied half a block, much of it surrounded by bare ground and gravel. Lots of cars parked on the gravel and a sidewalk of boards led from the parking lot to the church steps.

To reach the church Tom and Sterling drove down their street and up a side road leading to the north side of town. Sterling tried to finish dressing as they drove. Her cardigan slipped and fell onto the car floor. Preoccupied with finding the hole on the belt of her dress, she took little interest in the scenery. Until they reached the heart of Crossville.

"Look at that! Somebody dumped a ton of trash in the empty Cross land. Yuk," Sterling said.

"Happens all the time out in the county. Glad you had an alibi for last night, though." Tom deadpanned. "We are late, late."

"Dumping garbage on someone's property is not like digging little holes. What a low, stinky low thing."

Loud, off-key singing with enthusiastic organ accompaniment reached into the First Baptist Church parking lot. Sterling winched. The service was in full swing.

"I'm nervous as a nun in a whorehouse," Tom whispered as they jogged the steps to the double front doors of the church. He buttoned his blue suit jacket.

Sterling was too worried to laugh. Did she have a run in her hose? Did everyone know they had sex before church?

The way the congregation and minister stared as an elderly usher led them down the green-carpeted center aisle, their delicious sin seemed to glow like scarlet on their faces. The white walls and stained-glass windows on either side of the building went by in a blur.

JUSTICE TOMORROW

The usher waved them into a pew in the middle of the church. Sterling side-stepped in and stood next to a woman aged about fifty. The white blond hair under her hat frizzed with tell-tale signs of too much permanent wave. Happily, most of it hid under a blue hat that sprouted fake flowers. Smiling over her hymn at the late arrivals caused a mole on her left cheek to stand out.

To Sterling's dismay, Sheriff Boyd occupied the place next to the woman. He leaned forward slightly, patted the woman's arm, and thrust a chin in Sterling's direction. The woman, Mrs. Boyd Sterling presumed, offered her half the hymnal and kept on singing. She had a lovely voice.

Sterling accepted her share of the book with a sinking heart. She swallowed hard, panicked she wouldn't know a tune all Baptists should know.

No matter. The song ended. Beside her, Tom exhaled and took her hand as they claimed their places on the wooden pew. Sterling smoothed down her tight skirt, admired her cordovan leather gloves, and waited for the sermon.

The reverend resembled an angry grizzly with clipped brown fur and fiery black eyes. Standing behind the pulpit in an austere robe, he raised the Bible in both hands, ready to attack and maim.

"Acts, seventeenth chapter," he thundered.

Sterling risked a sideways glance at her lover. Her lover. She flushed, and he squeezed her hand as though he understood. She bowed her head, conjuring the magical sensation of resting in Tom's arms.

A slight movement on her right roused her. Mrs. Boyd leaned close. Sterling jerked her head around and they nearly bumped noses. Mrs. Boyd sat straight as though hit with an electrical shock. Had the woman been staring at her? Sterling frowned. She touched her cheek. Her glove came away with powder on it, so she knew she'd covered her freckles.

"In verse twenty-six, Paul tells us how God created the nations of the world from one man, and gave them seasons and boundaries–yes, boundaries–within which to live." The minister's deep voice blanketed the congregation, covering them with his words. "Yet today we have those who believe the races should mix and mingle. We have those who believe those boundaries set up by God Himself should tumble. We suffer those calling for an end to segregation. This is contrary to God's Word!"

To drive home his point the preacher pounded his Bible once and continued: "God made separate nations. These non-believers want to develop a mongrel country. Good Christians, God calls on you to stand against this!"

A murmur rippled the congregation. Sterling gaped.

"These minions of Hell want to defy the will of Almighty God! They will not prevail against His Mighty Hand." Another round of muttering answered the reverend.

"Now our nigras have listened to these devils, have turned from the plan God laid out. They are refusing to work, to shop in Crossville. They have fallen under Satan through the work of outside agitators!"

Sterling detected a little spit on the pastor's chin. Perhaps he was physically rabid. Tom tightened his grip on her hand. She compressed both lips into a small line of disapproval and stared at the pastor.

She ventured a glance around the congregation, and Jennifer Mullins caught her eye. She pretended to scratch her hairline and sent Sterling a conspiratorial wink. The man beside Jennifer scowled at her distraction. Alice Peterson nudged her husband, then threw Sterling a frown.

The organ heaved a chord which prompted everyone to stand and sing. Mrs. Boyd did not offer the hymnal this time and Sterling, too wrung out from the sermon, didn't pick one out of the pew rack.

Sterling kept her head bowed through much of the remaining service. The pastor announced the wedding of two congregants next week, then began a passionate appeal for sinners to fall on the altar. He begged them all to repent, be saved, and come into the love of Jesus.

No one came forward, so he gave up and offered a lengthy prayer of benediction. The organ burst forth again. People poured into the aisles.

Mrs. Boyd pounced at the first note on the pipes. She spun into her husband, shielded her lips with her hands and whispered. Her voice, however, carried several seats away. "You know the bride's in a family way. Her poor mother is beside herself."

Sterling attempted to use those few precious seconds to escape the pew, but she wasn't fast enough.

"I am so glad to meet you, Mrs. Foster. And welcome to First Baptist. I'm Peggy Boyd. You know my husband."

Sterling took the hand offered her, uncomfortable with Boyd lurking behind his wife. "A pleasure. I'm afraid I've been an awful bother to your husband."

"Now, Mrs. Foster, think no more about it," the sheriff interjected.

"At least I'm not guilty of dumping garbage on poor Mr. Cross's property. Just plumb mean," Sterling pouted.

Boyd's eyes nearly bugged out of his head.

"Haven't you seen it? There's a ton, I mean, a ton of trash piled up around the trees off Main like somebody just backed up a truck and plop!" She kept talking and scooting out of the pew.

Unaware of her husband's sudden agitation, Peg Boyd ignored his impatience to move. "If I can ask, where do you have your hair done?"

"I-I had it done in my hometown." She lowered her voice as they joined the stream of worshippers in the center aisle. "I simply could not abide mousey brown hair any longer."

"I own the beauty shop on Main. Least I will 'til I sell it to Maribelle Penix." Peg examined Sterling's hair and face. "Drop by when you need a touch-up."

"Yes, thank you." But no way in hell. She'd keep going to the next town to cover her red roots and get her hair styled. Sterling felt someone pat her arm as the wave of people flooded toward the front door.

"I was hoping you were a Methodist." Jennifer hissed in her ear.

"I am now. What are you doing here?" Sterling asked.

Jennifer introduced the glowering man behind her as her husband. "John's a Baptist and I'm Methodist so the family takes turns going to each other's church service."

"John, meet my husband Tom." Sterling gave John a polite nod. "Oh, hello, Mrs. Peterson."

Alice Peterson's frosty glance told Sterling news of her adventure in Callie's Cutoff had spread.

"Heard you had quite an adventure." Jennifer giggled.

Sterling lifted both eyes to heaven. "I had no idea Nancy and I would stir a fuss."

"You found the Johnson boy's hand."

"What? Good Lord. No!"

The white-haired woman in the aisle ahead of Tom swiveled to gawk.

"I wish I had yesterday back." Sterling moaned.

"I don't," Jennifer guffawed.

"Jennifer, come along," said her mother.

Tom shook hands with the pastor, who welcomed him to church. When it was Sterling's turn, the reverend grasped her hand in both paws.

"I waited at the altar. I prayed you would feel the call to repent your godless ways." His voice carried through the church and out the front door. The crowd's chatter faded.

Sterling pulled her hand back and summoned her most syrupy tone, "I also pray you'll repent your hateful ways. Good day, pastor."

A gasp reverberated through the crowd. The grizzled reverend gaped dumbfounded. People on the steps parted like the Red Sea as Tom and Sterling headed toward the parking lot. Her cheeks burned.

"Sterling! See you Monday." Jennifer waved from the top of the wooden staircase. "I'll make pimento cheese."

A few giggles. Then most of the worshippers went back to their conversations or made for the parking lot. One or two greeted Tom and Sterling. Others tried to steer clear of them.

Tom slammed her passenger door shut, walked around the car, and slid behind the wheel. "Jennifer pulled your bacon out of the fire again."

139

"God just punished two Catholics for straying." She gnawed on a fingernail then jerked her hand to her lap.

"Never again," he muttered and pointed the car down Main.

"Amen. Tom, Mrs. Boyd checked out my make-up and hair." Since they were too busy to talk last night, she relayed Gray's warning about the Alabama police alert.

"You think she was trying to figure out if you're the girl they're looking for?"

Once Tom voiced her fears, she felt ridiculous. Not possible. "Peggy Boyd's in the beauty business. She wanted to figure how I did my make-up. I'm not worried."

Tom took her hand from the car's bench seat and kissed it. "I don't want to take any chances."

"Well, we have to show up at church somewhere. From what Jennifer tells me about the new Methodist preacher we'll do better there."

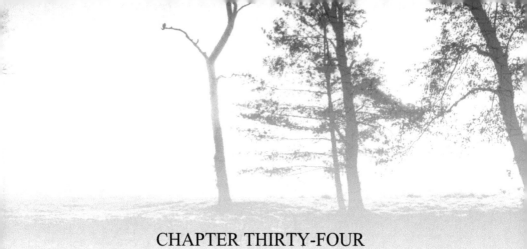

CHAPTER THIRTY-FOUR

Hands on hips, Sheriff Boyd monitored Tom and Sterling's drive out of the Baptist parking lot.

"She's got a lot of gall and freckles," Peg told him. "I swear, honey, I can't tell about her hair. But those pretty big eyes? Not a lot of natural gingers with blue eyes."

Boyd snorted. Maybe she wasn't the girl in the alert. Still, he didn't trust Mrs. Foster. She came off like one of those do-gooders. Independent. Bright. He would sure warn Penix and Murphy.

"The girl's asking lots of questions about the Epsons and Callie's Cutoff out where the Johnson boy died. Alice told her it was okay, but now she's thinkin' better of it. I heard Alice complaining to her daughter about Sterling Foster's snooping." Peg checked her lipstick in the mirror of her compact.

"You are listening on our telephone party line again?" Boyd gave her a sideways grin.

"I picked it up to make a call and listened enough to know someone was talking."

Boyd snickered.

What she said about Sterling Foster stuck with him, though.

Despite what Peg told him, the next time he had a minute he'd call Klansmen in law enforcement throughout Georgia, South Carolina, Tennessee, and Alabama to see what they knew about Mrs. Foster.

The rest of his afternoon and evening went to answering irate citizen phone calls about the trash on the Cross property.

CHAPTER THIRTY-FIVE

He the

Silver's brow furrowed. "Brother, are you sick? Burns infected?" He put his hand against Gray's forehead as they walked by the ruins of the church. Gray swatted it away.

"I'm fine. My hands just need to be stretched." He demonstrated.

"Something's eating you."

"I-I should never have suggested a boycott."

Silver threw back his head in a full-throated laugh. "That horse done left the barn."

"I appreciate your understanding." Since his meeting with Sterling, Gray had been off-center. Lost. And angry.

Even the young widow who had him to dinner last night raised out of bed and caressed his cheek. "You real good, baby. But whoever you thinkin' 'bout, it ain't me."

Sterling might have to leave – should leave. She might be a saint in his end of town, but he bet her heroics won few fans among whites.

Silver crossed in front of Gray. "You know this boycott's bringing the community together like Henry Johnson's death and the church fire didn't."

"And put Ajamu outta business."

"So far. But I'm still willing and able to fight with him."

"I know. I don't want to lose you. I lost enough already." Gray saw his life played out in the fractured, broken sidewalk under his feet.

"You need to get laid."

Gray laughed. "Not again."

"Man! You sick to the bone."

"Did Justice Tomorrow get Sterling's latest packet of information, film, affidavits?"

Silver polished his fingernails on his shirt. "I called yesterday when I drove folks to North Baileyton. Things are happy back at home. Real happy."

CHAPTER THIRTY-SIX

Sterling skipped her period. Four weeks since she got to Crossville. And the last time she had her period was—oh, no. She checked the November calendar hanging on the kitchen wall and counted twice. Tears blurred her vision of the dates. This couldn't be right. Although, it would explain why she woke up nauseated every morning, why her breasts felt tender.

Why had Tom refused to use protection when she asked? Catholic teaching? He said it didn't matter. Why had she believed him? Catholic guilt or heat of the moment? He'd played her and she went along because . . .? Great question. Why had she gone along? Damn the Catholic Church.

She imagined her parents' disappointment. They must never know. Never.

Fueled by a gnawing sense of urgency, Sterling threw herself into a frenzy of activity as Thanksgiving approached. Even without the worry of a pregnancy, she expected to get a phone call any day saying her grandmother had passed away.

Should she tell Tom about the baby? When? What would he say?

Better question — what did she want him to say? Did she really love him? She chewed a fingernail to the quick. Did she love her made-up life with Tom enough to make it real? Did he?

She would give up the child for adoption. The whole notion made her tear up and hug her mid-section. But raising a baby alone overwhelmed and frightened her – she never heard of a woman doing it, except as a widow. The shame of going home with an out-of-wedlock child kept her considering that option.

JUSTICE TOMORROW

When Gray signaled for a meeting close to Thanksgiving, she almost considered asking his advice about her problem. He always helped her figure things out. She hadn't seen him, even on the street, for weeks. Would their meeting be awkward?

And it was. In the beginning. Until he told her he found another witness. She hugged him in joy and found comfort.

"I talked with a farmer who lives up the road from Parson's on the left of the road as you drive out of Callie's Cutoff," Gray told her in a business-like tone. "He said that 'new white' deputy parks regularly off the side of the road near the entrance to the man's farm. I guess you can hide there from speeders coming out of Crossville. Anyway, the farmer said on the day Henry Johnson died he thought he'd have to dig the deputy's cruiser free from a rut. But the deputy rocked the cruiser loose and tore into the cutoff after a pickup truck full of yelping redneck whites."

"The new white deputy has to be J.T. Dawson." Excitement instead of dread filled her for the first time in weeks until she realized the witness didn't tell Gray enough. "Did the farmer say the deputy who tore into the cutoff after a pickup truck was J.T. Dawson?"

Gray's shoulders had slumped briefly, "But the man did say the deputy's cruiser came right back out of the cutoff like it was on fire."

"It's not enough. We have to be able to put J.T. Dawson in that cruiser."

"I know, Sterling," Gray sounded impatient. "The witness said he didn't notice any other car or truck. When he heard about Henry, he figured the officer in the patrol car was part of the ambush. He's scared, like all the Blacks who saw anything. He only talked to me because I'm a hero these days."

"I haven't been able to think of the right approach with J.T. Now I know. I'll handle him," she said.

"The case is coming together."

She told him what she'd learned about John Cross the fourth. "His life's a drag. Divorced. One teenage son. He's a Congressional aide whose last job sounds really fascinating: a subcommittee on sanitation and public health."

Gray thought for a minute as though something lay just outside his grasp. But Sterling had something more vital to relay: Mrs. Boyd's interest in her hair and freckles.

His Adam's apple bopped twice, the only sign of how he felt.

Sterling wandered over the old store, taking in the collapsing shelves, the odd canister still sitting on a wooden counter, the filthy windows, the swinging door to a side storeroom with one hinge missing.

"Do I have to tell you to be careful, Sterling?"

"Nice to know you care."

The words hung between them.

145

Finally, she said. "This is no fun sometimes."

"No goddamn fun at all."

After their meeting, Sterling wanted out of Crossville. When she was little, she and her big brother Danny used to count the days until Christmas. The end of the investigation became like Christmas to her.

She focused on enjoying things she never thought she would, like cooking with Jennifer, volunteering at the library with Rose, or lunch with Nancy. Still, hers was a life built on the sandy soil of lies and secrets. She craved bedrock.

Rather than worry, she pushed harder than she should.

Two or three times she drove to Parson's, going inside for a Coke while the attendant washed her windshield and pumped the gas. Even though she lingered around the counter to finish her drink, no one was friendly enough to chat up about Callie's Cutoff and Henry Johnson. Her fill-ups earned her free juice glasses etched with grapes. Glass souvenirs from Parson's.

During her cooking lesson on fixing Thanksgiving dinner, Sterling asked: "What would you do to hide a secret?"

Jennifer whirled on her so fast her pink apron flared at the bottom. "What did you find out?"

"I mean, if you saw a murder . . . or knew someone you love stole money or-or something. How far would you go to keep their secret?"

Strange, Jennifer sounded relieved. "I-I suppose I would have to keep a secret to save the family honor."

"Really?"

"Mother is right about this; you can't live down a bad family name. You must think about your children. See how I'm making this to thicken the gravy?" Jennifer whisked a white mixture of flour and cream so fast some of it sloshed out of the cup.

Sterling persisted. "Turning in a murderer isn't the same as saving the family name. It would be justice. Who's gonna get justice for Henry Johnson?"

To her surprise, Jennifer pursed her lips thoughtfully. "We talked about this in my bridge club. It's a shame—and nobody thinks murder is okay. But the folks who did it have friends they don't want to put in danger and loved ones they don't want to dishonor."

"Then they shouldn't have done the murder."

Jennifer stared into the skillet full of turkey drippings and the white flour mixture. "You better stir the gravy, not that pot of snakes."

"Doesn't it bother you?"

"I thought you were interested in my family history. I don't hear you talk about Callie or her sister Aunt Amelia?" Jennifer slammed a hand on her hip. "Why does the Johnson boy matter now?"

****

146

Sterling grew so desperate for leads she sought out a few bulldozer operators cutting crude roads through the Cross property. She bought an ice cream soda at the drugstore counter, sat down, exchanged a few pleasantries, and wound up with nothing but a memory of the first time her mother bought a soda for her.

Often while Tom was at the office, playing poker with John Mullins and a few men from his office, or at a Rotary Club dinner meeting, Sterling scooped up Aunt Amelia Epson's diary and headed for the living room.

Reading the diary made her feel useful and kept her from wondering what Tom was saying or doing. Sometimes when he related his conversations, she cringed to hear how much he had given away about the two of them and how little information he got in return.

"Now what harm did it do to tell John how we met?" Tom scowled. "I swear, every time I open my mouth, I feel like you're taking notes on what I did wrong. Back the hell off!"

She no longer pointed out problems with telling how they met or how, for example, a girl from Mississippi at the University of Georgia would meet and marry a man from Georgia at Vanderbilt University in Tennessee needed explaining to some folks. And he never told her why he left Georgia Tech for Vanderbilt. Tom couldn't keep his own stories straight.

Instead, she tried to limit his social contact unless she was present. She didn't worry about the real estate office. He liked his job there if his dinner conversation provided any sign. Tom sounded like a rising star in the land business, achieving success where he least expected to find it. His sales in little Crossville boomed.

Under the light of the living room lamp, settled amidst red throw pillows with her pen and notebook at the ready, Sterling longed for a break in the case, for the investigation to heat up. What she was stuck with, however, had more to do with a young Epson girl's forbidden love for the Cross boy. It was shaping up to be a post-Civil War feud over land.

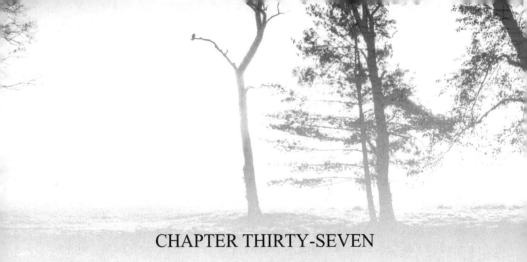

CHAPTER THIRTY-SEVEN

The only true success by their Justice Tomorrow team in the dying days of November proved to be Gray's boycott. Crossville felt the pinch more every day.

White store owners ran sales to attract customers. Blacks sent people to towns a hundred miles away to get what everyone said they needed. Most food they got out of their gardens anyway. White men raked fall leaves, repaired their own roofs, emptied garbage in the landfill miles away, while six or eight Black men piled in a car to earn a few dollars in neighboring towns.

White women cleaned their own houses, cooked their own meals, tended their own babies, and Black women scraped by on the quarters contributed by churches as far away as Atlanta and New Orleans. The much-anticipated Methodist Christmas Carnival slated for December fourth nearly had to be canceled for lack of workers.

Walking to lunch amid swirling November leaves and unseasonably warm weather, perusing books in the library, or shopping in the A&P supermarket, Sterling cringed at the hunched shoulders, sullen looks, harried expressions. People snapped at each other. Cars honked at jay-walking pedestrians. Her head hurt from pressure building in Crossville.

Strangely enough, the boycott stayed out of the local radio station airwaves and the newspaper. Nancy explained it when she and J.T. came over for dinner one night. She said all she had to do was mention the boycott, and the editor jumped down her throat with both feet. She expected the radio station staff had similar problems.

To talk with more people, Sterling got into activities at the Methodist church. She lunched with Rose, cooked with Jennifer, joined the 'radical' Methodist preacher's Bible study, and spent hours sifting through papers at the historical society with Harriet. At least with Harriet, she was able to grouse about the lack of progress.

Her only satisfaction came at night. Sometimes twice a night.

Yet she could not find a way to tell Tom about the baby. Her fears of raising a child alone coupled with his delight over being her first lover, his growing interest in local business, and her indecision about what she wanted to happen kept her silent. He never mentioned the case unless asked. It dawned on her that their pretend life had become real for him. She did nothing to dissuade him.

"I am about to make us a lot of money," he said one night. "I never made this much money on my own." He came through the front door a few days before the church carnival, slung his coat on the newel post, and plopped on the living room couch next to her. "I'm gonna be the last straw buyer, and I get a bonus."

"And . . .?"

"Now maybe you will have a little faith in your husband. I know the buyer. A little drum roll, please . . . John Cross the fourth! He is the secret buyer of all the land north of town, and he got it for pennies on the dollar —when he couldn't steal it from black farmers and had to buy it from small landowners like Penix."

"Apparently, there's no more need for secrets."

"Cross is coming to town to discuss his project." Tom's finger tapped an early December date on the kitchen calendar. "The minute the check arrives, we're gonna fix the right burner on the kitchen stove so my clever bride can use it."

She didn't bother to point out she wasn't really his wife.

Instead, she mapped out for Tom how to discover why Cross wanted to gain control of such a large parcel. She framed for him subtle questions to ask people in the real estate office and civic groups he'd joined. She even made him practice asking his questions, and she took the role of George or John or someone in the Rotary Club. Annoyed at first, he turned the game into foreplay. Not that she minded.

To Sterling's surprise, Aunt Amelia Epson provided part of the answer about land ownership the next afternoon.

Sterling thought of the diary's author as Aunt Amelia because she was getting to know her so well. The poor girl's handwriting, the age of the ink, and water spots on the pages challenged Sterling's attention. More than once she

149

drifted asleep amid the red pillows.

Today, however, half an hour into Aunt Amelia's harangue about learning music, Sterling bolted upright and re-read: "Dear Papa's dreadful row with Mr. Cross nearly resulted in blows. Mr. Cross was angry they did not include his land in the recent town incorporation. He called my honorable father and Mr. Anderson 'deceitful' to name the town Crossville when not a clod of dirt in it belonged to him. Papa rightfully responded no respectable town included land owned by negroes or land which might be given them."

Sterling found the entry curious. Was it true Cross land was not in the town limits? Nobody ever said so. Even if Aunt Amelia was right, so what?

Buoyed by this small revelation Sterling plowed through several more diary pages of social engagements, a complaint about her tutor Mr. Arnett, reports on crops, her father's desire for some land owned by John Cross.

Aunt Amelia finally rewarded her with another nugget on the feud: "A headache sent me to my room early after dinner. I did not mean to hear, but Papa's study is under my room. Mr. Cross called on Papa in foul temper about acres in the north both claimed. I am fearfully sad as Stephen Cross is a handsome young man whose eye has fallen on me. Will we be like the sad story of Romeo and Juliet which Mr. Arnett is reading to us?"

She called Tom and, amid news of her day, asked him if he knew about the city limits of Crossville. If they wanted to buy a house they needed to know. She hoped he understood.

Tom burst through the front door without taking off his coat, grabbed her off the couch, lifted her up, and twirled her. She squealed.

"A good day?" She managed when he set her down.

"John Cross the fourth has no land in the city limits of Crossville, which means he can do almost anything he wants. County zoning laws, such as they are, are a joke. For example, almost any vacant land can be a farm. You can do anything you want with a farm. George acted surprised I didn't know."

"A farm?" She rubbed her collarbone where his wool topcoat scratched her skin.

He laughed, ripped off his coat and his new suit jacket and flung them across a chair. "None of that matters, though. I heard a rumor about the land today, more than a rumor. It fits – the evictions, the new building going on in town, the silence of the Klan, the boycott hush-hush. Everything we've talked about."

"What?" She made hurry motions with her hands.

"A military base. There was a legal notice in the *Crossville Caller* about a military installation. Cross now has a parcel of land big enough for a large one—close to a thousand acres. Thanks to Presidents Kennedy and Johnson the military is getting funny about racial problems. They might not want to come to a town where there was a boycott or Klan killings. And I'm not real sure they'd want land that had been stolen from Black sharecroppers."

He expected applause, but she pursed her lips instead. "Crossville sits in the middle of two military bases. Why do they want one more? And right here?"

His hands and chin dipped toward her as though she were a child. "Bases can be all sizes and perform all kinds of functions – like an arsenal or motor pool. Doesn't have to be like Pearl Harbor or-r Ft. Bragg."

"Have you seen the ugly sheets of metal fence along the back boundaries of the Cross property?"

Tom headed for the whiskey. "Somebody saw pigs roaming behind the fence. I hope they were kidding."

"Who wants a bunch of pigs or weapons next to the A&P? Jennifer groused about the ugly fence. She'll stroke out over pigs."

"Honey, any kind of military presence means money for the town. Jobs. Housing. Full cash registers at the hardware, the record store, more houses sold . . .."

"I'll suggest Nancy call somebody at the Pentagon and ask what they're doing."

Tom kissed her cheek. "You are brilliant. Pretty. Getting to be a great cook. An all-around perfect wife."

"I hope I'm a perfect mother." It slipped out. Sterling froze.

He gaped at her a second. "Pregnant! You're pregnant?"

"I-I don't know for sure," she stammered. "I missed last month. I'm so tired every day, and for the last week I've been sick as a dog every morning."

"Pregnant." He folded her into his arms. "A baby. Oh God! Then it's not me."

Stung, she shoved him away, lurched into the wall to hold her up. "What the hell —? It is you."

"Oh my God, no. This is my baby, ours. I'm crazy about it already. I'm crazy about you." He threw his hands up to the sky. "Thank you, God."

Outrage still heaving in her chest, she blinked. Her hot rush of fury cooled. Tom wanted the baby. Wanted her.

"I-I have to finish dinner."

Tom trailed her down the hallway to the kitchen. At the entrance he thrust an arm across the doorframe to stop her, his eyes big as his grin.

"Honey, you never have to attend a PTA meeting. My proof of love: I'll go to every single one," he whispered.

He enfolded her in his embrace, and she snuggled into it as he babbled about their future.

"He'll play Little League baseball. I'll be his Boy Scout leader. He'll go to Auburn like his old man . . . or Harvard with your father."

"I thought you went to Georgia Tech and Vanderbilt." She frowned.

"And Auburn. I got around. Until I met you, I failed at everything. Even fatherhood. I got knocked out at my first Freedom Summer rally, remember." He urged her onto a kitchen chair. "You need to stay off your feet. What if it's a girl! I'll be her Girl Scout leader."

"I don't think fathers can be Girl Scout leaders." She wanted to dance around the kitchen.

"I'll be the first. I will be the best father. You'll be the best mother. We'll be great parents."

A pot of vegetables continued bubbling on a burner unheeded.

"Tom. I don't even know for sure yet." A tightness in her belly and her tender breasts told her otherwise.

"It's real." He cradled her face in his hands. "Boy, this commission comes along in time. We need to fix a nursery."

She stroked his cheeks, soaking in his warmth. "You know we can't live in Crossville, right?"

He kissed her. "No one's gonna like this Crossville when we're done." He kissed her again slower. "Honey, there are a million Crossvilles. I'll find us another."

Entangled in his embrace and light-headed from his kisses, Sterling did manage to move the pot off the stove. But the chicken Kiev in the oven burned by the time they got back to it, and she completely forgot to ask what he meant by nobody liking Crossville when they were done. Usually, no one in town realized Justice Tomorrow agents had been around.

****

Sterling couldn't seem to maneuver J.T. into talking about the night Henry Johnson died. She invited the Dawsons to dinner twice. The couples double dated when the new movie theatre opened in Crossville – but there was still no natural way to approach him. Tom had a better shot, but she hesitated to tell him about the witness Gray found, the leverage they now enjoyed with the deputy. Disloyal, perhaps, but Tom's carelessness and his acceptance of their undercover life made her wary.

Thanks to her work on the Methodist Christmas Carnival she found an excuse to get to knock on the side door after Nancy left for work.

Bleary-eyed J.T. answered several minutes after she knocked. He mustered a smile. His uniform shirt wasn't buttoned or tucked in, and his tousled hair needed a comb. "You're up early, Sterling."

"Sorry. You had the night shift. I tried to wait until a decent hour to come over."

He invited her inside. "Nancy's gone."

"I know. She loves her job."

J.T. grunted.

The neat and tidy house she'd first visited now sported the lived-in look. "I need to borrow any color linen tablecloths for the carnival. I'll wash them after they're used."

From his blank expression, she might as well have asked for uranium. "I thought I had more than I do, and I need them today. No, yesterday."

He scratched his head. "Uh, Nancy keeps such stuff in the closet over here. You're welcome to go through them."

"Thank you." She followed him toward a narrow closet between the kitchen and sunroom. It was the same type of closet she had in her house. He leaned on the kitchen doorframe as she squatted down to the bottom shelve to paw over tea towels, dish drying towels, placemats, and tablecloths.

"J.T., Nancy told me about what happened in Lexington. I wanted to say how much I admire you. You did what was right at an awful cost."

"What?" His hand slid down from the frame and his jaw clenched. "That's none of your business."

"Maybe. I know, but I'm proud to be your friend. I know it doesn't pay the bills . . ."

"No, it doesn't pay the bills. Or get you a good job — hell, any job." One of J.T.'s hands fisted.

"Still, it must feel good in your soul knowing you stood up for what's right. I'm sorry if I said something to make you mad. I-I was only trying to say, well, you know." She dropped her eyes and turned to go.

"Ah-h, look, Sterling, I'm sorry if I snapped. That's not like me."

When she looked at him again J.T. offered a half-grin. "I get it. And I didn't mean to get in your personal business. But there's so much going on in Crossville. So much of the same thing you had to face in Lexington."

J.T. shifted his weight. "Maybe."

Sterling nodded. "The march. The church burning. The murder of the poor Johnson boy."

Panic seemed to light up J.T.'s eyes. "You want some breakfast? I think, Nancy left some biscuits and sausage gravy for me. Want to share?"

"No, I'm about ready for lunch. I just came to get the tablecloths and, since you were here, to, ah, well, tell you what I told you."

"Thanks," he mumbled but his eyes and smile seemed more relaxed.

153

"I wish a man like you knew who killed Henry Johnson."

All the color left J.T.'s face. "I'd be in a tough place, wouldn't I?"

"Depends on who did the murder." She shot back. "Or who might have seen you drive into the murder scene and drive out."

"I-I'm glad I don't know anything." His eyes grew cold and never left hers.

"Not every day's gonna be like today, J.T. Not every sheriff's gonna be like Boyd. And there's no statute of limitations on murder."

Her words dropped into an uncomfortable silence. His lips remained clasped in a tight line. His eyes narrowed.

She might have said too much. "In case you don't know already, Nancy is proud of what you did. She'd follow you to the ends of the earth."

"I know. But like you said, it don't pay the bills."

She smiled. "Thanks for the tablecloths."

****

A Ferris wheel covered with lights circled in a clear blue sky over the Christmas Carnival while loud calliope music blared throughout the Methodist Church grounds. Unless the wheel came to a standstill, the riders would be trapped in an endless loop.

A metaphor for this investigation, Sterling fumed. She leaned against Tom as he drove to the carnival. "We've got to move this case forward."

She didn't tell him Justice Tomorrow might pull her any day.

The closer Tom and Sterling drove to the carnival, the more cars and people they saw. All Bell County appeared to be there. He found a parking spot and they walked two blocks to the church.

After waiting in line, Tom forked over two dollars to walk between Christmas trees onto the church carnival grounds. Sheriff Boyd, with Peg on his arm, waved as they headed toward the merry-go-round.

"Hello there, folks." The sheriff touched the brim of his hat.

"Nice day, sheriff, Mrs. Boyd," Tom replied.

"Isn't this exciting?" said Mrs. Boyd. "I think it is a success already, even with the talk of the trash some fool keeps dumping around the county and the bone you dug up."

Boyd flushed.

"Bone?" Sterling said. "What about our bone?"

Boyd patted his wife's hand and grinned. "I haven't heard anything. Just a call asking where you found it. Kinda routine. Whoa! Apple pie! Come on, Peg."

Jennifer Mullins found them right away, gushing. "What great weather! I can do without a sweater. And the iced tea table is getting lots of customers. Thanks for helping us set up, you two."

Tom's hand went to the small of his back. "I think I pulled something," he quipped.

Jennifer guffawed. "I am so excited. Mother says the Cross property will make Crossville grow and grow."

"With pigs on it?"

Jennifer rolled her eyes.

And she'd be rich from the family investment in local businesses and the housing development Cotton Estates she'd mentioned while they were cooking. Sterling squinted. "I thought you didn't like this small town."

"Won't be small too much longer. John agrees," Jennifer craned her neck. "Listen, I've gotta run the ring toss booth. Come throw something."

Bright red, green, and silver garlands, loud music, happy smiles, friendly shouts, childish laughter — the crowd caught the carnival mood. Sterling's spirits lifted too.

"Isn't it a little early for Christmas?" Tom whispered.

"It is December. Have a little holiday cheer." She landed a playful punch.

Cakes, pies, cookies, tarts – Sterling lost count of the desserts spread over tables along the church's outer brick wall. Tables stood on the opposite side full of casseroles, chickens, potato salad, ham. People with plates piled high with food passed, and she realized she was hungry.

"I'm starved." Tom had to yell in her ear over the talk of carnival-goers and music of fiddlers on a small stage next to booths selling jams, Christmas ornaments, quilts, and candles. "I'm gonna get us something to eat."

She heard a shout, people hurried toward it, and she discovered a sack race underway.

"Good turnout isn't it?" Harriet Cook elbowed her way from the crowd to hug Sterling. "Everyone's had to work extra hard since the help didn't show up. Whew! Everybody in the county must have crawled out of the woods to come."

Which made Sterling think. "Harriet, you know any of the Murphys? Penixes?"

"Know them all. There's one over there." The older woman frowned. "Troublemakers the bunch of them. You can always tell Jim Penix's around by the smell of homemade brew. He and Angus Murphy make it. Sad to say, he's the only one of the Penixes worth the powder and lead to blow up. He's getting iced tea — the one with the striped shirt untucked in the back."

Penix looked familiar. "He hang out at Parson's?" Sterling asked.

"All of them do." Harriet took her by the arm. "Believe I'll go get some tea. Want some?"

On their way to the iced tea service line, four people said hello to Harriet and stayed to greet Sterling. Meeting Penix could be interesting. She wouldn't be reckless but daring. There was a difference.

155

Harriet popped in line in front of Penix. "'Cuse me. Got to get a new glass."

Sterling had never seen one, but Penix resembled a pig stuffed into pants. A flat nose separated two pinhole eyes that waggled atop a double chin. He probably broke his nose in one or two fights. Harriet introduced him to Sterling. He grunted.

"Pour her a glass of tea. She just got here, and she's parched."

"Shore, Harriet. How's your cousin Claud?" Penix poured tea all over the table and handed it to Sterling with a smile that revealed two missing bottom teeth. A small inhale proved Harriet correct about the pure alcohol scent of homebrew.

"Move it," someone in the back called.

Harriet hushed him with the wave of her hand. "You can wait a minute, Wally." She turned back to Penix. "Claud is mean as a snake, same as you."

Penix chuckled. "Ain't seen him in a coon's age."

"You still rocking on Parson's porch?" Harriet asked. Sterling took a careful sip of tea.

"Not for overly three months," he said.

"For a fact? That colored boy was killed in Callie's Cutoff about then," Harriet pointed out.

"So?" Penix glared at Harriet.

"Parson's pops right out at you when you come out of Callie's Cutoff," Sterling ventured.

"It do." Penix shifted his considerable bulk.

"I thought the first time I saw it how everybody at Parson's could count all the cars and trucks on the road." Sterling observed as she waved at Rose Anderson.

"I reckon."

"Ever see an Imperial LaBaron? I always thought that car was so nice," Sterling said.

Penix perked up. "Never did. But I saw a Lincoln Continental. At Parson's."

Sterling's hand flew to her throat. "My goodness, you did? When?"

"Back in September, it seem like. Parked by the store a long time. I went over to see it up close. It shore was a nice machine." Penix's mouth smacked at the memory.

"Was it blue . . . or white? I love those colors in a car." Sterling cooed. An Army officer with Alice Peterson jabbering in his ear joined George Thompson and his wife at the cake judging table.

"Oh, it was a pearly white."

"I hear a Continental has seats soft as butter. Did it?" Sterling clutched both hands around her glass.

156

"It did." Penix was caught up in the tale. "I'd have seen more, but the man inside gave me a dirty look then took off. I kinda held it agin them Carpenter boys they made him take off."

"Wouldn't you love to be rich enough to have such a car?" She tittered even though a sudden leap of logic made her heart crash against her ribs.

Penix scowled at Sterling. He must have made the same connection.

"Your Aunt Gertrude shake her bursitis?" Harriet asked.

"No ma'am. She's still ailin'." Penix's brows crashed together as his body angled away from the two women.

"And how's the Postmaster? You, Murphy, and a couple of the boys still playing poker with him in the Post Office on Fridays?" Harriet gave him a conspiratorial smile.

"Nobody 'pose to know," he muttered sheepishly.

Harriet laughed. "I know a lot more than I say. You say 'hey' to Gertrude for me."

Someone cut the grass so uneven Sterling wobbled. The sugary tea or the conversation set her teeth on edge. After a few steps, Harriet whipped around to her.

"Don't jump to conclusions—he might mean any day of September, not only the day poor Henry died."

"I know." She watched Penix and J.T. exchange furtive glances as they passed. "Let's go."

Sterling waved to Nancy and J.T. as she muttered to Harriet. "At least we might have a place to begin."

"Well. I've got to go see about the one-legged race." Harriet excused herself.

As soon as she disappeared amid a group of children munching on cookies, Sterling made her way to Nancy.

"Wonder how much the carnival's raised this year for the starving children in Africa mission? The boycott's got attendance down," Nancy surveyed the crowd.

Maggie shrugged. "How's the great Crossville journalist?"

"Having a ball. I got to do real news."

"Haven't seen the *Caller* yet. Good catch seeing the legal notice about the installation," said Sterling.

"Pure luck. Who reads those public hearing notices in tiny print? I wanted the recipe printed next to it. Wish I had gone to the hearing."

"Aren't they boring things?"

"A matter of form most of the time." Nancy sighed. "George didn't even go to this one. Nobody ever shows to comment. Just slam, bam, thank you, ma'am, and everybody goes home. But we still don't know exactly what the project is since nobody at the hearing asked and I can't get John Cross to

157

comment."

"Did you reach anybody at the Department of Defense?"

"My story quotes a Department of Defense spokesman as saying they have no plans to build a military base in Crossville 'at this time'." She squeezed Sterling's arm while J.T. acted fascinated by the plate of cookies he carried. "I'm gonna follow up. Took the guy at the Pentagon a while to come back with a statement, and the major who called me was very careful about what he said."

"That's the military for you," Sterling murmured and started to mention what the sheriff said about the bone they'd found.

Instead, Nancy hid her hand by her side then pointed a finger toward Alice Peterson and the army colonel with her. She swung back to Sterling and folded her arms with a cock of her head. "Do tell. I hear Alice hosted another colonel at her house for dinner a while ago. I'm calling the Pentagon again."

Finger bone forgotten, Sterling pursed her lips. Maybe Jennifer and Nancy were right.

"You notice the way the roads on the Cross property are being laid out? Not paved, mind you, only dirt and gravel," Nancy pointed out. "Meanwhile, the Epsons and Andersons are pouring money into businesses and laying out housing subdivisions. Almost like they know something."

"There you are. Hi, Nancy. I've got us enough for lunch and supper." Indeed, Tom carried two of the biggest plates of food Sterling had ever seen. "Hey, J.T. I spotted an empty picnic bench under the tree over there. You want to join us?"

"No." J.T. strode off. "We're on our way home."

Nancy and Sterling exchanged questioning glances behind J.T.'s back. His wife hurried to catch him.

The weathered wooden picnic table Tom picked out seated ten people. He paid no attention when she sat next to him and picked up her fork.

"S-o-o good." He said between bites.

Sterling only hummed her agreement since her mouth was full of fried chicken.

Between forks of scalloped potatoes and bean salad she repeated her conversation with Penix. Tom kept eating.

"I need to talk to J.T. about being in the cutoff, but — Tom, we should get out of town as soon as possible." She heaved a sigh and laid her fork aside. "I'm gonna cook like this someday."

"Marry me." Tom gave her a loud kiss.

"You have no romance in your soul." Sterling landed a playful swat. "You only care about your stomach. I'll carry our plates to the kitchen."

Tom swung his legs out of the table and put both feet on the grass. "I'll wait here. Unless you want me to win you a teddy bear at the milk can toss."

As she handed in her plates at the back door of the church, she caught sight of him walking toward Jim Penix and two other men talking and smoking under a neighboring tree. They didn't act glad to see him. Nothing she could do. If there ever was. Was Tom fooling her or was he really so thick-headed? She didn't want to go over, so she called him to leave. After a minute he glad-handed the men and left. She wanted to kill him.

Tom walked to the car with a spring in his step and the keys twirling around one finger. A bad feeling crept in. Sheriff Boyd approached the circle of men, then his head swiveled to her. Tom got into the car, started it, and tried to back out of the parking space. He had to wait for a few cars to go by. The carnival traffic was still bad. Out of habit she also checked the rearview mirror. The knot of men jawed, scowled, and popped their suspenders.

Tom didn't notice her twitch of fear. "One of the three men I talked with is Murphy, Angus Murphy. You remember he's the man I told you George sent me to out to Parson's to meet and sign a deed over to Cross. The other is someone named Penix. I came at them just now like I knew all about what happened in Callie's Cutoff with Henry Johnson."

"Oh my God, Tom!" That explained the naked hostility.

"No, it's okay."

Sterling's stomach lurched. She put a protective hand over it. "I just quizzed Jim Penix. They're not stupid."

"You should have told me. Anyway, I don't think they thought anything of it. I kind of drew them in. They were saying all kinds of awful things about the Blacks in town. The boycott, how the niggers weren't grateful, stuff like that. I-I threw out how damn brave of 'somebody' to do what they did to Henry Johnson. After . . .."

Sterling moaned.

"Murphy saw it all from Parson's parking lot." Tom scowled at her reaction and looked over his shoulder to see if he could pull out onto the street. "He talked about the Lincoln Continental he was looking at when he saw the Carpenter boys in the back of a pick-up whizz by. He claimed he heard them whooping and hollering a half-mile up the road. Anyway, a county deputy tried to pull out behind them, but he got stuck in a rut where he parked off the side of the road and didn't get Callie's Cutoff until long after the Carpenters disappeared into the cutoff. And guess what?"

He finally pulled into the stream of traffic. Sterling wanted to tell him to drive toward Atlanta and keep going. "What?"

"J.T. Dawson was the deputy driving the cruiser! He was the one chasing the Carpenter boys in that pickup into Callie's Cutoff on the day Henry Johnson was murdered. Penix and Murphy both used J.T.'s name. And after Sheriff Boyd stood there in his office the day you found the finger bone and said J.T.

wasn't on duty near there that day."

Tom's inexperience marked them both. He didn't even realize what he'd done. It should be clear, even to those dumb white hicks at the carnival, that she and Tom knew way too much about the murder of Henry Johnson.

"We have to write all this, witness each other's statements, date it." She admired his earnestness, and, to be honest, felt a little jealous he'd found the critical pieces of the puzzle instead of her. But he just killed the mission. Once those men reported Tom's conversation to Sheriff Boyd, she and Tom had to leave town or risk getting killed. They would be a danger to Boyd.

She stared ahead and leaned on her elbow in the open window of the passenger door so she could see the sideview mirror. Merciful Mary, what now?

"They're Klan, no doubt. And they know Gray's responsible for the boycott, Sterling."

"I figured they'd learn sooner or later. I was hoping for later." She chewed a fingernail. "Those men watched us drive off, you know."

"Who cares? They don't suspect anything." Arrogant, defensive.

She dropped it. The oily slosh in her gut told her it was time to leave the postcard perfect town she'd grown to love. Not tomorrow. Now.

Gray. She needed Gray.

****

Angry calls from Murphy, Penix, and some of the other boys lit a fire under Sheriff Boyd the Monday after the carnival.

Jim Penix went on and on about Harriet Cook and both Fosters. Boyd had his misgivings about Sterling, but Tom didn't worry him. Especially since George Thompson vouched for the boy. And poor old Harriet had odd notions, but she didn't care one lick about anything living. As far as he knew, Harriet only cared about her husband after he died.

His search for information about Sterling didn't take as long as he feared. By Tuesday he had his answer. An Alabama lawman said the red-haired woman they sought asked a lot of questions about two colored boys killed during all the trouble over Blacks' voting — he remembered the girl's blue eyes.

Best of all, she'd gotten shot. In the arm – the right arm by the way she held it when he last saw her. The Alabama man acted plumb aggravated when he found out she and the colored boy running with her hadn't died in the woods. Boyd put his feet on his desk the way he did when he had a problem to solve. He'd search out a way to see if her arm had a scar on it.

Sterling Foster was a civil rights troublemaker, the girl in the warning. He'd bet his last nickel. If he had to guess, the Black boy who saved the little girls from the church fire was her accomplice. No warrants were out for either Sterling Foster or the colored boy — and he was the one started the boycott. Solve a lot of problems to get rid of him. He didn't want to arrest him or Sterling Foster. He wanted them to disappear.

Tom Foster. The man seemed smitten with his wife. George Thompson needed him, and Boyd hated to cross George. The way Murphy and Penix reported Foster's questioning it so ham-handed that Boyd thought Tom might have wanted them to know what he was doing. He sighed and scratched his head. This whole mess was getting outta hand.

Simplistic thing to do was watch the Foster woman. From what he knew about Tom he wasn't a threat to anyone.

A few more days, he told himself. He reached for and tore the green paper wrapping around a roll of antacids in his side drawer. Keep things together a few more days. His ringing phone echoed through his office. Shit. Not more.

Boyd understood why Cross had to dump garbage on his own property, but Lord have mercy, pigs? Every time he picked up the phone somebody bitched about the trash, the pigs, or the new corrugated steel fence. Especially the Methodists since the land abutted their church.

The phone rang incessantly. Probably Jim Penix or Angus Murphy. He wished those boys had full-time paying jobs. Penix and Murphy visited his office so often he ought to find work for them here. There was the problem in Crossville -- too few jobs for white men. He rubbed his beard stubble, then snatched up the irritating phone.

"Sheriff, me and Murphy got to thinkin' we oughta go see Harriet Cook. You know she and that new preacher at the Methodist Church talk all the time about niggers gittin' rights," said Penix. "Maybe we oughta go see that damn preacher too."

Boyd heard such talk about the new preacher but not Harriet. It did fit the woman's contrary ways. He put a hand over his forehead. Penix and Murphy were probably three sheets to the wind on their own homebrew right now.

"Harriet and the Foster woman asked me some mighty funny questions at the carnival—and so did Foster!" Penix went on. "Murphy and me, we'll pay the Fosters a little visit."

"Do nuthing. You can watch the Foster woman, but that's all. She's the one I want to know about." Boyd tried to be patient. He heard a car go by somewhere close when he hung up. Penix must be in the phone booth at Parson's.

Another call kept nagging in the back of his head. A Baptist elder called to talk about cleaning out the church attic, but they got to chatting about other things. The elder, who served as County Clerk, mentioned Mrs. Foster combing through land deeds in his office. Turns out she checked recent sales and transfers back a whole year. The sheriff said he had no idea. Still, her search made him anxious. He didn't know what Sterling Foster found on those deeds, but she had no call to meddle.

On top of all that, a note on his desk said to call some professor. Jesus Christ. Sterling Foster's old bone had attracted attention. No time for such crap. The sheriff dragged the back of his hand across a cheek. Yep, he needed a shave.

A few more days, Lord.

****

Sterling fell into the habit of visiting the historical society so frequently that Harriet presented her with her own key and parking spot behind the Emporium. They bonded over history, but Sterling liked Harriet for her feisty attitude and down-to-earth good sense.

On the Wednesday after the carnival she decided to tell Harriet about her baby girl – she thought of the child as a girl. She wanted to talk with a woman about what she needed to do besides seeing a doctor.

The day Sterling drove to a neighboring town to have her red hair roots retouched, she thought of calling her mother collect and telling her she'd married her true love. Talking on her party line at the house was risky. But her mother would have too many questions, including when she was bringing her new husband home.

Harriet's news blew away any thoughts of the baby. To Sterling's dismay, Harriet took it upon herself to visit Gertrude Penix, the ailing aunt of Jim Penix, and quiz her on what the man told them.

"He was at Parson's the day Henry Johnson died. Gerty doesn't think it fittin' for him to spend so much time with Sheriff Boyd and that shiftless Angus Murphy," Harriet reported. "And he saw Deputy Dawson hot foot it into the cutoff and come whipping back out a few minutes later. Here, I wrote it all down."

Grinning with pride, she handed over a letter detailing what she learned so it would be on the record. Ever the historian. The queasiness filling Sterling's stomach had nothing to do with her pregnancy. If Penix knew what his Aunt Gertrude told Harriet, then Sterling's friend might be in danger. And the danger was greater since Tom's ill-advised conversation at the carnival on Saturday. "You need to stay out of sight, Harriet. Don't stir this anymore."

Harriet pooh-poohed her. "Gertie's so addle-brained with her homemade

162

JUSTICE TOMORROW

medicine she'd confess to killing the president, and not know what she'd done. But maybe I'll dig out some old boxes in the storeroom and unearth anything about land ownership. Can't get into trouble there." She pointed to a carton she'd hauled to a table. "Here."

Harriet's hand shook enough to rattle the papers she gave Sterling.

"Now we know Penix's story is true, there's more questions," Sterling said. She decided at the last minute not to tell Harriet what Tom or Gray had learned. The fewer people who knew anything, the better.

"Who was the man in the Continental?" Harriet murmured as she considered a crumbling page she'd laid on the table. "Darn. I need gloves. You too."

"What did the Continental man have to do with Henry's death or the land business?" Sterling asked. "You think Continental man is the boss of the land deal? Harriet?"

"Hm?" Harriet pulled a shoebox from a top shelf. "Anything new on the land evictions?"

"Nothing much. I went over county deeds. Did you know Tom was right? Cross began buying up land a year ago."

Too late. Harriet's attention had fled to whatever papers and letters lay inside the deteriorating box.

A worrisome feeling followed Sterling as she left the Emporium to join Nancy, Rose, and Jennifer for lunch. She tried to appreciate the surprisingly warm day. Few were left for her in Crossville. Two of the trees across the way showed only the odd red, yellow, or orange leaf hanging on for dear life. Once Sterling reported to Justice Tomorrow, she felt sure she and Tom would be pulled out of town.

Penix leaned against the front of the Post Office. She smiled in his direction. The hateful scorn he sent in return stunned her. Her body jerked, her vision narrowed, sharpened. She wrapped her blue wool coat around her against a sudden chill and strode across the street with her head high.

Afterwards, a weird sense of being watched rose in her nearly every day, although she rarely saw anyone. Once she spotted Penix on her way to the real estate office. Another time Tom noticed Murphy when they stood on their front porch. Frightening at first, feeling watched became wearisome. She had to remind herself to stay alert. Especially on the rare times she met Gray.

Two weeks later she pulled her car into her parking spot next to Harriet's at the Emporium. These days parking in the back made her life easier since

Penix or Murphy often lounged in front of the Post Office or opposite it on the park bench among the evergreens. And since she came every day with her arms full of books or research papers, it also proved convenient.

She stepped out of the car, dropped the keys in her purse, and came to a standstill. The back door was ajar. Not like Harriet. She shuffled the book to her other arm and touched Harriet's car. Cold and no strange noises came from the Emporium.

Frowning, she stood off to the right and pushed open the heavy door. Nothing happened. She felt foolish. "Harriet—?"

A stinging smack to her cheek knocked Sterling to the floor. Her book flew across the room, the loose papers in it flying everywhere. She cried out, flipped to her side, and crawled toward a broken cane chair. Two men in white hoods loomed over her.

The taller man grabbed her by the back of her hair, hauled her to her feet. He reeked of alcohol. Ears ringing, she screamed and reached behind her with one hand to free her hair. At the same time, she raised one arm to protect her face. The second man struck at her with his fist, but her arm absorbed most of the blow. Still, her head snapped sideways. Her first assailant let her drop to the floor.

Blood dripped from her lip. Things were out of focus. But she had escaped the worst. Surely someone at the Post Office heard the ruckus. The man who'd held her hair jerked her upright and patted her cheek. She grabbed a quick breath then fell limp. He pulled her to her feet again.

"Right there." He chuckled and hoisted her up on his right shoulder.

Her hand clawed weakly for support. When he cocked his arm, she shifted her weight and drove her knee into his balls. He howled, bent double, and dropped to the ground with his hands on his groin.

His fat companion jerked and stared, "What the fuckin' hell?"

Sterling careened into the back wall, casting around for an escape. She gasped for air.

"Bitch!" The second attacker whipped around and fisted his beefy hands. Panting, she stepped away from the wall, positioned her feet, and raised her fists. With a bellow, he lowered his head and barreled for her like an enraged bull.

At the last second, she leaned aside matador-style. As he charged by, she chopped the side of her hand against the vertebrae of his neck. His momentum carried him into the wall. He crashed, dropped, and lay still. The smell of liquor and urine wafted up. She fell against a stack of heavy boxes.

The first man groaned again, rolled over and tossed his hood on the floor along with whatever he ate for breakfast. He rested his forehead on the wood floor, clutching his balls. Penix. The unconscious man had to be Murphy.

"Harriet!" Sterling cried.

The storeroom spun faster every time she moved, so she waited until her personal Tilt-T-Whirl slowed. Then she launched herself from the rear wall to the front of the Emporium. Since neither of the two men stirred, she inched along the wall until she reached the curtain.

"Harriet!"

The fabric curtain over the entrance to the front weighed so much, and there was so much of it. She fought through it. Blinded by the sunlight from the front windows, she stepped behind the front counter and tripped over Harriet's body.

Her arm broke most of her fall. Still, her forehead clunked against the counter's edge. She howled in pain, half-falling, half-kneeling on the floor next to Harriet.

Blood matted Harriet's hair pooled on the floor around her head. She lay on her back. Was she breathing? Sterling fumbled around the countertop. Where was the telephone?

Behind her, one of the men in the storeroom cursed, scraped a foot or box against the floor.

Sterling staggered to her feet, went hand over hand around the counter, and weaved to the front door screaming, "Help! Help me!"

Two women coming out of the grocery heard her cries and came at a trot. From across the street and down the block where he'd been the day of the protest J.T. bolted toward her. She shrieked his name. The barber sprinted toward her from his shop across the grassy strip. A man in a white butcher apron came out of the A&P and jogged where two shoppers pointed.

"Sterling!" J.T. grasped her in his arms.

"Harriet's . . . there." Sterling pointed. Pounding hammers, whirling colors in her brain sickened her. She grasped her head in both hands to keep it from exploding. J.T. rushed into Emporium, gun drawn.

"Oh my God," squealed a woman who'd been at the A&P.

Blood on her hands. Sterling swiped it on her skirt. Where did it come from? A scalp wound. "Harriet. Behind the counter. Two men . . . in storeroom."

The barber tried to get her to sit on the ground, losing the comb from his front pocket in the process. An elderly woman thrust a floral-print handkerchief to her head to stanch the bleeding.

Through the front window, she saw J.T. bend, almost disappearing behind the front counter. He leapt up and plowed through the curtain. A clatter, thud, slam sounded in the back.

"Help him," she appealed to the barber and the pasty-white butcher.

The barber released her to an older woman in a black coat and ventured inside. He stopped to the side of counter, and one hand flew to his mouth.

"Honey, here. Let's get you warm." The woman removed her own coat and wrapped it around Sterling. Its heavy wool warmed her. The world no longer threatened to buck her off. More people arrived to gape inside the Emporium

J.T. threw back the curtain and ordered the barber away. He almost had to shake the man to get him to obey. Head hanging, he escorted the barber toward the front door.

"Harriet?" Sterling asked though she knew.

"I'm sorry. She's gone." J.T. hung his head as though it was his fault.

She gasped, along with half a dozen others in the growing crowd behind her. One woman in the crowd pressed a wad of tissues in her hand. She dabbed at her throbbing head, letting the tears flow. Someone in the rear wept, then another.

"What about the two men who killed her? The ones who attacked me?" Sterling demanded.

"Did you catch 'em?" The butcher yelled in outrage. A siren echoed down the street.

"Th-there was nobody in the storeroom. I checked. Or the parking lot out back." J.T.'s voice was hoarse, though loud enough for everyone standing around to hear. "Somebody got sick back there, boxes tossed round, and some blood. No men."

Sterling stiffened, "What? Not possible."

J.T. pointed at the butcher, then the barber. "You go 'round back and stand in the parking lot. And you watch the door. Don't let nobody in until the sheriff comes. Folks, y'all need to get back, stay outta here. Keep away from the door."

He motioned to Sterling, and she followed him inside whispering, "There were two men in white hoods. They couldn't have gotten far. One was out cold, and the other had his balls so far up his throat he'll walk hunched over."

"You saying you took them out?" J.T. sounded incredulous.

She drew her lips into a thin line. "They were drunk. I smelled it."

J.T. put an arm around her, led her to a long table, and made her sit. Books and papers lay scattered all over the tabletop. Sterling snuggled into the coat and thought Harriet would have a fit at the mess.

Dragging a handkerchief out of his rear pocket J.T. pressed it against her bleeding forehead. He hissed, "I don't believe for one minute you cold-cocked a grown man and kicked another so hard he vomited. Don't give a shit how much they'd had to drink. Who else was here?"

"N-no one."

He put a finger close to her face. "You tell such a stupid story to someone else, and you're in trouble. Who was with you?"

The truth dawned on her. Maybe the blows to the head made her slow to understand. "It was Penix and somebody else. Probably Murphy. You let them get away."

"Who else was there?" he insisted. "Tom?"

She stood, took a shaky breath, then stuck a stiff arm in front of her. "Get away from me."

He ground his teeth, blocked her from leaving, "You wanna end up like Harriet? Listen, you walked in the back, two men punched you. You didn't see who it was. When you came to, you found Harriet. Got sick. That's all. We'll talk—"

"Shit, J.T.! What's —?" Sheriff Boyd, flanked by two deputies, strode into the Emporium and halted. Planting his feet wide apart he crossed his arms. "Mrs. Foster?"

She had no trouble letting sobs buy her time to think.

J.T. told the story. "She let herself in the storeroom entrance – her car's parked in the rear. She saw two men in white hoods. One tall, one medium height. She can't remember anything else except waking all bloody, coming out front, and finding Harriet. She was screaming and I ran over."

The sheriff grunted, walked behind the counter, hands on hips. For a few moments, he hunched to inspect Harriet's body. Then he stood, pushed back his hat, and grabbed a deep breath.

"Deputy Dawson, take Mrs. Foster to the doctor, get her checked out. She looks like a bleached sheet."

"I can take myself."

Boyd flexed his hands as he appeared to vacillate between strangling or shooting her. "Deputy, get a —."

"Wait! I'll take her." Jennifer Mullins shouted, straining against the arm of the deputy posted at the front door. "Sterling, I'll get you a doctor."

Boyd waved Jennifer in. Sterling sagged into her embrace with a sigh of gratitude.

"Anything missing? This a robbery?" Boyd asked around the room.

"I-I don't know." Sterling's voice quivered. "I can check."

"Later. Look later," Jennifer tightened her grip around Sterling's waist. "I'll stay with you 'til Tom gets home."

"Wounds to the head bleed like a stuck pig. May not even take stitches." The sheriff sounded sorry the injury wasn't worse.

Jennifer put her arm around Sterling's waist to guide her outside. She waited until they crossed the street before whispering, "You don't think they stole Aunt Amelia's diary, do you?"

167

Sterling could only shake her head no. She hadn't the energy to say she'd taken it home to read instead of giving it to Harriet.

CHAPTER THIRTY-EIGHT

Sheriff Boyd hunted down Jim Penix and Angus Murphy in no time. The damn fools went home. After listening to Deputy Dawson's private accounting of what happened at the Emporium, he couldn't wait to slap those two around.

When he tried to talk to Murphy, the man's scrambled words and sentences made no sense at all. Fuming, he grabbed the man by the scruff of the neck and hauled him into the cruiser.

With Murphy mumbling and cursing in the back, Boyd drove to Penix's shack. Wasn't it enough he had some University of Georgia professor asking about the damn bone those women found? Thank God he was easily put off. Now Boyd had two outta control drunks killing people. And he was so close to the finish line.

By the time he fought through the discarded bottles, sticky floors, dirty shirts, putrid dishes, and the hunting knife dug in Penix's wall, Boyd figured his wife left him again. In a dark room where a television set provided light and entertainment, Penix drank whiskey fast as he raised his arm.

Penix's blood-spattered white hood lay drooped off the back of the couch. The damn idiot left it in plain sight. Boyd swept it into his hip pocket, still searching for a place to sit. He settled on the cleanest thing he found, a footstool by Penix's feet. The pure ethyl alcohol smell from Penix's homemade brew overpowered the decay of baloney molding on a nearby plate.

"The bitch caught me off guard a-and fooled ole Murphy into hitting his own head," Penix whined.

"By herself?" Boyd raked his hands through his hair.

"She's stronger than she —."

"You and Murphy were drunk."

Penix stuck out his chin. "We'd had a few. Figured it was time to teach them women a lesson. We didn't mean to kill nobody. Harriet hit her head when Murphy smacked her."

Sheriff Boyd let it slide. "How'd you get away?"

"J.T. hustled us out the back, pushed us through a hole in the fence to the Mobil gas station." Penix offered the sheriff a drink from his Mason jar then lifted in a toast. "Gave J.T. a gallon of homebrew. Sheriff, we got to kill—."

Boyd slapped the liquor away and slammed a fist on a nearby table. "I'm takin' you to my uncle's fishing cabin at the lake. You stay put or I'll shoot y'all myself."

He hauled Penix to the cruiser and kicked him in the back with his friend.

By the time he left the cabin, he rested easy about Murphy and Penix. They had no way back to town from the lake except to walk—and he knew they were too lazy to do that.

Some good came outta this, the sheriff mused as his cruiser headlights showed him out of the backwoods and onto the state highway to Peg. Least he knew he could trust J.T. Dawson all the way. He let out a breath and relaxed a little.

Two days until the announcement. They filed all the deeds. The big fence was built. He'd watch Sterling Foster himself for two more days.

CHAPTER THIRTY-NINE

News of Harriet's murder and Sterling's assault spread through the Black community fast as lightening. Everyone liked Harriet Cook and appreciated what Sterling had done the night of the fire. And they wondered why the Klan—who else—targeted those two white women.

Ajamu's young men deployed to doorways and fences around the South End. Reverend Johnson went house to house praying with families, calming fears. The news hollowed out Gray's stomach. He grabbed Silver from a conversation with Ajamu and hurried him into the woods to talk.

"You know what we ought to do, brother," Silver's expression went flat, dull.

"What? Fire those guns you helped Ajamu stock? Harriet and Henry Johnson aren't enough dead people? Spilling Sterling's blood isn't enough for you?" Gray broke off a stick and beat a few pine limbs half to death. His head swiveled to his younger brother seated on the ground against a tree trunk.

Silver shifted on his hip and then slid a knife from his pocket. He unfolded the eight-inch blade, fisted the white handle, and stabbed the thick limb of a fallen oak on his right. Thunk. Thunk. Thunk.

Gray shivered in the cold, fought to keep a scream from rising out of his chest and into the woods. He had to go keep an eye on the old postmaster soon.

He'd only been a little younger than Silver when he wriggled the same knife out of his father's pocket, flicked the blade open, and shinnied to the top limb of the tree to cut his father's body down. The knife sliced the ropes to free his father's hands and feet. Then he'd thrown it away. Silver found it, pocketed it.

Now Silver broke the silence. "You have to get Sterling outta here."

"She never should have come." Gray concentrated on the darkening sky.

"Harriet's gone, I got no way to contact Sterling. Why don't you signal Foster? Meet up and find out what the hell happened. This mission may be compromised."

"She won't go 'til we all do. Remember what I said, what I called us? Sterling and the brothers. She damn sure won't go without your say-so." Silver made it sound like a compliment.

Gray kicked a pinecone into a tree trunk.

Silver rose, brushed off his hands on his pants. The folded pocketknife dangled from a finger. "We got most of what we came for. The people around here got pride and hope. They got brotherhood and solidarity."

"Which goes away the minute the boycott fails. Then Ajamu steps in." Gray heaved a sigh as deep as the wind stirring the leaves and took a stab in the dark. "He still smuggling in guns and ammunition? Are you helping him?"

After a while Silver said, "We all broke Justice Tomorrow's rules."

The wind whipped leaves and twigs aside. A storm stalked the woods like a giant pursuing a victim.

"We're ready when they come this time." With a smile, Silver handed the knife to Gray. "By rights this is yours."

Gray's arms hung by his side. Silver snorted, shoved the knife in his brother's right pants pocket, and walked back the way he'd come.

Weariness as strong as death overtook Gray. His shoulders slumped, and he brushed dirt off both pants legs. For a moment he fantasized about a long hot shower, decent clothes, a steak, perhaps an evening filled with symphonic music to cleanse the soul.

Silver vanished amid blowing leaves and bowed limbs. The knife weighed on Gray until he thought he'd tip over or break.

He had to go to work. But he longed to feel safe, to know those he loved were safe.

CHAPTER FORTY

Two large windows, each boasting the name "Homestead" in black letters, graced the front of the building and a row of three-foot-high box shrubs ran along the foundation. The red front door at the head of the three front steps also carried the firm's name for those who missed it on the windows.

Sterling parked her car at the closest meter to the office. Although it was unseasonably warm, she had chills, so she wore a coat. She observed a dirty canvas hood over the parking meter directly in front of the office that read: Reserved for John Cross.

She'd only taken two days bed rest, so she figured on dizziness and weakness. With a sigh, she shoved the car door open. Each muscle whimpered and screeched. The red, scraped, and swollen side of her face throbbed, the ten stitches taken along her hairline covered by an oblong white bandage itched. There was no way to disguise her swollen lip and little way to cover her black eye.

Tom tried to persuade her to stay in bed. Nothing on God's earth could prevent her from joining Tom at the real estate office today. Her throat closed. What did John Cross plan for the acres bordering the prettiest town she'd ever seen? Her fingers tingled in fearful anticipation.

Two middle-aged women coming out of the county offices saw her, nudged each other, cringed. Sterling tilted her chin. No more hiding under bedcovers shivering, grieving, and dissolving into bitter tears for Harriet. Time to fight for her friend and her friend's town.

A host of folks had called or dropped off fried chicken dinners, macaroni and cheese casseroles, and a host of cakes. Tom thanked them all, explaining that Sterling felt too ill to come downstairs. She refused to answer the phone, although several people called. She heard Tom flat-out refuse J.T.'s demand to go upstairs and talk to her. Nancy phoned and visited twice. Sterling refused to see her. It wasn't her fault J.T. let Harriet's killers go free. And she had to get over it for the sake of the mission. But right then she did not have it in her to pretend.

From the south of town, the rumbling noise of trucks and military-grade machinery on the road jolted her. She paused at the curb and placed her hand on the hood of her car to lean on and boost her onto the sidewalk. The hood vibrated. The noise grew louder. It had to be a big convoy. A man coming out of the bank stretched his neck toward the racket. Sterling fed the parking meter and held onto it for a moment to watch the military trucks pass.

Except the convoy veered into the middle of the Cross property. Truck after truck. Papers, cardboard milk cartons, a banana peel—trash blew off the top of the trucks onto the streets where puddles from the rainstorm yesterday turned them into soggy messes.

The man from the bank stepped closer to the sidewalk edge. "What the hell's this?"

Sterling's stomach lurched. A long Army-green truck filled with more garbage paused in the street, negotiated the turn into the Cross property too sharply, and for a moment teetered on two wheels.

People spilled out of the A&P, the bookstore, the library, and Methodist church. One or two fanned the air in front of their faces or held their noses.

John Cross's work with the Congressional sanitation and public health subcommittee, the strange garbage dumped on Cross land, the unpaved roads on the property, the ugly metal fences—all made sense to her now. Even the pigs, a final slap at the town. Her hands and lips trembled. One foot in front of another, one step up, then another. Turn the Homestead doorknob, push.

Four empty desks with ringing telephones on each one heralded her arrival. The secretary who usually occupied the first seat kept a jar of peppermints and always offered Sterling one. Everyone must be in the rear conference room where she heard voices.

On her previous visits Sterling had appreciated the potted plants on the desks, the colorful posters of local homes hung along the walls, even the blue and yellow afghan draped across a wing-back chair in the lobby. Today she plodded as though sticky tar coated the polished wood floor. Inside the doorway, she watched two women and five men around a punch bowl and plates of cookies. George and most of his employees wore smiles and paper party hats.

"Sterling. Darlin', are you okay? What happened to you was awful. Does the sheriff have a lead on the crooks?" George's words tumbled over her. "Tom,

174

get your wife a chair. Great you're here to celebrate with us today."

"It's a garbage dump. In Crossville's front door," Sterling announced from the doorway. "The Cross land is a military landfill. Army trucks are rolling in now. Trash all over the place."

"What!" cried the peppermint secretary.

The man who sat next to her stammered, "G-George?"

George's thick lips bobbed open and closed. "Well, yes. The contract with the Army was signed a few days ago."

"Acres and acres of trash." Sterling pointed her fury at George. "It stinks all the way across town."

Several people groaned. Tom shoved a chair under Sterling. Her knees gave out.

"What about all the jobs? You said jobs were coming in." The speaker had framed photos of his two little girls on his desk.

"There's jobs. Running dozers, moving the trash heaps around, weighing metal for resale. Tending the pigs." A voice boomed from the doorway. "And security!"

George Thompson all but leapt in the air. "Mr. Cross."

"Sorry I'm late. I wanted to make sure the foreman had things under control." John Cross walked into the middle of the room and put a folder on a table there. A faint hint of decay reached Sterling's nose as he hurried by her. Or maybe she imagined it.

Cross's dark brown, unruly eyebrows overshadowed hazel eyes and black rimmed glasses. His hair, cut short, blended from white at the temple into brown along the sides and in back. He extracted a pack of Lucky Strikes from the inside pocket of a blue wool suit. The smart cut of his expensive jacket did little to hide his scrawny build or thin arms. He wrapped an extraordinarily long finger around the cigarette, touched a lighter flame to it, and took a long drag into his lungs. Satisfied, he greeted Sterling's barely concealed hostility with amusement.

"You must be Mrs. Foster. I am sorry about what happened."

He didn't look at all sorry. In fact, he sat on the edge of the table, leaned back, and smoked with a smug, self-satisfied air.

"What about all the money people have put into Crossville?" A woman by the punch bowl croaked. "Their stores in the middle of town? Their shops?"

He waved his hand to scatter the smoke. "What about it?"

"They'll be ruined." The man who spoke sounded dull, lifeless. "Not today. Not tomorrow. But a stinking landfill all along the north edge of town will kill business. Destroy housing on nearby streets. The town will wither."

Cross took off his glasses and polished them with his handkerchief. "Part of what you said is true. The price of progress. The business district will fade. But the workers in the landfill have to live and shop somewhere. More stores will pop up elsewhere."

"The County says there has to be woods or farms on the land. A landfill is not a farm." The man from the front desk slapped his palm on the table.

"The landfill has woods. And we have farm animals. That's all the county needs to call it a farm." Cross tilted his head and blew smoke up to the ceiling.

Sterling's hand covered her mouth. The man from the front desk painted an all too real picture of life in little Crossville after a 600-acre military landfill became fully operational. She flashed on Jennifer Mullins, Alice Peterson, Rose Anderson Collins, and all the others whose lives in Crossville suddenly turned to garbage.

"Why?" She stood. "You're related to many of the people who live here."

Cross chuckled. "Have you examined the size of your husband's check? He not only gets a commission as my buyer, he bought into the company."

Sterling whirled to Tom.

"I became a stockholder in a public company buying land for military use. Landfills are only a small part." He enunciated each word.

"No money in small military landfills." Cross flicked ashes into a silver ashtray on the table. "Things failed to come together as I'd hoped. We had to have an operation on my farm by Oct. 25 before new federal regulations went into effect."

"So, someone dumped trash and shooed a few pigs on your property weeks ago . . . to-to make the whole property eligible for the old landfill rules?" Too sick to stand anymore Sterling plopped on a chair again.

"Now the Crossville landfill is grandfathered into the old, less-stringent landfill rules." Cross clapped George on the back. "You will all be delighted to know our financial advisor and banker is coming from Atlanta to present your checks."

Cross couldn't use a local bank, Sterling realized. A local banker would not stand for ruining the town. She glanced at Tom, who had the decency to act ashamed.

CHAPTER FORTY-ONE

Tom knew about this project. Or part of it at least. Her chin trembled with her misery. He let this betrayal happen right before her love-fogged eyes.

"I'm curious, Mr. Cross," she said. "Is all this petty revenge on the families who quarreled with your great-great-grandfather?"

"Let's call it a bonus." Cross lost his smile and slid off the table. "And a challenge. We had to post a notice of hearing. But I had already laid the groundwork with the only people I know who read the tiny legal notices in the paper. They expected a military site and that's what they saw advertised in the legal notices. The garbage disposal site is a military installation, although it belongs to us . . . all of us here."

"George, you can't approve a project you own a part of," said Tom.

"No, I am an honest man. I never presided over or voted on anything to do with the Cross project." George tried to sound offended. "I did not attend the zoning meeting."

"You can ruin an entire town, stink it up, make it unlivable!" Sterling pivoted to the stunned real estate employees. "And you're willing to let it happen? Do nothing?" Tom brushed her arm. She shook him off.

Cross clapped his hands and his sweeping gesture took in the cookies and punch on a side table. "Let's celebrate. George, pour me some punch."

"I don't feel like celebrating," said one man.

"We gotta do something," said another by the punch bowl.

"I'm calling the county attorney," said the secretary.

"Go home. Rest. And for God's sake, call Nancy. She's frantic to talk to you," whispered Tom.

Sterling nearly decked him. Her heart pounded against her chest. "I may go by the Emporium to see . . . see what needs cleaning."

She must leave a meeting signal for Gray. She had to tell him of Tom's deception and her screwup in letting Tom deceive her. Even though Justice Tomorrow hadn't summoned her, she was packing and leaving town.

"See you later." He leaned over to kiss her cheek, but she brushed him aside.

Cross chuckled. She picked up the coat she'd tossed on a chair and left. Behind her, a few employees of Homestead Realty ate cookies and raised punch cups in a stale room devoid of cheer. In the outer office telephones continued to ring, and no one answered. She rubbed her forehead, her sorrow evolving into a headache.

A muscular, older man in a cashmere topcoat opened the front door for her. He hadn't buttoned the coat, so the gusts of wind caused it to flap around his legs. He gave her the once over in a familiar way.

As she passed him her vision narrowed, her breathing became faster, shallower. Colors, lines, details around her sharpened.

"Are you all right, ma'am? Nasty cut you got." The man's tenor voice resonated in her chest.

Did she know him? He looked so familiar. "I'm fine. Thank you."

Sterling gagged. She ran to her car and passed a black Buick without looking behind her, remembering only later that a white Lincoln Continental sat in the space reserved for John Cross.

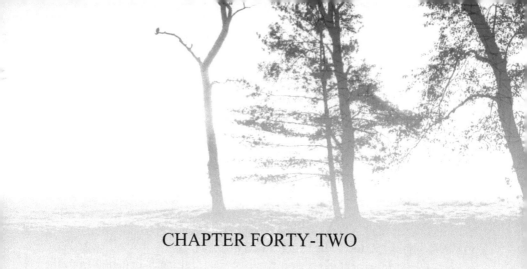

CHAPTER FORTY-TWO

Sheriff Boyd picked his teeth in the rearview mirror, swiped the front ones with his tongue. Dodging the paper air freshener dangling from a string looped over the mirror, he clucked at his image in satisfaction. Today he drove his own tan four-door sedan again but wore a pinched-front hat low on his forehead. The rudimentary disguise succeeded. As she drove to town, Mrs. Foster ignored him. Nor did she see him when she left the real estate office, parked in front of her house, and stomped inside like she wanted to kill.

Boyd drove by, hid his parked car in a dirt lane near the Dawson's house, grabbed a rain slicker off the passenger side. His blood zinged with the thrill of the chase until he felt under the front seat for a thermos and pulled out Penix's bloodied white hood. Goddamn. Careless. Bad idea to leave the thing. He stuffed it deep in his back pocket and untucked his plaid shirt to cover it.

Skirting the houses and vacant lots, Boyd clutched his slicker and thermos as he searched for and found a place to hunker in a clump of bushes on empty land across the street from the Foster home. He'd keep an eye on Mrs. Foster today and tomorrow. The job fell to someone else from then on.

He used the radio to check in with his right-hand man in the department, and Alvin gave him an earful about Sterling Foster's dust-up at George's office. His blood pressure shot up. Everywhere she went she caused trouble, violated God's law on the races, and sassed a man of God in his own church. She asked too many questions. Might already know too much.

It worried him that she pitched a fit at the real estate office. Got everybody pissed at John Cross and George Thompson. Mad folks did troublesome things, upset plans. She and whoever she worked with ticked him off five ways to Sunday. They sashayed into his town with their godless ways and stirred up trouble where there was none. Made his gut burn to think of a white woman in the middle of colored trouble.

Boyd shifted on the grass to get more comfortable. Good view of the old store, although the filthy windows would keep him from seeing a party inside. He wiped the sweat off his forehead, glanced at the darkening sky. Crazy weather. Fit right in with what was going on in town.

Nancy Dawson knocked on the Foster's door but got no answer. It was clear someone was home. Rude. Mrs. Dawson ought not fool with trash like Sterling Foster. Maybe Mrs. Dawson thought the best of everybody and refused to see the evil next door. His Peg inclined that way.

The Foster house sat like a sleepy pile of wood, shingles dangling from the roof, shades covering the windows, no lights inside. Almost like the house itself waited in grim expectation.

The threat of rain settled an ache deep inside his bones. Muggy and warm enough for spring in November. Tornado weather.

He went over everything he knew about the Fosters, what addle-brained Penix told him as his gaze roamed over house, the street, the old store. Boyd cursed himself for a fool. Everybody in town knew the store was once used for Klan meetings, so there would be a big temptation to use it as a place for anti-segregationists. Plus, it was close to the Foster house.

Boyd's gut told him he had something. A wolfish grin crossed his face. They'd meet soon after Harriet's murder. He knew it. He might catch Sterling Foster, the colored boy, and whoever else they worked with. Perfect place to bury them all.

He needed back-up. And back-up happened to be handy. Taking a chance on being spotted, Boyd sprinted across the street and up the steps of Dawson's front porch. He rang the bell, banged on the door.

Nancy Dawson kept both hands on the door after she opened it. Her body went stiff as a fire poker. "Sheriff Boyd. Did you hear about the garbage dump—?"

He waved both hands in front of her. "Where's J.T.? I need him right now."

Nancy called for her husband and walked down the hall to fetch him without asking the sheriff to sit. Boyd clapped his hands together in front of him, rocked up on his toes.

J.T. hurried down the hall tying his robe, his eyelids drooping. One cheek bore the marks of the wrinkles in his pillowcase. Boyd forgot the man had pulled night duty again.

The deputy's voice sounded sleepy. "You find Penix and Angus Murphy? Those goddamn asses left me a thank-you jug of their homemade whiskey on the porch and—."

"I picked them up and took 'em to the fishing camp." Boyd tried hooking his thumbs in his gun harness then realized he was in jeans and a shirt. "Come on."

"I'm your man." J.T.'s fingers rubbed his beard stubble.

A flush of pride filled Boyd. He'd taken a chance on this deputy, and it paid off. "I got a lead on the nigger who set fire to the church."

"Set fire to their own church?" The muscles around J.T.'s mouth twitched.

"Wanted to start a race riot. Some Yankees helped."

"Sheeet," J.T. swore.

"Got a tip there's a meeting in the old store today or tomorrow." Boyd figured he could call his gut feeling a legitimate tip. "We got to put a permanent stop to all this. You hear? A per-ma-nent stop."

For a second, he feared J.T. didn't get it —or didn't want to get it.

"I hear." His Adam's apple bobbed. "How many?"

Good question. "Two, I'm thinking." Boyd stepped in closer to confide, "The feds let me know Ajamu might try to bring in armed fighters."

"I was at the briefing you gave."

Boyd jutted out his chin. "Well, this part's for your ears only. We got a couple in town right this minute."

J.T.'s lip curled. "Who?"

"Ama-jam-ma Who-the-hell-ever, for one. Ah-h, Feds asked me to watch him." Boyd found losing a few hours' sleep slowed him a step. "You and me got a chance to get rid of these folks."

"Lemme get me my damn pants." J.T. clenched his fists.

"Got no idea how long it's gonna take." Boyd jerked a thumb toward the store.

"You clear it?" J.T. hollered from the bedroom. "Or do we want company?"

Shit. "I'll use your phone. You and I are off duty."

While he was on the phone with the dispatcher making sure he and J.T. wouldn't be disturbed, the deputy came out of the bedroom in uniform. Too late to make him change, but didn't the boy know off-duty meant street clothes?

"Go around back of the store, hide in the weeds, come in the door when I call — or if you see something suspicious. Careful on the first step at the top. Always been loose, and I don't reckon age fixed it. I'm goin' in the front."

"Ready, Sheriff."

With a satisfied nod, Boyd left, ran up the street, and knelt on one knee at the corner of Dawson's property panting like a Kentucky Derby winner. After a minute, he glanced back, and a blur of color told him J.T. had moved from his side door toward the store. Boyd lost him amid the weeds.

The sheriff slithered closer to the store. The tall grass and briars, limp in the

181

humidity, brushed his knees and shirttail. He glanced up. Thunderous dark sky. Air so still he heard bugs crawl.

A raindrop plopped on his head. Another. It was as easy to wait dry inside as wet outside, so he tiptoed up the front step, eased open the door, cleared it with his weapon, and slipped in.

Ten feet to the left of the counter where customers once left empty Coke bottles, Boyd spied two good-sized barrels shoved in a dark corner. Was a time he ate sour pickles out of them. He sat on the floor behind one, satisfied his hiding place afforded a view of the side room, the trap in the floor, and front door. J.T. covered the back.

He fell silent as the Grim Reaper and wished for an old-fashioned sour pickle.

CHAPTER FORTY-THREE

All the window shades pulled down made the house dark as a cave and matched Sterling's mood as she paced.

She failed to watch out for Tom, and she failed to get J.T. to talk. The complexity of the case blew her mind. But she got the pieces of this mystery straight.

John Cross evicted Black farmers from their land, bought more land on the cheap from poor whites, filled key players in town with visions of a big money-making development, then laughed at them. George Thompson must have gotten rich as an investor who helped Cross through zoning and property acquisition.

The success of the plan meant keeping the community quiet and off-balance while they were grabbing Black farms. The attempted murder of Reverend Johnson and the resulting death of Henry were only diversions, as Gray suspected. Did the people involved in the murder go after the pastor again with the church fire —or burn it as revenge for the march? Or both?

And Tom. Sterling's stomach roiled. After investing in John Cross's company, he acted like putting money in a private company while on a case was okay. He talked of the money they needed. Then he claimed Cross duped him like he had the others in the real estate office who invested and acted as straw buyers. Was the father of her child naïve, greedy, or crooked? Or a combination?

Sterling wanted to believe the best of him. No man had ever been so thoughtful of her, so attentive and loving. He took pride in his business, worked for the cause they both believed in, and tried to fix the mistakes he'd made. Not everyone had a talent for investigatory work.

Still, she must tell Gray everything —including Tom's involvement in the

Cross development.

Feeling a little better, she picked up Aunt Amelia's diary to distract herself while she waited for the meeting. She settled into a comfortable position on the couch, clicked on the table lamp and flipped to the last entry she had read. Forbidden love continued blooming between Aunt Amelia and Stephen Cross.

Despite the water and age stains, Sterling learned Aunt Amelia had seen Callie talking with the colored boy Lucius in a way not considered proper while Lucius and his mother served at Easter dinner. She scolded her sister and Callie brushed her off. Best of all, Stephen Cross and Aunt Amelia stepped up their courting. The two met several times at the home of friends since neither "dear Papa" nor Stephen's father approved of their courtship.

Sterling smiled. A real love story to enjoy.

Apparently, the romance between Aunt Amelia Epson and Stephen Cross flourished in secret for two more entries, known only by her older sister. Callie also had a secret admirer whose name Aunt Amelia did not know or perhaps didn't share with her diary. Their tutor, Mr. Arnett, appeared in few sentences and only with complaints. In between the recounting of hurried meetings and fervent touches were brief mentions of land disputes between John Cross and "dear Papa". Clearly the disposition of land did not command Aunt Amelia's attention as much as love.

Sterling's eyebrows shot up. Aunt Amelia wrote that her father had asked Mr. Cross for a price on over four hundred acres near the stagecoach station, land that lay along the front of the new landfill. Aunt Amelia said she wrote about the acreage because it was so large. Hoping to read a comment on the land later, Sterling hauled herself up from her nest of pillows, dug around on a nearby table, and found a notebook she used to record every time Aunt Amelia mentioned land.

Once she fell into a rhythm, it became easier for Sterling to read Aunt Amelia's hideous scrawl. She skimmed the report of local vexation with Cross. He apparently thought it was good business to donate property to emancipated slaves. Thus, they earned a living and patronized his stores and mill. Other landowners did not agree with him. A loud argument involving Cross, "dear Papa," and several other landowners was reported by Aunt Amelia only because it happened outside church after services "in front of the ladies." The women were scandalized. Sterling skipped the accounts of daily living and news of returning Confederate soldiers because they interfered with the romances in Aunt Amelia's diary.

Sterling's interest peaked again at an entry detailing a carriage accident where a buggy driven by Stephen Cross ran into the family carriage driven by "dear Papa." Stephen apologized by saying the buggy horse bolted and offered to make restitution. But "dear Papa" alighted from the carriage in a rage, and lots of shouting and fist-waving followed, according to Aunt Amelia.

Several more entries without mention of love or land. Then:

"May 22, 1865 – Dear Papa and Mr. Cross had a pleasant exchange in town today. Papa asked Mr. Cross to sell him four hundred acres adjoining those of the negro Anders. At first Mr. Cross was unwilling. He wished to gift the land when he freed his slaves John Turner and Robert Barron. Papa gave him a price, and to my delight, Mr. Cross agreed. Then he tipped his hat to Callie and me and said, 'For your daughter's sake I will agree to this sale.' Perhaps the families will reconcile! Stephen and I barely concealed our joy at this turn of events. Callie became ill on the ride home. Paul Miller returned from a prisoner of war camp missing his left arm."

Sterling frowned, flipped to the next page, then the next. The dates weren't consecutive. Aunt Amelia skipped an entry for the next two days. Unlike her. The girl wrote with religious dedication every day. Sterling twisted the book toward the living room table lamp.

Someone had cut out the missing pages. Her finger along the inside spine found sharp edges. No ragged tear.

She moved on to the next entries. From what she gathered, she had missed a lot.

Lucius and his mother banned from the house. Mr. Arnett dismissed – Sterling hoped for failure to teach penmanship. No, Mr. Arnett had been instructing several Negro boys to read, including Lucius. Aunt Amelia reported Callie so "fearfully" upset she and "dear Papa" quarreled.

Three more pages gone. Sterling growled. It was like reading a novel where the author wrote alternate chapters.

The next entry revealed Aunt Amelia and Stephen planned to elope. Something happened in between entries to make the two families angry again. The lovers felt their families would be "wholly" reconciled once they married.

Aunt Amelia missed a day of writing, since Sterling found no page cut along the spine.

Whoever cut out the diary pages must not have seen the next entry. She skimmed Aunt Amelia's lengthy expressions of grief, desolation, and abandonment to find the cause.

"After supper, we heard a knock. Mr. Cross burst into our family sitting room without being announced. He so startled Mama, Papa, and I that we fell mute. 'A present for you and Stephen.' He threw papers at my feet. 'I recorded these today for my former slaves, John Turner and Robert Barron. I've come to tell you my son Stephen has gone to live with his cousins in Mississippi. I'll not have a defiant son under my roof. Epson, you stole my acreage on the north side because I would not serve in your Confederate regiment—don't think I have forgotten. And now your family knows too.' He looked at me with something akin to sadness. 'Stephen is gone to marry a woman in Mississippi or never see me again. I am sorry if this brings you pain. But your own foolishness is the cause.' Mr. Cross said to dear Papa, 'You have one daughter of courage and virtue. You failed to control the other, sir, and we are both the poorer for it. You have no land from me, and I have no son in my house.'"

Several words were scratched out, and Aunt Amelia concluded: "The paper deeds I press between these pages are the only wedding present I shall ever receive, for I'll have no husband but Stephen."

Stephen must have obeyed his father and married the bride Cross picked out. Sterling had seen a copy of John Cross's will naming his son Stephen as his only heir.

What Aunt Amelia revealed dazzled Sterling. She recognized the names Turner and Barron. Unless he lied to Aunt Amelia and her family, old John Cross deeded land to his former slaves, the acres John Cross the fourth stole from their descendants to create a military landfill.

The deeds Aunt Amelia "pressed between these pages" proved the black farmers owned the land they tilled for generations — and John Cross's landfill was dead.

Sterling dropped the diary with a huff. Crap. Didn't take much of a detective to figure who held the missing diary pages and the deeds. Jennifer literally dangled them under Sterling's nose. She bet the farm Jennifer had the deeds and the missing diary pages taped behind the dreadful gold frame from her attic.

She had other questions, like what happened to Callie Epson. But first things first.

The phone rang again. She tried to ignore it, but the noise dragged her from the diary. She wandered into the study to pull aside the blind and count the raindrops on the windowpane. Thoughts of Tom crept in, she thrust them aside. Time to see Gray.

She hesitated in the kitchen, then wheeled back to the study. In case J.T. or Nancy happened to be watching the back, Sterling climbed out the window and entered the store through the trap door.

As she eased her arms up and pulled herself into the store, she felt a familiar sensation. She crept behind the counter, letting heightened senses overtake her.

CHAPTER FORTY-FOUR

G ray took his time, traveled in a circular route, and even sloshed through the stream behind the store to be certain no one followed him to the store. He'd felt eyes on him earlier.

He stood in the woods, sheltered by a pine, to study the old building. It seemed sad, worn, and forgotten in the rain.

Under the piles holding up the foundation, Gray thought he detected a movement, a shadow between the weeds and briars. The trap door opened. Then closed.

Sterling was early. He grinned. She had news.

Moving sideways, he crouched and made his way through the undergrowth to the side window. He'd left it open for an occasion like this one. Half-way there he paused, frowning. The showers muffled sounds and the dim light of a rainy-day blurred vision, but he thought something moved on his left near the door.

After several minutes, he dismissed it as nerves, swiped the water off his face, and dropped to his knees, crawling the rest of the way through the weeds. A stack of wood under the window rose so high he only had to climb it, and high step over the windowsill.

Water dripping from his clothes sounded like cannonballs in the damp storeroom of the silent building. He sniffed rotten wood and decay, waiting to move until his eyes adjusted to the poor light. Then he picked his away around broken floorboards, rat droppings, and cracked glass bottles to the entrance of the shop side of the store.

He waited. Nothing except rain on the tin roof. Felt strange. Nothing to pin it on. Maybe his jitters stemmed from how badly he wanted Sterling out of

Crossville.

He grabbed the door frame, leaned inside the empty shop. "Sterling."

She must have been sitting or stooping at the far end of the massive store counter. She popped up with a ready smile. "You're early."

"How are you? I can't see." Gray walked in, straining to see the side of her face. "Should I worry?"

Sterling chuckled. "Penix and Murphy are sissies." She circled behind the counter and headed for him, tapping the wood with her knuckle to punctuate every word. "Did you see the garbage trucks?"

"I don't care." He stepped toward her, his hands itching for a reassuring touch.

"I figured out how to stop it —."

Gray held up his open palms. "I don't care."

"I've found diary entries validating some of the Black farmer's claims, Gray. We can keep out the landfill."

Why was she so insistent?

She kept on. "We have hard evidence of one man involved in killing Henry Johnson. There were more."

"We can't——."

He wanted to shake her silly. "You need to leave, Sterling. Tonight."

The air behind him moved, a shadowy presence became solid in his peripheral vision. Sterling's breath caught; her nostrils flared. She staggered backward across a puddle half-way behind the counter.

A gun's barrel dug into Gray's side. He froze. With a sideways glance, he knew whose firm hand held the weapon.

"Sheriff Boyd," Sterling said.

A torrential downpour pounded the roof. Water coming through the leaky ceiling dripped like tears in some places, waterfalls in others. The temperature began dropping almost as fast as the rain.

The sheriff shoved Gray forward with one hand. Sterling backed further until the counter hid half of her.

Good. She gave herself a chance.

Gray cast about for a weapon.

"J.T!" Boyd shouted.

CHAPTER FORTY-FIVE

A hinge screeched. The back door opened to reveal a stony-faced J.T. Dawson holding his weapon with both hands. Sterling's heart sank.

J.T. skittered sideways until he took himself out of the line of Boyd's fire. His gun pointed at Sterling.

"Perfect timing, deputy," Boyd crowed.

"J.T." Sterling's voice shook.

"Nancy's trying to get hold of you about her tablecloths," J.T. said. "Your friend Nancy?" The sight of the .38 Colt in J.T.'s hand caused his words to garble in her head.

Boyd shoved Gray. He stumbled on a loose board. "Who killed the Johnson boy? You said you knew, Mrs. Foster. How?"

The sheriff's tone scared Sterling as much as his gun. A man calm as Boyd could uncork a great deal of violence.

"You," she answered. An eerie calm and righteous indignation rose in her. A hand stroked her abdomen in silent mourning. "I found the epaulette from your uniform buried near the tree."

Boyd's dry chuckle barely rose over the rain on the roof. "Damn. I searched everywhere for it."

"It's long gone."

Boyd cursed.

"John Cross set it up." Sterling said, taking a slow, careful step toward J.T. "His car was at Parson's. He was waiting to see what happened."

"Never mind about Cross," the sheriff snapped.

"He gave the orders. You never were the boss around here. Cross told you to kill Reverend Johnson, but you failed." Boyd and J.T. stood ready to take everything precious from her – at least they'd give her the truth about Henry

Johnson and about the land grab before she died.

"Cross had the money, the idea, the inside dope. But I give the orders. I make things happen round here. Right, J.T.?" Boyd grabbed Gray's shirt with his free hand.

"J.T. in the Klan too?" She threw him an accusing look.

The sheriff chuckled. "Any time he wants."

"Like you said, Sterling, things aren't always like they seem," J.T. rasped.

Sterling awarded him a contemptuous groan. Gray's brow furrowed, he squinted at the deputy.

"Poor ole Tom," Boyd said. "He's gonna be heartbroken when you turn up dead."

A soft, barely audible exhale arose from the deputy.

"I know Tom invested in the company— but is he in on it? Did he know about the landfill from the beginning?" She had to know.

"The boy knows business. That's all he knows."

Sterling forced her feet closer to J.T. She had to deal with the deputy.

"You may kill a teenage Black boy without the FBI caring, sheriff, but not a white woman." A pregnant white woman. She gritted her teeth against thoughts of the baby who would die with her.

"Oh, I don't think they'll care long." One corner of his mouth drew up.

"Sheriff —." J.T.'s weight shifted to the other foot.

Gray coughed. His eyes ranged the floor, settling on something that she couldn't see.

He needed a distraction.

Without warning, Boyd slammed his gun butt into the side of Gray's head. He dropped to the floor out of her sight.

A screech – hers? She fell forward, grasped the counter, and knocked over a glass bottle.

Boyd stomped once to plant his boots, sending a spray of water in the air. With a growl, he drew back to kick the black man on the floor.

Sterling snatched the bottle and threw it at Boyd with a desperate grunt. It bounced off the sheriff's cheek. His head jerked to Sterling for a split second.

CHAPTER FORTY-SIX

Boyd's kick sent Gray sprawling at the sheriff's feet. As he hit the floor, the world banged loose inside Gray's skull. But lying on his back gave him a blurry view of the bottle striking Boyd and the sheriff's head swiveling around.

Gray whipped a leg around and slammed it against Boyd's shins.

Boyd yelped. Gray's heel lashed out again and connected with the sheriff's kneecap. Already off-balance, Boyd's eyebrows shot up, his mouth became an "O", and his arms wind-milled in the air. His gun fired, flame bursting out the barrel as he hit the floor, then clattered across the floor.

Sterling screamed.

Had Boyd shot her?

With speed born of fury, Gray rolled to his right, grabbing for the loose piece of board he'd spotted. Boyd aimed a sideways boot that scraped Gray's waist and hip. The instep of the sheriff's boot hit the pants pocket holding his father's pocketknife. Gray hardly felt it.

"Shoot!" The momentum of his kick carried Boyd onto his back. He flipped to his belly and crawled for his gun. Gray swung the broken board and smashed it down on the sheriff's fingers.

Boyd screeched. Gray swiped the pistol further out of Boyd's reach with the board.

"Shoot, J.T.! Shoot the bastard!" Boyd said, lashing out with his fists, blocking one of Gray's blows with his arm, and knocking the wood out of his grip.

Boyd scrambled to his feet. Gray scooted back far enough to reach for his knife.

****

The sheriff's bullet whizzing by her right ear shocked a scream from Sterling as she inched ever closer to J.T. He gaped at her, then his attention bounced from the fight to her. His body and gun whipped back and forth looking for a clean shot.

She couldn't see Boyd and Gray, but she heard curses, howls, the sound of flesh hitting flesh over the noise of the storm outside. Her focus riveted on J.T. Her life depended on it.

"Don't do this, J.T. Please." Sterling raised her voice. "I'm begging you." She moved another step, held her hands out in front of her in a prayer pose, elbows bent. Her fingers trembled like her legs.

"Stay outta this, Sterling." J.T. warned.

"I love Nancy. We're friends." One, maybe two more steps and Sterling would be close enough.

A guttural and savage howl followed a painful scream. Mouth open, J.T. rose on his toes a little to see better.

She moved in, used the side thrust of her prayerful hands to knock J.T.'s gun aside while she aimed a knee for his groin. As he twisted to partially block the blow, his gun fired. Behind her, a man shrieked.

Sterling lost all reason. J.T. shot Gray. She launched herself at the deputy with fists and feet flying, intending to do as much damage as possible before he killed her. She landed a fist to his nose, blocked his return jab.

"You crazy. . ." He swiped at his bloody nose and leveraged his weight to shove her away so hard she fell on the floor. Then he twisted back to the fight. And froze, slack jawed.

Panting, Sterling crawled to the counter and used one arm to help her kneel, rise, and peer on the other side.

Gray sat astride Sheriff Martin Boyd stabbing his chest over and over, both hands on the knife handle.

Above the sounds of thunder and rain, short, rhythmic thuds followed by a series of sucking slurps filled the air. Gray hummed, not a tune, but a mindless chant as he continued his unholy rite. Sterling's hands covered her ears. But she couldn't look away.

"Jesus Christ," J.T. breathed.

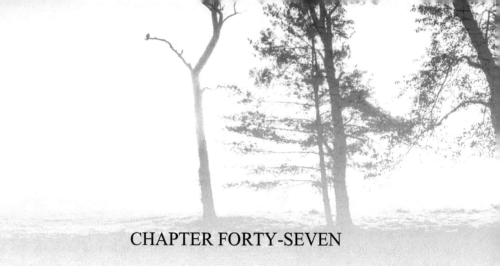

CHAPTER FORTY-SEVEN

Blood splattered near Sterling's hand, startling her out of paralysis. She stumbled around the counter to Gray.

Gray's knife struck Boyd with a thunk. It came out sounding like a boot in mud. Thunk, suck, thunk, suck. Gray worked like a machine.

Sterling knelt by him. "Gray." At last, she reached and clasped her hand around his fists on the knife handle.

His head turned a fraction, his eyes focused on her, and he allowed her to take the knife. With an agonized shudder, he rolled off Boyd and into a growing puddle of rain mixed with blood. He lay panting, staring into the leaky roof.

Thunder. A bolt of lightning sizzled across the sky, flooding the dim store.

The carnage looked worse in the light. The half-eaten deer covering her in an Alabama hole flashed across her mind. Sterling gagged.

J.T. flopped against the counter. "Shhh-it."

"Gray, are you hurt?" She moved over to rest a hand on his chest. She checked him up and down for wounds.

"I'm ... no." He blinked once, twice, pulled in a deep breath. Sterling helped him sit. Touching his cheek, she forced a tiny smile. He heaved another sigh.

"You have to get out. Run." She stood, offered her hand to help him up.

"Come with me —"

"I'll leave Crossville right behind you." Sterling held onto Gray to keep him steady, folded the knife, and shoved it in his pocket.

"You both gotta stick around."

Dread surged through Sterling, turning her legs to concrete pillars.

"You both disappear right after this, and folks get suspicious. Stay, but don't go out a lot." J.T. dabbed at his nose.

Air eased out of Sterling's mouth. She relaxed her grip on Gray's blue checked shirt, let him stand alone. "J.T., Gray is my colleague."

"Colleague?"

"We're private investigators," Gray mumbled.

"Private, huh. You-u know you were stabbing a dead man, don't you?" J.T. said. "I shot him when Sterling knocked my gun."

Gray shook his head. "I —"

"You mean, Boyd's got J.T.'s bullet in him?" Sterling asked.

The consequence of that hit both men at once. They stared at each other for a second.

"Well, we've got to dig it out. Get rid of it. Otherwise, the cops can match it to your gun." Gray took out his knife, the snick of the blade almost masking his shudder.

"Can you?" J.T. dragged himself up off the counter.

"Don't come around here. Too much blood. I can get it."

All Sterling's muscles tightened. She squinted, but suddenly she did not see a man, only a half-eaten deer. She wheeled toward the front of the store. Though the window grime, the tall weeds, and downpour the street was hard to see. Nevertheless, she concentrated on what might lurk outside. Nothing was worse than what lay inside.

She took her mind away, pretending to be the scout as her brother Danny in battle fatigues, his face coated with camouflage paint and his helmet pulled low, led a patrol in some distant country.

"Got it," Gray called.

Sterling jerked like someone punched her. She grabbed at her side. Instead of going to Gray, she licked her lips and scooted to the next window for a new vantage point. The Mekong Delta dissolved into a Crossville street.

"You need to get cleaned up, Gray. Go jump in the creek behind here. You can go home like you went for a walk and fell in the water," J.T. said. "Wash off the blood. Ditch the bullet. Creek's deep in places this time of year. Be pretty cold."

"We have to explain the hole in his shoulder," Gray said. "And your gun firing, deputy."

Sterling hugged herself with both arms. "J.T., sorry —."

"Damn right." He spit it out word by word. "You bloodied my nose and bruised my cheek. And you didn't trust me."

Her teeth chattered. "How did . . . how was I to know —."

"Jesus! How could you think I would hurt you?" J.T. stomped off a few steps running a hand through his hair. His rebuke stung.

Gray angled his body so J.T. couldn't hear. "No matter what he says, get clear. I-I don't want anything happening to . . . I need you."

Sterling tilted her head. As quick as she saw love and tenderness, it vanished. Standing in the store with his hands on her and their shoes soaked in blood, she knew they'd be forever cowards if they ran right now. She waited in silence.

"No, Gray. I'm done." This time she slammed the door.

"Sterling . . ." His nose almost touched hers. "We will have our own agency someday like we planned. Sterling Brothers Limited, remember?"

She shook her head. The noise of rain on the tin roof rose and fell in deafening waves.

J.T.'s hand slapped his thigh. "Y'all, this—this is a damn mess right here. Only thing I can think is pray for lightning to strike."

Another roll of thunder. Sterling caught the glimmer of an idea in the flash.

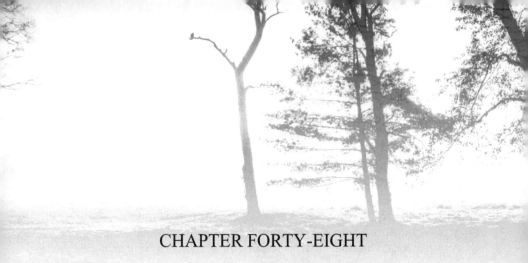

CHAPTER FORTY-EIGHT

Was it afternoon? Early evening? Sheriff Boyd must have died hours ago instead of only minutes. Sterling watched Gray high-tail it until the tall grass, fog, and mist closed around him. A spirit to feel, but never see again.

She ducked and ran from the back of the store through the weeds to her own kitchen door. She opened the back door and felt the screen door hit her rear. As she checked the red kitchen clock she careened through the kitchen, dripping wet, shaking with fear, leaving blood and water on her clean floor.

Only an hour since she first left the house. One hour. How was it possible? She grabbed for the kitchen faucet knobs twice without being able to turn them. At last the hot water flowed and, whimpering, she scrubbed pieces of Sheriff Boyd from each finger and palm.

Through the kitchen window she glimpsed the store. Out of focus, grey, veiled behind sheets of dark clouds and rain. Forever blood red in her mind. She scoured her forearms and elbows with a vegetable brush.

Nancy burst through the screen door of the kitchen without knocking. Startled, Sterling whirled from the sink, arms and hands dripping water. Nancy clung to the screen door frame. Neither woman said anything. Nancy's splotched cheeks showed how she'd reacted when J.T. fetched Penix's gallon of homemade whiskey and told her about Sheriff Martin Boyd.

"Hurry," J.T. called from the bottom of the backdoor steps.

Without a word, Sterling opened a cabinet, handed over three Parson's glasses etched with grapes. Nancy snatched them, stiff-armed the backdoor screen, and handed them to her husband. Sterling remained paralyzed in the middle of the kitchen floor.

"Get those clothes off—all of them. Underwear too." Nancy bustled back into the kitchen like an old pro at covering up a bloodbath. "Where's your washer? I'll clean around here. Haul yourself into the shower. And mind that bandage on your head."

Sterling obeyed.

Standing under the blessed hot water, she opened her mouth, let the shower spray fill it — and tasted blood. She spewed it down. Water circled the tub drain along with the pinkish traces of Boyd's blood. Like her hopes and dreams. She felt the wet gauze bandage on her hairline and remembered Nancy's warning too late.

A sob burst from her, and another then another until her weak knees folded and she scratched at the tile walls for support.. Without thought she slid into the tub, burying her cries in crossed forearms lying on upraised knees. She could have died. Gray could have died. Her baby could have died. Their part in the murder would haunt Nancy and J.T. forever.

The hot water soothed her at first, then the shivering returned so strong, she couldn't rise. Every crevice of her body felt bloody. She itched to be clean. Scrubbing once didn't do it, so she lathered again.

This time she caressed the small bump in her belly as something real and tangible to her. She had responsibilities. Yes, she belonged in Crossville. People called to her on the street, Jennifer offered her recipes, Rose asked her to substitute at bridge, and Nancy laughed at her dumb jokes. She knew where everything was on the A&P shelves. But it all died with Sheriff Boyd.

Like always when she felt at home, she had to go. Her tears mourned a fantasy.

She ripped off the bandage, dressed the angry stitches, found clean clothes, and dried her hair. With a deep, cleansing breath she walked downstairs to a kitchen that carried no hint of what she'd dragged in. Neither did she. Mourning passed into doing what must be done to survive, to build a life for her child. She smelled yeast rolls and something with cinnamon. Warming heat from the oven eased her.

"Set the table for four." Nancy hurried in from the alcove where the washing machine churned.

"Let me call Tom. With any luck, someone will listen on the party line."

"Never happens when you want it to," Nancy quipped.

How normal they sounded.

"Hey, Tom." Sterling dialed up her cheeriest tone. "What time will you be home? Nancy came over to wash clothes, so we decided to eat together. We're setting our table for four tonight. We're hoping J.T. will be back from wherever he and the sheriff went in time for dinner."

"I've got a few things to do first. Be another hour or so." He paused. "You want company tonight?"

"Misery loves company. Nancy and I have been slaving over a hot stove for two hours already. Perfect thing for a rainy day. Made yeast rolls." Sterling glanced at Nancy. She scurried back to check the laundry.

"Town's in an uproar." Tom's voice dropped away.

In the second of silence between them, Sterling smiled. Occasionally, it was hard to tell if someone listened on the party line, but not this time.

"Sterling, I swear I . . ."

"See you soon, honey." Sterling hung up and gave Nancy a nod.

"I put some rum and Coke in glasses – let's go have a little taste in the living room." Nancy dried her hands on a kitchen towel, pointed toward the hallway with a nod.

Just the thing, a little liquor to take the edge off.

"Your clothes are in the wash. I added vinegar. Hope it works on blood. Probably ruined your jeans. E-everything's ruined."

Sterling grabbed Nancy's shoulders. "Take a breath."

"I can't stop, or I'll think. And if I think, I'll scream. If I scream, I'll never stop."

"J.T. saved my life. The sheriff was going to kill me. Now we've gotta work together to save all of us." Sterling pulled Nancy into a hug. She felt cold.

"I-I never saw so much blood. I'm scared to death."

"Me too," said Sterling.

"Who are you?" Then she screamed, "Who are you?"

Sterling wanted her to know. Still, the energy to tell Nancy the whole truth fell far beyond her.

"Private investigator. Someday, someday soon I hope, you'll have a great story to write." She tried a smile.

Nancy wheeled into the living room, grabbed one glass on the nearby table, and guzzled half the contents.

Sterling followed. "What happened to having a little taste?"

"You do this for a living?"

"Not after this assignment." To her surprise, tears pricked Sterling's eye.

"But you have done it?"

"Lots of times. Successfully."

"What about Tom?"

"Best he never knows what happened. He wouldn't be able to keep this secret. The fewer people who know, the better." She dropped her voice.

"Why did J.T. shoot Boyd?" Nancy cried. "Why did Boyd go crazy?"

"Do you really want to know, to put that picture in your head? God knows I wish I didn't." Sterling's tone oozed misery. "I never should have agreed to meet Boyd in the store."

Nancy stared. "That's all you're going to say?"

"You have enough secrets to keep."

"I guess." After a few moments, Nancy added, "You have to go away."

Sterling clasped Nancy's hand and said nothing.

CHAPTER FORTY-NINE

"Hey, Nancy, Sterling? Where are you girls?" J.T. called from the kitchen door.

When the two women reached him, he peered at them through the screen with a small smile. "Got a break. We – I mean, I — found a Klan hood stained with dried blood in the corner by two big barrels. Belongs to Penix or Murphy. I know 'cause I picked it up in the back room at the Emporium the day Harriet died and gave it to the sheriff. Some boot prints around it, so the sheriff must have had it. I dropped it out the back door. Penix and Murphy are as good as caught."

Nancy's low moan shamed Sterling. But it mustered no pity, dismay, or sadness. A man died today, and two men were framed for a murder they didn't commit – although J.T. pointed out that they killed Harriet Cook and helped murder Henry Johnson.

Was it justice? Sterling had no doubt. Was it legal? No doubt there either. She had to live with it. They all did. A whiff of burning wood reached her. "The fire?"

J.T. rubbed his nose carefully. "Yeah, homebrew lit up everything. Soaked everything, and I mean everything, real good. Shoe prints, blood stains – fire's already got some. I got to get on scene."

"Be careful," Nancy said. "I love you!"

Did she and Tom have a love like J.T and Nancy? Sterling's hand brushed her stomach. They had something. She watched J.T. walk over to the store's back door.

In the kitchen, Nancy stirred something on the stove. Yellow swirls of butter, lots of it, danced with her spoon and sloshed over the pan.

"Did you hit my husband in the nose and bust his cheekbone?"

"A giant misunderstanding."

"Good. He deserves it for not telling me what was eating him all this time, for not telling either of us what was going on after Harriet died. Hope you knocked some sense in him."

Sterling turned off the stove, grabbed the crook of Nancy's arm. "We got enough melted butter. Let's go have a real drink in the living room. Dinner's about ready . . . .. I hope it reheats well. But those rolls will rise in time to bake for dinner."

"He didn't tell me until yesterday how he drove up on Henry Johnson's murder. It wasn't until after they found the body that J.T. put it together—what he saw in Callie's Cutoff that day." Nancy gulped. "It's made him crazy for months."

Sterling gave her a gentle push toward the living room then peeked around the shade out the opposite side window. Wisps of smoke drifted out of the store's window, blended into the gloom. She let the shade drop back and followed Nancy.

"Are you some kind of civil rights agitator?" Nancy asked.

Sterling collapsed next to her against her favorite pile of pillows. "I gather evidence quietly, write it down, and leave. Someday those who murdered black people will go to trial."

"You have to know who J.T. saw in Callie's Cutoff when Henry Johnson died. J.T. will tell you. He's not a man to let such a thing slide. The sheriff thought he was. I knew better. Huh! My mom and dad know better."

"Who did he see? John Cross? The Carpenter boys? Penix, Murphy, the sheriff?"

"All of them and two deputies—Alvin is one of the deputies," Nancy said. "What about John Cross?"

"I saw his car outside the real estate office today. Just like the car Penix described to me once. Cross parked outside Parson's the day Henry Johnson died, watching and waiting to see what happened in Callie's Cutoff. He ran the local Klan from Washington, but there's no way to prove he killed anybody. I'm certain Cross knew about the ambush and waited nearby."

"Is there anyone who can make the dump go away?" Nancy cried. "Or does Cross get to mastermind a murder and make millions off ruining the town?"

Sterling eased against the back cushions. "I don't know about the murder. But I know someone who might know something about Cross and his land. She's gonna need help."

"Who?"

Sterling grinned at Nancy.

201

CHAPTER FIFTY

Gray dove headfirst beneath the knee-deep water of the creek running behind the store. The cold didn't bother him at first -- terror kept him warm. He used a rock to scrub as he walked through the water.

Was anyone lurking in the woods? Not today. It was luck, but the storm tilted the odds in his favor. He removed his blue-checkered shirt, scoured it on rocks, then dragged it to get rid of the blood.

One last time he turned toward the store, and nearly tripped over a submerged tree limb. The building lay behind a curtain of distance, dying leaves, pine needles, and heavy rain falling in sheets. Too soon for the fire to begin. Odd he believed the deputy—a sheriff's deputy—could pull this off. Probably because he believed Sterling would help him.

Gray blessed the canopy of trees hanging over the water and shielding him from houses, fields, and a street as he ran through the creek. He pumped his arms and slapped the shirt around him to stave off the cold.

Once he stumbled and sank in a deep pool. Rather than frighten him, the water closing over his head made him feel clean, filled him with hope for survival. He ducked under again, rubbing his hair, ears, and every fiber of his clothes. He refused to end up like his father on the end of a white man's rope.

When he could make out the back of a few South End buildings, he jumped out of the creek bed and ran through a muddy field. He tried to put his shirt on. It whipped about, and his stiff, disobedient fingers lost their grip. The wind snatched it away.

With a curse, Gray jogged toward the general store. He judged where it was by its misshapen roof and the light in the barbershop next door. Underneath the store's roof overhang, he gathered his breath and leaned out to see the street. Nobody braved the weather to walk on the sidewalks or drive on the street.

The bite of the wind between the store and the barbershop next door grabbed at his bowels. A clap of thunder and the heavens opened again. Gray forced his legs to run, his arms to swing about and beat his back for warmth as he crossed the street for home.

In the street, distant car headlights shone, and he raced for the sidewalk hoping the driver did not see who it was. Pricks like tiny ice picks stung his feet and legs as he went around back to the stairs leading to his room. He only paused to remove his muddy shoes.

Tiptoeing the whole way through the outer door and down the short hall, he shut the bedroom door as quiet as trembling hands allowed. Blessed warmth from an old radiator covered him like a lover. He shed his pants, socks, and underwear inside the doorway, wiped himself down with a towel then draped his wet clothes over the radiator under his one window. His teeth rattled so loud from the cold he barely heard the sizzle of his clothes on the radiator.

His search in a chest of drawers for clean clothes yielded a prize. Under his other shirt, he found a small bottle of whiskey kept as a treat. He took a big gulp and welcomed the fire spreading through him. Warmer now, he grabbed a wash rag to mop the damp footprints in the hall and doorway.

"Mr. Gray? Mr. Gray," called his landlady from downstairs. "You there?"

Feet still tingling with pricks of cold, he hobbled closer to the downstairs. "Yes, ma'am. I fell asleep. Just woke up."

His landlady harrumphed. "Musta been sleeping hard. I hollered for supper. Come on down and git you some ham and biscuits."

To his surprise, his stomach growled. Getting something to eat risked seeing tiny lines streak across his landlady's brow and hearing a lecture about the evils of liquor. "Thank you, ma'am. I'll be there directly."

He ate his ham and biscuits at the kitchen table without her disapproval. An awful stench rose from the stove, but he hadn't the nerve to ask her about it. Lips pressed together his landlady hummed to herself as she stirred the black iron pot. After a minute, her head bobbed, and the 'kerchief she wore on it slipped a little to the left. She added a powder which made the god-awful stink worse, then smeared the foul-looking mixture on a rag, rolled it, and handed it to him.

"Put this poultice 'round your eye and nose where it swellin' up." The lines on her forehead faded as she shooed him off. "Git on to bed."

Gray sighed his gratitude. Once upstairs he washed down his dinner with more whiskey. Holding the poultice to his aching cheek, he crawled under two blankets and shivered. His mother, a statuesque woman who valued learning as much as life, would be disappointed that he abandoned his studies so close to graduation. His father, who punched a white man for insulting his wife and died for it, would be proud. And Sterling? What did it matter what she thought? She was gone. He stuffed a corner of his pillow in his mouth and screamed.

CHAPTER FIFTY-ONE

Red and yellow-tipped flames from the old store attracted the attention of someone driving down the street at last. The fire's speed in such wet weather surprised Sterling. The homemade whiskey Murphy and Penix left J.T. proved highly flammable.

She and Nancy raced onto the front porch as fire engines wailed into view. Firemen unrolled hoses and tromped all over the ground surrounding the store. Sheriff's Department cars screeched to the curb and deputies raced around the store to secure the scene. Sterling released a soft breath. No worry about authorities finding strange footprints or wondering about trampled weeds.

During the initial confusion, sirens, and red lights someone yelled for Nancy. From the back of the store two deputies assisted a bloody J.T. and loaded him into a sheriff's car. Nancy jumped in beside him for the trip to the hospital.

Tom drove onto the street and had to park a block away. He ran home hollering for Sterling to get out of the house in case the blaze spread. His alarm gave her an excuse to duck inside and gather some of her valuables in a suitcase to take outside.

Tom walked beside her to his car, trying to talk to her, whispering his regret whenever he could. When the firemen contained the danger, she went back into the house, bustling around giving the volunteers cool drinks.

At last she went upstairs to get volunteers some towels to wipe their faces on. Tom followed and cornered her in the bathroom.

"Give me a chance to explain."

She tried to get past him, but he refused to remove his arm from the edge of the sink.

"I invested in the company for the sake of the investigation. All of us at Homestead Realty bought stock in Cross's company. It was expected."

JACKIE ROSS FLAUM

He made a certain amount of sense. "Why didn't you tell me?"

"This right here, Sterling. You doubt me. You have from the start."

"I doubted you as an investigator, not as a human being. How was it not important to tell me Cross had a company you bought into?"

He shrugged. "I was hoping to use my ownership in the company to get information about it, about what he was up to."

She wanted to believe him. "People died to give Cross the land."

"How can I fix us?" He leaned close.

"Did you know what Cross planned, Tom?" A whisper.

He crossed his heart. "I had no idea how massive it was."

"Did you know the project was a dump?" She couldn't wrap her mind around it.

"Yes. All the company owners just got huge payments from the new military dump." He reached in his pants pocket for a paper and opened a green paper check, so the numbers were plain. "Cross fooled us."

More like blinded them with money. The figure she saw made her grasp the bathroom sink. "H-How did he fool so many people?"

"Most people want to believe, especially when a man is promising them money like they never thought possible. I saw enough money to build a real future for my baby. Cross was slick, and he had George's seal of approval," Tom admitted. "I thought I was too smart to be conned."

"But dumping trash in the town's front yard on land stolen from poor Black people?"

Tom threw up his hands. "Cross had the land before we got here."

She gritted her teeth, wishing she took everything in as fast as it hit her. Murder, a cover-up, a pretty little town ruined, Gray gone for good. A ruined career. Somehow Tom's investing in a garbage dump seemed minor. Every agent violated one or two rules on this case.

"I spent a lot of time in the library, talking to people on the phone who knew about garbage dumps, and called a few lawyers on zoning," Tom said. "Let me try to fix it."

She shook her head. He took both her arms and for a second tried to hold her. His anger softened. "I, ah, I went by the office, brought home all the papers I had on the deal. Ah, a few folders from George's drawers—somehow the lock had fallen off them. Maybe I can spot something we can use."

Sterling left the bathroom. She couldn't bear to hear anymore.

Several hours later, firemen stomping out the last embers of the blaze, and deputies acting on what J.T. told them located the charred remains of Sheriff Martin Boyd. In a flurry of activity sheriff's deputies assumed control of the murder scene and its environs. The state police arrived. And, later, FBI agents headquartered in Atlanta appeared.

JUSTICE TOMORROW

To Sterling's dismay, their house and porch became the de facto headquarters for law enforcement investigating the murder and fire. Why all the investigators for a fire and murder — even the murder of a sheriff? The question nagged while she served coffee long into the night.

At various times all the law enforcement agencies questioned Sterling, keeping her nervous stomach near the tipping point. Tom glowered and growled at anyone who upset his wife. She found it helpful and, to her astonishment, endearing.

She didn't have much to tell them. The discovery of a military dump on Crossville's doorstep and the gloomy weather caused her to draw all the shades and hole up at home. Later in the afternoon Nancy had come over. The two of them washed some clothes, tried a new roll recipe for a planned couples' dinner, and had a few drinks.

J.T.'s performances, most of which she missed, must have been impressive. Sterling bit her tongue to keep from cheering as he talked with the state detective in her living room. According to J.T., Boyd picked him up and said he would meet Murphy and Penix in the old store. Since several deputies knew the sheriff went hunting for the pair after Harriet's murder, J.T.'s story rang true.

Meeting the two men in the old store struck him as odd, J.T. told investigators, but Boyd went in the front door and stationed him out back with orders to watch. He walked around some then laid low in the weeds when Penix and Murphy slipped in the back way. At first, laughter. Suddenly loud voices, arguing – about what he couldn't tell. Then he heard crashing, swearing, fighting. Alarmed, he rushed inside but got whacked. He came around and crawled through smoke toward the back. Rescuers discovered him midway down the stairs.

Nancy told deputies some of the truth. She gave them the time the sheriff knocked on the door for J.T. She heard the sheriff mention Murphy and Penix. She also recalled glancing out Sterling's kitchen door to see two white men running behind the store but thought nothing of it. There were no more credible witnesses, so the acting sheriff sent officers to bring in Murphy and Penix.

Meanwhile, the FBI discovered two teenage boys who saw a colored man running through the creek from the direction of the store. He jumped in deep water a couple of times, which they thought powerful strange in the weather. Then the colored man waded up the creek out of sight. The boys gave vague descriptions that the FBI agent filed. The agent also noted he found the glassy-eyed teenagers camped in a pup tent drinking whiskey stolen from their fathers.

But the report galvanized Sheriff Boyd's deputies once they connected it with a call previously relegated to the round file. In the uproar following news of Boyd's murder, the sheriff's office was flooded with tips from good citizens. Deputies kept a log of even the most minor and unlikely calls. A woman noticed a tall person hiding under her oak. A motorist driving through the colored section after dark saw "a bare-chested drowned Black rat" running across the street from behind Ferry's store.

When she learned of those reports, Sterling cringed as though the Grim Reaper had tiptoed up behind her. God knows when such things might pop up to bite you.

The fire next door to her house smoldered for hours while the firemen kept watch. Near midnight a deputy carried in paper sacks of evidence: a jug of the type Penix used for his brew, and broken pieces of glasses given away at Parson's where Penix and Murphy hung out. Sterling served more coffee while a state police detective listened to where and how the deputy found the evidence inside the bags.

"Seems we need to find these boys and have a talk," suggested a soft-spoken state detective. He swung to the acting sheriff.

The man stiffened. "We'll find Penix and Murphy. I figure we can handle the case from here."

The state policeman didn't seem to realize what he was hearing. But Sterling, serving hastily made sandwiches, knew the acting deputy was saying, "Go away." Soon after, the state police detective and his fellow officers found themselves on their way back to Atlanta.

After the last lawman left her house, Sterling struggled to bed. Tom crawled in beside her, drew her next to his warmth, and whispered, "I need you, Sterling."

"I-I need to think." She turned over, her back to him. After a moment he eased out of bed and went to the next room to sleep.

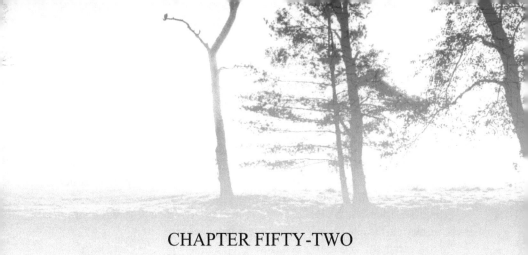

CHAPTER FIFTY-TWO

Blood dripped from her arm as Gray laid Sterling in the hole dug in the Alabama woods. He dragged the deer over her as an offering to the braying men and dogs. She remained silent and immovable; her soul tethered to Gray's words.

"I need you to be still, Sterling." Gray had whispered as the deer's blood mingled with theirs.

"I need you, Sterling," he'd said yesterday with Sheriff Boyd's blood staining them both.

Sterling jerked awake, panting, sweating, patting the mattress, and flinging off the covers. Her eyes flew around the room until she caught light around the edges of the white bedroom window shades. The stench of charred wood from the fire next door filled the room. Her hand groped the bed in search of Tom.

Where was he? Then she remembered. Hugging herself, she burrowed deep under the covers. Her future, once so clear, now loomed cloudy and unfathomable. Hard to think today that it was so much less than she'd hoped for. Lost homes, loves, jobs, illusions. Her mistake falling for Tom—if it was a mistake — paled beside the death, destruction, and betrayals of yesterday. She hurt all over, wounded too deep to measure. Everyone in Crossville must be feeling lost and afraid this morning. Thank God it wasn't raining anymore.

Jennifer Mullins would be her first visit this morning. Jennifer used her, and she had to answer for it. Sterling skipped her usual shower. She'd bathed twice last night. Instead she got up, yanked a comb through her hair – always a chore with curly hair – and dressed in an over-sized blue work shirt and tight jeans. Another month the jeans wouldn't fit at all. She took the steps one at a time, still struggling to fasten her jeans button. At the foot of the stairs she halted.

Brows furrowed in concentration, Tom sat in the living room chair with a full ashtray of cigarette butts at one hand, a pencil behind one ear, and a mug of coffee in his free hand. Neat stacks of papers and library books sat all around him. A shaky metal TV tray put more piles of paperbacks and paper within his reach.

He didn't notice her until she said, "Studying for finals?"

His head jerked. "Oh . . . morning. I, uh, I'm going over all these contracts, filings, and stuff on Cross's company and the dump. Shoulda done it earlier."

"Hmm-m . . ." Sterling mumbled.

Tom lifted the book he was reading. "I made a few calls last night, stopped at the library yesterday – that's where I learned about the fire."

"What a tragedy." Her stomach hurt.

"Boyd's death? Somebody did us a favor."

"No, I-I mean, this town. The people who invested in it, who live in it — the farmers. They lost everything. Their land, livelihood, even their houses. Those shacks set way in the trees? Cross tore them down."

"Sterling . . ." Tom began.

She headed for the kitchen in search of coffee, cereal, and a place to feel sorry for herself.

He followed. "I think I found something."

"Something?" She fumbled in the cabinet for a cup.

"I think so. 'Course there's the little problem of getting everybody to agree – mostly Cross." Tom poured himself more coffee.

He had her attention.

"There's no getting the houses back," he went on. "And I can't see Cross giving back a single acre he took from each Black farmer. There might be a compromise."

A smattering of hope. "Can Cross afford to have the dump and give back the land he took from the farmers?"

"A stretch but, yeah."

Sterling wrinkled her nose. "But it stinks! An-d it looks god-awful."

"Honey, bulldozers can dig deep pits for the garbage and cover it up. It's a new idea but makes sense. I talked to somebody about it yesterday, read up on the idea early this morning. Or maybe it was last night. To make it real simple, you dig a deep pit for garbage, sprinkle lye or something to break it up—hell, it could be fairy dust for all I know about it now. Then you bury it, dump more trash in the same spot, repeat, and repeat."

"Like making lasagna," she mumbled.

"Set it back far enough from the main road, decorate with a bunch of trees, flowers, and a nicer wall than Cross threw up."

"Decorate?" She chuckled, her spirits lighter.

"Trouble is, Cross has so much land he doesn't have to go to the trouble or expense of layering the shit to satisfy his military contracts." Tom got up, retrieved her neglected coffee cup by the stove, and filled it for her. "We might appeal to the county zoning board and claim what – nobody read the tiny, longwinded legal ad in the newspaper about the change in land use? Probably won't work, since Cross filed the notice, and nobody filed an objection to a 'sanitation, beautification, and development' project. I think people who had a mistaken idea of what was happening planned to enjoy any business it brought."

"Like the Andersons and Epsons?" she asked.

"It stands to reason."

"They knew it was a dump?" The idea intrigued her. "I can't believe it."

"Me either. They must have been told it was something else. Or, like me, they thought it was a small project back in the woods. Now, I haven't researched much about a legal appeal. I've got a better idea."

One of her eyebrows arched.

"The stockholders in his company can make Cross cooperate."

He explained about shareholders and voting— Sterling had trouble following his discussion of company finances so early in the morning. She took a sip of coffee. "What's the problem?"

"Four of us Cross stockholders want the town back to normal," he said.

"Not enough?

"I'm sure two stockholders, George Thompson or his nephew in Atlanta, wouldn't vote to cost the company so much money. Cuts in on company profits, which translates to company dividends, which means shareholders like George, Cross, and me make less money." He scratched his chin thoughtfully. "We need a big-money investor, someone who will find the value in keeping the town."

"Know someone?"

"Nobody I'll go to unless I have to." Tom's top lip curled. "If I do, the mother of my child is the person I want with me."

Sterling laughed. "Very sweet. But let's go back to George. Can't we fry him somehow? He used his official job to make money from a zoning request. Hold the threat of jail over his head to get him to vote with you. It can't be legal."

"We have to prove it. Hell, first we have to find him. He's not returning anyone's call that I know of. Takes time, and trucks are rolling. The easiest way is to figure how to make it worthwhile for the company to bury garbage, set the landfill back from the road, and surrender land," said Tom.

Sterling sipped her coffee. "What if Cross doesn't legally own the land? What if the Black farmers he evicted still own it?"

"That would void the contract with the military. You can't use what you don't own or rent."

"Simple?"

"Nothing is simple with the law. You got lawyers, filings, court dates, and such. In the end, though . . .." Tom shrugged

Sterling smiled. "And your law degree is from . . ."

"Vanderbilt University."

"Ha-ha."

"No. Well, Sterling, I went to law school. I don't really like the law."

"You're full of surprises."

Tom shoved his coffee cup aside. "Court cases – especially as many as the farmers have – are expensive. I know there are folks in Crossville to pay the farmers' legal fees, but . . .."

"The cases will tie up the landfill operation for years. The military might move on." Sterling chuckled.

"Yeah, we could use it." He folded his hands on the table. "How do we get proof the black farmers really own the land they farmed so long? Does Gray have it?"

"No, but I'm pretty sure I know who has what we want." Sterling left the table to put her cup in the sink. "Gray'll be gone today. Maybe he left already."

"Gone?" Tom brightened.

"And so am I. I'm going to get proof you can use in your stockholder plan."

"Life with you will never be dull." Tom laughed. Sterling kept on walking, but his voice followed. "I know you're still mad. But I'm gonna make it right. I'll win you back."

CHAPTER FIFTY-THREE

Through the greying lace curtains of his upstairs bedroom, Gray watched county patrol cars ease down on either side of the wet street. Once in a while a sheriff's deputy got out, knocked on doors, or questioned random young people on the street. How long until his turn? A deputy's voice rose from the street below. He shouted at a skinny man Gray didn't know. Instead of leaning back from the assault, the man stood erect and immobile.

Gray's gut clenched. He rubbed his forehead. One more time he'd play dumb and drunk for the man. One more time. He found his bourbon, dabbed a drop on his tongue. Enough to create a lingering odor.

The sun broke from the clouds and shone through his window just as the knock came.

"Mr. Gray! Mr. Gray, deputy sheriff wants ya," Mrs. Carson called from the foot of the stairs.

"Yes ma'am. I'm coming." Gray made sure his feet made enough noise, so the officer heard and did not storm through the little house after him.

A dark-haired deputy, who announced himself as Deputy Alvin Hankins, stood barely a foot inside Mrs. Carson's house, filling the open front door space like a misshapen boulder dressed in tan and black.

"I knows you," said Mrs. Carson.

Gray remembered seeing him around town, but Hankins never looked so big. He'd never noticed the big hand or the bushy eyebrows that nearly grew across the man's nose.

"Y'all come in and set yourself, Deputy Hankins." Mrs. Carson gave a tight wave of her hand toward the sitting area to the right of the stairs. She carried her tiny body erect and stiff as she led the way.

JACKIE ROSS FLAUM

Hankins did not remove his black-brimmed cap or wipe his muddy shoes when he walked into the house. He remained standing beside Mrs. Carson with his fingers hooked in his equipment belt. "Your name Gray?"

"Yassir." Gray put a steadying hand on the back of a cane-backed chair.

"Gray what? What's your name?"

"Socrates Gray."

"Socrates, huh?" Hankins snickered. "Where y'all from, Sock-ro-teez?"

"Mississippi. I come to work. I does odd jobs at the Post Office — and for Missrus Cook 'til she . . ."

"How long you been here, boy?"

Gray scratched his chin. "Month?"

"You go out last night, boy?"

Mrs. Carson made a disgusted noise deep in her throat. The officer's attention shifted to her and back to Gray.

"I drank a little." Gray studied the ground, heart pounding.

"A little?" Hankins leaned down a bit to glimpse up in Gray's face, and Gray fought the urge to rub the bruise on his cheek.

"This here fool got hisself stinkin' drunk, ran out across the street in the rain then come hollerin' back a minute or two later like he was touched in the head," Mrs. Carson huffed.

"Ah, you see all this?" The deputy asked the landlady.

"And I shore wish I ain't never seen it!"

"Boy, you go running in the creek?" Hankins whipped around to Gray.

"No, sir." Gray clashed his hands together to mask the shaking.

Mrs. Carson sniffed, fingered the bun in her hair, and stiffened her spine.

"Auntie, you say he went across the street?"

"I seen what I seen." Mrs. Carson drew herself up and spoke as though each word was distasteful. "He woke me a-hollering. I heard him upstairs for a whilst then he run down them back stairs and 'cross the street. I gits up and sees him out that front winder. It a'raining so hard I seen nuthin', then of a sudden, here he come again. I won't have such in my house. No sir. I am a God-fearin' woman."

"Yes, ma'am." Gray dipped his head lower, listened to Hankin's breathing and tried to figure what the man would do. Suddenly the deputy clapped his hands and Gray flinched.

The deputy chuckled, wagged his finger at Gray. "You hung-over."

Gray winced. "I ain't feeling myself."

"Sheriff Boyd got killed down at the old general store last night. You know anything about that?"

"No sir!"

"We're wanting to know where everybody was last night." The deputy

214

planted his feet shoulder-width apart.

By 'everybody' Gray knew he meant every black male.

The deputy leaned toward Gray. "You know anything about the killing, boy?"

Gray shook his head slowly.

"You see anything else, Auntie?"

Mrs. Carson drew herself up and closed her mouth. Her lips nearly turned white.

"Well, you think of something there's a re-ward." Hankins rubbed his two fingers together to show he meant paper money.

Mrs. Carson walked to the front door, opened it, and after a moment, Hankins clucked to himself and strode out. She shut it with care, shuffled to the kitchen and banged the skillets and pans. She manhandled the damper on her wood-burning stove until the fire inside the stove belly burned red.

Gray exhaled slow. He eased into the chair nearest him with a ragged sigh.

Two plates hit the tablecloth on the kitchen dining table near the stove. "Eat some breakfast." Mrs. Carson opened a drawer and flatware rattled. "I 'pect this ain't the last of it. You gotta git on to the post office."

CHAPTER FIFTY-FOUR

Jennifer Mullins opened her front door so slowly the massive white gardenia wreath hanging there did not wiggle. "Sterling, you poor thing. I heard about the fire."

"Can I come in?"

"'Course." Jennifer stepped aside and led her into the living room. Her posture was perfectly correct, almost stiff. "How're you feeling? Aren't you afraid those men will come after you?"

"Why should they? I don't know who they are."

"Maybe they think you do. Coffee?"

Sterling shook her head, sat on the edge of a green floral chair which matched a nearby sofa, and inspected. The rose-colored ceramic ashtrays in the shape of gardenias made her smile. A comfortable room, but Jennifer cleared her throat like she was anything but relaxed.

"I made a delicious coffee cake. Want to try it?"

"Jennifer, I thought we were friends. Stop pretending you don't know why I'm here. It stinks like the garbage dump."

Jennifer's shoulders sagged. "Nobody knew what John Cross planned. He called it a military installation."

"He wasn't lying. We just pictured a military installation like an airbase." Incredible. So many people were hoodwinked, Sterling thought.

Jennifer hung her head. "I don't think you understand how things were before Cross brought his proposal. Sure, my family owns lots of property. But you can't eat land. All you can do is pay taxes on it unless someone wants to buy it."

JUSTICE TOMORROW

"And no one wanted to buy it until Cross came along," Sterling said.

"He held out the real possibility for the first time in ages that someone in this dead town would want to," Jennifer said. "You can't sell land unless people have jobs. Then they have money to buy houses, shop, or build businesses on land you own."

"Nobody thought to ask specifics about the installation?" Sterling asked.

"John, my daddy, my uncle—everybody asked. Cross owns a lot of land around his planned landfill acres, and he showed them blueprints for his own housing and shops there. He started laying sewer pipes! A landfill that didn't pose a threat to his other projects was no threat to the town—or so it seemed."

"Jennifer, all he has to do is let the pigs roam on the surrounding land and he can expand the dump—which is what he will have to do to satisfy his contract with the military."

"I know. Now. Please understand, Cross's development promised to bring millions of dollars to our town. Jobs for everyone – jobs for Negroes too. My family invested thousands of dollars in improvements in Crossville. It's what my people have done for generations. My ancestors cleared this land, laid out the town as it is now."

"That's why you ripped out pages of Aunt Amelia's diary? Why you took the deeds that proved the Black farmers really did own their land?" Sterling asked. "To get jobs for Negroes."

"Don't be—."

"Your family probably put everything they had into the new housing development, the new hardware store, fixing up the A&P. Painting over every dirty board and rock. You thought keeping the deeds secret protected your investments and ensured the Cross project went through. Everyone gains— except the black families who lost what little they had. Then you got suspicious about what Cross was really up to. Or felt uneasy somehow."

Jennifer played with her wedding ring.

"What made you question what was going on?"

"It wasn't the secrecy about it. Developers play things close to the vest. My uncle and my husband always do." Jennifer quietened her busy fingers and folded them in her lap. "But Cross measured each word he spoke. He reminded me of a sneaky weasel."

"And he is a Cross."

"Maybe . . . I never believed the military needed to build here. Not so close to what they already have."

"Why did you let me near the diary?" Sterling wondered. "You dangled that gold frame at me."

"Hideous, isn't it?"

The two women smiled.

217

"I'm betting you kept the deeds and torn out pages from Aunt Amelia's diary taped under the brown paper in that frame."

"They're in the chest of drawers over there now. I know what I did was wrong, Sterling. Some people, Rose or maybe Nancy, will say, 'Oh, it's just some Negroes. What are their pitiful farms compared to the welfare of the whole town?'"

Sterling started to defend Nancy but thought better.

"I know those people—played with their kids growing up. Mr. Anders' son, Al, got killed in a car wreck . . ." Jennifer wet her lips. "A very fine man."

More than casual friends by the way she emphasized each word of the last sentence.

"I bumped into him when I graduated from college and went abroad for a month with friends. Imagine recognizing someone from home in Paris? We backpacked – all five of us -- around Europe."

"You refused to stand up to your mother or your friends in defense of a bunch of poor colored people. Even for the sake of a friend?"

Jennifer's sharp snicker pained Sterling. "My mother's a segregationist. Her life, her position in this town, everything she feels about herself depends on her roots. And, well, you saw the way Rose acted when I mentioned an old rumor about my aunt running off with a former slave. She was incapable of speech for two whole minutes."

"Callie did run off with Lucius. And her tutor helped."

"I read it in the diary and I —." Jennifer's hands twisted.

"Who killed her?"

"Aunt Amelia never came out and said. She only mentioned how her father –."

"Dear Papa."

Jennifer gave her a crooked smile. "'Dear Papa' led the search for his daughter Callie and came back with the news of her death. I removed the pages where Aunt Amelia describes finding out about Callie and Lucius, about their plans to run away with Mr. Arnett's help. Aunt Amelia was a true child of her time. Callie horrified her by favoring a colored man, but she kept quiet out of love for her older sister – and the threat of Callie spilling the beans about Stephen."

"Did she say anything about who killed Callie?" Sterling leaned forward.

Jennifer shook her head. "She wrote of a horrible suspicion too dreadful for words. And how distraught her father acted after Callie died, drinking and muttering for weeks about blood on his hands. She knew her father killed Callie. She never referred to him as 'Dear Papa' again."

"That's all she wrote about it?"

"She mentioned her father misplaced his cavalry sabre and scabbard. And she expresses wonder when her father gives such a lot of land to several of his hired men in gratitude for their help searching for Callie. You know, my family has looked for the sabre and scabbard. Made by John Griswold & Co. of New Orleans and presented to 'Dear Papa' for his service to the Confederacy. From what she wrote, Aunt Amelia thinks he lost them while he and his men searched for Callie. I think—well, it's too awful for words to believe he killed his own daughter."

Sabre wounds might pass for arrow holes by those willing to believe. Epson probably took only his most loyal men in the search party. Men with the last names of Penix and Murphy. Men given acres of Epson land in gratitude for their service.

"I also took out the page where Aunt Amelia wondered why anyone thought Callie was in love with Arnett," said Jennifer. "You'll want to see it. The pages mention more land John Cross gave away and names the former slaves who got it."

"I bet Aunt Amelia's dalliance with Stephen was no big deal after Callie died." Sterling mused.

"When he came to offer his condolences like everyone else in town, Aunt Amelia said John Cross referred to Callie as, 'Your foolishly brave sister.'"

"John Cross knew about Callie and Lucius?" Sterling found it shocking. The John Cross she'd read about surely used it against the Epsons somehow.

Jennifer shrugged.

"Why did Stephen allow all the suspicion to continue about him? I thought he left town," Sterling said.

"According to Aunt Amelia, Stephen pretended to leave, but ran to a cabin in the woods owned by the Epson family. He and Aunt Amelia were together when Callie died. He was protecting her—and pretending to be gone was his only way back into his father's good graces." Jennifer wore a sly grin. "I cut out those pages too. My maiden aunt may have been unmarried, but she was no virgin."

The slamming kitchen door cut off their giggles.

"Jennifer? Why haven't you answered my calls?" Alice Peterson called.

"In the living room, Mother."

"Why are you avoiding me? It's your bridge club, isn't it? I know what ridiculous notions you girls are talking about," Alice's plaid A-line skirt swished to a halt.

"Morning, Mrs. Peterson." Sterling rose.

She raked Sterling up and down with her eyes. "I see you're feeling better. I haven't seen you since Harriet . . . died."

"I'll be at the service tomorrow." Sterling touched her bandage as though she just remembered it was there.

"I miss Harriet." Alice's hard expression slipped into sorrow. "She was worth a thousand other people."

"Jennifer and I are talking about my research on your family, Mrs. Peterson."

"I thought you quit after the sheriff arrested you."

"He didn't arrest—." Sterling pressed her lips together and began again. "You'll be pleased to hear your family history might be important in saving Crossville from the dump."

Alice grabbed the pearls around her neck and hung on. "Really."

"She read Aunt Amelia's diary."

"My God, Jennifer!"

"I found deeds tucked inside," Sterling rushed to say. "Those papers, plus other things Amelia Epson wrote about the Cross land, proves John Cross has no claim on much of the land he's now using for a military garbage site."

Alice Peterson's mouth moved but nothing came out.

"I know that if you or Jennifer had read the diary first you would have recognized its importance and taken the deeds straight to the county courthouse to be recorded again. The originals burned in the courthouse fire after the Civil War. You would have stopped the garbage dump in its tracks." Sterling went on.

Jennifer's eyes filled with tears.

"Thank God you allowed me to read the diary. I'm disappointed so many of the pages were unreadable. Moths, water damage, and just plain old age, I suppose. Anyway, congratulations." Sterling said.

Alice found her voice. "Well, I-I guess . . . do you believe John Cross's awful dump can be, ah, dumped?"

"My husband thinks so. He's one of the Cross company stockholders. I am so proud to be your friend," Sterling concluded with a flourish.

"This is such good news." Jennifer patted her mother on the back. "Sit, Mother. I'll get some coffee for us."

"No, no. I-I have to go home. Your father will be delighted to . . ." She scrutinized Jennifer for a second. "Are you sure?"

"See for yourself, Mother. Sterling brought these over." Jennifer walked to the credenza along the far living room wall, opened a drawer, and took out two

JUSTICE TOMORROW

pieces of yellowed paper wrapped in tissue. Alice held out her hand for them.

"Harriet would make you put on white gloves before you read them," Sterling breathed.

"Yes, she would. The old crank." Alice sniffed. Lifting a deed, she held it to the light, turned it over, examined it. At last she announced: "It's genuine. Anyone would be a fool to doubt it. I've seen enough of old John Cross's handwriting to recognize it. Jennifer, Aunt Amelia has come to our rescue."

She dropped the deed back on the tissue paper and took her leave. Sterling watched her go in amusement. The kitchen door slammed. Jennifer snickered.

"She acts like she's never seen those deeds." Sterling didn't bother to hide her astonishment.

"We were both in a bad place. And Mother's already mad about my Methodist Bible group discussing racial justice. She and her friends think it's not Christian." Jennifer brightened. "I made a chess pie if you'd like a piece."

"I don't want anything, Jennifer. Look how tight my jeans are. I'm going before you foist any baked goods on me."

"What about the deeds?"

Fury rose from the bottom of Sterling's toes. "You need to finish this. What if I hadn't gotten interested in your family history? What would you have done?"

"I-I don't know."

"How did you know I would catch on to what I read?"

"Oh, Sterling. I hoped, prayed, gave you hints, and cooking lessons."

Sterling grabbed for the front door handle. "Jennifer, why didn't you pull the deeds yourself?"

"I couldn't let everybody know what I'd done. I hid the diary and the deeds and let those people lose their homes. I might have been arrested or sued for being a fraud."

Fraud? Probably not. Still, Jennifer's attack of conscience wasn't all about brotherly love and Jesus. "I found them, and you're a big hero. Get your coat. I'm calling Nancy and giving her a big story. We are going to the county courthouse and file these deeds as soon as the press arrives."

Jennifer stared in open-mouth horror. "You're not going to the courthouse dressed like that?"

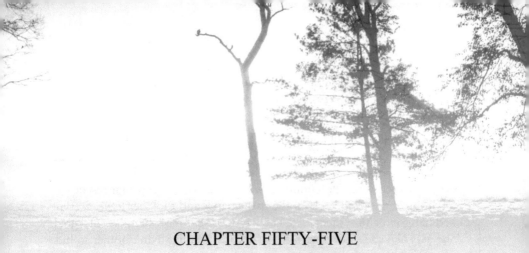

CHAPTER FIFTY-FIVE

Gray finished breakfast with his landlady and forced himself to go outside the boarding house. Was anyone watching? He closed a blue cardigan around him tight with both hands while scanning the dilapidated brick and wood buildings around him.

Not many folks about. Maybe the weather, but more likely the police sweep was keeping folks inside. Water rippled in the potholes. An old Chevy sedan splashed through a puddle and someone inside hollered at him. His head whipped around, but the car passed.

Lowering his head against the breeze, he crossed the road in a jog and scooted between two cars parked in front of the grocery. Usually, three or four vehicles and drivers waited there for passengers every morning since the boycott began. They traveled together to nearby Leesville and North Park, so people could work or buy goods. Gray frowned as he headed toward the red and blue barbershop pole.

Carl swept the floor of an empty place.

"You closed?" Gray peered toward the back.

Carl leaned on a broom almost as tall as him. "Na." His head bobbed toward the sidewalk where sheriff's cars still patrolled and young men foolish enough to hit the street got questioned.

"Yeah, they come to Mrs. Carson's. I talked to 'em. I -I had too much whiskey last night."

"Uh-huh." Carl pored over the ads for hair products tacked on the dingy yellowed wall all whopperjawed. He tapped the broom on the floor twice. "Ain't nobody here but you and me. Sit up in the chair and I'll give ya a trim."

"You cut my hair last week."

"Git up there."

Gray's gut churned. Carl hummed as he flapped a faded white cloth cape in the air and let it drift slowly over Gray's lap, then tied it around his neck.

"'Member I live out back a this shop." The big knuckles on his arthritic fingers moved over his selection of combs until he found one he favored. "Don't sleep good. Old age, I reckon. I look outta my bedroom winder in the dark, wishin' my Bessie was here, wishin' things was different. Most nights I see nothing 'cept God. Last night I seen you. Missin' your shirt."

Gray jerked. Carl's hand bowed his neck. The clippers buzzed.

"Brother, you come from the crick like the devil was on your tail. Now I hear the sheriff got hisself kilt in that old store runs behin' that same crick. Store caught fire an' burnt clear up." He unplugged the clippers, blew on Gray's neck.

Gray hesitated a split second. "You think they know who did it?"

"Well, folks is afraid it was one of us." He took the barber's brush off a nearby tray and wiped the hairs off Gray's neck. "So's the po-lice, but they ain't saying."

"I was drinking, got caught drunk in the storm, and fell." Gray reached around, untied the cape, and yanked it off his neck.

"Hmm-m," Carl mused. "Found me a shirt on the edge of the crick this morning. Blue checkered." This time his eyes held Gray's. "I had to step in muddy footprints to git it."

"Got a sour stomach and a headache this morning." Gray set his jaw.

"You walk like you beat up inside."

"Too much whiskey'll do it." Gray's shaky hands dug into his pocket for some coins to pay the bill. His fingers brushed his father's knife.

"Uh-huh." Carl's head slowly bobbed to a rhythmic but tuneless hum. "Well, they axed me, an' I says I was sleepin'."

"Did you?"

"They real serious. They talked to Silas Ramsey—he simple, always was. He tells them what he knows without them hardly axing. When he said nothing, them deputies beat him, so's he piss blood." Carl clenched his teeth. "Maybe Ajamu's right. The boycott be working but folks getting hungry for more."

"I-I gotta get to the Post Office, Carl." Gray had no good answer to Ajamu today.

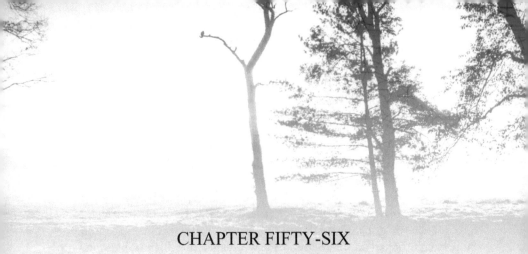

CHAPTER FIFTY-SIX

A shaken Crossville buried its amateur historian and closet integrationist, Harriet Cook, on a cold, overcast December day. Behind the cemetery, a breeze whispered through a tall stand of pines to underscore the weeping of people below. Huddled next to Tom for warmth, Sterling dabbed at tears and tried to swipe the earthy smell of the open grave from her nose. Or perhaps the stench came from the nearby garbage dump.

"You'd think the cold would freeze the stink," said Tom quietly.

Folks who filled the little cemetery behind the Methodist church bowed their heads for the final blessing. Sterling, however, seized the moment to take inventory of the mourners and congratulate Harriet on the turnout. All the town notables made it except George Thompson, who had vanished. Probably just as well, since he had no more friends in Crossville and lots of legal questions to answer.

"Amen." The Methodist pastor wiped the mud from the grave off his hands with a towel he kept in his pocket.

"Amen," intoned the crowd. Nobody moved until the pastor invited them back to the church's Fellowship Hall for a "greeting of friends."

Immediately Sterling felt a tug on her arm. A white-haired woman she usually saw at the A&P whispered, "Imagine discovering those deeds in an old diary. I declare, you and Jennifer Mullins are a wonder."

"Mildred, do you think I might find something in my mother's old papers to help?" The woman next to her said.

"You should go see."

It saddened Sterling, but she got it. Too much had happened in Crossville to give Harriet a proper bereavement period. The murder of Sheriff Boyd. The investigation of his death and Harriet's. The manhunt for Penix and Murphy. The military garbage dump. The discovery of deeds questioning the ownership of land Cross used to build the dump.

Still, Harriet deserved to be mourned. Sterling trudged away from the two women trying not to feel resentment. Her shoes sank in mud churned up from the soggy grass by the mourners who led the way to Fellowship Hall.

With Tom's hand on her elbow and everyone's eyes on her back, they dodged puddles and stepped around the side to Fellowship Hall. The church bulletin board advertised a bake sale next week, a women's study on servanthood and slavery, and a plea to help in the children's Sunday School classes. Along with everyone else, they piled their coats on a chair or hung them on hat racks in the foyer, then followed their noses.

A blast of heat and conversation greeted them once they opened the doors to the large dining area. Several people already claimed wooden chairs at tables covered with white tablecloths. On the other side of the room long tables were filled with desserts, breads, casseroles, fried chicken, a baked ham, a roasted turkey, vegetable dishes, cups of coffee, and glasses of tea. Lines of mourners moved around the tables chatting and filling their plates.

Amid a crowd of people with plates and cups Sterling spotted Nancy and J.T. Dawson listening to Rose. Poor Rose talked a lot and said nothing. In the middle of a group of young women, she heard Jennifer Mullins' voice. No doubt Alice Peterson hovered nearby, close to her daughter, ready to swoop in if she made a mistake or said something wrong.

Tom steered her into the line for plates and food, but they soon found themselves surrounded by people offering congratulations.

A middle-aged woman in a black skirt asked, "Do you really believe the colored people can stop the garbage dump, Mr. Foster?"

"I hope——." Tom began.

"Why would they want to?" Sterling's rather loud voice silenced the clatter of silverware and voices.

The woman blinked, "Pardon?"

The people closest to her stepped back. Hostility and shock rose like summer heat. Mourners murmured under their breath and shook their heads at the shame of it. But Sterling couldn't shut up. "Why would black people help a white town that kills their children, burns their church, and steals their land? A town where they have no say in anything."

"Disgusting notion," muttered one young woman whose thin, pale cheeks now shone red hot.

"Wh-at? What kinda talk is this?" stammered a local farmer who hovered over the fried chicken platter.

"Straight talk, sir. My wife is speaking frankly." Tom said. "We gotta ask ourselves – what's in it for colored people if they help the town?"

"They live here! We treat them real fine. 'Sides', how they gonna make a living?" the farmer speared a chicken leg with a lot of force behind his fork.

The barber shrugged. "They're doing mighty fine right now without Crossville."

"Tom makes a point." The bald man who owned the bookstore spoke up from half-way across the room. "Harriet once told me Crossville drew its boundary to make sure colored people didn't live here."

"You aren't saying —." A short blond man sputtered.

"He's saying we need a favor from the Black farmers. A favor means give and take," Sterling said.

"If the Black farmers don't take back their land, stopping the dump will take years– and still not get done." Tom put down his plate and talked to the silent hall. "Meanwhile, the garbage piles up until it doesn't matter. The town's a stinking hole."

A ripple of angry muttering spread through the hall.

"Mr. Cross's garbage dump will have lots of jobs for Black people. Am I right, honey?" Sterling didn't have to fake her admiration for Tom right then. "Maybe they won't want to see those jobs go away."

Tempers were heating up in the room.

"Oh, pshaw. Those nigras would love to get the land. Farming is all those folks know." Rose inched her way into the conversation next to Jennifer.

"They might reach a deal with Cross and take money for their acres. Then our so-called military installation would operate and grow." Tom's upper lip curled.

People mumbled, nudged each other.

"Those colored people will never get a dime – and they won't get no land neither. No judge in the county would be on their side. It ain't right." The owner of the five and dime store shook with such visible anger he grabbed the edge of the dessert table for support. "We'll sue Cross."

"On what grounds?" Tom asked.

Jennifer walked over to the desserts. "Listen, y'all. We all want to keep our town from ruin. We've got to do something."

One of the young women she'd been standing with came over to Jennifer and added, "Sterling and Jennifer are right. We have to work together."

"I ain't 'workin' together' with no coloreds," the dime store owner snapped. He gave Jennifer a disdainful once-over. "It ain't fitting."

Her cohort shrank into the crowd and a moment later, Jennifer followed.

JUSTICE TOMORROW

"Way I see it, we either reach a deal with the coloreds to get this fixed or learn to love the smell of garbage." Tom's voice carried.

The A&P butcher trailed him. "Nigger-lovers."

Tom whirled on the man. "How you gonna keep the A&P open when the air coming in the doors smells like rotten meat? To say nothing of the rats bound to come crawling in the store from the dump next door."

"Somebody ought to call Reverend Johnson at Mt. Moriah and start talking," Sterling suggested.

The hall erupted. Harriet's wake transformed into a boisterous de facto town meeting. Sterling chuckled to herself and edged away from the table. She'd only snagged a pimento cheese sandwich, but she moved to leaned against a wall to eat.

Alice Peterson met her gaze across the hall with pursed lips and arms folded across her chest. At last she heaved a sigh, looked heavenward, and shook her head at the ceiling. Perhaps Alice knew her friend better than Sterling thought. Harriet would approve of this wake.

Two hours later, full of chicken casserole and pleased with the discussion, Sterling caught Tom's eye. He raised his hand in her general direction with a slight grin and fell to whispering with his co-workers from the real estate office. Despite herself, the delicious memory of his mouth on hers made her lick her lips.

She sidled to the edge of the hall, avoiding knots of people speculating about the murders, arguing over the dump, and weighing the cost of allowing Blacks to have a say in the town. Overheated and drained, she walked toward the door where it was marginally cooler.

In the outer foyer, Jennifer Mullins smoked a cigarette and stared into the gravel parking lot. The two women gazed into the Georgia evening in silence for a long time. Jennifer stood rooted to the spot; Sterling shifted from one foot to another. Sterling glanced at her friend and it dawned on her she read Jennifer wrong—or half wrong. Jennifer adored her mother and wanted to please her so much she'd shove aside everything else. Suddenly Sterling wanted to leave, to have her own mother as close as Jennifer had hers.

"I gotta ask," Sterling thrust a hand on her hip. "Why pick me to do your dirty work?"

Jennifer exhaled a cloud of smoke. "You're not afraid of what people think."

Gray's face flashed through her mind and her heart squeezed in pain.

"I saw you at the fire," Jennifer went on. "How you saved those colored girls."

"You thought I could save the town, save you."

Jennifer took another drag from her cigarette.

"You're a grown woman. Save yourself." Sterling snapped.

CHAPTER FIFTY-SEVEN

The morning after Harriet Cook's funeral Gray lay in bed dreading to deal with the Postmaster. He'd been in the barbershop often enough to know Carl Poke loved gossip. His report to Justice Tomorrow was already late. Nothing more to do here. He ought to grab Silver and hightail it out of Crossville.

Sterling. He had to stop wishing for Sterling. He wanted to be alone. Instead, he got a visit from Silver.

"Man, you're sweating. You sick? Or get a little roughed by the po-lice yesterday?"

His little brother had a bump under one eye. Gray raised up on one elbow. "You get in a fight?"

Silver touched the sore spot with his hand and winced. "Pigs looking for Ajamu. Can't find him. They act like he's got something to do with the sheriff's death."

Gray flopped on the pillow and turned to face the window. Silver plopped beside him on the bed.

"But listen here — Sterling and one of her friends filed old deeds to our farmers' land at the county courthouse. Big story in the county paper. Proves those brothers own the land they farmed, the land filling with Army garbage right now. They've got the way to stop it." Silver nudged Gray's arm with his elbow. "Way folks is walking around here you'd think God suddenly painted 'em white."

"I need sleep."

Silver sent him a fisheye. "What's keeping you awake?"

"Sterling."

Silver's eyebrows shot up. He lowered his voice. "Good God. No wonder

I can't get Foster to meet with me. He's busy. You don't think . . .. Sheriff Boyd?"

Gray whipped his head around and snarled, "I don't think anything — and you don't either. We're leaving tomorrow. Next day for sure."

"Uh-huh." Silver rose. "I'll tell Foster."

"No." It came out sharper than Gray meant.

"Why?"

"It's best we don't see other members of the team. Things in town are a little –."

"—tense?" Silver said.

With a forced grin, Gray tossed the blanket off and swung his legs over the edge of the bed. "Oh, more than that, I think. Just figure a way for us to get out quietly. We don't want to run out. Can you fix it, please?"

Silver snapped his fingers. "My Aunt Lois was real poorly last time I saw her. And I hear my main man Gray's leaving for Macon for a new job."

His brother left humming a Motown tune and Gray flopped back in bed.

Things would work out, get back to normal. No, never normal again. His eyes popped open, toured the faded, peeling patterned wallpaper around his room, and he came around to something he hated to think about. Why hadn't Penix and Murphy been arrested? Wasn't that Sterling's plan? Gray's stomach flopped over. Law enforcement would never rest until someone paid for Sheriff Boyd's death.

The thing is, who really killed Boyd?

The question was academic, a distraction. Still, he told himself to work on one thing at a time. Altogether, what he remembered happening in the store sounded like an English mystery about a murder on a train. All the suspects took turns killing the victim, so no one person was guilty of murder.

He relived it in slow motion. J.T. had his gun pointing in the sheriff's direction. Sterling pushed his gun aside, causing it to fire. The bullet hit Boyd in the back – it had been the devil to dig out — and he pitched forward. Was Boyd alive at this point? Gray hadn't stopped to wonder. He swung the knife into Boyd's stomach as he fell. Then, a blur. He must have shoved the sheriff to his back and straddled him to finish the job or redecorate the corpse. He would never know which.

Gray shivered. He'd still be stabbing the sheriff if Sterling hadn't been there. After a little distance, his madness worried him. At the time, however, he recalled nothing but deep satisfaction, and holy revenge. And a feeling Carl was right — maybe the time for peaceful protest had passed. Maybe it was time to follow Ajamu.

Gray longed to be with Sterling. He imagined sitting next to her as they went over things, debated violence versus pacifism, feeling her warmth. She would let him talk it out, straighten his thinking. But she was gone. The terrible emptiness inside told him he'd found the most tender wound. She'd never work with him, never see him again. To be fair, Gray hadn't given her the information she needed to make any other decision.

He pushed off the covers and got ready for work. Be late and the Postmaster would skin him alive.

CHAPTER FIFTY-EIGHT

As Sterling shuffled by the living room in her robe, Tom slapped the morning newspaper onto the sofa cushion beside him. It startled her. "Happy birthday."

She'd forgotten. In all the work she'd been doing she'd forgotten her own birthday.

"I'm twenty-one. Guess it's time to stop counting birthdays."

Why was Tom still at home? He'd been busy the last week meeting with lawyers and bankers trying to stop the Army's garbage dump from ruining Crossville. No need for him to go to his real estate office. With George still missing and the dump operational, no one in Crossville could sell a home or business. The escalating pile of garbage was stinking up the whole North End of town.

She sighed. The whole town was in an uproar about how best to cooperate with the Black community. In the days following Harriet's funeral and burial the division grew between those who favored concessions to save the town and those who refused to consider such a thing no matter what happened to Crossville.

Since she joined a group petitioning for a meeting between Black and white community leaders, they said hello passing each other in the hallway or kitchen.

"I let you sleep late," Tom said. "I figured you wore yourself to a frazzle collecting money for the farmers' lawsuit."

"Raised a hundred and thirteen dollars yesterday."

Tom applauded. "Now your feet hurt."

Her ankles were swollen. "A little."

"Take a day from making half the town hate you. Rest."

Tempting. "You're dressed to kill. Nice new suit."

"Important meeting this morning with an investor. From Atlanta. You keep the car, I've got a ride."

"Okay." By now Sterling knew when Tom was lying. She let it pass.

Being in the same house was a strain. At least when Tom was home, she didn't dwell on her parade of nightmares like the motion of Gray's knife, the unseeing deer's eye, the frenzied braying of hunters, Harriet's cold skin, or life as a single parent with no income. The nightmarish uncertainty of life with no Gray. No one to soothe all the what ifs, help her sort her options.

She pictured Gray beside her now. He never forced her to see things his way, never judged. Instead, he asked questions, wanted to hear what she thought, nudging her to find her own mind. She missed him, but the break was his choice as much as hers.

"Sterling! Hey." Tom snapped his fingers in front of her. "What's been going on with you the last few days? When you aren't gone, you're sleeping. You napped three hours after Harriet's funeral, slept until ten yesterday, and last night you clocked twelve hours. When you're awake you act like you're on a fire ant hill."

"Fire ant . . . about how I feel."

"Is it the baby?" He patted the space on the couch beside him. "I can't wait to tell my father he will be a grandfather. He thought I couldn't do it."

She ignored his invitation and threw herself into the big chair opposite him so hard its front legs came off the ground.

Tom acted like he didn't notice the slight and filled her in on what he called the progress stockholders made in persuading Cross to scale back the dump. But he kept stalling on the most important point—the expensive new way of layering the garbage. Meanwhile, the military trucks rolled on with their putrid cargo. The white shareholders would be in court asking for an injunction to stop the flow of garbage tomorrow morning.

"There would be no problem if Cross found a way to make a little more profit. He'd collapse like a pyramid of cards. Greediest bastard I ever met, next to my father," Tom said.

"How much profit is enough? You already said he was making a ton of money," Sterling cried.

"Money isn't measured by the ton. It's measured by power, influence, and the model of your car."

"If we found a smidgeon of proof, Cross would be in jail for setting up Henry Johnson's death," she fumed.

"Oh sure," Tom sneered, "just like the cops have caught Murphy and Penix for killing Boyd. They won't be finding those two ole boys. Somebody's already gotten them out of town."

"Seems like everybody from the acting sheriff to the barn cats is looking for them," Sterling said. "They can't have too many friends after what J.T. said about the murder."

"You'd think so," Tom said. "But the local cops are all over the South End questioning every colored boy. Beat one pretty bad when he wouldn't tell them where Ajamu was. They brought him in, but the FBI made them let him go."

"Why are they questioning Black men?" Sterling's stomach clenched.

Tom shrugged. "Rumors mostly. Two drunk kids saw a colored man running in the rainstorm. And some man driving through the South End saw a Black man with no shirt crossing the street. Anyhow, the Sheriff Department's in a mess, Reverend Johnson and his folks are protesting the sweeps. The FBI agents left, but state cops have come back in a big way. County police are in charge, but they act nervous."

Sterling's lips pursed. "I thought the FBI went back to Atlanta."

"They stayed, but really stayed quiet. You're thinking of the state police. But they are back too."

"Something's not right," she mused. "Too many police."

"What?"

"Well, think about it. State, federal, local – that's a lot of firepower even for a sheriff being murdered," she said.

"It wouldn't be enough to investigate corrupt local county cops," Tom said.

"Who says!"

Tom grinned as though he knew what her reaction would be. "I heard rumors. They're saying Sheriff Boyd was part of Cross's scheme. Some house-cleaning is going to happen."

Sterling gaped at him, hoping J.T. wouldn't be caught up in the upheaval.

"Sterling?"

"Why haven't we been called out of Crossville?" she cried. "This assignment is over—we know who killed Henry Johnson."

Tom laid the folded newspaper on the nearby table. "I'm glad we're still here. For the first time in my life, I want to finish something. I want to see Cross back off the landfill, I want to guide the stockholders in his little company."

"This house reeks of smoke. The whole town smells of something rotting, and-and there's a split in town. Everybody's walking on eggshells."

"It began with the boycott. Gray did the coloreds no favors there," he said.

"Neighbors okay with talking to the Black farmers and community leaders aren't speaking to those who aren't willing to talk with them. I saw a shoving match in the bookstore between two old friends."

"Not the nice little town we moved into, huh."

"It was nice because we're white," she said.

"It's still wonderful for me. I found something to do that I like and I'm good at, I earned a little respect for myself, not for being my father's son. And I fell in love."

She barely heard him. Sterling's heart pushed into her throat. She shook her head to rid her memory of blood on the floor of the old store, then got to her feet. "I need coffee. Want some?"

His hand snaked out for her wrist. His heat, his intensity startled her as he stood up near her. "What do you want, Sterling?" A plea.

"I want to forget everything." It came out so low she wondered for a moment if she said it aloud.

"Forget me too? And our child?" Tom lightly stroked her hair near her bandage. "You've been through a lot. I should have seen it. Be patient. I found my calling, my place. Turns out, I'm a great businessman. I like it the same way you like investigating crimes. With a little help, this project will make me so rich no one will ever threaten us."

"Rich isn't safe, Tom."

"Hell, it isn't. You checked our bank account? I can do whatever I want."

It suddenly hit her. "You would tell me if Justice Tomorrow warned us to leave. No one's called to say my grandmother died?" Angry red splotches heated her face.

"Of course not. We'd be gone." He sounded so earnest. The flash of panic she saw must have been hurt. She relented, gave his arm a gentle squeeze. "I-I'm sorry. Some of it's me – I've got a bad feeling."

Tom rubbed his birthmark. "I've got a lotta respect for your gut."

Sterling noticed his gesture that always meant guilty. "You and I know this isn't our home. Tom, everything we have is based on lies."

"It is not a lie that I love you." He pulled her close, rested his head atop hers.

She searched for his familiar warmth and comfort. Today it wasn't there. Tom had been her refuge. He was there for her when Gray refused to be. She leaned on both men for the strength she should have had. She never really stood on her own.

A car honked. "Gotta run. Don't forget we're having a birthday dinner tonight with Nancy and J.T." Tom kissed her forehead, grabbed his briefcase, and left the house whistling.

CHAPTER FIFTY-NINE

One full suitcase already sat at the edge of Sterling's bed. How is it she needed one suitcase to start a case and two to leave? It was even more curious because her overflowing bag contained no physical evidence or witness statements. Those had been sent to Justice Tomorrow long ago.

Sterling planned to be home for Christmas. She held up a shirt, tried on a skirt, and compared two pairs of jeans to decide how to best hide her pregnancy through the week in Boston. She couldn't hide the bump much longer.

What did she want to happen after Christmas? Did she want the rest of her life filled by Tom? He was the safe, easy answer. Her baby deserved a father and a mother. But she had no respect for the father of her child. Could Tom change? Did she dare risk her life on that possibility? She and Tom had talked about going home after this assignment ended and talking with their parents about getting married. Now . . .?

A knock on the front door startled her. It wasn't Nancy, she always came to the back. It might be a salesman. Sterling hopped down the stairs. No encyclopedias today.

When she cracked the door, the distinguished-looking man who stood on her welcome mat removed his hat to reveal brown hair streaked by white. She recognized him as the gentleman she'd met leaving the real estate office on the day the garbage dump opened. He wore the same camel cashmere coat.

"Excuse me, is Tom Foster here?"

"No, I'm sorry. Can I help you?"

The man's eyebrows shot up. His brown eyes widened then narrowed. "I'm supposed to meet him – I thought we were meeting at his house. May I come in?"

"He said he was meeting an investor from Atlanta. You must be him. He thought the meeting was at the real estate office," Sterling said. "I'm sorry, Mr.---"

"Foster. I'm Tom's father, Brian Foster."

Same eyes, same hair, same build. No wonder he looked familiar when she saw him at the real estate office.

"I'm Sterling. Please, come in. Your son looks like you."

Brian Foster gave her his hat, shrugged out of his coat, and glanced over the foyer.

"How did you find Tom?" She hung his coat and hat on the hooks next to the door.

"Tom and I don't talk, as you might have guessed. I'm a banker and came to save his ass. Again." Brian gave a dry chuckle.

"C-come in, please." She tried to picture Tom looking like his father in a few years ahead, but the image wouldn't come.

"I've had private detectives searching for months," Brian went on. "They finally found him. When I arrived, he ran out of the real estate office without saying a word. I started to come over earlier but decided to wait him out. Two days ago, he called for help—as I knew he would."

The fight or flee instinct warred in her. The mission must be compromised, maybe far more than she suspected. Sterling's hand went cold.

"May I get you some coffee? I'll call Tom."

"No, don't bother. I'll go to his office. But I would like coffee first." His eyes scanned the house as he walked down the hall. He cleared his throat.

"Have a seat in the living room while I get it." Sterling's stomach flopped. "Do you take it black, like Tom?"

"Yes." Brian perched on the edge of the sofa as though he feared his pants might crease.

"I'll be right back." Sterling nearly broke a coffee cup in her nervous haste to return to the living room. Grabbing a peek at herself in the kitchen window she fiddled with her hair, but there was nothing to be done about her dirty jeans and torn shirt. She planned to look nicer for her first meeting with her child's grandfather. He didn't strike her as Mister Warmth. Carrying two cups and saucers to the living room she found him holding one of the fake wedding photos.

He returned it to the bookshelf and accepted the coffee. His lips pursed, sipping as though dreading to touch them to the cup rim.

Sterling sank onto the edge of the only chair in the living room. "Tom said this morning he had a meeting but didn't say it was with his father." She felt a little dizzy.

236

JUSTICE TOMORROW

"I-I'm at a loss. None of this makes sense," said Brian. "We argued about niggers getting rights, and he stomped out of the house. Then I hear he's been hospitalized -- injured in riots outside agitators stirred up among the poor ignorant coloreds. When I telephoned the hospital, he'd disappeared. No call for months. No letter. Nothing."

For all the emotion he showed, Brian Foster might have been discussing the weather.

"I'm sorry you and Tom haven't spoken."

"He's my only child. What's he doing here? How is he involved with John Cross's military garbage site?" Brian's voice remained cold and level.

"Tom invested in the Cross company, as did all the other people working for Homestead Real Estate. No one, including Tom, knew what the Cross property would be used for or the extent of it. He's developed a real love for Crossville. As you might imagine, everyone in town is upset at a huge, stinking dump next to the center of town."

Brian clucked. "Invested? That's Tom. Jump in without checking the depth. This time he got lucky. He can make a lot of money."

Brian Foster appeared at the end of a narrow tunnel in Sterling's mind, his every color, smell, and gesture magnified. The danger didn't strike her as physical, but still deadly. She scooted as far back in the chair as she was able.

"Why the devil is he siding with the niggers and trying to derail the project he invested in? It's a great deal."

She understood why Tom and his father didn't get along. "Why do you care about this dump site?"

"The Cross company is woefully under-capitalized. My bank is going to finance Cross's project, thanks to Tom. We stand to make a fortune, and so do our stockholders." Brian grimaced, "A lawyer friend of mine called to say Tom asked their advice on stockholder rights. Perhaps Tom really has lost his mind."

"Tom's grown into his own man."

Brian frowned. "He may not be aware, but Cross's loans will put our family back on solid financial ground again. Missing this deal, well, I can't allow it to happen. The Foster name is an old, honorable one. Our reputation's at stake, not to mention our fortune."

"He hasn't told me --."

"I don't mean to be rude, the detectives I hired haven't been able to provide me with much information. Who are you?" Brian's cup and saucer clattered onto the bookshelf.

237

"I'm Sterl—."

"I know your name. But who are you?" Brian jabbed a finger at the wedding pictures. "I know you aren't his wife. I was on the first pew at his wedding, his real wedding. His wife lives three doors from me in Atlanta, although she's been in California since Tom ran off."

Sterling blinked. His words rattled around her head like steel balls in a tin box.

Apparently, Brian didn't notice her shock. He paced. "Tom's father-in-law is a major stockholder of my bank, the man who bailed our family out of a difficult situation. He and his daughter have been very patient and understanding of my son's, ah, apparent mental collapse over the last few months."

Sterling's mouth moved. Nothing came out.

"They might not understand this behavior, however." Brian's right arm swept the room. "They will not tolerate his scuttling such a lucrative deal, much less his living in sin!"

Her feet, her fingers lost feeling.

"I don't know what he's told you. But all this --" Brian waved his arms about "-- must disappear. How much will it cost for you to leave town, pretend you never knew Tom?"

She forced her legs to lift her out of the chair, carry her to the front door, and fling it open. "Listen to your son when you find him, Mr. Foster. Good day."

Brian huffed to his feet. She pitched his coat to him and shut the door. His feet abused the front stairs in a series of loud clump-clumps that pounded through the closed door.

Sterling leaned against a wall and stared ahead at the dark wood floor of the hallway, hearing nothing but the echo of Brian's voice and seeing nothing ahead of her. An agonized scream banged inside her chest, her brain.

A gullible idiot. A cliché. A fool. No better than those girls she pitied as a child when her mother dragged her to deliver old clothes at the church's Magdalene House for unwed mothers.

Gradually, her heart slowed. Her cheeks continued radiating heat like she'd been slapped, but her knees grew strong enough to hold her. Her spine stiffened and her fingers tucked themselves inside fists. She would face Tom and his lies. Someday. Someday when her smarts and will to fight had brought her success. Someday when her heart had grown as hard as steel. Outside she

238

heard Nancy slam the car door and start her car engine. The sound galvanized her.

Sterling ran upstairs for her suitcase, stuffed things into it, and carried it downstairs. She threw on her coat, grabbed her purse then tossed the suitcase in the backseat of the car with her coat. Numbly she drove to the bank, cashed a check big enough traveling money but not large enough to raise an eyebrow, and plotted a route out of Georgia. Every aching fiber of her longed to be down the road. Yet she drove to the Emporium.

A full sun shone, though the wind stirring the pines and oaks would freeze anyone sitting under them. No wonder the bench in front of the Emporium, usually occupied by one or two men, remained empty. Winter finally claimed its rightful place after the unseasonably warm weather and the wet chill of recent weeks.

The sun irritated Sterling. The cold, dark shadows covering the back where she parked suited her better. What a great birthday. She unlocked the Emporium, compelled by a need she did not fully understand. Maybe she sought momentary sanctuary, a respite from feeling foolish, used, not good enough. Abandoned. The Emporium with its warm memories represented a safe space for deciding who she would be after Crossville.

She opened the back door with hopeful reverence. Inhaling through her nose, she summoned thoughts of Harriet with the hint of lemon polish and old books. The chaotic stair step of boxes against the walls and the jumble of odd tables and chairs welcomed her. The velvety fabric dividing back from front, the papers cascading from shelves, place settings of china, display cases of earrings in small white boxes — all familiar, homey, ordinary things.

"Harriet." She told the silence. "I'm in trouble."

From the light of the front windows, she saw a cluttered table. No one had disturbed the books and papers she'd been reading the morning Harriet died. Useless. Worthless. What had she managed with all her research and investigating? The vision Harriet had for Crossville was farther away than ever, the town splintered. She and Justice Tomorrow found Henry Johnson's murderer, but it came at a fearful cost to Crossville. To everyone involved.

The windows of the store needed washing, the counter and displays wanted dusting, and the floor begged for sweeping. Out of habit, she flipped on the lights and the front door "open" sign. Since Harriet had only a distant cousin, what would happen to the historical society and Emporium? Jennifer's attic might grow more crowded.

CHAPTER SIXTY

Wishing to avoid a tongue-lashing, Gray checked the empty alley behind the Post Office, crept quietly into the back door, and closed it with a small snick. He immediately saw the Postmaster had not sorted any mail, something that made his eyebrows shoot up. Then he heard urgent, hushed voices in the back, in the side room where the Postmaster took his coffee.

Frowning, Gray grabbed a broom and listened. The quiet words weren't clear at first, then his stomach clenched and his grip on the broom handle tightened. Three men, no four counting the Postmaster. They were talking about Sterling.

"We figure she's the nigger-lovin' agitator we heard about. I knowed it – I bet the sheriff knowed it when he told us to watch her," said one man's voice. Flesh slapped against flesh. "I bet she had somethin' to do with Boyd getting killed."

"She wasn't nowhere around. She and her husband live next door to the old store is the only thing I know of." The Postmaster's voice sounded flat.

"Sheet! I bet she met a nigger in the old store!" Splat. Someone spit on the floor. "Klan used to meet there in its hey-day too!"

"Goddamn," breathed The Postmaster.

"I'm gonna kill the bitch," the second voice growled.

A third man grunted. "Damn right. Y'all know to count on me and the boys."

"I know where she lives," said the second man. "Seen her goin' round town — and workin' next door."

The first man's voice rose. "Listen, you got to help Murphy and me. Why would we kill Boyd!"

"I-I don't know how long I can keep y'all here, Penix." The Postmaster didn't sound unsure of himself.

"Call the boys and let's go on over to the bitch's house," said the first man. "Here's the phone."

To Gray's dismay, the Postmaster told the operator to call a man Gray didn't know. But when the man answered, the Postmaster told him to get his gun and come. But Gray didn't hear where.

"All this trouble started with them two women, Harriet and the Foster bitch," the first voice whined when the Postmaster's call ended. "Listen here, we tole some other boys and when we say, they're okay with helping." The rest of the words were garbled.

Fear swirled around Gray, closing his throat, keeping him from swallowing. He had to warn Sterling. Get her out of town. A rivulet of sweat coursed down his back despite the chill in the air. Moving slowly and watching his step to avoid the creaking third board in the floor, Gray made his way to the back door, opened it carefully, then took a deep breath and slammed it.

"Good day to you, sir," he called in his usual way.

Feet scuffled before the Postmaster came out of the side room, his features contorted in anger. "You lazy sonvabitch!"

Gray bowed his head, spread out his hands, palms up, to plead. "Ain't never gonna be late again." He grabbed a broom as much to steady his hand as to sweep. "You see, I stay two no, three hours, mor'. I work real hard, sir. Sweep out front then empty this here trash . . .."

The Postmaster yanked the broom away from him. "Git your lazy ass out."

"But-t, sir . . .."

"Git!"

Gray kept his head down and his eyes on the floor, expecting to hear the whoosh of the broom as it swung to hit him or the thud of feet as the men in the back came to chase him. Instead, he made it outside unscathed.

Sterling's car occupied its parking place next door. Something right, thank God. He veered toward the Emporium.

"Don't you never come back, boy," yelled the Postmaster.

Cursing under his breath Gray trotted to the alley fence and slipped between the slats like a whipped dog. Safely on the other side he slid to the ground, peeked through a crack, and prayed the Postmaster wouldn't notice Sterling's car.

But old albino pivoted, stared at the vehicle then slowly backed away and slammed the post office door behind him.

Terror launched Gray off his haunches. Sterling was going to need more than his help. A car barely missed him as he raced across the street. He pumped his arms, panic breathing in and out. Ajamu and his young men jerked to attention as he ran toward the barbershop.

CHAPTER SIXTY-ONE

The bell over the Emporium door tingled and Rose swooped inside. She unbuttoned her tan wool coat and took off her matching brown gloves as she caught her breath.

"Sterling, I've been trying to get hold of you. When I saw the lights and the sign on the door, I declare I couldn't believe my eyes. Never thought you'd want to be here after what happened." Rose joined Sterling at the table, shoving aside the books and papers to make room for her purse.

"W-what else can I do?"

"Aren't you afraid the murderers will come back here?" Rose whispered as though the suggestion would make it happen.

"I never thought . . . ."

"Maybe being here might help you remember who hit you and killed Harriet." She looked like she was hoping Sterling would burst out the names of the killers in a glorious moment of insight.

"I can't. I've tried. They wore white hoods. I only know the tall one had a double chin, one was fat, and both men smelled like liquor—homebrew."

Disappointed, Rose pressed. "Some folks are saying it might be the same men who killed poor Sheriff Boyd. Whoever murdered him dropped a white hood in the field out by the burned-out store. You just said the men who attacked you had hoods."

Sterling held her head in both hands. "I want it all to go away."

"Don't we all." Rose smoothed back an errant strand of hair as she glanced about. "I never understood what Harriet saw in this place. It's so dark and backs right up to the colored section of town. It's a wonder it hasn't been robbed."

"Wasn't a Negro man who killed Harriet." She bit off each word. "Wasn't a Negro man conned people into having a garbage dump in the town's front yard. But it might be Negro men saving this town."

JUSTICE TOMORROW

Rose slid out of the chair to her feet and Sterling followed suit. "Keep talking like that and nobody will vote for your husband for County Commissioner."

County Commissioner? Tom never said a word. She guffawed. One of many things Tom had neglected to tell her.

"Sterling, honestly." Rose pressed her lips together then huffed, "Well. I wanted to tell you how sorry I was about your grandmother passing. I never listen on the party line, of course, but when I picked up the phone the other day to make a hair appointment, I heard Tom talking to your mother about the funeral."

Sterling's stomach lurched into her throat. Tom lied to her again. Justice Tomorrow warned them to get out days ago. "We-re leaving tonight."

Rose patted her hand. "I figured as much. Well, who knows what you'll come back to! You, Nancy, and even Jennifer talk like . . . well, I expect Nancy gets her queer notions from being raised in Kentucky or having a newspaperman for a daddy."

Suddenly Sterling had to get out. She felt for her purse.

"Now, you were reared in Mississippi. And Jennifer—." Rose paused, cocked her head. "Honey, you all right?"

Danger seeped through the walls, the windows, the backroom, weakened her knees. Sterling checked the front door, then the back for an easy escape route.

Before she made a move, the front bell announced a middle-aged man. He sported long sun-streaked blonde hair, wispy mutton-chop whiskers, and limped in using a cane. At first, he frowned, but when he spotted the women, he unleashed a grin full of teeth and charm.

"Excuse me, I'm looking for Sterling Foster." The man's pale eyebrows lifted as his hazel eyes darted from one woman to the other.

Sterling froze. Rose beamed, introduced herself, and, after a long second or two, nudged Sterling. "Here she is."

"Sorry to bother you. So much excitement around here. Everybody's running . . . Well, I've been to the sheriff's office – the state police are taking over, I guess, and nobody knows what's going on. I am very sorry about the sheriff's death. However, I need to determine where the bone came from."

"Bone?" Sterling parroted. "The one Nancy and I found in Callie's Cutoff?"

"I've scanned —," the man paused, then began again. "Sorry, I'm Dr. Jonas Oliver, chair of the University of Georgia Department of Anthropology." He carefully enunciated the last word as though the women might not understand otherwise.

Rose's eyes fluttered wide. "Professor, so pleased to meet you."

243

Sterling edged around the table toward the front door. This was not the Professor Oliver she remembered.

All at once, the Postmaster cupped his hands against the front window to peek in then jumped back like he'd touched an electrical current. On the other side of the glass, a startled Sterling scurried to the door in time to open it and watch his fat thighs slap together all the way into the Post Office.

Professor Oliver jerked. "Something the matter, Mrs. Foster?"

The postmaster never came outside in daylight. Harriet joked about it. She'd only seen him when she mailed letters. Sterling came in and shut the door. "No-o. Please, sit, professor."

Showing all his teeth again the professor pulled out a chair for her and moved forward as though he meant to force her into it. She sat, skin tingling from scalp to toes. Rose slid into the seat next to her.

"Mr. Cross has not only given the department permission to study his land, but access to his family papers and, ah, such." The professor cleared his throat as he sat beside Rose. "You and Mr. Cross share an interest in the local legend of Callie Epson. A member of his family was suspected of the murder. Now decades of frost upheavals and your discovery might shed light on the legend."

Rose covered her mouth. Still, a giggle escaped. "Jennifer will be thrilled."

The money in her purse would buy Sterling enough gas to reach the safe house on the far side of Atlanta and a ticket to Boston with a lot left over. Except she would call from the next town to warn Jennifer. For friendship's sake. Sterling ventured another peek out the front window at the trees, the grass, the empty park bench.

"I brought a new, ah, machine, with me – resembles surveyor's equipment. It helps us locate bones in the ground," Professor Oliver said. "You know, Mrs. Foster, you look familiar. Did you take my class?"

Sterling swung her attention to the professor, fear twisting her stomach. "I-I took a history class from Professor Oliver." There was no such thing as a machine to locate buried bones. How was he fooling anyone, even Rose, with such a story? Who was he?

The man grinned like Sterling won first prize. "Well, about the bone. Once the state police determined the bone was old, an easy assessment, they assigned it and the metal to the university for study. It was easy to determine that the metal fragment is part of a Griswold-made sheath from the Civil War. The finger probably got jammed in it somehow, thus ensuring its survival when other bones decayed to dust."

"Tell me, did Sterling and Nancy find an Indian bone?" Rose asked.

"Indians are in Bell County. I have a book on it somewhere." Sterling rose, took a half step back, checked around the room. She might sprint to the back

JUSTICE TOMORROW

and her car before the fake professor could catch her. She eased around the table.

"Oh my no. It's a Negro bone dating back to the Civil War. We suspect we will find more of his body – and it was from a male. The bone had markings on it as though someone had cut or shot a fragment away." The professor asked, "Don't you find all that fascinating, Mrs. Foster?"

"Oh-h yes." Everything the so-called professor said was ridiculous and impossible to determine. Who sent him? The police? The Klan? The Peter Pan collar on her blue blouse tightened around her throat. Sights became loud, sounds fell around her in a colorful array.

A dog barked out front. Funny, there were usually several dogs barking and running loose around town. And, people. Always people walking by. Not today. A shadow traveled across the length of the window like death passing over.

"We can't be sure until we've gone over the area." Oliver went on. "I really can't say much more."

"I-I'm sorry . . .." In her hurry to leave Sterling knocked over a display of earrings. "I have to go. My grandmother died and . . .."

The back door slammed. Something heavy and wooden raked the floor and thumped against the back. Everyone gaped in the direction of the noise. More wood scraped against wood. A grunt. Glass shattered.

"Missrus Foster!"

Sterling's mouth dropped.

Gray ripped the curtain aside. His slack jaw and wide eyes told her it was too late to run. A soft cry escaped her.

"Who's . . .?" Rose demanded.

Gray shoved the phone across the counter at Sterling. "Git the sheriff. Them two white men they lookin' for is comin' in your back door. I seen 'em at the Post Office — and heard them talk 'bout you so's I come right over!"

"What?" Rose lost all color.

Sterling's shaking hands picked up the receiver and tapped on the button to clear the line. "It's dead."

"They say they gonna kill you," said Gray.

"I knew it," Rose wailed.

"Wait! H-how do you know all this?" Professor Oliver's chin jutted out.

"Gray does odd jobs here and the Post Office." Sterling stammered.

"You heard men plotting to kill Mrs. Foster?" The professor gripped the table with both hands.

A series of bangs rattled the back door. Rose squealed in alarm.

"Get out the front door. We'll make a run for it across the street," Professor Oliver said. "They won't try anything in broad daylight in the middle of town."

Sterling grabbed a deep breath. Following the professor may not be a good idea but staying in the Emporium wasn't an option. She herded Rose and the professor forward.

The back door thudded as something struck it, then thudded again

"Sterling." She almost missed the sweet desperation of Gray's whisper. "I want to-to tell you, you have to know —."

Gray had an odd air about him, a soft glow in his eyes. Amid her terror, a calm claimed her.

"Are you two coming? We'll go out together. Mrs. Collins, go to the window and watch to see if you recognize anybody on the street." Professor Oliver put his hands on her shoulders and rotated her body to the window. When she obeyed, Professor Oliver strode toward Sterling and Gray.

CHAPTER SIXTY-TWO

Sterling backed into Gray. Professor Oliver, or whoever he was, must have seen a chance to make his move. She raised her hands to defend herself.

"What are you still doing here, Sterling? You should have been long gone!" Professor Oliver hissed at them.

Sterling sagged with relief.

"Both of you get to emergency shelters." The professor went on. For Rose's benefit he added loudly, "What you say, boy?"

Shelters. Something must be wrong to send them underground.

"Gray, a car's waiting for you and Silver at Brown's farm." He palmed a car key into Sterling's hand. "My car's the green Dodge near the Post Office. Head east, read the instructions – you'll know where."

She tucked the car key safely into her bra, her fingers cold against warm skin. Sterling knew the problem. But it cut to the quick to hear Oliver say it.

"Justice Tomorrow's compromised. A dangerous threat's been detected."

"Foster." Gray's tone chilled her.

"Stay low for six or seven months," the professor said, then yelled to Rose, "See anything?"

The next crash from the storeroom sounded like the back door splintered. Rose screamed. The professor lunged for the front door.

Sterling grabbed Gray's arm to whisper. "The *Ashland Daily Independent* building where Nancy's father works."

"Six months. Noon." He covered her hand with his own.

"There's two men in white hoods! One's sitting on the bench to the right." Rose squeaked and pointed. "And, the other's behind a tree!"

Suddenly another huge thud and crash from the rear. The door hit the floor. The profanity of men climbing through the wreckage propelled everyone out the front door.

"Go left!" Professor Oliver sprang forward without his cane.

The four of them careened outside screaming, hollering, bumping into each other. Arms pumping and legs churning, Sterling ran behind Rose's flapping coat and glanced sideways. Sunlight glinted off something beside the park bench. Oh, God. The hooded man had a gun. She put Rose between her and the gunman — nobody wanted to kill Rose.

Penix and Murphy burst from the Emporium spewing profanities loud enough to roust hell.

More screams and shouts. From doorways and shops, the five and dime, the bookstore, barbershop, and A&P, people streamed into the street to find out about the commotion, then scrambled back inside at the sight of armed men.

Desperately Sterling shoved Rose behind a full rain barrel at the alley's entrance and ducked down beside her. A shot cracked over the yells and shrieking. The bullet popped a chip off the Emporium's wood façade, followed by a thud-thud as Gray and the professor dropped flat to the sidewalk.

Everything fell silent. Nothing stirred, not even the air. Sterling pressed against the damp barrel wood, smelling the rot and making herself small as possible. The barrel didn't completely hide both women, but it was safer than the sidewalk or running.

Someone's boot trampled beside her. With a cry, she started, grabbed Rose's hand to run. It was Silver.

"Stay down," ordered Silver. Behind his hip, he gripped a pistol. Sterling gasped.

CHAPTER SIXTY-THREE

Sterling's head tilted to Silver. "Don't do it."

"Tell it to the man." Silver hissed.

"I'll stand up, go out on the sidewalk, I swear to God."

Silver glanced at her and swore.

Rose wept and buried her face her hands. Sterling eased from the fat barrel enough to close her hand around Silver's wrist. He twitched. She slid her hand down his hand and covered the muzzle. After a second, he released it. When she stuck it in her belt and pulled her shirt out over it, she glimpsed Ajamu in the shaded sidewalk near a bright white planter to her right.

"Put it down, Ajamu." Silver raised his empty gun hand.

Hard sole shoes scraped the cement sidewalk. Then a surprised "What the . . ." came from the Emporium followed by a series of curses. A cry and a few screams echoed from down the street toward the A&P. Sterling hugged the rain barrel like a lover.

A Black man's voice, which sounded like it came from across the street, yelled, "We in ever alley an' street."

Now as curious as she was terrified, Sterling eased her head to one side of the barrel enough to see one of the white-hooded gunmen shift from one foot to the next. The gunman motioned with his head toward a second man nearby who cradled a shotgun. They shifted their stances as though feeling uneasy then fled off to Sterling's left. She leaned out a little further from the barrel to see a confused Penix and Murphy on the sidewalk in front of the Emporium. Behind them near a rain barrel stood the Methodist preacher and Reverend Johnson.

"We ain't afraid." Penix raised a rifle to his waist and pointed it at the ministers.

"Then you ain't counting. Look around." Another Black man shouted from behind a tree in the grassy strip.

"Penix, the whole town's watching. It's broad daylight."

Sterling peeked in the direction of the voice and discovered the barber who had spoken at Harriet's funeral. He stood in front of his shop beside a Black man Sterling once saw raking Alice Peterson's leaves.

Someone stepped next to Rose, drawing a terrified squeal from her. Sterling grabbed her shoulders and discovered the white butcher standing beside their rain barrel with Silver.

Rose sniffled. "What's happening?"

While she didn't dare rise far enough to get a good view, Sterling saw that several whites and more Blacks were slowly encircling the Emporium.

A gun cocked. Sterling ducked back behind the barrel, sucking in a breath. God, where were the county deputies? She hunkered down, braced for shooting.

"Whoa! Whoa! Everybody whoa!" A man's deep voice sounded far away, maybe on the far side of the Emporium. Nothing moved but Silver's shoes as he stepped back. "Let's all of us settle down. I'm Lieutenant Colonel Mattison of the state police outta Atlanta. But lookee, here's Deputy Dawson. You know him. You know he's fair."

"Penix! Murphy! Boys, you need to tell your side of things. Y'all willing to die before you do?" It was J.T.'s voice. More shoes scraped on the cement sidewalk. "Huh? Boys? It ain't right for it to end this way. We gotta get it straight."

The air around Sterling felt so heavy it was hard to draw it in.

"Now, listen y'all. We're gonna take Penix and Murphy, give 'em a chance to explain. You may think things is cut and dried, but it ain't," J.T. called. "All y'all go on home."

Sterling made the sign of the cross. Rose murmured low, praying to the ground.

Swearing, grunting, panting. A scuffle. The stench of sweat and fear, anger and hate overpowered the scent of the pines. Sterling risked a look around the barrel in time to see Gray disappear into the Emporium while several uniformed police officers wrestled Penix and Murphy away. Her Black and white protectors disappeared down alleys too, into buildings or through back fences. The butcher helped Rose to her feet.

"Mrs. Foster? Mrs. Collins?" Professor Oliver bounded off the sidewalk, dusting himself off as he came to Sterling's side. He helped her rise and whispered, "Incidentally, I am a professor, and you did find a Griswold sheath."

J.T. came out of the Emporium, checked both ways before stepping onto the sidewalk and motioning the professor and the butcher to bring the women

250

JUSTICE TOMORROW

inside. "Sterling, you and Rose okay? Rose, sit there. Can someone get water?"

"Why's this happenin'?" Rose cried and leaned on Professor Oliver as he led her to a table along the wall. A display table of china rattled as they brushed by.

Sterling stumbled into J.T.'s arms. He thanked the butcher and directed a deputy to take his statement at another table. She collapsed on the first chair she came to. With a shudder, she folded her arms on the table in front of her and let her head fall on them.

"You gotta tell me what happened." J.T. pulled a chair close to her.

"Is it over?" She whispered.

J.T. cleared his throat. "Couple of state police folks in Atlanta been wondering about Boyd and his department for a while. Skimming county money. Kickbacks on speeding tickets. And they got questions about the Cross development. They just asked me to help. I'm the newest man in the department and, I guess they figure I'm ah, pretty clean."

"What about the other men with rifles? Are they gonna come back?" she sniffled.

"Na. We'll go by their houses and pick 'em up after a while. White hood or no, I recognize Deputy Alvin Hankins. He helped kill the Johnson boy. I know the other man too," J.T. sighed. "May take a while, but Crossville's gonna get straight."

"And the men who saved us?"

"What men?" J.T. acted surprised. "You mean, the new Methodist preacher and Reverend Johnson?"

"The ones in the alleys." Had she been able to command her feet she would have leapt up. "Negro and white together."

J.T. shook his head. "I never saw anybody but the two preachers. Maybe another officer saw them. Or maybe Rose."

"The only thing Rose can describe is the dirt behind the barrel."

"Let it go, Sterling," J.T. whispered.

"They risked their lives. Saved me . . . Saved . . . People have to know, J.T. They have to know how Negro and white men came together."

"Tell me how Harriet's handyman Gray warned you about Penix and Murphy. How you, Rose, and the fella I haven't met ran outside to get help. You and Rose took what cover you could behind a barrel in the alley until we got here. Who is that man over there, anyhow?"

"A professor from the University of Georgia. He came to see me about the bone Nancy and I found." She produced a tiny smile. "Nancy may have a good story about it."

J.T. squeezed her hand.

"I won't let this go, J.T."

251

"Never thought you would. I promise the heroes today will get their due. All of them."

He didn't flinch when she cast about for on-lookers, lifted her shirt, and passed a pistol to him under the table. "Toss this for me?"

"I've done worse." He grasped the butt and stuck the gun in his belt.

She smiled. "I'd like a job as a police investigator someday."

"Anybody asks, I'd say you'd be good," he chuckled. "And my word might count for something these days. Listen, we got enough for now. You go on home."

"Don't trust Tom. Ever. Tell Nancy." She whispered as she stood. "And tell her — tell her I . . ." Tears pooled in her eyes.

"I'll let her know." His eyebrow arched. "Get some rest. Take a few days. I'll have a deputy drive you home."

"I want to walk, clear my mind."

He squinted at her. "Really?"

"Bye, J.T." Sterling kissed his cheek and he squeezed her hand.

Out back, she took a deep, cleansing breath. Pine. For once it smelled like Christmas morning in Boston. She got her suitcase from her car, carried it through the alley and transferred them to the green Dodge parked near the Post Office. A half dozen police officers were strung around the crime scene as she drove out and turned toward Main. People gaped at the activity around the Emporium and never paid her any mind.

Six months, she told herself as the familiar sites of Crossville slipped by her car window. In less than six months, she'd be a mother. She'd have to use that recommendation in her suitcase from the Boston YMCA to get a clerk job, but she could support herself until the baby arrived. At the end of six months, she'd be standing on her own two feet when she met Gray. They'd use J.T.'s recommendation as a start. And they'd build their own detective agency: Sterling Brothers Ltd.

ABOUT THE AUTHOR

Award-winning author, public relations manager, and speechwriter Jackie Ross Flaum attended the University of Georgia and finished at the University of Kentucky. She began her career as a reporter for *The Hartford Courant* in Hartford, Conn. After moving to Memphis and abandoning reality for fiction, she won first place for romantic suspense in the 21st annual Duel on the Delta and second place in the spring 2019 *Short Story Land* online competition.

She's had short stories in the award-winning anthologies *Mayhem in Memphis* and *Elmwood Stories to Die For*. Her short stories have also appeared in *Stories Through the Ages: Baby Boomers Plus*, *Backchannels* literary journal's spring 2020, and the crime writers' anthology *Dirty Low Down Vote VII*.

Her novella, *The Yellow Fever Revenge*, was released on Amazon in the middle of the 2020 pandemic.

Jackie's happily married, has two daughters, four grandchildren, and one disobedient dog.

Currently, she is president of Malice in Memphis a Killer Writing Group.

Justice Tomorrow is the first story in the Sterling Brothers Ltd. Mystery series featuring Madeline Sterling and Socrates Gray, partners since the dark days of investigating the murder of civil rights workers.

Follow Sterling and Gray in ***Price of a Future***, coming in the fall.

Made in United States
Troutdale, OR
01/21/2025